SHADOW OF CTHULHU

CHRONICLES OF CAIN BOOK 6

JOHN CORWIN

RAVEN HOUSE

THE MAD WORLD

The god killer has escaped from her chains on Prometheus's Rock.

Aura from Dimension Beta killed Athena and unleashed eldritch horrors on Gaia Beta with the Apocalypse weapons stolen from Hephaestus's lost armory on Oblivion. She executed a plan that Cain never saw coming and even fooled the gods.

The gods are too busy fighting minions of the Elder Things in the divine realm to care about an escaped elf, no matter how dangerous she is. Since no one else will track down Aura Beta, Cain decides to take on the task himself. After all, tracking down hard-to-find individuals was his bread and butter before Hannah changed his life.

What starts out as a straightforward task quickly turns into a nightmare. Reaching Prometheus's Rock requires going through minotaur and centaur country. Beyond that is the land of the giants. But these dangers pale in comparison to what lies ahead.

Aura Beta is on Gaia Beta, a world overrun with eldritch horrors, and plans to invade Prime. Cain would usually assassinate such a dangerous person but killing Aura Beta is only a temporary measure. Thanks to the bargain struck with Athena, Auras from all dimensions are now immortal. If they die, they come back to life at midnight.

Cain has no choice but to wade through a sea of monsters so he can capture Aura Beta and put an end to the madness. Otherwise, Gaia Prime will fall, and the Elder Things will rule the human worlds.

BOOKS BY JOHN CORWIN

Join the Overworld Conclave for all the news, memes and tentacles you could ever desire!

https://www.facebook.com/groups/overworldconclave

Or get your tentacles via email: www.johncorwin.net

Fan page: https://www.facebook.com/johncorwinauthor

CHRONICLES OF CAIN

To Kill a Unicorn

Enter Oblivion

Throne of Lies

At The Forest of Madness

The Dead Never Die

Shadow of Cthulhu

THE OVERWORLD CHRONICLES

Sweet Blood of Mine

Dark Light of Mine

Fallen Angel of Mine

Dread Nemesis of Mine

Twisted Sister of Mine

Dearest Mother of Mine

Infernal Father of Mine

Sinister Seraphim of Mine

Wicked War of Mine

Dire Destiny of Ours

Aetherial Annihilation

Baleful Betrayal

Ominous Odyssey

Insidious Insurrection

Utopia Undone

Overworld Apocalypse

Apocryphan Rising

Soul Storm

Devil's Due

Overworld Ascension

Assignment Zero (An Elyssa Short Story)

OVERWORLD UNDERGROUND

Soul Seer

Demonicus

Infernal Blade

OVERWORLD ARCANUM

Conrad Edison and the Living Curse

Conrad Edison and the Anchored World

Conrad Edison and the Broken Relic

Conrad Edison and the Infernal Design

Conrad Edison and the First Power

STAND ALONE NOVELS

Mars Rising

No Darker Fate

The Next Thing I Knew

Outsourced

1

It's the unexpected things that kick you in the ass.

The hairs on the back of my neck prickled, but it was already too late. Something hard met my backside and sent me flying. I tucked and rolled across the torn earth. A tall stone wall stopped my forward momentum. I gained my feet quickly, but it seemed my attacker was in no hurry to finish me off.

He was huge—ten feet tall and bulging with muscles. He wore a ridiculously short loincloth that barely covered his junk. His height and hairy balls weren't the most notable thing about him, however. His bull head and the large, curving horns really drew my attention. The minotaur pawed the dusty earth with a hoof and glowered at me. Then again, he could've been smiling. I wouldn't have known the difference.

"That was but a kick, human. The next blow comes from my horns if I'm not satisfied with your explanation as to why you are here in our lands."

I blinked. "So, your policy is donkey kick first and ask questions later?"

"Do not compare me to a lowly donkey, human." He bared his unnaturally sharp teeth, and the ring in his nose clinked against them. "Your kind brings death and misery wherever you go. That is why we have a labyrinth to dissuade visitors."

I'd been all over Feary during my days with the Oblivion Guard but had rarely visited this part of the world. The cities in this area resembled those of ancient Greece in all their glory but were primarily populated by creatures lost to legend and myth. It was no coincidence that it was geographically relative to Greece on Gaia.

I held up my hands. "I'm not looking for trouble. I'm traveling to Prometheus's Rock."

He pawed the ground again. "There are other ways to reach that place, human."

"Yeah, but that would mean going around your labyrinth and over goblin-infested mountains." I pointed straight ahead. "This is the shortest and safest route."

"How safe is it if it costs you your life?" He stepped closer. "Go back whence you came or die."

I blew out a breath. "Maybe if you just escorted me through your city, I'd be out of your hair in a few hours, and you wouldn't have to resort to murder."

"Humans are not allowed in Minos!"

I hated name-dropping to the point of loathing, especially when the name was mine. But it seemed like if there was ever a good time to do it, it was now. "I'm Cain Sthyldor."

His eyes flared, and his chest heaved with a bellow of rage. "How dare you show your face here, criminal!" The minotaur reached over his shoulder and drew a great, iron war hammer. By great, I mean the thing was seven feet long with a hammerhead big enough to turn me to paste in a single blow.

"That's not the reaction I was expecting." I backed up a few feet and glanced at the ground to my right where I'd left sigils that would lead me back out of the maze.

"Cain, what's that noise?" Hannah's voice echoed through the stone corridors. "Did you find a minotaur?"

I'd left her and Aura in one of the many gardens inside the maze while I scouted ahead and marked out the route. It seemed I'd have to beat a hasty retreat to them if I wanted to remain in one piece.

The minotaur's gaze darted toward her voice. "How many of you are there, evil one?"

I backed up a few more steps. "I don't know which Cain Sthyldor you're thinking of, but I'm the one who freed minotaurs from slavery in the Beast War."

He stomped toward me, eyes glowing with bloodlust, war hammer swinging easily in one of his hands. "You freed minotaurs?" He bellowed. "You murdered my people, griffins, and other beasts, trading their lives for riches. The fae tried to stop you and finally banished you from Feary!" His teeth clacked together. "You are a war criminal!"

My thoughts turned to the orc historian Raghat and the warning he'd imparted last time we'd spoken. The fae had ordered him to alter the historical record of our little adventure in the Dead Forest, and it seemed they'd also spread heavily doctored versions of the Beast War. They were trying to make me public enemy number one in Feary.

I probably deserved to be called a war criminal, but only because of deeds I'd performed under orders for the Oblivion Guard.

I cupped my hands and shouted, "Hannah, stay where you are."

She shouted back, but her words were drowned out by the furious roar of the charging minotaur. I summoned my staff, and the bright-blade hummed to life. The sight of it didn't slow the minotaur in the slightest.

Even though I hadn't worn Death's cloak in a month, I still felt naked without its protection. My brief time serving as the Grim Reaper had made me grow accustomed to the supernatural strength and reflexes it had given me. Having the abilities of a powerful deity, no matter how briefly, had spoiled me.

Now, I was just normal ol' me—completely reliant on magical tattoos that gave me a little extra boost when the odds were stacked against me. I still couldn't believe this beast had gotten close enough to donkey kick me in the ass. Then again, the labyrinth was enchanted in ways that were supposed to make a trespasser's head spin. Disorient them so they'd become trapped forever, living out their days among the food-filled gardens. The disorientation aura was playing havoc with even my well-tuned senses.

The fact that a minotaur had confronted me meant that I was somewhere close to the city entrance. Unfortunately, I might not have long to celebrate my success.

I powered the invisible tattoos along my body and dodged to the side just as the charging beast lowered his head and swung the hammer. I swung the brightblade at his heel, thinking a mild nick might be enough to bring him down. His size should have hindered him, but he was deceptively quick on his hooves, spinning away from my blow. His shoulder rammed the wall. If it had been ordinary stone, it would've cracked, but the enchantment prevented it from suffering even a scratch.

The minotaur gripped the war hammer in both hands and swung it back over his head. At first, I thought he meant to throw it, but instead, he slammed it to the ground. A shockwave of earth and air crashed into me. I tumbled backward in a storm of dirt and debris. Somehow, I planted my brightblade in the ground and anchored myself to keep from plowing into the wall behind me.

The minotaur was already charging again.

I threw out small shields about ankle and shin height. He shattered the first and second one, stumbled against the third, and slowed his roll considerably when he struck the fourth, roaring in pain. The shields couldn't stop him, but the delay was enough for me to take a deep breath, wish I hadn't gotten out of bed that morning, and climb to my feet.

If I'd learned anything during my brief encounter with this minotaur, it was that he had zero finesse, relying instead on brute force and rolling over his opponents. His size and strength gave him that luxury. But as a battle tactic, it was stupid. If it weren't for his catlike reflexes, I would have already crippled him.

I readied my blade, knees bent, shoulder angled toward the oncoming threat. The minotaur lowered his head the moment he entered striking distance and swung the war hammer in an overhead arc with his left hand while his right arm swung out as a counterbalance. I remained perfectly still, waiting for the right moment to act.

The beast's accuracy was spot-on. If I'd been a stake, he would've pounded me into the ground in one blow. Just as the hammer was about to land, I saw the opening I needed. I deactivated the brightblade, ghostwalked forward, thrust the staff up, and tapped the beast in his great, big, hairy balls. I probably could have neutered him on the spot with the brightblade, but I wasn't looking to permanently ruin his sex life.

The war hammer dropped. The beast bellowed and grabbed his privates as he dropped to his knees and rolled over onto his back.

Before he had a chance to recover, I put a foot on his chest, and the brightblade sizzled to life, hovering just over his neck. "Yield."

Eyes watering in pain, he glared at me. "I am no coward. Kill me, or I will rise and smash you into oblivion."

I lowered the brightblade to his crotch. "How about I slice and dice your nethers and let you live."

"No!" Sweat beaded between his horns. "This is why the fae call you the Butcher. You have no mercy."

"I don't know what stories the fae peddled about me, but I assure you that I did not slaughter minotaurs, griffins, or any other beasts." I kept my eyes locked on his. "I'm the one who started the uprising. Granted, I did it for my own selfish purposes, but everything worked out."

"Why should I believe you?" the minotaur growled.

I wished I had a plausible answer, but I didn't. I could kill this guy, skip the bullshit, and possibly sneak my way around the perimeter of the city, perhaps hugging the wall and using a camouflage blind. The only problem with that tactic was my knowledge about Minos was close to zero. The entire city might be a maze, or it might have a nice, convenient way to sneak around the perimeter without being seen.

The minotaur thought I was a war criminal. Not killing him wouldn't prove much. In fact, he'd probably think I was trying to deceive him by playing nice. The best course of action was to knock him out and try my luck inside the maze.

I banished my staff and backed well away from the minotaur. "What is your name?"

His nostrils flared, but confusion replaced the anger in his eyes. "My name?" One hand cupping his jewels, he rose slowly to his feet, but didn't reach for his hammer. "I am Taurin, human. I am the guardian of the maze, defender of Minos."

"That's your day job?" I frowned and made a show of looking around at the colorful foliage. "How many invaders do you get through here in a week?"

He stared blankly at me.

"In a month?" I folded my arms over my chest. "How about a year?"

He mumbled something under his breath.

I cupped a hand over my ear. "I'm sorry, what was that?"

"One," he growled.

I put a hand to my chest. "Little ol' me?"

He nodded. "You are the first in many years."

I frowned. "Um, so what do you do with all your free time?"

His nostrils flared. "I tend to the gardens."

During our journey through the labyrinth, Hannah, Aura, and I had found ten large gardens, each one flawlessly maintained. In addition to flowers and shrubs, there were fruit trees and rows of vegetables, presumably planted to feed any who became trapped within these walls.

"Well, they're lovely. My companions and I were very impressed, especially with the tomatoes. I've never seen them so large and red."

His chest puffed out with pride. "I make a very special fertilizer with my own manure."

That was a bit of information I could have done without. *Note to self: Don't eat the tomatoes.*

Taurin's bullish eyebrows pinched. "Where are your companions?"

As if on cue, Hannah and Aura stumbled around the corner, eyes wide.

"Holy shit, Cain, it's a minotaur!" Hannah leaped in front of me, spreading her hands as if to shield me. "Don't worry, I'll keep you safe!"

"You have a child and an elf with you?" Taurin flinched as if the conflicting information assaulting him right now was more than he could handle. "And why does the child act as a protector?"

Hannah raised a fist. "Just try and attack Cain. I dare you!"

I put a hand on her shoulder. "Hannah, we're just talking about gardening."

She blinked, mouth falling open. "Huh? Then what was all the pounding and bellowing about?"

Taurin seemed to regain his purpose, reaching for the war hammer. "No humans are allowed in Minos, but especially not the war criminal, Cain Sthyldor."

Aura snorted in disbelief. "Cain is a lot of things, but a war criminal?"

"Well, he did murder all those women and children," Hannah said. "That's basically a war crime."

"Oh yes, I'd forgotten about that." Aura hissed a breath between her teeth. "Okay, so you got us there, but he hasn't killed any kids in a long time."

Hannah winced. "He killed Sigma."

Aura frowned. "Yeah, but Sigma was trying to kill you."

"He was still a kid, so technically—"

I held up a hand. "Can you two stop digging my hole deeper?"

"He murdered many humans?" Taurin lowered the hammer. "How many?"

"Oh, countless humans," Hannah said. "God, all those mechanists he slaughtered probably numbered in the hundreds."

The minotaur pawed a hoof in the dust. "And yet he also slaughtered beasts."

"Beasts?" Aura shook her head. "Do you mean sentient beasts?"

"Yes." He stomped the ground. "He slaughtered many in the Beast War."

"No, Cain saved the beasts. The fae just spread false rumors about him because they hated him for inciting the beast uprising." Hannah nodded as if suddenly sure I wasn't a mass murderer. "Cain might have killed a lot of people, but he totally helped free griffins, cecrops, and a bunch of other intelligent creatures."

Taurin looked at Aura uncertainly. "Elves are known for their honesty. Even to this day, we trade with elves because they have always helped my people. What say you of Cain?"

Aura winced, because she sure as hell wasn't an ordinary elf. She'd betrayed me and Hannah, then did a one-eighty and started helping us. "Cain is not exactly a good person, but many griffins call him Liberator because he started the rebellion that led to the Beast War and forced the fae to emancipate all sentient creatures."

"Cain is the one known as Liberator?" Taurin shook his head. "I thought that was Torvin Rayne, the Great Drow."

Hannah groaned. "That dude was pure evil."

Aura nodded in agreement. "Torvin hated Cain, and he'd never do anything to help anyone except himself."

Taurin stared blankly at the maze wall with the look of someone deeply conflicted.

"We are on a quest to save an elf," Aura said. "She was taken by the gods and bound to Prometheus's Rock."

The minotaur clenched his teeth. "The gods are cruel. What they give with one hand, they take with another. Poseidon, in his anger, caused Pasiphae to fall in love with a white bull that should have been his sacrifice. Though the stories only mention the original minotaur, they do not tell the tale of his twin sister or how Pasiphae secretly sent her away."

Hannah gasped. "Wait, this woman fucked a bull and got pregnant? Pretty sure my high school biology teacher would say that's impossible."

This was a can of worms I didn't want to dive into, so I waved a hand. "Taurin, you've been lied to by the fae. The question is, will you help us pass through Minos so we can rescue our elf friend?"

He straightened and turned to Aura. "Lady elf, I accept your word and will gladly aid you."

Aura blinked several times before answering. "Um, great! Can we go now?"

Taurin lifted his hammer and sheathed it over his back. "Yes. Follow me."

He turned, and we headed forward into minotaur central.

2

Aura had, of course, lied to Taurin about our quest. We weren't going to Prometheus's Rock to save an elf but to track down Aura's evil doppelganger, Aura Beta, who'd laid waste to Gaia in Dimension Beta before coming to Prime and killing Athena right at the end of an otherwise very successful venture.

She'd slain the goddess with the sword Soultaker, trapping her soul with the undead army inside even though her body remained alive. Mars had then killed Layla with Soultaker and healed her body to give me a reason to find a way to free Athena's soul. I'd taken on the mantle of Death, stopped a zombie uprising, prevented three of the four horsemen from starting the apocalypse, and found Thanatos, Greek god of death who'd enchanted Soultaker.

Freeing souls from the sword required the blood of the killer. Hermes had gone to retrieve blood from Aura Beta, but she was no longer chained to Prometheus's Rock. I'd gone to my Aura and used her blood. Thankfully, it had worked to revive Athena, but the goddess had attacked Mars the instant her soul was reunited with her body. It made me think that even though the blood of Aura Prime and Aura Beta was mostly identical, something might have been off.

But that was water under the bridge. Aura Beta was a complete psychopath who was free to wreak havoc again. She'd been driven mad from using Panoptes, a ring that let her see many places at once and travel to any of them. One of those places had been a warehouse filled with apocalypse weapons from Hephaestus's lost armory on Oblivion Beta. She'd used those weapons to lay waste to Gaia Beta and then set out to murder the goddess who'd cursed her bloodline.

So long as she was free, she was a menace to all the other dimensions. I possessed Panoptes, which was the only way I knew of to access the warehouse with the apocalypse weapons, but for all I knew, Aura Beta had a backup stash. It was imperative that we find her and put her somewhere she could no longer be a threat to Prime. Someone who'd lured the gods out of the divine realm and murdered Athena was too dangerous to be free.

I wasn't usually one to give up my life of sipping mangoritas just to go on a quest, but securing the insane elf had become my top priority, so I didn't have to worry about being stabbed in the back.

So, here we were in Feary, traveling to Aura Beta's last known location. I'd wanted Layla to come as well, but she'd disappeared after her resurrection, and I hadn't seen her since.

"Tell me more of this elf friend." Taurin glanced back at us. "Why would the gods punish her as they did Prometheus?"

"She insulted Athena," Hannah said.

The minotaur snorted. "The gods are unforgiving and cruel." He led us unerringly through twists and turns in the labyrinth, to another of his well-tended gardens where plump, red tomatoes hung low on the vines. Taurin plucked three and handed them to us. "Taste the fruits of my labor."

I imagined his labors, i.e., taking horse-sized shits and spreading them over the soil around his tomato plants. I took a bite of the tomato anyway. Sweet, tangy juices burst across my tongue. I sighed in appreciation. It was one of the best tomatoes I'd ever tasted. "I'll bet these sell well in Minos."

"Unfortunately, no." His huge shoulders slumped. "Centaurs and minotaurs are primarily carnivorous. I would have to hide my face in shame if they knew I also enjoy salads. Only cervitaurs are primarily herbivores."

Hannah giggle snorted. "That's the silliest thing I've ever heard. I love salads."

"Does anyone else know about your gardens?" I asked.

Taurin nodded. "My mate. But he thinks salads are disgusting."

Aura inspected a row of huge cucumbers, then turned and waved a hand at a row of lettuce. "Such a shame to have all these veggies go to waste."

Hannah snapped her fingers. "Dude, you could make so much money if you sold these. Organic food is huge on Earth."

His forehead pinched and his bull ears twitched. "How could I possibly sell anything in the old world? The nearest mushroom portal is far outside the labyrinth."

"It's super easy." Hannah smelled the tomato and sighed. "I used to live with foster parents who had a farm. They showed us how everything worked from picking the produce to transporting it to the farmers market."

Taurin scratched behind his left horn, a perplexed look on his face. "What use would I have for old world money?"

Hannah reached up—way up—and patted him on his huge forearm. "It's not about the money. It's about doing something you enjoy." She patted her tomato. "It's obvious this is your passion."

He puffed out his chest. "I do very much love this! My mate complains that I spend all my time in the labyrinth."

Hannah frowned. "What else is there to do for fun in Minos?"

Taurin's gaze grew distant. "Well, gladiator tournaments with battles to the death are very popular. There are the those who go into the mountains and hunt dangerous game. And my people are always training and preparing for war in case the mountain goblins or trolls attack."

Aura blinked. "War?"

"In case the orcs or goblins ever decide to enslave our people again." He raised a huge fist. "Minotaurs, centaurs, and cervitaurs formed an alliance to keep our foals and calves safe from such threats."

I wasn't surprised. Centaurs and minotaurs had been used as soldiers, gladiators, and guards by the slaver races for centuries. They had been bred for battle and brainwashed, which had made it quite a challenge during the Beast War since orcs, goblins, and drow had used their slaves to protect them. Minotaurs and centaurs had died protecting their masters. Some had died at my hands, but it hadn't been by choice.

That, however, would remain my dirty little secret since I wanted to make it through Minos alive. I nodded in what I thought was the direction of the city. "Can we keep going? I'd like to get to Prometheus's Rock by nightfall."

Taurin looked away from Hannah who was explaining logistics and intermodal transportation to him. "It is best that we do not venture into the city. I cannot guarantee the safety of any humans once inside, as they are strictly prohibited. Instead, we will use the underground labyrinth to traverse it."

"Underground labyrinth?" Aura looked uncertain. "Um, is it safe?"

"Safe enough with me as your guide." He approached the statue of a cervitaur buck in the center of the garden, reached between its legs, and pulled something. Stone grated against stone as the statue slid aside.

Hannah peered at the statue. "Is that a deer centaur?"

"They're called cervitaurs," I said.

She kept talking. "Taurin, did you just pull on its junk?"

Taurin released the generously proportioned penis on the statue. "Junk?"

"Its huge honking dong." Hannah walked over and touched the stone phallus. "Why is it so ginormous?"

The minotaur stared at her blankly. "That is quite small." He reached down toward his loincloth as if to prove the point with a size comparison.

"Hold up." I threw up a hand and avoided looking at his crotch. "We need to get moving."

Taurin seemed disappointed even though his skimpy outfit left little to the imagination. "Very well." He motioned toward the spiral stars leading down into the ground. "Proceed."

I led the way into the darkness below. The brightblade hummed to life in the pitch black, revealing a chamber hewn into the gray stone. Connecting corridors led in five directions. The tunnels were tall and wide enough to accommodate minotaurs and centaurs standing three abreast.

Small crystals embedded in the ceiling flickered on, negating the need for the brightblade. I snuffed the humming energy and banished the staff as I strode toward one of the nearby tunnels. The crystals flickered on, revealing a fork ahead. The labyrinth below was markedly different than the one above.

Taurin clopped down the stairs after the others, tugging on a chain on the wall. The cervitaur statue grated back into place. He headed toward the northeast corridor without hesitation, following its downward slope further into the ground. The unsettling effect of the disorientation enchantments from the aboveground labyrinth faded away, leaving my senses clear for the first time in hours.

Even though I could have memorized the path, I didn't want to take any chances and did my due diligence by tracing the floor with sigils every so often. Simply marking walls with chalk might have been an option down here, but in the labyrinth above, the walls couldn't be marked due to the protective enchantments.

Walls in the garden labyrinth also randomly shifted positions, rearranging the maze and making it more difficult to retrace my steps if I hit a dead end. The sigils tracked any alterations in the layout by recording the changes and allowing me to puzzle out which way the new corridor led.

Taurin stepped wide around an area. "Follow me exactly lest you trigger a trap."

Hannah looked at the section of floor which looked no different than the surrounding area. "What happens if you step there?"

"A pit," Taurin replied without looking back.

I summoned my staff and examined the area through the true

sight scope. A faintly glowing outline revealed the triggers. Like the garden labyrinth, this one relied on magic instead of mechanical devices to activate traps.

Keeping the true sight scope to my eye, I scouted the path beyond Taurin. Maybe he planned to guide us safely through, or maybe he didn't. I'd tried to give him a reason to trust me by not killing him, but mercy didn't always work against a determined enemy. I didn't count him as an enemy, per se, but he'd certainly considered me a threat after learning my name.

I hadn't stayed alive for so long by blindly trusting people who'd tried to murder me only moments ago. Taurin, however, had very little to gain by killing us, so the odds were in our favor that we'd soon see the other side of the labyrinth and hopefully be that much closer to Prometheus's Rock.

I hadn't expected the trip through Minos to be such a hassle. I'd severely underestimated how difficult it would be to traverse the labyrinth and hadn't realized humans were persona non grata in these parts.

I wasn't normally one to take mushroom portals, especially on Feary where pixies would report my presence to the high fae, but I'd seriously considered using one this trip since Prometheus's Rock was so far from civilization.

Then, I'd discovered that not only were there no portals within hundreds of miles of the rock, but that portal travel to the area was restricted. I'd contacted Pyroeis about flying over Minos or through the mountains, but he'd informed me that the labyrinth enchantments prevented air travel over Minos. Any griffins who tried to fly over would become so disoriented that they risked crashing into the mountains or plummeting to their deaths.

To make matters even more difficult, the mountains were infested with goblins and orcs who could easily shoot down griffins with ballistas or arrows. Despite the dangers, Pyroeis had still offered his services. I'd refused, thinking I could simply slip through Minos unnoticed using my vaunted Oblivion Guard training. That had been a foolish assumption on my part.

So, here we were on foot in an underground maze with a minotaur tour guide. If he led us safely to the other side, then getting donkey kicked in the ass was a small price to pay.

Time dragged on as we followed him through twists and turns. Time and time again, he led us safely around trap triggers that were only visible through my scope. We crossed a long stone bridge over a raging underground river. It gave me unpleasant flashbacks to crossing the glass bridge spanning the screaming river into Hel even though this river was tame by comparison.

Giant stone aqueducts spiraled up from the river and into the chamber's ceiling about fifty feet above. Water rushed up the half-pipes, defying gravity and presumably delivering water to the city.

Hannah stopped to marvel at the constructs. "Wow, how do those work?"

Taurin stood next to her. "Magic, of course. The aqueducts deliver water to canals that run throughout the city. They were gifts from the elves centuries ago, before our city was sacked and our people were taken as slaves."

She grimaced. "That got dark real fast."

Taurin glanced around furtively. "Let's not waste time. There are those who—"

"What is the meaning of this?" A voice echoed from the other side of the river.

I located the source an instant later. A centaur with thick horns curving up from his forehead glared at us. "Are those humans?"

I didn't know how good the centaur's eyesight was and hoped he couldn't see us clearly. "Aura, buy us some time," I hissed.

She frowned. "How?"

"You're a fucking elf!" I motioned toward him. "Go talk to him."

"Oh, yeah." She slipped around Taurin and strode toward the centaur. "We're elves, sir."

"Elves?" The centaur clopped toward the bridge. "They don't look like—" He peered around her and paused. "Oh, I guess they are."

I'd quickly traced sigils on Hannah and myself, casting illusions that made our ears look pointy. Granted, there were other things that differentiated elves from humans, like supernatural strength and speed, but this would probably get us past a nosy centaur.

Taurin put himself between us and the newcomer. "Balfeus, is it not early for the afternoon inspections?"

"Someone found a hydra egg in the eastern canal this morning." The centaur peered suspiciously at us. "We nearly had a disaster on our hands the last time that happened."

"Another hydra egg?" Taurin peered down at the river. "That is the third one in as many months. But the river flows too fast to be a suitable habitat for a hydra."

"We suspect the mother is somewhere near the mouth of the river." Balfeus tapped his fingers on the bridge railing. "We are mounting an expedition to find and destroy the creature before the nuisance turns into an infestation."

"How in the world could an egg survive a trip downriver?" Aura said. "Wouldn't it be smashed on the rocks?"

"Hydra eggs are hard as stone, Lady elf." He tilted his head. "Your accent is quite strange for an elf."

"I—we're not from these parts." Aura cleared her throat. "We're from Faevalorn."

Balfeus pursed his lips and nodded. "We do not receive many visitors from afar. What drew you to our remote city?"

"We're traveling to Prometheus's Rock and thought it would be interesting to traverse the labyrinth along the way." Aura shrugged. "Taurin offered us a tour of the underground, so here we are."

Balfeus grunted. "Would you not rather see the actual city instead of this boring underground?"

"We will eventually make our way there, but this is pleasant for now." Aura turned to Taurin. "Can we continue on? We would like to make it to the rock by sundown."

"Of course." Taurin turned to Balfeus. "I hope you discover the source of the eggs."

"Oh, we shall." The centaur touched the haft of a giant battle-ax on his back. "Fighting a hydra will be glorious." He spun toward me. "But first, I will see these humans drowned!"

I summoned my brightblade a heartbeat before he lunged at me. I threw up a shield and blocked him, then leaped back to give myself some space. "We're elves, not humans!"

Balfeus bared his teeth. "Do you think I am not trained to recognize illusions when I see them? Your ears are flickering!"

Aura jumped between us. "I am most certainly an elf, and these people are under my protection!"

"Then you have broken covenant." Balfeus unslung his battle-ax. "The elves of Alnora enchanted our labyrinth to keep out humans. They promised they would never allow them in Minos."

"I'm not from Alnora." Aura held up her hands pleadingly. "Look, we're just passing through."

Balfeus glared at Taurin. "Have they bewitched you, brother? I know you are not capable of such treason."

Taurin opened his mouth to reply, but Hannah stepped in front of him. "I am a demigoddess and have forced him to do my bidding. Now, let us pass, or I will kill him and you." Her forehead furrowed in concentration, and her eyes began to glow white.

Balfeus's eyes flared wide with anger and surprise. "Have not the gods punished us enough? Now they send their illegitimate progeny into our midst?"

Hannah threw up her hands in exasperation. "The gods didn't send us, you idiot! This is just the fastest way to get to Prometheus's Rock!"

Balfeus roared in frustration, then abruptly turned tail and ran.

Hannah blinked. "Well, that was easy."

"Wait, brother!" Taurin threw up a hand as Balfeus reached the end of the bridge and stomped on the ground. The section of stone sank into the ground, and the bridge rumbled. Taurin leaped twenty feet to the other side just as the center section dropped out from beneath us. He gripped the edge, but the rest of us dropped straight into the raging river below.

3

Frigid water closed over my head, and the rapid current snatched me like a leaf caught in a sudden wind. I'd been tossed into rough seas, whitewater rapids, and frozen oceans more times than I could count as part of my training but getting dumped into a force of nature powerful enough to crush you to paste was never pleasant.

The twenty-foot fall dunked me underwater briefly, but I'd already scouted my next steps during the fall. Water sizzled and boiled around the brightblade as I fought my way back to the surface. A rock directly in my path was just waiting to break my bones. I had other plans.

Activating the sigils tattooed on my legs, I gave myself extra strength and thrust myself sideways. I had a grappling hook in my utility belt, but there was no way I'd pull it out in time, so I stabbed the brightblade into the rock as I passed it. It didn't penetrate deep, but it dug a glowing groove in the side and slowed me just enough so I could grip an outcropping with my hand.

Without hesitation, I banished my staff and flung out a hand to catch Aura by the hair as the current carried her past. She shouted and gurgled as water filled her mouth. Hoping her hair wouldn't tear out by the roots, I dragged her close enough to wrap my legs around her waist and bring her close to the rock.

Coughing up water, she clung to the side of the rock next to me. It was too steep to climb to the top, but it was the best we could do for now.

I frantically searched for Hannah and spotted her clinging to another rock near the base of the bridge. White light poured from her eyes and mouth, boiling icy water into steam. Her survival instincts had kicked into high gear. Beams of energy speared from her and into the bridge supports, melting the stone to slag. Taurin raced along the bridge, diving to safety next to Balfeus as the structure collapsed into the river.

The rocky slopes along the sides of the river were too steep to climb. Our only way out was to either ride the river to wherever it went or for me to cut handholds in the slope with my bright-blade. Somehow, I didn't think we'd have time for that since Balfeus would probably just be waiting to cut us to pieces at the top.

If I could just get Hannah to focus some of her energy on the cliff, she could probably cut us a ramp in less than half the time it would take for me to use my brightblade. The problem with that solution was that when Hannah's powers unleashed all at once like this, she had almost no control.

Still, it was worth a shot. "Hannah!" The roar of the river drowned out my words, so I used an amplification spell. "Hannah!" My voice boomed loudly. "Cut us a path on the riverbank!"

She instinctively glanced our way, slashing the top of the rock we were holding onto. Molten stone flowed down the sides, threatening to burn our hands to a crisp.

"Fuck!" I released the rock just before the magma reached my fingers, yanking Aura along with me.

"Cain!" Hannah cried out in despair, and the deadly energy flowing from her eyes and mouth abruptly cut off. "Cain!"

The river gripped me and Aura, rushing us toward an uncertain fate where it vanished below the surface at a wall of rock. The odds of surviving past that point were slim to nothing, so I took the only other route available to me and started kicking my legs frantically.

Aura seemed to figure out what I was aiming for and started swimming as if her life depended on it—which it most certainly did.

Hannah slumped and slid off her rock. Expending so much power all at once had done what it usually did and knocked her out. I suddenly had two rapidly closing windows of opportunity to save myself and save her. I started swimming as if two lives depended on it, flung out a hand, and gripped the edge of an aqueduct.

Aura latched on next to me, putting herself in the way. "Get up there!" I gripped the hem of her pants and hoisted her onto the mouth of the stone funnel. She yelped and was suddenly whisked away as the enchantment took her and the water spiraling upward.

My arms were exhausted, but I fished the grappling hook from my utility belt and latched the enchanted hook firmly onto the lip of the aqueduct. Hannah floated facedown a good forty feet out to the side and nearly past me already. I shoved off and swam toward her even as the river carried me at a steep angle.

There was no way I'd reach her before she floated past me, but I had no more tricks up my sleeve. Or did I? I would've slapped myself for not thinking of it, but I didn't have time. I traced the fastest sigil of my life and cast a row of small shields in front of Hannah. She bumped against them and began sliding sideways, but away from me.

"Fuck!" Using a trick I'd only recently begun to use, I motioned with my hand, pulling the threads of the sigil to telekinetically move the shields toward me, curving the one furthest away inward to keep Hannah from sliding around the side.

The grappling rope snapped taut, still a dozen feet from Hannah. Using all the willpower left in me, I dragged the shields closer and closer until, finally, I could reach out and grab Hannah's shirt. I pulled her to my chest and flipped her on her back so that her mouth was above water. Wrapping my arms around her upper stomach, I yanked them in and up. Water spurted from her mouth.

I did it again and again, each time expelling more water. "Breathe, gods damn it!"

Hannah heaved and water streamed from her nose and mouth. She coughed weakly. I didn't know how much longer the grappling hook would hold, so I decided she was breathing well enough, and began using my free arm to pull us toward the aqueduct.

My arms were frozen and exhausted. My legs were leaden with fatigue. I cursed myself for not having put an automatic reel enchantment on the rope, but it was certainly too late now. My dazed mind ran through the inventory of my utility belt, but there was nothing inside that could help me. The only other possibility was to use the ring of Panoptes to travel out of here.

It occurred to me that I'd never tried to take anyone with me while using the ring. If it didn't work, Hannah wouldn't have me holding her anymore and would be lost to the current. Surely if the ring allowed me to travel with items from the warehouse, it would allow me to take something living right?

There was no choice but to try.

I usually kept the ring duct taped to the handle of my staff, but I'd stuffed it into my utility bag during the fight with Taurin so it didn't accidentally fall off. I reached below the frigid waters and into the pouches on my belt, trying to remember which one. My fingers closed around something familiar. Something I hadn't touched in ages, and it sent chills down my spine as a voice echoed in my head.

Cain?

Cthulhu?

Somehow, the cursed pearl that Fred had given me all those years ago was back in my pouch. It had linked me to Cthulhu, poisoning me every time I used it to boost my magical powers. The curse had nearly killed me and almost cost Hannah her freedom. There was no way in hell I would've put the thing in my utility belt.

I am coming, Cthulhu said.

Panic fueled newfound strength in my arms. I struggled with every ounce of my being to reel me and Hannah over to the aqueduct. Cthulhu's minions used underwater tunnels called deepways and could access just about any place in the world that was covered by water. The deepways even linked Gaia to Feary and Oblivion, meaning one of his creatures was probably zeroing in on me right this instant.

I lost track of time as I slowly inched closer and closer to the aqueduct, Hannah limp in my arms. I had to reach safety before—but it was too late. Tentacles wrapped around my waist.

Hannah and I were thrust up and out of the water. We landed on the aqueduct and would have been whisked upward, but the grappling hook and tangled rope held us firmly in place as water rushed past us, sending spray into my face. Tentacles gripped the sides of the funnel, and a massive octopus slapped a tentacle against my face.

My master says—

The grappling hook popped free of the aqueduct. Hannah and I shot up the spiraling funnel, losing contact with the tentacle before hearing Cthulhu's message. We sped up the spiraling aqueduct, riding a waterslide in reverse, our bodies pressed hard against the curves from the anti-gravity enchantment.

We shot through a hole in the chamber ceiling and burst onto the surface of a canal about the size of a small stream. The water here flowed lazily compared to that of the river but was still strong enough to knock someone over. The canal was about fifteen feet wide, and the sides extended another five feet above the water. My feet found the bottom. I planted them and held onto Hannah to keep her from being dragged away.

Despite the strong current, I was able to stand in the hip-deep water. The bottom of the canal was slick, and my feet lost their purchase. I was too tired to fight it, so I leaned back and let my feet slide along the bottom. Just ahead, a stone bridge arched across the canal. Next to it, a ramp led up and out of the water.

I used what little strength I had left to push us at an angle toward the ramp. Once there, I dragged us out of the water just enough so I could lean Hannah against the wall. I was damn tired, but now was no time to rest, so I crept up the ramp and peered over the sides. There wasn't much visible except mud and torn up earth.

Judging from the hoof marks, blood stains, and the auditorium style seats and platforms surrounding us, it seemed we were in the gladiator arena. The canal split into four directions, sectioning the arena like a pie. Thankfully, there were no battles being fought, and the seats and platforms were empty.

A horn sounded in the distance. Shouts and battle cries rose in response. It seemed Balfeus had raised the alarm.

A flash of red hair drew my attention back toward the nexus of the canals where Hannah and I had emerged. Aura was crouched over the side, looking down into the water.

"Aura." I called out just loudly enough to be heard over the water.

She flinched and spun around, eyes wide, then staggered over to us. "Cain, I thought you were dead!"

"Almost." I motioned her down into the ramp area to keep hidden in case someone happened into the arena. "Didn't you see us a moment ago?"

"I hit my head hard on the way up the aqueduct and barely managed to drag myself out of the water." She rubbed her head and showed her bloody fingers. "I crawled over there to see if there was a way back down."

"Is there?"

She shook her head. "I'm sure Balfeus saw us go up the aqueduct, so that war horn they keep blowing is going to lead a small army here any minute now."

I nodded. "We've got to go." I scoped out our surroundings and shook my head. "Going on foot is too dangerous. I'm exhausted, you're walking like a drunk, and Hannah is unconscious." I nodded at the water. "Let's drift in the canal until we reach the northern side of the city. Maybe we'll luck out and end up near an exit."

"Yeah, but there's more labyrinth on the other side of the city, isn't there?"

I took a deep breath, closed my eyes, and let my senses tell me what I needed. "This is flowing west. We need to go back to where the canal splits and get in the northbound flow. I'd rather take my chances in the labyrinth than face a squadron of bloodthirsty centaurs."

Aura nodded. "Sounds like a plan." She pointed toward the four-way split in the canal. "There's another ramp like this one over there."

I really needed a moment to rest my arms, but now was not that moment. Putting more power into my body sigils, I hefted Hannah and shambled up the ramp and across open ground to the north-bound canal.

Aura stumbled after me, wincing with every step. "Gods, my head hurts."

We made it to the other ramp and walked down it. I eased into the water, holding Hannah faceup against my chest, then floated on my back and let the current take us. Aura drifted behind us on her stomach.

We passed beneath several more stone bridges and emerged into the city proper. I imagined that the underwater river ran beneath the center of the city, dividing it into north and south. The canals likewise split into four main tributaries which branched into even smaller streams that delivered water throughout the city.

I couldn't see over the sides of the canal, but the clopping of hooves on cobblestones told me that despite the war horn still blaring in the distance, there were plenty of nearby citizens not heeding its call. Movement caught my eye as a female centaur walked across one of the bridges ahead. If she so much as glanced this way, she'd see us.

Ducking underwater wouldn't work with Hannah in her current state, so I quickly cast a cloaking blind in front of us and motioned Aura to come closer so she could also hide behind it. The centaur chomped on something that looked like a fried rat on a stick and continued across the bridge, eyes straight ahead.

I breathed a sigh of relief as we passed beneath the bridge. It looked like we were going to make it without being spotted.

A pair of young centaurs fishing in the canal on the other side of the bridge looked at us with wide eyes. The camouflage blind was in front of us and did nothing to hide us from the sides.

There was a moment of inaction, and then the centaurs shouted. "Humans!"

Their cries echoed through the mostly empty streets.

"We're elves!" Aura shouted back, revealing her pointy ears.

The centaurs blinked in confusion, but there was no taking back their shouts of alarm. We were already past them and nearing the next bridge. I saw a wall in the distance and realized we were close to the city exit. The canal branched in two directions at the wall, probably forming a moat that surrounded the entire city. Judging from the sound of galloping hooves and shouts echoing in the streets around the canal, the cries of the young centaurs had already raised an alarm.

I'd barely be able to haul Hannah across dry land, much less fight minotaurs and centaurs. But like so many things in life, I didn't have a choice.

4

Getting Hannah on her feet was priority one. I traced a sigil on her chest and powered it. Electricity buzzed and her body convulsed. Hannah shrieked and flailed, nearly nailing me in the face with her elbow. I pinned her arms the best I could, but she wasn't the weak teenager I'd rescued from a demigod assassin all that time ago. Her goddess strength overpowered me, and I was too tired for this shit. I pushed her away to keep my face from getting elbowed.

She went underwater for an instant, splashed to the surface, spluttering, and looked at me. "Oh, shit. I passed out, didn't I?"

I nodded. "Yeah. Now get your bearings, because we're about to have to make a run for it."

Shivering, she nodded. "Where are we going?"

I pointed to the last ramp, which was coming up fast. "Somewhere up that way."

"Okay." She gripped my arm to keep us from floating apart.

Aura drifted over to us. "Is there a gate blocking the exit, or is it wide open?"

Having not seen the gate on the other side of the city, I had no idea. "Just be ready for anything."

Aura groaned. "If there's a closed gate, I'll be ready to die."

"Is chasing down Aura Beta really worth all this?" Hannah swam toward the ramp.

"She destroyed Gaia Beta, disintegrated the Rlhala, and killed Athena." I forced my tired arms to push me through the water. "She might have another cache of apocalypse weapons and I don't think she'll hesitate to use them on Prime now that's she's free from the rock."

"Where's she going to go?" Hannah said. "You told me there aren't any mushroom portals for hundreds of miles around because travel to this area is restricted. She's probably hunkered down in the wilderness."

"She was also clever enough to murder Athena." I shook my head. "She outsmarted the mechanists on her world and then destroyed it with apocalypse weapons. She's full of rage and determined to finish what she started. I, for one, refuse to underestimate her. The sooner we find her, the better."

"Well, when you put it like that, I guess you're right." Her lips pressed into a line. "I just didn't expect the journey to be so hard."

I reached the ramp after Hannah and dragged myself out of the water. My limbs were cold and numb. Even with magic assisting my body, it was all I could do to trudge up the ramp. I hated to even consider what I was about to do, but there was no choice. The cursed pearl could give me the extra energy and stamina to make it out of here alive.

I can use it just this once.

But if I used it once, what was to stop me from using it for the next emergency or the next? Using it to amp my powers had slowly poisoned me with magic cancer until I'd become a shadow of my former self. I'd been ignorant of the side effects back then, but now I knew what would happen. Tapping into that tainted power even once would give Cthulhu power over me.

I clenched my fist and closed the pouch with the pearl. *Fuck Cthulhu.* I'd rather die on my own terms before giving into his temptations again.

The adventuring clothes I'd purchased for this expedition were already drying out. Water steamed around me as the gear heated to shed water. Every step became a little lighter as sodden cloth lost excess weight. Hannah's and Aura's were doing the same thing. The clothing had also been guaranteed to keep us warm in cold conditions, but apparently the frigid waters of the underground river had overwhelmed the enchantments.

As heat from the warming spells seeped into my bones, I found a bit more strength waiting for me. I'd endured worse during my training for the Oblivion Guard, but in the decade since leaving, creature comforts and mangoritas had softened me.

I crept to the top of the ramp and peered over the wall. A herd of centaurs rushed in our direction, weapons drawn. Their equine lower bodies gave them a speed advantage we couldn't hope to overcome. We had to avoid a footrace at any cost.

A long, raised drawbridge guarded the way out of the city and back into the labyrinth. Even if the drawbridge were lowered, a portcullis blocked the gate on the other side.

Seeing there was no other choice, I summoned my brightblade and pulled Panoptes from my utility belt. The ring allowed the bearer to see many places at once—something mortal minds couldn't bear for long. Wearing it caused dizziness, fatigue, and if used too much, insanity.

Aura Beta had done just that, turning her obsession with killing the gods into an insanity-fueled crusade that had caused her to destroy Gaia Beta before coming to Prime and killing Athena. According to Noctua, moderate use of the ring would prevent me from going mad, but I wasn't about to take her word as a guarantee.

Hannah and Aura didn't know about the ring. I hadn't seen a reason to tell anyone, so I was about to catch hell for this—provided it worked.

Hannah peered at the ring as I slipped it on. "What is that?"

The world split into multiple frames, each one slightly blurry and overlapping the one next to it like a honeycomb. In one frame, I saw Hannah and Aura. In the next, the warehouse where the apocalypse weapons were stored. Several frames were black. A heavy snowstorm clouded the view in one frame and sunbaked desert dunes shimmered in the next. By concentrating on a particular frame, I could travel to it. So far, I'd only ventured to the one with the warehouse.

I gripped Hannah and Aura by their wrists, concentrated, and took us into the warehouse.

It would have been the perfect escape, except I arrived alone. One of the frames displayed a confused Hannah and Aura looking around wildly since I'd just vanished right in front of them. It was a good thing I hadn't tried this while rescuing Hannah, or she would've been abandoned in the river, sucked underground, and drowned.

I needed to consult Noctua again and specifically ask if taking living beings through the ring with me was possible since inanimate objects traveled just fine. The ring was already making me dizzy to the point of nausea, thanks to my state of exhaustion.

I considered running to the aisle where the apocalypse weapons were stored, but using one risked annihilating Minos. Hannah had proven adept at controlling Earthmaker, but she was in no shape to be wielding it now.

I took off Panoptes and the dizziness faded. I ran over to a stash of med kits, pulled out a stamina potion, and downed it. Energy flooded my body. I'd pay dearly for it later, but it'd get me by for now.

I grabbed two duffel bags with emergency gear, slung them over my shoulders, then slipped the ring on and traveled back to Hannah and Aura.

Hannah gasped. "Cain, where in the hell did you go?"

"No time to explain." I took off the ring and secured it in a utility belt pouch, then unzipped a duffel bag and handed her and Aura clockwork rifles I'd liberated from mechanists during our adventure on Gaia Alpha. I grabbed magazines marked blue and handed them each one. "These are shock rounds. They should put the centaurs down for a while."

Hannah snapped the magazine into place and spun the clockwork mechanism to load the chamber. The guns were constructed of old brass and stained wood with redundant pipes and gauges along the sides that did little except satisfy the mechanist aesthetic. The bullets were powered by liquid mana instead of gunpowder, and some even had rocket fins to allow them limited guidance to a target.

Then I pulled out my ace—an M72 LAW rocket launcher.

Nub weapons were typically my last choice in any situation. I had an oblivion staff, dueling wands, and plenty of magic for most situations. But when it came to big explosions, the nubs had the best gear in the smallest packages, hands down.

The centaurs were only a few blocks away and closing fast. I peered through the scope on the LAW, aimed it at the portcullis, and fired. The rocket roared toward the target, leaving a trail of white smoke. The impact was glorious. Splintered wood rained down. The chains securing the drawbridge snapped and it slammed to earth.

With the stamina potion fueling my body, I dropped the empty LAW, brandished my clockwork rifle and motioned toward the gate like a soldier in a war movie. "Go, go, go!"

Hannah slung the duffel bag over her shoulder and started running. Aura took off after her, and I brought up the rear. Arrows zipped through the air. Centaurs brandishing war hammers, battle-axes, and maces galloped after us, war cries on their lips.

I glanced back and realized I'd forgotten to grab the other duffel bag, but it was too late now. I fired a shock round at the lead centaur. The bullet caught her full in the chest. She danced like a puppet, and her legs folded. Her horse ass flipped over her head, and she rolled to a stop. Cervitaurs and centaurs right behind her skidded to a stop to avoid trampling her.

Another centaur swooped in from the side, swinging a flail over his head. I nailed him in his rump, and he went down in a heap. I took down three more of our pursuers as we raced for the draw-bridge. I'd hoped the rest would give up, but they only roared battle cries and charged.

Many of them looked young enough to be children. I imagined that was because the bulk of the fighters had gone in another direction while searching for us. These were the ones who weren't old enough to join the army just yet.

"They're fucking relentless!" Aura shouted as she fired and downed several more.

There was no way to outrun the centaurs, so I stopped, knelt, and began firing. Every shot hit a target. Hannah nailed three more in four shots. Aura took out a dozen trying to flank us. Within a few seconds, only a few stragglers were left standing.

"I'm out," Aura said.

Hannah tossed her a magazine from the duffel bag, then tossed me one before ejecting the one in her rifle and reloading. She tossed the empty mags into the duffel bag. "Clear."

I nodded. "Clear."

Aura raised an eyebrow. "You two really have this fighting stuff down, don't you?"

Hannah chuckled. "Cain doesn't take me out for ice cream. He teaches me how to survive and kill."

"I teach you how to defend yourself." I watched the last few standing centaurs and cervitaurs as they milled about uncertainly, then I stood and started backing toward the bridge. "Let's go."

"Well, I don't think we killed anyone." Aura caught up to me. "I'm surprised you chose non-lethal when they would have killed us if they could."

"They might've broken their necks when they fell," Hannah said. "I mean, all that horse flesh falling on the human part can't be good for you."

"You sound like you hope someone died." I glanced back at her.

"They were trying to kill us." Hannah kept a wary eye on the centaurs. "Nothing wrong with killing someone who wants you dead."

"We're trespassing in their territory. They don't like humans. It's okay to respect that even when we're defending ourselves."

"But why?" Hannah looked confused. "Did humans take them as slaves too?"

I frowned. "Not that I know of. Humans were once enslaved by orcs and goblins, but I think they were treated better than the so-called sentient beasts."

"So, it's a jealousy thing." Hannah scowled. "Then again, humans are kind of despicable."

"Agreed," Aura said without hesitation. "But the ones who live on Feary are a lot different than the ones on Gaia. The ones here have never been at the top of the food chain, so they're not as arrogant or entitled as the ones we know and love."

We navigated the smoking kindling that had once been the portcullis, then ran across the bridge. I considered our future options. There was no way in hell we could come back this way. We'd have to cross the mountains or find a town on the coast and hire a ship. There nearest fast-travel mushrooms were hundreds of miles away from our destination, which was why I'd chosen the one near Crete since it was considerably closer.

I reached into the duffel bag hanging from Hannah's shoulder and fished out plastic explosives.

"Whoa." Hannah's eyes lit with excitement. "Are we blowing the drawbridge?"

I kept digging through the supplies inside but couldn't find one critical component. I took the bag from Hannah and set it on the ground, then sifted through dozens of magazines, health kits, and more before concluding that I hadn't packed the one thing necessary for the explosives to work.

Hannah frowned. "Where are the detonators?"

I looked up at her. "You tell me. You helped me pack the duffel bags. I made sure every bag I packed was fully stocked."

Hannah grimaced. "I thought I double-checked, but I don't remember."

I tossed the explosives and magazines back into the duffel bag. We were in the clear for now, but the war horn I'd heard earlier sounded closer. The drawbridge was made of thick timber. We'd only packed one emergency rocket launcher in each duffel bag, and without the detonators, the plastic explosives were useless. I summoned my staff and ignited the brightblade.

"Do we have time for this?" Aura glanced furtively at the city.

"We've got the other half of the labyrinth to go through. If we don't take down the bridge, they'll storm in and chase us down before we escape." I dug the brightblade into the wood. It was like cutting through frozen butter with a table knife. "The wood must have a strengthening enchantment."

"I told you two rocket launchers are better than one." Hannah glared at the bridge as if trying to activate her powers again. "This is taking forever!"

"Cain, let's use our head start to our advantage." Aura gripped my forearm. "Maybe the citizens of Crete don't know the labyrinth as well as Taurin."

I rolled my eyes. "Of course they do."

Hannah raced ahead into the first section of the maze.

"Where are you going?" I shouted.

She didn't respond.

"She's got the right idea." Aura huffed. "Stop being stubborn, Cain!"

"We're never going to outrun fucking centaurs!" I was nearly a quarter of the way through the bridge. "They can't jump the moat."

"Can't they?" Aura measured it with her gaze.

"It's damned near fifty feet wide." I shook my head. "I don't think centaurs can clear that distance."

Hannah's shouts echoed from the labyrinth.

"Well, shit. Is she in trouble already?" I gritted my teeth. "Go check on her."

A mass of centaurs, minotaurs, cervitaurs, and some taurs I'd never seen before thundered into sight and began shouting at the sight of their stunned comrades.

"Now we're fucked," Aura said.

I banished my staff since there was no way in Hel I could finish cutting up the bridge in time. "Yeah, we're fucked."

Hannah ran out of the maze, still shouting. I braced myself for whatever was chasing her, but then she grabbed my arm and dragged me toward the maze. "Let's go!" she said. "I found a way out."

"You what?" I was trying to grasp how she'd already found her way out of the labyrinth unless it was considerably smaller on this side of the city, but I ran after her since there were no other options.

We came to a garden. A minotaur statue stood to the side of a spiral staircase leading underground. I glanced at its massive dong and grimaced. "Same kind of secret lever?"

She nodded. "Just give the dick a good yank and you're in!"

"That's what she said," I muttered darkly.

"Fastest way to a man's heart." Aura hurried downstairs and the rest of us followed. I found the chain underneath and tugged it. The minotaur statue grated back into place.

Crystals hummed to life, lighting a chamber intersected by five corridors. We were back in the underground maze.

5

I'd carefully watched Taurin when he'd led us through the underground labyrinth on the other side of the city. This section of the maze looked remarkably similar to the outer section on the other side of the city. Was it possible the path on this side was identical to the other?

There was only one way to find out.

It would probably take some time for our pursuers to realize we'd gone underground. Or they might never realize we had. But one wrong move down here, and we'd end up trapped. One of us could escape to the warehouse with the ring, but that didn't do us much good since there was no way out of the warehouse.

Once again, I summoned my staff and peered through the true sight scope. Then, I headed in the same direction Taurin had taken on the other side of the underground maze. "Wait here, and let me scout ahead." I headed around a curve, took a left, avoided a trap trigger, and reached a dead end. Apparently, the route wasn't identical on this side.

I went back to the others and studied at the other corridors. Four more choices. Three too many. Some might lead me for miles before reaching a dead end. There might be dozens of other branches along the way, none of which led where I needed to go.

"Maybe we should split up," Hannah said.

I shook my head. "The true sight scope is the only thing keeping us from walking into traps. If a wall closes us off from each other, we're fucked."

"Agreed." Aura scuffed her shoe on the stone floor. "I'd rather be trapped in the aboveground labyrinth where I can see the sky and eat delicious veggies from the gardens."

I retraced Taurin's route in my head and realized my mistake. "Be right back." I took the opposite corridor that Taurin had taken on the other side of the maze and followed it. I only had to go a few hundred yards before determining it was the right way. This side of the maze was identical but reversed from the one on the other side.

Hannah looked at me expectantly when I rejoined her and Aura. "Figure it out?"

"Yep." I waved them on. "This way."

"How?" Hannah shook her head. "Was it the sigils you left?"

"Nah." I started walking. "I memorized the route and reversed it."

Aura caught up to me. "Please tell me you used magic. Because I have a good memory, and there's no way in Hades I could've memorized the route through the maze."

"Memory sigils." I tapped one of the invisible tattoos beneath my head of hair. "For when you really have to remember something."

She looked a bit relieved. "Well, now I don't feel so bad about myself."

Hannah made a face. "It's not all about you, Aura."

"I know." Aura held up her hands defensively. "I've just never been one of those people who can walk into a room and notice everything right away like Cain does. Nor can I memorize a freaking miles-long route through a maze."

I motioned them to keep moving. "Can we get going now?"

Hannah bowed deeply. "Lead the way, almighty memorizer of mazes."

I spun on my heel and set a brisk pace. By using the true sight scope and following a flipped version of Taurin's path, I led the others on a long, twisting route. We eventually reached a dead end.

Hannah looked alarmed. "You messed up, didn't you?"

Aura walked to the wall and revealed a chain that was hidden in a slot in the wall. "No, we're right where we need to be."

Hannah blew out a sigh of relief. "We must be under a garden near the end of the aboveground maze."

"Yeah." I just hoped an army of centaurs wasn't already there waiting for us. "Wait here." I pulled the chain, and a statue above grated out of the way.

A hulking minotaur rushed downstairs, a pair of female centaurs, centaurides, close on his heels. The centaurides wore thick leather armor on their human torsos with longbows sheathed to their horse part, and broadswords on their human backs. A cervitauride trotted down after them.

My brightblade hummed to life. Hannah and Aura brandished their clockwork rifles.

The minotaur held up his hands defensively. "Cain!"

"Hold fire!" I held up a fist. "Taurin?"

The minotaur nodded. "I noticed you were using sigils to mark the path I led you on, so I surmised you might be able to solve the puzzle yourself."

I shrugged. "It's just reversed."

He nodded. "And you were able to avoid triggering traps by using your staff."

"Yeah." I glanced at his three companions. "How'd you even know we went underground?"

He displayed a leather bracelet on his wrist. "This allows me to control aspects of the maze and detect when things are changed. When you moved the statue, I felt it."

"All of Minos mobilized for war simply because of two humans and an elf?" One of the centaurides stomped a hoof. "What has our society come to? They look harmless!"

"Forgive me for not introducing my companions." Taurin waved at the others. "This is Thelea, Ismolis, and Kalith."

Kalith, the cervitauride, bowed slightly, her pointy doe ears twitching. The centaurides acknowledged us with curt nods.

Hannah regarded them uncertainly. "Um, so why did you bring your friends?"

"Once he told us about you, I insisted he let us aid you," Kalith said. "I have long been opposed to the ban on humans and believe we should be reaching out to other species, not withdrawing into isolation. It's time for the labyrinth to be dismantled, and for our priestess to lead us into a new age."

"I do not agree with the teachings of the priestess." Taurin scowled. "But I also believe that you should not be hunted down and murdered just because you are human. And if Cain is truly the Liberator, then that is doubly true."

"If we allowed your deaths, we would truly be the monsters some claim us to be." Kalith shook her head sadly. "Taurin used the bracelet to manipulate the labyrinth and draw your pursuers away. I suggest we depart immediately so we might aid in your escape."

Aura furrowed her brow. "How exactly will you aid us?"

Thelea patted her horse back. "You will ride us."

"Oh, that's cool!" Hannah clapped her hands. "I didn't even know riding a centaur was a thing!"

"We are centaurides." Thelea narrowed her eyes. "Centaurs are male."

Hannah blinked. "Oh, I thought you'd be called mares."

Thelea and Ismolis glowered.

Kalith laughed. "That is actually a terrible insult."

Hannah paled. "Oh, god, I'm sorry! I never met a centaur—I mean centauride—before today."

Kalith touched a hand to her own chest. "I don't mind being called a doe, but the proper term is cervitauride."

Hannah looked sheepishly at Taurin. "Are female minotaurs called minotaurides?"

"Indeed." Thelea pursed her lips. "The man-child has figured it out."

"Man-child?" Hannah giggled. "What is this, the Jungle Book?"

I sighed. "Can we get on with this?"

Ismolis stomped a hoof. "Agreed. There is no time to waste." She turned and trotted up the wide spiral stairs, tail twitching in agitation.

We followed them upstairs to the aboveground labyrinth where Taurin led us to the exit. A grassy savannah extended as far as the eye could see, framed by steep mountains to the east and west. There was no way the three of us could have made it far across the open expanse before the army of Minos caught up to us.

Ismolis gripped my arm. "Mount me."

"Yeah, Cain, ride her!" Hannah snickered and climbed onto Kalith's back.

Aura rolled her eyes. "Girl, you sound like Layla now."

I hoisted myself onto Ismolis. The leather armor on her horse back wasn't quite as good as a saddle, but there were stirrups to brace my feet on. I located loops at the waist of the leather armor on her human torso. "Is this where I hold on?"

Ismolis nodded. "You are perceptive."

Hannah located the same loops on Kalith's armor and gripped them. "Why do you have stirrups on your armor?"

"They are for our elven allies to use," Ismolis said. "They have helped us repel goblin hordes in the past."

"Oh." Hannah stood in the stirrups and settled back down. "That makes sense."

Aura hopped onto Thelea, and without further ado, our steeds galloped south, leaving Taurin without so much as a goodbye.

"Taurin seemed awfully intent on killing me earlier." I braced my feet in the stirrups to alleviate the pounding my ass was taking. "Why the sudden change of heart?"

"He is a gentle soul," Ismolis said. "Violence has never been his preference."

"Gods be damned, he seemed pretty fucking violent when I ran into him in the labyrinth."

"Because that is what our society has beaten into our heads." She shrugged. "He came to me because he was torn about what to do with you. Did he do as society expected and show the others where you were, or did he follow his better judgement?"

If Taurin was a gentle soul, I was glad we hadn't run into the ones leading the hunt for us.

Ismolis and her companions covered a lot of ground over the next hour, finally reaching the coast where columns of white stone jutted from the black sands. Rusted chains hung from most of them, making it apparent that more beings than just Prometheus had been imprisoned on these shores.

"It is a travesty what they did to Prometheus." Ismolis said. "He gave his creations fire so that they might thrive, but Zeus wanted the mortals weak and entirely dependent on him."

I looked out at the rocks as I dismounted. "Which one was Prometheus chained to?"

She pointed to a column of stone that stood taller than the others, its peak stained almost black. "There."

"These other rocks were not used by the gods," Kalith said. "The merfolk use them to chain up invaders. They do not allow the goblins or other mountain folk to fish their waters."

Hannah hopped to the ground. "Merfolk can walk on land?"

"Some of them, yes." Kalith turned toward Minos. "We should go before we are missed."

I nodded at the trio. "Thank you for the help."

"Fare thee well, Cain." Ismolis galloped away and her comrades with her.

I summoned my staff and examined the bloodstained rock where the Titan, Prometheus, had once been bound—his liver devoured every day by an eagle. We'd finally reached the starting point of the quest—the last place Aura Beta had been seen—at least by Zeus, Mars, and Hermes. Tracking her down was going to be extremely difficult given the elapsed time since her escape.

The dangling chains were shiny and untarnished unlike the rusting remains of those on the other rocks. They'd no doubt been forged by Hephaestus and created to be inescapable. There were no locks, no keyholes that I could see, but I wanted to examine them up close and in person.

The beach was about twenty feet below the side of a cliff, but there were enough ridges and slopes to make the descent easy in comparison to some places I'd scaled. We walked along the clifftop until we were even with Prometheus's Rock. Even with the height of the cliff, the rock towered over us by a good forty feet.

My grappling hook and rope had snapped off at some point during our escape in the aqueduct, but I had all the spares I needed in the warehouse. I took out the ring and slipped it on. "Be right back."

"Cain, wait!" Hannah reached out a hand, but I'd already traveled away.

I now stood in the warehouse, but I could still see Hannah and Aura in the other frame. By willing just my consciousness through, I could listen to them, even move about and spy on them. That was how Aura Beta had infiltrated Sanctuary, by following me with the ring. Once her consciousness had been through my wards, she was free to bring over her body.

The ring had limitations, but it was a powerful and addicting tool. Even with this momentary use of its powers, I felt the dizzying madness burrowing away at my consciousness. Keeping it on for too long would probably drive me as insane as Aura Beta.

I took off the ring and sighed with relief as the vertigo receded and my vision stopped swimming, then went over to the emergency stash and grabbed the rock-climbing gear. I made a mental note to put more bags with explosives in here so I wouldn't suffer a debacle like the one back in Crete. Despite my constant preplanning, there were so many other things I could have stored here that would've made this adventure a lot easier.

I blew out a breath. "Next time I'm storing dirt cycles."

With the ring on once more, my view split into a honeycomb of frames, showing me the beach, the dark places, the winter and desert worlds, and the warehouse. I'd tried envisioning Sanctuary and other destinations, but the ring only allowed travelling back to the last place I'd been.

I concentrated on going to the beach, and suddenly, I stood in front of Hannah and Aura.

Hannah gripped my forearm. "Cain, you need to tell me how in the hell you're doing that right now!"

I slipped off the ring and held it up. "Panoptes."

Aura blinked. "All-seeing?"

I nodded and tucked it into my utility belt.

"Oh no you don't." Hannah tried to reach into the pouch.

I diverted her hand with a quick flick of my hand.

She glared at me. "What's Panoptes? How does it make you vanish?"

Aura narrowed her eyes. "Cain, did you get that from my evil doppelganger?"

I knelt at the edge of the cliff and started hammering in a spike. "Yep. It's what made her go insane. It's how she was able to get into Sanctuary, knock out Aura Alpha, and join us to go see the gods without anyone knowing."

Hannah regarded me with judging eyes. "Why didn't you tell me about it, Cain? I understand you not wanting Aura to know, but..." Tears pooled in her eyes. "You don't trust me?"

I gave her a look, then resumed pounding the spike deep into the rock. "That's a dumb question."

"Cain doesn't trust anyone, Hannah." Aura sighed. "After all we've been through—"

"Shut it, Aura!" Hannah's fists balled. "You have no room to talk."

Aura backed up a step. "Are you seriously still upset about the past?"

"You betrayed us because you wanted to use me as a puppet for the Ender faction, you fucking bitch! Of course, I don't trust you. But I trust Cain with my life!" She dropped to her knees next to me. "And I thought he trusted me with everything."

I secured a rope to the spike and tested it. "Let's rappel—"

Hannah gripped my shirt and went nose-to-nose with me. "Cain, why didn't you trust me with this?"

"It's not about trust." I met her gaze with a stony gaze of my own. "I don't have to explain every little thing to you or anyone else. Just trust that I will do what's best."

"What's best for you?" Hanna released my shirt and wiped away her tears. "I guess you're best at looking out for number one."

"That's not true, Hannah." Aura stood to the side, well out of reach of her. "I don't think Cain would be chasing down Aura Beta if he didn't care about others."

I stood and brushed dirt off my pants. "This isn't about saving others. It's about not letting her murder us in our sleep or destroying Prime with apocalypse weapons."

Hannah remained on her knees, eyes to the ground. "I—I don't understand you, Cain," she said in a quiet voice. "I thought you loved me. I thought we were a family."

Her words stabbed me like a knife to the heart, and I hated the strong emotions that evoked. "We are, Hannah. But that doesn't mean I'm not going to keep secrets from you."

"Then I'll keep secrets from you, asshole!" She threw a clump of dirt at my legs. "Don't ask me about anything anymore! We're done!"

6

Hannah and I argued plenty, but this was obviously hitting her a lot harder than usual. Deep down, I understood why even if I didn't agree with it. Keeping secrets was just something people did, especially if they'd been a trained assassin most of their life.

I tried to refocus on the task at hand, but knew I needed to nip this argument in the bud before it derailed everything. "Did I need to include you on this mission, Hannah?"

She frowned. "I don't know. You just asked me if I wanted to come."

"Yeah, I did. Because I trust you. Because I thought it would be a growing experience for you."

"You didn't ask me to come," Aura said.

Hannah flicked her gaze to her. "Shut up."

Aura backpedaled.

I continued to press. "I could have left you a note and gone, but I didn't."

"Is it because Shae left?" Fresh tears trickled down her cheeks. "Because you knew I was depressed and lonely?"

I almost said no, but she and Shae's relationship had come to a nasty end. Shae had returned to Gaia Alpha to train with Cain Alpha, and Hannah had been beside herself with grief and regret. It hurt my soul to see her like that but admitting to it felt shameful. That shame was all thanks to my training in the Oblivion Guard and my adoptive father, Erolith. Guardians weren't supposed to allow emotions to guide their actions, but I'd broken that code countless times with Hannah.

So, I swallowed the prideful part of me that didn't want to admit emotions affected me and nodded. "Yes. I wanted to spend time with you and make you forget about Shae."

Hannah's lips quivered, and a smile broke through her tears. "Fuck you, Cain. You're the worst dad ever." She lunged and gripped me in a tight hug. "And the best. God, you make me so angry!"

I patted her back. "So, I'm not your big bro anymore?"

She shook her head without moving it from my chest. "No, you're way too much like a dad to ever be a brother. I realize that now. A brother wouldn't hide so much shit from me."

I'd tried to resist all the familial titles, but this one felt like it fit better. I tried to gently escape her embrace, but she shook her head and held on tight. "No way. I need this hug."

Aura sat down on a rock, apparently resigned to let the family drama play out.

I broke the awkward hug with a statement. "Panoptes drove Aura Beta insane."

Hannah let go and backed up. "How?"

I took out the ring and put it in her hand. "Try it on."

She slipped it on and gasped, staggering back. "This is trippy." Hannah wrenched it off her finger. "It's yucky but cool at the same time." She hiccupped and projectile vomited tomatoes nearly ten feet through the air. Eyes wide with surprise, she looked at me. "I don't know why that happened."

"Bad drugs, I guess."

Aura watched us in open-mouthed horror. "Cain, what does the ring do besides turn Hannah into the girl from The Exorcist?"

"It allows you to see multiple places at once. You can travel to those places, which is what I did." I put the ring away. "But the more you use it, the more of your sanity it claims."

"Aura Beta must have gotten it from the lost armory on Oblivion Beta." Aura stood. "Guess it's no better for mere mortals than most of the weapons in there."

"Yeah. Nothing from that place can be used without paying a price." I helped Hannah to her feet. "Now, can we get going?"

Hannah wiped her mouth with the back of her hand and nodded. "Yeah, I'm feeling better now."

"Can I try it on?" Aura said.

I shook my head. "No."

Aura slumped. "Gods be damned. I didn't realize you two still hated and distrusted me so much."

"I don't hate you, Aura." I tested the rope and handed it to Hannah. "You made up for a lot, but broken trust takes a long time to mend."

"Yeah, it's not like the movies." Hannah clipped on a belay and rappelled smoothly down the cliff, just like I'd taught her. She was a fast learner in everything except how to control her god powers.

Aura looked hurt. "You treat me like I'm dead weight."

I pulled up the rope, tied the duffel to it, and lowered it to Hannah.

As if to prove her point, Aura launched herself away from the cliff and rappelled to the ground in two bounces. "I used to be a highly skilled infiltrator and bounty hunter. I'm not totally useless."

Hannah rolled her eyes.

I took a moment to enjoy some alone time at the top of the cliff while I considered my life choices. My emotions had gone almost numb during my short stint as the Grim Reaper, but now they seemed to be careening back the other way. I'd let my emotions dictate who to invite on dangerous missions. I should have done this alone instead of weighing myself down with others.

Hannah called up from below. "Cain, what are you doing? Are you thinking about running away from us?"

"Yep." I took a deep breath and slid the rope through the belay. "Unfortunately, I have to go down there."

I joined the others at the bottom and faced them. "Any other grievances I need to address before we track down a murderous world killer?"

Hannah shook her head. "No, Dad."

The word knocked the wind out of me for a minute. I hated to admit that a part of me liked it nearly as much as another part of me despised it. "Thanks, Daughter."

I'd hoped saying that would shock her out of calling me Dad. Instead, she giggled and grinned like a maniac.

I groaned.

Aura stared glumly at us. "Well, I feel like a real third wheel now."

"You invited yourself, Aura." Hannah huffed. "Get over it."

"I really felt like we were friends!" Aura threw up her hands. "Did you treat Aura Alpha like you're treating me?"

"You're like a semi-friend," Hannah said. "And no, we treated Aura Alpha better because she technically wasn't the one who betrayed us."

"But she betrayed your alts!"

"Yeah, but not us." Hannah shrugged. "I mean, it's weird, but I'm still mad at you, not her."

Aura turned to me. "What about you, Cain?"

"Meh." I shrugged and turned away from them so I could study Prometheus's Rock through my scope. Scaling it looked treacherous, but it was necessary if I was going to find a way to track Aura Beta.

"Fine. Time to pull out the big guns." Aura unslung her backpack and withdrew a dark wooden box.

Hannah reached out to touch it, but Aura slapped her hand away.

"Ow!" Hannah balled her fists. "What is that thing?"

I swiveled and ignited the brightblade. "Hannah, back up!"

Aura's eyes flared. "Gods damn it, Cain, what are you doing?"

"Open it slowly," I growled. Was it possible Aura Beta had replaced Prime? The box was carved with intricate sigils, most of which I didn't recognize.

Aura huffed. "You know I'm immortal, right?"

"Yeah, but you'll be dead until midnight."

She scowled. "Fuck you." Aura traced a sigil on the front and opened the box. Inside, were three frosty glasses, each one holding beautiful golden liquid. Aura glared up at me. "Are you still scared, Cain?"

I banished the brightblade and stepped forward. "Are these mangoritas?"

She nodded. "This is an ancient elven lunchbox. I figured you might enjoy mangoritas on the trip."

I nodded. "Gods damn you, Aura. You know my weakness."

Aura lifted her chin in victory. "Apologize to me and you can have one."

I hated apologizing, but sometimes it was just necessary. "I'm sorry I mistrusted your intent."

Hannah groaned. "God, Cain, you're pathetic!"

Aura handed me the freezing cold glass, then plucked a curly straw, an umbrella, and a plastic pirate sword from the lunchbox. She slid the sword through a slice of pineapple and cherry, then placed it in the drink, opened the miniature umbrella, and placed it on the other side. Smirking, she dunked the curly straw deep into the golden cocktail.

She patted my hand. "Enjoy."

"Pathetic!" Hannah threw up her hands. "Aura, you conniving little bar wench!"

I took a sip and groaned in ecstasy. "Gods, it tastes fresh."

Aura closed the lunchbox and patted it. "This keeps any kind of food as fresh as the moment you made it."

I sighed in appreciation and set the glass on a flat rock so I could resume looking at Prometheus's Rock through the scope.

Aura sidled up next to me. "Are you glad I came along now, Cain?"

"Yep."

"Pathetic." Hannah blew out a breath of disgust. "What now?"

A glint of metal on the side of the rock caught my eye. "We go closer." I banished my staff, picked up the mangorita, and started walking.

The fine black sand was so loose underfoot that it made progress slow. That was fine by me, because it gave me time to enjoy the mangorita. The tide was creeping in slowly but surely, waves crashing against rocks that had been on dry land only moments ago. It seemed this entire area would be underwater soon.

That was bad news in more ways than one. It meant all signs of footprints in the sand had long since been washed away. It meant we didn't have long to inspect the rock. It also meant that we'd be in territorial waters of the merfolk of this region. If they were really stringing up goblins and other intruders, I didn't want to be around here for long.

I picked up the pace and reached the rock about halfway through my mangorita. Even without the scope, I was able to confirm my theory. The metallic gleam belonged to spikes hammered into the rock. Rope hung from a spike far above, but most of it seemed to have been hacked off with a serrated edge.

"Someone climbed it already." Hannah tugged on the lowest spike and walked around the rock to follow the pattern. "Why didn't they hammer them in straight up?"

I took out a hammer and spike and tested it on the slick, white stone. Despite hitting it with all my strength, the spike didn't so much as chip the rock. "It's magically hardened. Whoever did this found the weak spots in the enchantment and nailed in spikes where they could."

The spikes I'd brought were enchanted to penetrate even the toughest rock or hardening spells, but Prometheus's Rock was protected by god-level magic. The spikes used by the last person to scale the rock were identical to mine. That wasn't uncommon in the magical community where only a few shops sold such enhanced gear.

There were shops aplenty that sold magical adventuring gear in Feary, but I was positive these spikes had come from the same shop I used on Gaia. Since the rope and spikes were enchanted to resist weathering, it was hard to tell how old they were. I suspected they hadn't been there for long.

Hannah frowned. "You think someone climbed the rock and freed Baura?"

I raised an eyebrow. "Baura, as in Beta Aura?"

"It's easier than spitting out her name and dimension every time." Hannah shrugged.

"Good enough." I took another sip of mangorita and savored it despite the encroaching tide. "Anyone who had to use climbing gear to scale the rock wouldn't be able to free Baura from the magic chains." I handed my mangorita to Aura. "Don't spill a drop."

She craned her neck to look way up the rock. "You're going up there? Why?"

"To look for Baura's blood."

Aura frowned. "Wouldn't it have washed away by now?"

I hadn't planned on explaining my theory, but decided it was worth it if only to avoid a slew of questions. I ran my hand along the smooth stone. "There are almost no pits on the surface. No crevices. But there are a few weak spots in the enchantment as proven by whoever hammered these spikes in." I pointed at the blackened top of the stone. "The top is stained with Prometheus's blood even though the enchantment should prevent it from being stained.

Hannah snapped her fingers. "Prometheus was a Titan."

"Exactly." I pointed out the cracks in the rock where the spikes had been hammered. "His struggles eventually cracked the rock and weakened the enchantment in places. That's why his blood stained the top."

"I still don't see how that's helpful," Aura said.

"It means that there might be cracks on the surface up there." Hannah crossed her arms and looked smug. "It means that Baura's blood might have gotten trapped in one of those cracks and not been washed away by rain."

"Oh." Aura pressed her lips together. "I don't see how rain wouldn't get into every little crack if blood got into it."

"Rain would splash against the surface and be repelled by the functioning parts of the enchantment, right, Cain?" Hannah looked like a student expecting a gold star for her fridge. "Blood is thick, and with her lying on the stone, it would seep into tiny fissures that rain couldn't reach."

"Exactly." I gripped the lowest spike and hoisted myself up. Using my best Schwarzenegger voice, I said, "I'll be back."

Hannah grinned. "Get to the choppah, Billy!"

I started climbing. The spikes were spaced far apart due to the random location of the weak spots in the rock—so far, in fact, that when I'd climbed about fifty feet up, the next spike was too far to reach without jumping and grabbing it. I paused to consider how the previous climber managed to hammer a spike in an area that was impossible to reach from this one.

There was no evidence to suggest it, but it was possible they'd used the stone's impervious enchantment to their advantage. I fished in my utility pack and pulled out a small suction cup. I pressed it to the smooth stone and powered the sigil on the side to enhance the grip. It remained affixed when I released it and even when I tugged on it. It certainly wouldn't hold my weight, but there were larger suction cups designed to scale smooth surfaces that would do the trick.

Hannah shielded her eyes with a hand as she looked up at me. "Cain, what are you doing?"

"Just confirming a theory." I removed the suction cup and put it back in my pack, then leaped to the other spike, grabbing it with one hand, then yanking hard to launch myself to the one just above it so I could rest my foot on the first one.

"Aren't you going to use a safety rope?" Hannah shouted.

I reached for the rope dangling from the top of the cliff and tested it with my weight. It seemed secure, so I clipped my belay onto it and used it to scale to the top. Once there, I glanced out at the ocean. The tide was nearly halfway to the base of the rock. I had maybe fifteen minutes before the others would be standing in ankle-deep water.

I removed a tiny vial containing Aura's blood from my utility belt and dripped the crimson liquid inside onto my finger. Then, I traced a simple sigil and powered it. Aura's blood trickled in thin lines in several directions, stopping when it reached what I was looking for. Since Aura Prime's blood was virtually identical to Baura's blood, the spell was able to seek out any fluid matching it.

I followed each line and found miniscule fissures at the end of each one. I attached the smallest needle I had to a syringe and carefully inserted it into a fissure. After a few minutes of gentle prodding, I was able to extract drops of watery blood. I squeezed the blood into a clean vial, then went to work on the other fissures.

Within ten minutes, I had enough watery blood to possibly make a tracking spell work. Due to Aura's immortality curse, her blood tended to survive longer outside her body than was normally possible. If this blood was still viable, then finding her would be much easier.

One might wonder why I didn't simply use Aura Prime's blood to track Baura. That had been the first thing I'd tried. It was also how Aura had found out about my plans to track down Baura and invited herself on this adventure. Although Aura's blood was virtually identical to the blood of her alts from the Alpha and Beta dimensions, the tracking spell pointed only to her when I used it. There was something that differentiated her blood from that of her alts.

Fitz, my friendly neighborhood shaman, said it was likely that the different dimensions existed on a slightly different frequency of space time, which was how they occupied the same physical place but were still separate. It meant that Aura's blood was missing that intangible frequency that could be used to track Baura.

That was the theory, at least. Fitz and I still hadn't figured out how Aura's blood had worked to free Athena from Soultaker even though Baura had been the one to kill the goddess. It did, however, possibly account for Athena's insane behavior after being freed. Then again, she, an immortal goddess, had been trapped in a realm where she was violently killed in battle and resurrected every day. It was enough to break the psyche of anyone.

Motion in the ocean drew my gaze. The high perch of Prometheus's Rock gave me an excellent vantage point. I wouldn't have seen the fast-moving objects otherwise. Using my scope, I zoomed in. Triangular fins jutted above the surface, drawing foamy wakes in the salt water. Their trajectory would take them right to us.

I wasn't particularly worried about sharks. They weren't any larger here than the ones on Gaia, as far as I knew. It was just odd that they were moving with such precision right toward the rock.

One of them leaped from the water, arcing a good twenty feet through the air. That was when I realized they weren't sharks at all. They were merfolk, and not the beautiful, alluring kind that lived in the oceans north of Faevalorn. These had human torsos and the back fins and lower halves of sharks. At the speed they were traveling, they'd be here in minutes.

If we didn't reach the cliffs before then, it'd be our blood in the water.

7

I leaned over the side of the rock and shouted down at the others. "Get back to the cliff. The merfolk are coming!"

"Do we really need to worry about them?" Hannah called back up.

I cupped my hands. "They're shark people, for fuck's sake!"

"Oh, shit!" Hannah looked at the ocean then back to me. "What about you?"

"Just go, I'm coming!" I stuffed the vial of Baura blood into my utility belt, gripped the rope, and rappelled pell-mell down the side of the rock.

Hannah and Aura were already trudging through the thick sand back toward the rope on the cliff. The ankle-deep water slowed their progress to a crawl. I reached the end of the rope and swung over to the nearest spike. The shark fins were less than a half mile away and moving fast.

I dropped from twenty feet up. The thick sand and water cushioned the fall. Slogging through the now knee-deep water, I fought to catch up to the others. Even with their head start, I didn't think they'd reach safety before the merfolk caught up. I considered climbing back up Prometheus's Rock but spending the night up there didn't appeal to me.

Alternatively, I could simply use Panoptes to slip into the ware-house and then move unseen to the cliff. But doing that would still leave Hannah and Aura as targets. I cast a look over my shoulder and confirmed my fears. I had maybe a minute before the merfolk caught up. At my current slog through the ever-deepening water, I'd still be a good distance short of the cliff.

Aura and Hannah would still have another thirty yards to go by then as well. I wasn't keen on fighting merfolk in their natural element, but if I slipped back to the warehouse quickly, I could retrieve Tidebringer and shift the odds in my favor. I reached into a pouch and put on the ring. The instant dizziness as my vision split while moving through the knee-high water nearly tripped me up. I traveled to the warehouse and tore off the ring. I was in the last place I'd been in the building near the emergency stashes. The apocalypse weapons were three rows down.

Still reeling from the side-effects, I ran down the aisle, turned left, and raced to the stash of apocalypse weapons. Aside from Soultaker, which was now stored in the vault beneath Sanctuary, I hadn't even touched them. I'd learned that the immense power vested in them was addicting. The more you used them, the more you wanted to use them.

The great trident, Tidebringer, hung next to the war hammer, Earthmaker. I gripped the trident and immediately realized some-thing was off. The apocalypse weapons, Earthmaker, Tidebringer, Soultaker, and Airbender, had been crafted by Hephaestus, the blacksmith of the gods. They were perfectly honed. Perfectly balanced.

This thing in my hand right felt like a dead lump of steel compared to Tidebringer. I gripped Earthmaker and confirmed that it was also a counterfeit. Airbender as well. That was all I had time for since the merfolk were about to chow down on Hannah and Aura. I put on the ring again and slipped back to the ocean. The merfolk were well past my position and closing fast on the others.

The water was up to my stomach already, slowing progress even more. Shark fins ducked below water and then emerged in front of Hannah and Aura. They could eat Aura for all I cared. She'd reincarnate at midnight. Hannah, however, would not. The merfolk wouldn't be much of a problem if Hannah could control her powers, but considering the girl had already drained herself dry in Minos, it was unlikely she'd have any juice left.

The merfolk rose as if standing on two feet. Their faces were human, but their eyes were black as pitch, and their skin was slightly grey. They wore skintight fish scale armor over their chests and heads which probably reduced water drag. None of them brandished weapons. Then again, they had shark teeth.

Hannah unslung the clockwork rifle and leveled it at them. "What do you want?"

A mermaid stepped forward, her dark eyes locking onto me for an instant before turning to Aura. "You!" she hissed. "Vengeance shall be ours!"

Hannah put the rifle butt to her shoulder. "Don't come closer, or I'll shoot!"

Aura backed up a step and unslung her rifle. "Why? What did I ever do to you?"

"Do not feign ignorance, murderer!" The mermaid stepped closer, apparently unconcerned about the rifle.

"Wait!" I shouted, struggling against the sand and water. "That's not the same person!"

One of the mermaids ducked underwater, and I knew exactly what was going to happen next. I resisted the urge to draw my brightblade, because if I was right, this misunderstanding could be corrected. I took a deep breath. She leaped out of the water, gripped my arm, and dragged me under. An instant later, we emerged next to Hannah and Aura.

The mermaid wasted no time questioning me. "How did you vanish earlier?"

"Magic." I wiped salt water from my eyes. "Hannah, Aura, lower the rifles."

"Not a chance," Aura said.

"Do you really think you have a chance at hitting them while they're in water?" I put my hand on the rifle barrel. "You saw how fast she just dragged me over here."

Hannah dropped the weapon slightly, but not enough to submerge it underwater. "What's going on, Cain?"

I turned to the mermaid and pointed at Aura. "Did someone that looked like her attack you?"

The mermaid scowled. "They didn't look like her. It was her!"

"No, it was her twin who was imprisoned on Prometheus's Rock." I backed up a step to give myself a little bit more space between me and her. "We came here to find out who freed her and where she went."

The mermaid narrowed her eyes.

The merman next to her tilted his head. "That would explain why she returned here unarmed except for that strange device." He looked at the rifle.

The second mermaid nodded. "I agree with Calder. This elf does not have the same look of madness about her."

The water was deep enough now that every wave made us bob in the water to keep from going under. I pointed to the cliff. "Can we talk up there? We're not comfortable in the water."

The lead mermaid pressed her lips into a thin line, then nodded. The next instant, I was dragged underwater and propelled forward at incredible speed. My head broke the surface, and I went airborne alongside the second mermaid. Her shark tail morphed into human legs just as we reached the top of the cliff.

I landed lightly alongside her. Aura landed in a heap next to Calder, and Hannah showed off with a superhero three-point landing.

Their leader faced me. "I am Rille, the leader of our reef. This is Calder and Maya."

"I'm Cain. This is Aura and Hannah." I pointed them out and turned back to her. "Tell me what Aura's twin did."

Rille waved an arm at the ocean. "This is where we come to hunt for mussels and other shallow-water prey. One day, we heard the cries of the elf and came to investigate. She was starving and in agony." Rille shook her head. "Unfortunately, there was nothing we could do as it was impossible for us to climb the rock and just as impossible for us to free her from the same chains that bound Prometheus."

Calder pointed to the chains. "The gods dangled her over the side instead of laying her on the flat top, which was even crueler than what they did to Prometheus. She would look down at us, screaming for help or for a taste of the food we had collected, but there was no way to reach her."

"The great eagle feasted on her liver daily, killing her. But she would come back to life, screaming at the top of her lungs." Rille shuddered. "When the eagle returned one day, she went absolutely mad, kicking at it with her feet. The eagle snapped at her, and its beak cleaved through her wrist. She dangled by one arm as we watched, then jerked violently, dislocated her shoulder. Screaming in agony, she pushed with her feet until she tore off her arm."

"Gods be damned." Aura hissed. "She tore off her own fucking arm?"

Rille nodded. "She fell, striking the sides of the rock and hit the water, lifeless. We placed her on the cliff and left her, knowing she would revive again. When we returned the next day, she was gone, and we thought that was the last we would see of her."

I already knew where this was going. The apocalypse weapons were gone and only Baura could have known how to access them. She must have used Tidebringer on these poor people.

Rille continued her story. "The elf returned nearly a week later and waited by the shore. We thought she returned to thank us, but instead, she screamed curses, blamed us for not helping her, and then she threw strange blue orbs into the water. The sea began to boil and explode into steam all around us. Our people were hurled into the air, boiled alive, and churned into bits by her magic." Tears filled Rille's dark eyes. "Most of our hunters died. Those of us who survived fled to the reef."

"She murdered so many of our people." Maya's fists clenched.

"Why would she blame us when there was nothing we could do? She killed my mate!"

Not all of the weapons in the lost armory had been swords, hammers, or tridents. Some were orbs. Why Baura had chosen to use orbs instead of Tidebringer was a mystery, but she also wasn't entirely sane, meaning logic didn't always apply to her decisions.

I wasn't familiar with the blue orbs and didn't remember where they'd been stored in the warehouse. "Did the orbs return to her?"

"We were too busy fleeing for our lives to notice," Rille said. "It was absolute pandemonium."

"Wow, what a bitch." Hannah clenched her fists. "She's an absolute psycho, Cain. We have to stop her."

"I am so sorry she did that." Aura set down the rifle. "Baura murdered a goddess and was put there for punishment. She's incredibly dangerous and insane."

Hannah frowned and turned to me. "I thought Baura stashed all the stuff from the lost armory in that warehouse you mentioned."

"As far as I know, she did, but I just discovered some items are missing." I blew out a breath. "I went to the warehouse to get Tidebringer so I could use it to protect us, but it's not there. Earthmaker, Airbender, and Tidebringer are gone, replaced by cheap fakes."

"Oh, shit." Hannah's eyes widened. "You're telling me that batshit insane elf has the weapons again?"

I nodded. "I'm surprised she didn't use Tidebringer instead of weaponized orbs."

"Maybe using something so powerful would have drawn the attention of the gods," Aura said. "The orbs probably wouldn't."

"Seems plausible." The gods had known when the weapons were used on Oblivion but hadn't intervened since that world was already post-apocalyptic. Surely they would have stopped her from using them on Feary Prime.

Hannah's face paled. "How did she steal the weapons if she doesn't have Panoptes?"

"No idea." I shook my head. "I picked up each of those weapons when I first found them in the warehouse, and they were real. This was the first time I picked one up since then."

"But why fakes?" Aura stared out at the ocean as if trying to find the reason there. "Was it to fool you so you wouldn't realize it right away?"

"Maybe."

"Earthmaker? Tidebringer?" Rille looked concerned. "What kinds of weapons does this elf possess?"

I sighed. "Hephaestus made world-building tools that can control air, water, and earth. In the wrong hands, they can be used to destroy worlds. Suffice it to say that Baura is the last person you want controlling them."

"World-destroying weapons?" Maya shuddered. "She could destroy the sea?"

"She could turn Feary into a broken, dead world." I looked out at the rock. "We have to find her quickly, because there's no telling what she has planned."

"Make the tracking spell, Cain." Hannah patted my utility belt. "Do it now before that crazy bitch starts wrecking the world!"

"Tracking spell?" Rille tilted her head. "Is that why you were on the rock?"

"Yeah. I needed her blood to track her." I pointed to Prometheus's Rock. "Do you know who attached the climbing rope to the rock?"

Rille shook her head. "It wasn't there a few days ago, and suddenly it was."

I didn't know if I should be concerned or not. I'd suspected that someone had climbed the rock to aid Baura, but this new information tossed that idea out of the window. Had someone else climbed the rock for the same reasons I had?

That was the least of my worries. For now, I needed to see if my efforts would yield a working tracking spell.

I searched the rocky ground and found a flat piece of granite that was about as large as the palm of my hand and a quarter of an inch thick. I took it to a nearby boulder that would suffice as a table.

The merfolk started rapid-firing questions, but I was too busy preparing a workspace for the spell.

I dusted off the top of the boulder, placed the piece of granite on it, then set the vial of Baura's blood next to it. The blood was thin and watery, but as long as some of the red blood cells were still alive, it would suffice. I just hoped that her immortality extended to her blood.

Just to play it safe, I cleaned the granite with a purifying potion before going to work. Without pure, thick blood, I needed as few impurities seeping into the sigil design as possible.

Once that was done, I pulled out another device I rarely used. Drawing sigils with my fingers was usually sufficient, but the thin blood required special handling. A thin stylus carved from dragon bone and engraved with power runes would amplify the efficacy of sigils drawn with it.

I dipped the dragon bone stylus tip into the blood as one might dip a quill into ink and then began painstakingly tracing the tracking sigil on the granite piece. Keeping the lines perfect despite having to constantly dip the stylus in blood required absolute concentration, so I blocked out all the chitter-chatter around me and continued working.

Hannah and the others must have gotten the hint, because they walked away to give me some space after I continued ignoring any questions directed my way. This particular tracking spell was more complex than the quick ones I'd used with fresh blood, because it needed as much power amplification as I could squeeze into it.

Once I was done, I cleaned the stylus and tucked it away, then placed my hands on the sides of the granite. I closed my eyes and envisioned Baura right after she'd slain Athena. I looked deep into her insane eyes and willed the sigil of her blood to reunite with its owner.

I placed my hand over the sigil and focused my will into it. Then, I waited for the tug of a direction on my consciousness. That tug never came. Despite pouring everything into it that I could, there was nothing.

The tracking spell had failed.

8

I focused my will into the sigil once more, but it wasn't working. The blood was too old, too watery to be of any use. The salty ocean water had probably killed the blood cells.

Hannah and the others approached. "What's wrong, Cain?"

"The blood was useless." I tossed the stone into the ocean. "We're fucked."

Rille tilted her head. "Would more blood help?"

I shrugged. "As long as the cells are still alive."

"Come with me." Rille led me to a large boulder near the cliff's edge. One side of it had been hollowed out into a small cave by the elements. The inside was dark with blood. "This is where we placed the elf after her escape. She bled dry inside."

I ducked into the opening and ran a finger along the stone. Crimson sludge covered the tip. The blood was old, but it was concentrated. Most importantly, there wasn't any salt water mixed with it.

I found another small piece of flat stone, cleansed it, and dipped the stylus directly into the pooled blood. After another laborious procedure, I produced the tracking sigil and imbued it with my will.

The spell tugged on my mind, drawing my gaze to the west.

A sigh of relief escaped my lips. "It works."

"Thank the gods." Aura knelt next to me. "Where is she?"

I pointed in the direction. "Somewhere over there." I rose to my feet. "The reading is faint, so she's a good distance away."

"That is giant territory." Rille bared sharp teeth. "She is well out of our reach."

"No!" Maya dropped to her knees and slammed her fists against the sand. Tears filled her eyes. "I must avenge Kairi."

"How?" Rille knelt next to her. "You know we cannot remain for long on dry land. The ocean owns us."

"I do not care." Maya rose slowly to her feet, resolve filling her black eyes. "I will hunt down the evil one who killed our friends and loved ones. We will imprison her for eternity in our deepest dungeon."

Hannah looked concerned. "What happens if you leave the ocean for too long?"

"We die." Rille put a hand on Maya's shoulder. "There is no seawater for hundreds of miles. We all crave vengeance, but the elf is out of our reach."

The last thing I wanted was another tagalong. I didn't know how Baura managed to do what she'd done, but she needed to be stopped ASAP or Feary and Gaia would likely meet the same fate that Gaia Beta had suffered. Utter annihilation might only be hours away, and I didn't want our pace slowed by merfolk.

"What if she brings seawater with her?" Hannah said. "We could put some in a bucket."

Rille's brow furrowed. "That has been done before, but it is impractical."

I held up a hand. "Hannah, stop being so helpful. We need to go right now before Baura gets too far away."

Hannah frowned. "But it'd be really cool teaming up with a mermaid."

"But impractical, I'm afraid." Aura shook her head. "Baura has an arsenal of world-ending weapons. There's no telling what destruction she might unleash or when."

"I appreciate your help, but we don't have time to stand around figuring out how to keep landbound merfolk alive." I checked my utility belt to make sure everything was secure, then turned to Aura. "You dropped my mangorita, didn't you?"

She rolled her eyes and pulled out the preservation box. "Cain, I sealed it and put it away when you started climbing the rock. Somehow, I knew we'd be running for our lives." She pulled out the drink, popped off the lid, and put the pirate sword, umbrella, and curly straw back in. "You're welcome."

I took a sip and sighed. "Thanks."

"What is this mangorita?" Rille stumbled over the word. "A potion? Why does it require such intricate ritual parts?" She peered at the straw as if it were dangerous.

The ambient magic in Feary translated most languages into the native tongues of the listener, but some words had no equivalents. The merfolk, like most denizens of Feary, spoke Faeicht. Thanks to the influence of humans from Gaia, words from the thousands of languages in our world had lodged themselves into the fae language. Mangorita was not one of those words.

Hannah spoke before I could answer. "It's a potion that puts Cain in a good mood."

Rille nodded. "I can see why that would be necessary. He does not seem like the cheerful sort."

"Oh, believe me, he's not." Aura put away the preservation box. "Sometimes I wonder how he has any friends at all."

I took another long sip to stop myself from saying something hurtful, then took the stone with the tracking sigil on it and started following its pull westward.

"Cain, wait! I want Maya to come with us." Hannah caught up to me. "It'll only take a minute to get her some seawater."

"I'm done waiting. You and Aura can stick around and help her if you want, but we've wasted too much time already."

"Aura has two more mangoritas, Cain." Hannah stepped into my path. "Do you really want to leave those behind?"

I considered it as I detoured around Hannah. "If Baura isn't stopped, there won't be any more mangoritas. I'll give up two of them for now if it means ensuring a supply in the future."

"Okay, that's a fair point, but wouldn't it be cool to have a mermaid on our team?"

I shook my head. "Nope."

A shouting match erupted behind us as Maya argued with Rille about coming with us. I glanced back and saw Aura hurrying to catch up to us.

Hannah sighed long and loud, then started walking alongside me. "We've had an orc and a gorgon on our quests. I just thought, why not a mermaid too? I mean, you'd probably even get to have sex with her."

I glared at her, but she wasn't wrong.

"Come on, Cain, please?" Hannah clasped her hands like a beggar.

I shook my head. "Maya is focused solely on revenge. That's not a good mindset for tracking down an insane immortal elf who could annihilate us with a single blow from one of her apocalypse weapons."

"Cain is right." Aura jogged until she drew even with Hannah. "It would only lead to problems. Besides, Cain had sex with a gorgon, and I don't think he can top that even with a mermaid."

"Why are you two so focused on my sex life?" I blew out a breath. "If it's such a big deal, I'll be celibate until we're done with this quest."

Hannah snorted. "You're a slut, Cain. Admit it."

I couldn't disagree. "We've got more important things to focus on besides my private activities."

"They're hardly private," Aura said with a smirk.

"Do you write about your experiences in your diary, Cain?" Hannah snickered. "I'll bet you could make some good money if you published them."

I rolled my eyes.

"No, he'd probably offend people who don't like sex in their adventure tales." Aura laughed. "All slaying, no laying is what they want."

"It's not my fault some people don't like sex." I stopped myself from saying anything else. "What we need to do is figure out how

Baura got into the warehouse. I need to inventory everything to see what's left."

Hannah's grin faded. "You think Baura might have another Panoptes?"

"I don't see how she could." I shrugged. "Unless we missed one when we destroyed the weapons from Prime or Alpha."

"If she had a backup ring, where did she hide it?" Hannah ran a hand down her face. "It's doubtful she kept it on Feary, meaning she probably stored it on Gaia or Oblivion. But if that's true, how did she get to either place? Mushroom portals?"

I'd been trying to piece together Baura's movements. The nearest mushroom portal was days away by foot. That meant during the week after Baura's escape she'd traveled to a mushroom portal and then used it to go wherever she'd hidden the ring so she could enter the warehouse, steal the weapons, and replace them with fakes. That was a lot to accomplish in such a short period of time, especially considering she'd returned to murder merfolk.

My thoughts went back to the beginning—back to the Dead Forest. Shub-Nuggerath's cult had infested the forest, thanks to a bargain made long ago with the high fae. The only way to purge the monsters was by destroying the forest itself. My plan to spread toxic wastes across the forest would have worked given time, but Baura had used Airbender to create a storm that destroyed the forest in a day.

Unbeknownst to me, that had been the first time I'd seen her use one of the apocalypse weapons. She'd used it to help me because I'd struck a bargain with Athena to free Dusa and Aura of the curses she'd placed on their bloodlines centuries before. That bargain drew Athena from the divine realm and to a place where Baura could kill her. Baura might have been insane, but she knew exactly what she wanted and how to get it.

Aura's curse had been twofold. First, she was immortal until her forty-first birthday. That didn't seem so bad, but the second part of the curse was so vile and depraved, that only a god could have contrived such a punishment.

Every female in Aura's bloodline was fated to give birth to twin girls on their fortieth birthdays. One year after birth, one daughter would be sacrificed body and soul to the gods. The other would take up the curse, becoming immortal until the cycle repeated while their mother became mortal and barren.

Baura had waited until Athena relieved her bloodline of the second part of the curse. Before Athena could also revoke her immortality, Baura had struck her down with Soultaker. I suspected Baura had intended to escape by using Panoptes, but I'd stolen it while she was unconscious.

For someone who was batshit insane, Baura had pieced together a remarkably coherent plan. She'd helped us when she needed to, spied on us with the help of Panoptes, then kidnapped Aura Alpha and replaced her at the very last moment, thus avoiding the classic blunders of impersonating someone for too long. She'd known that I would have suspected something or seen the creeping insanity in her eyes if she'd taken Aura Alpha's place too soon. By doing it at the last moment, she'd escaped all suspicion and barely had to talk to me.

Considering all that, it made perfect sense that Baura would have had a backup plan in case things went wrong. She must have figured out a backup method for entering the warehouse with or without Panoptes. The decoy weapons were just another layer in her deceptions, another way to throw me off the trail a little longer.

If she didn't have another Panoptes, I really wanted to know how she'd gained entry to the warehouse. The only door in or out of the place was secured by a keypad that I'd been unable to hack. The mithril main door was impenetrable. Noctua had told me the warehouse was one of many scattered across Gaia, each one used by a mysterious organization to secure dangerous artifacts. I didn't know how Baura had originally discovered the warehouse, but it was possible she'd gained physical access to it from the outside and then set one of Panoptes many eyes to watch it, thus granting her access.

When I traveled to the warehouse using Panoptes and then left it, Panoptes showed me the last place I'd been. It stood to reason that unless the ring was attuned to the warehouse before Baura possessed it, she had somehow entered from the outside.

Baura would have instantly known upon awakening on the rock that she no longer wore Panoptes. After her escape, she would have theorized that someone had taken the ring and thus had access to the warehouse. She would have gone straight to the warehouse and replaced the apocalypse weapons with quickly made duplicates so the current owner of the ring wouldn't suspect anything.

That theoretical scenario made the most sense.

Baura might be insane, but she somehow remained remarkably cunning and calculating. As for her escape, I suspected she'd intentionally goaded the eagle into biting off her hand. To completely tear off her other arm to escape was akin to a wolf gnawing off its own paw to free itself from a trap.

I couldn't afford to make a single mistake when it came to apprehending Baura. I had to take her by surprise before she had a chance to unleash apocalyptic destruction on the world. I already knew what I'd have to do when I caught her. There was only one prison that could possibly hold her, even though it meant an eternity of torment.

Hannah tapped me on the shoulder. "Deep thoughts by Cain Sthyldor?"

"I think I worked out how Baura gained access to the apocalypse weapons." I explained my reasoning to them.

"She intentionally got the eagle to bite off her hand so she could escape?" Hannah grimaced. "I have a question: What does that eagle eat when no one is imprisoned on the rock? And livers taste gross, so wouldn't that be as much of a punishment for the eagle as it was for Prometheus and Baura?"

"Thanks for asking the important questions, Hannah." I snorted.

"Your theory makes perfect sense," Aura said. "I just don't understand how Baura is still able to function if the ring has made her so insane."

"That's a good question." Most people would have been reduced to gibbering zombies, especially those without training in mind resistance. Then again, Aura had been a handler for my former assassination agency. "How much psychological training did you have?"

"If you're asking if it was enough to help me overcome an insanity-inducing magical ring, then I'd say maybe." She pursed her lips. "I was an agent for Eclipse before I became a handler. They regularly tested us, sometimes even kidnapping and torturing us to make sure we wouldn't give up information about the agency. The psych training was intense."

I grunted. "That might be just enough conditioning to keep Baura from going completely off the deep end."

"I just can't believe Hermes would be so stupid and only chain her up by her wrists." Hannah shook her head in disbelief. "This is a woman who could jump into a volcano and still reincarnate."

I turned to Aura. "If I cut off your arm, would it grow back?"

"Only if I died soon after." Aura winced. "If you cut it off and I healed before dying, then it wouldn't."

Hannah shuddered. "Maybe Hermes didn't realize how her immortality worked."

"Or he was just in a hurry." I shrugged. "He didn't seem to enjoy Zeus and Mars bossing him around."

"Can't blame him. They're total assholes." Hannah narrowed her eyes and turned to Aura. "If Baura is so resilient and dangerous, doesn't that mean you are too?"

Aura glanced at her. "Hannah, I was a handler for a supernatural assassination and bounty hunting agency. You might think of me as just a harmless bartender, but I'm not. I managed to be friends with Cain for years before he discovered I was also his handler."

Hannah scowled. "How is it that Baura seems so much more dangerous than you?"

"Because all sense of morality has been wiped away by insanity," I said. "She's gone complete psychopath."

Hannah turned on Aura. "I don't know. I think Aura is a psychopath considering how she betrayed us."

Aura threw up her hands. "I'm done talking about that."

I closed my eyes and felt for the pull of the tracker. We hadn't walked very far, so it was hard to tell if we were much closer. It was also starting to get dark. I picked a cove of boulders on a hill about a mile distant from our stopping point. While Hannah and Aura bickered, I thought about everything else I could've placed in the warehouse to make this trip easier, like motorcycles.

I also wondered if there was a way to set the other eyes in Panoptes to watch places that would be useful. Placing one in Sanctuary so I could zip back there whenever I wanted would be great. Another one at Voltaire's would be even more amazing. Unfortunately, Noctua hadn't known much about the ring or how to control its eyes.

I took the ring out of my utility belt and examined it. It was just a thin sliver of metal, barely noticeable unless you were looking for it. I'd only noticed it at the last moment on Baura before she'd killed Athena. For something that was about vision, the ring was almost unnoticeable.

Most of Hephaestus's inventions were fashioned to resemble what they did. Tidebringer was a trident, Soultaker a sword, Airbender a weather rod, and Earthmaker a war hammer. Why did Panoptes look like nothing but a cheap ring? It hardly seemed in keeping with the blacksmith's signature style. Then again, the ring was about seeing and not being seen.

I slid on the ring and suffered through the initial bout of dizziness. Then, I examined the ring. It looked the same. Focusing my will, I sent a simple command. *Reveal yourself to me.* The ring shimmered and I nearly recoiled in horror and surprise.

9

The thin sliver of metal expanded to a wide black band covered by countless eyes. Some looked human. Others had vertical or horizontal pupils like those of cats and goats. Some rotated crazily until only their whites were visible. Others were hazy and clouded with blindness.

"What's wrong, Cain?" Hannah had stopped because, apparently, I'd stopped walking.

I held up the ring. "Do you see the eyes?"

She frowned. "No. What are you talking about?"

Reveal yourself to her, I commanded.

Hannah gasped and shrank back. "Holy fuck balls, Cain! That's nasty!"

Aura turned around and walked back to us. "What is?"

I revealed the eyes to her, and she recoiled. "Ew. Can you feel the eyes on your skin?"

Fighting the dizziness, I touched one of the many eyes and felt moist flesh. "Yeah."

Aura pursed her lips. "Well, the name makes a lot more sense now. Can you see through all of them?"

"Seeing through just a few of them is hard enough." I rotated my hand for a better look. Some of the eyes stared unblinkingly, but many were twitching, looking in seemingly random directions. I refocused on the split views of the warehouse and other places viewed by the ring and counted them. Out of thirty-one frames, only five of them weren't blank.

There was the warehouse, the winter landscape, the desert, a forest, and a white place. I counted the number of blind eyes and reached forty-three before giving up. There were simply too many eyes to count them all. It seemed the blind eyes might be the ones looking at the black places. Either that, or there was nothing but a void there.

I focused on one of the blind eyes that stared unblinkingly. *Stop looking.* It blinked, then began twitching and rolling wildly. One of the black frames vanished. A staggering wave of dizziness hit me, so I tore off the ring. It once again became the seemingly innocent metal circle.

"Are you okay?" Hannah gave me a look of concern.

I nodded. "Some of the eyes are blind, but I figured out how to make them stop looking."

"Can I try the ring, Cain?" Aura's face indicated she already knew the answer.

I didn't disappoint. "No." I tucked it into a pouch. "Let's get going."

We reached the hill with the cove of rocks and set up camp in between them. While Hannah prepared dinner, I set wards and a camouflage blind around the edges of the campsite. I didn't think there was much to worry about in this stretch of land since the giants seldom left their forest, but it was always best to play it safe.

I slipped through the opening between the boulders and entered camp. There wasn't much to it—just the tall, narrow tent that I'd used on our adventure into the Dead Forest. It barely looked large enough for a single person to fit inside, but it was a fae tent—deceivingly small on the outside, but large on the inside.

I went inside and pushed aside the back flap. It opened into a full-sized dining area with a small kitchen next to it. A washroom and bedroom branched off to the sides. Hannah pulled two plates from a heating box and set them on the table while completely ignoring Aura.

Aura grumbled and began making her own plate. "Wish I'd stayed at home."

"Would've been better." Hannah shook her head disapprovingly. "That's what happens when you invite yourself on someone else's adventure."

I ate quickly, then went outside and scaled one of the tall boulders for a better look at the surrounding landscape. There were still unanswered questions about Prometheus's Rock, and I suspected clues might still be around.

The merfolk didn't know who'd climbed the rock or when. The only reason someone would have climbed the rock after Baura's escape was because they were hunting for clues, or they knew how to make a tracking sigil from blood. I wondered if the gods had sent a minion after her since it seemed doubtful they'd do it themselves. On the other hand, the gods had their hands full with the war in the divine realm and Athena might still be having mental issues after resurrection, so maybe they didn't care about tracking down a lowly elf.

I summoned my staff, flipped up the scope, and surveyed the surrounding territory. I switched through the various modes, searching for auras and heat signatures. All I found were animals. Whoever had climbed Prometheus's Rock was far away from here by now. Then I realized I was probably looking in the wrong place.

The other person or persons probably would have thought the same exact thing as me when they saw the cove of rocks on a hill. It was the perfect camping spot, and it wasn't far from Prometheus's Rock, meaning it was the first place they would have seen.

I climbed down and began inspecting the area around the rocks. The grass prevented footprints, but the scope on my staff picked up faint traces of old sigils. These were simple, premade sigils someone not versed in magic could purchase from the same adventure supplies store where they'd bought the climbing gear.

It seemed highly doubtful that someone sent by the gods

wouldn't know how to make basic security sigils. Tracking sigils could be purchased just as easily as security spells, but they weren't very good. Then again, skilled trackers didn't need to heavily rely on magic to find their quarry. I could probably pick up Baura's trail without a tracking sigil, but it was much easier this way.

I banished my staff and knelt, checking for signs that only an experienced hunter would notice. The ground was covered in thick grass. The dirt beneath was firm enough to resist footprints, but that wasn't what I was looking for. I leaned over and put my eye level to the top of the grass. Some of the blades were slightly more depressed than others. There were also traces of transference, mostly small streaks of white where salt had rubbed off footwear. The rock climber had been soaked with saltwater like me. The gear was designed to quickly dry, but that didn't mean it shed the salt from the water.

The faint tracks headed toward the forested hills. There was only one set of tracks, meaning only one tracker on foot. They weren't a skilled magic user, but they were obviously skilled at hunting if they knew which way to go without a tracking sigil.

I went inside the tent and snatched another mangorita from Aura's backpack without anyone noticing, then went outside and scaled back up a boulder to watch the sun set. When darkness claimed the land, tiny flashes of light blossomed in the distant forest, probably willow-wisps. A howl rose in the distance and was answered by a chorus of howls.

Something with glowing yellow eyes skulked around the base of the hill, then dashed away as it frightened prey from hiding. A soft breeze carried whispered promises.

"Come to us, my love."

"We will show you pleasures in a soft bed of leaves, sweet thing."

"Your wildest fantasies are our pleasure."

The wild fae of the forest loved to lure travelers to their dooms. It was like the "Hot young singles in your area" ads on the internet, except in this case, you'd end up becoming part of a tree or being slowly eaten by carnivorous plants. The wild fae avoided Faevalorn and other fae cities because their kin, the high fae, frowned upon the murder of their subjects. This far out, however, anyone was fair prey.

To most seasoned travelers, it was simply background noise, easily ignored. As long as you didn't enter into any agreements with the wild fae, they couldn't directly harm you, but it was still best to steer as clear of them as possible.

There was just enough moonlight for me to perform my next tracking trick. I fashioned a sigil in the air and suspended it between opposing thumbs and forefingers, like a photographer framing the perfect shot. The spell filtered the silvery moonlight where it painted the grass, revealing the faint glow of phosphates left from the salt dried on the clothes of the other hunter.

The trail faded a hundred yards or so out, but it was enough to see that the other tracker was making a beeline in the same direction I was. They had a solid head start on us, which meant they'd probably reach Baura before we did. I hoped they knew what they were getting into, because their prey was just as likely to become the predator.

I released the sigil, then lay on my back, staring up at the stars. The constellations were different on Feary than they were on Gaia. There was Athena's shield to the north, Zeus's lightning in the west, and Mars's sword to the east. Like most constellations, it required a lot of imagination to see any of those shapes in the stars.

I closed my eyes and blocked out my surroundings. The whispers of the wild fae faded. The susurrus of the night breeze through the grass and trees went silent. The howls of predators and the screams of prey no longer echoed in the night. It was just me and the beating of my heart. The calm void welcomed me into its embrace, and I slept.

THE TINGLING of my protective tattoos woke me just before sunrise. Remaining low on the top of the rock, I rolled onto my belly and scanned the landscape. The flash of horns and war armor caught my gaze. A small army of various taurs—centaurs, minotaurs, and cervitaurs—milled around the cliffs near Prometheus's Rock. One of them cried out as they discovered the blood-soaked cave where Baura had bled out.

"Those fuckers are relentless." I blew out a breath, then swiftly lowered myself down the side of the boulder and went inside the tent. Hannah was asleep in the bedroom and Aura was sprawled on the floor in the dining area.

Aura shivered and woke with a start before I even got close. She looked up at me. "What's wrong?"

"Our hooved pals are apparently still chasing us." I went into the bedroom and nudged Hannah.

She sprang from the bed and landed on her feet, fists raised. Hanna blinked in confusion. "Cain?"

"Good reflexes."

"Well, you trained me to sleep with one eye open."

I nodded. "Obviously not good enough, because you'd be dead by now."

Hannah sighed and lowered her fists. "What's going on?"

"We've got company coming. Be best to vacate the premises immediately."

"Oh, shit." She scooped up clothes from the floor and dumped them into her duffel bag, then pulled fresh ones from inside.

I went into the dining area, grabbed my bag, and pulled out fresh clothes. I'd wanted to bathe, but that would have to wait. There was no doubt in my mind that the centaurs would spot the boulders on the hill and immediately identify it as an ideal vantage point to survey the surrounding area.

Aura was already dressed and heading outside by the time I changed. Hannah came out of the bedroom a moment later, tying her long hair up into a bun to keep it out of the way.

"I kind of regret not shaving my head like I wanted." She rubbed her tired eyes. "It's such a pain keeping up with it. I'm just glad I showered last night."

I grunted. "Shave your head, grow a goatee, and you're all set."

"Is there a spell for growing a goatee?" She rubbed her bare chin. "I'm in!"

We hurried out of the tent flaps. I traced a sigil, and the tent folded up into a small square, which I slid into my backpack.

Aura was peering around the curve of the boulder toward the beach. "Some of the centaurs are pointing at Prometheus's Rock, and others are really worked up about the place where Baura bled out."

"Good. We need to get a head start before they decide to come up here for a good vantage point." I slipped past her and hugged the boulder to remain out of sight of the beach. We made our way downhill and jogged toward the forest, which was a good mile away and up a steep slope.

"This reminds me of Tokyo," Hannah said. "That was scary."

Tokyo hadn't been scary, but Hannah was still young and prone to excitement. I'd been through narrow escapes so many times that it barely fluttered my nerves at all anymore.

Aura's forehead pinched. "Tokyo?"

"Side job," I said. "Got it from the freelance job board."

"Why are you doing freelance work?" Aura seemed at a loss. "Did you get bored?"

I didn't really want to answer the question because it was none of her business.

Hannah winced. "Sorry, Cain. I forgot she was here."

"Wow, that hurts." Aura shook her head. "Will I ever be able to make up for what I did? Or will you two hate me forever?"

"We don't hate you, Aura." Hannah smiled gently. "You've done some good things since then, but considering that you lied to Cain for a decade about who you really were, then used him to hunt down me so you could capture and indoctrinate me as a god-killer weapon, well, that still really bugs me."

"When you put it like that, it sounds worse than it is," Aura said.

"Worse?" I gave her a look. "It was exactly that bad. You're just lucky you and your alts are the only beings I've discovered so far who can make a perfect mangorita."

Hannah smirked. "It's your one redeeming quality."

I was glad we'd gotten off the subject of Tokyo. I'd taken the job because I thought it was connected to Alistair, a murderous necromancer I desperately wanted to slash to steaming bits with my bright-blade. Unfortunately, the Grim Reaper, Fate, and Time wouldn't allow me to do that. The necromancer in Tokyo had been an acolyte of Alistair's, as it turned out, but she wasn't nearly as skilled or depraved as her master.

Even so, she was still murdering people to use them as her zombie minions. I'd been only moments away from pulling the trigger and ending her when we'd been attacked by ninja zombies.

Hooves thundered in the distance. It seemed the herd had moved away from the beach. We hurried up the next hill, desperately trying to reach the other side before being spotted. We were nearly to the top when shouts from behind indicated that we hadn't quite made it.

I turned and spotted a grizzled palomino centaur rearing up on hind legs, a battle-ax flashing as he waved it from the top of the hill where we'd spent the night. His comrades spilled around the edges of the rock. I zoomed in with the scope on my staff and saw the blood-lust burning in their eyes.

They wouldn't stop chasing us until we were all dead.

10

The forest was perhaps a quarter of a mile away, and it might be our only chance at escape.

Hannah clenched her fists. "What now?"

I turned toward the forest. "Run."

Hannah sprang forward with all the grace of a cervitauride, bounding down the hill without missing a beat. Aura blew out a breath before sprinting downhill after her. I powered the sigils on my body for some extra power and hurried after them, my backpack jangling with every step. Running downhill while dodging tripping hazards and boulders was no mean feat for mere bipeds, but we made it to the bottom and then raced up the next hill toward the forest.

It was a long distance to cover, especially uphill. Once we reached the top, we'd have to scale a rocky ledge. I doubted even Hannah would have the stamina to overcome these obstacles, but we really didn't have a choice.

I glanced back. Our pursuers had vanished behind the hill we'd just left, meaning they'd be thundering down it any time now. I didn't see how we could possibly make it uphill to the forest before they caught us. And even if we made it into the forest, that didn't mean we'd be able to hide.

I considered our sparse options—hiding behind a camouflage blind, turning to fight and praying Hannah's powers came online, and last but not least, a deus ex machina where we were saved from an impossible situation at the last minute by divine intervention.

The whooping war cries of the centaurs grew louder. I looked over my shoulder and beheld something that might have been awesome in a movie but was horrifying in this situation. One of the centaurs had a freaking rocket launcher. It seemed they'd taken it from the duffel bag I'd inadvertently left behind. I didn't know how in the hell a centaur would know how to use a LAW, but now wasn't the time to inquire.

"He's got a fucking rocket launcher!" I shouted to the others.

There was a loud boom as the rocket launched and hissed through the air. I quickly wove sigils and threw as many shields into the air as possible with the faint hope that I might be able to detonate the rocket mid-flight before it came close enough to reduce us to body parts.

But I didn't need to worry because the centaur's aim was so far off, the rocket soared overhead and slammed into the large shelf of rock near the top of the hill.

"What the fuck?" Hannah stared, mouth agape at the cloud of smoke. "How does a centaur know how to use a rocket launcher?"

Using an M72 LAW wasn't as simple as pulling a trigger. There were several steps needed to prepare it to fire. I didn't have time to consider her question for much longer because the centaurs were already roaring up the slope toward us. A low rumble from above drew my attention in the other direction.

Weakened from the exploding rocket, the rock shelf collapsed. Loose shale and slabs of granite slid downhill. Right behind it came everything that had been sitting on top of the rock shelf—boulders, rubble, and a pair of giant sequoia trees.

Suddenly, centaur army didn't seem quite so bad.

"Run east!" I shouted.

Hannah stared at me. "Which way is east?"

"This way!" I took off, running parallel to the oncoming landslide. The ground shook so hard beneath our feet, it was a wonder we managed to keep upright as we ran.

The whooping and cheering of the four-legged assholes coming after us changed tone as they turned tail and ran downhill, away from the tumbling boulders and slabs of stone. Some of them lost their footing and tumbled head over horse ass.

We barely scooted out of the path of certain death, but a pair of boulders collided, sending one of them careening right at us. I grabbed Hannah's shirt and yanked her back an instant before the boulder would have smashed her to paste. It whizzed by so close to us I felt the wind on my face.

Hannah gasped and fell back into me. "Holy shit. I didn't even see it coming!"

Running with a limp, Aura caught up to us. "I think we made it."

The giant sequoias slammed into the earth, sending dust and gravel into the air. The centaurs were already at the bottom of the hill. The minotaurs I'd seen among them earlier were no longer there. As bipeds, they probably hadn't been fast enough to outrun the rolling rocks. I was just glad they hadn't run sideways like we had, or they'd be on top of us by now.

Aura put a hand to her side. It came back wet with blood. A sliver of rock had penetrated the protective clothing and lodged into the flesh just above the waist. Gritting her teeth, she pulled it out.

"You okay to keep going?" I asked, as if we had a choice.

She nodded. "Merely a flesh wound."

Hanna grimaced. "Uh, it looks more serious than that."

"Doesn't matter." Aura steeled herself and started uphill, wincing with every step. "We need to put more distance between us and those centaurs."

"Agreed." I pulled a wad of stanching gauze from my utility belt and adhered it over Aura's wound. The heavy bleeding would soak it in minutes, but it was better than nothing. "Let's go." I turned up the slope and began the long trudge to the top. The centaurs milled about on the plain below, looking stunned and rudderless. The palomino, however, was more than ready to go. He gesticulated wildly at us. Two centaurs broke from the group and began searching the rubble, presumably for survivors of the landslide. The rest of them galloped on a diagonal intercept course toward us.

It had been their own faults for the deaths caused by the landslide, but they wouldn't be likely to see it that way. If anything, they'd be even more enraged. I'd intentionally avoided killing them in Minos, but if they kept coming after us, I'd no longer stay my hand. It was about time to make them afraid of pursuing us.

The only problem with that plan was their sheer numbers. I could snipe a few of them, but not all of them. Judging from their balls to the wall pursuit of us, picking them off might not even scare them away. If anything, they'd be willing to die as long as some of them reached us. Once that happened, I'd be forced to fight on foot.

I'd dueled plenty of bipeds and won, but I wasn't sure if I could take a creature who had the advantage of height and four legs, much less a group of them. For now, escape was our best option. Aura's injury, however, was quickly draining her of blood and energy. I suspected we didn't have long before she either bled out or became too tired to move. We needed to find a place to hide ASAP.

I ran uphill past Aura, reaching the rocky ridge near the top of the hill moments later. There was very little underbrush in the forest since the giant sequoia trees cast too much shade to allow smaller plants to thrive. There were a few giant mushrooms and ferns but not enough vegetation to provide a hiding spot.

The only chance at concealment would be a hollow in a tree. Even then, it was likely we'd be found quickly. I closed my eyes and felt the northerly tug of the blood tracking spell. It felt marginally stronger, but not by much. Given our current circumstances, there was really only one way to play this.

I dropped to a knee and scanned the area with my scope. Several fallen trees and a thicker layer of ferns to the west offered the best chance for my gambit. I ran my fingers across the ground. The hard-packed dirt would still leave traces of our passing, which was just what I wanted. As soon as Aura and Hannah reached me, I told them the plan.

Aura shook her head wearily. "You might have to kill me, Cain. Maybe they'll leave my body alone. I'm going to bleed out before much longer."

"But you're the only one with the proper skills to make sure Hannah makes it." I opened her hand and put an anti-pain potion in it. "Drink this."

She popped the cork, tilted back her head, and drank. I removed the already blood-soaked stanching pad from the wound and put two more over it to keep the blood from dripping. It was imperative that she not leave a trail of blood for the plan to work.

I put my hands on Aura's shoulders and looked her in the eyes. Her face was pale as death. "You can do this. Just get to that ridge over there and you should be safe." I pointed to a ridge about three hundred yards north. "Hannah, do exactly what Aura tells you to do, okay?"

She looked up at me with big, worried eyes. "What if it doesn't work? What if they come after us?"

"Then pray that your god powers come to the rescue." I shooed them away. "Now, go!"

Aura straightened as the pain potion kicked in. "Let's go." She began carefully balancing her way along the roots of a tree, avoiding the ferns and other vegetation. Hannah gave me one last look, then followed.

I cast four shield sigils, shaping each shield like the bottoms of our boots and bound them to move with my boots. The centaurs needed to believe we were all still together.

I twisted my boots on the ground and started running south. The shoe shields flattened the ferns as they raised and lowered in time with my steps. I shook the bloody stanching pad as I passed by ferns, sprinkling them with blood. Once I reached rocky ground, I walked along the rock, leaving no trail except a couple of drops of blood.

I continued running, leaving hints of my passing as I went, then stopped and crept to the edge of the ridge for a look. The centaurs were nearly to the top. Once they entered the forest, I'd lose sight of them, so I needed to act fast. I continued following the curve of the ridge until I was out of sight of the eastern slope, then dispelled the footprint shields.

A pair of large rocks near the end of my fake trail weren't ideal, but they'd do in a pinch. I shoved them over the edge and watched them bounce and roll down the hill at an angle until they came to a stop. It would hopefully appear as if we'd gone down the slope. With that done, I hopped onto a large tree root and ran back into the forest, skipping from root to root.

I buried the bloody gauze in a shallow grave so I wouldn't chance leaving a trail, then continued onward. A small rise offered a decent view of the forest to the southeast, so I stopped and looked for our pursuers. I caught a glimpse of them heading in the direction of the false trail I'd left, the palomino centaur in the lead. He stopped and inspected a fern, then pointed ahead and continued walking.

It was difficult getting a headcount of the remaining centaurs, but it looked as if they hadn't split up. It had been a long while since I'd had to fool an expert tracker, but it seemed my skills weren't too rusty after a decade or more of disuse. Half of the success, of course, relied on Aura and Hannah leaving no traces. It seemed they'd done their part well.

Keeping to the giant tree roots, I took a roundabout path to the ridge where I'd directed Aura to go while also stopping to make sure the centaurs hadn't reversed course. The trees were widely spaced, allowing for a good view of the forest as I climbed the rise toward the ridge, but I didn't see any signs of our pursuers. It was possible they'd started down the slope where I'd tossed the rocks.

Any tracker worth their salt would immediately realize that those tracks had been made with stones and not feet. Whoever led them was obviously good enough to spot the blood and faint footprints I'd left. It seemed likely that they were at this very moment looking down the slope with suspicion.

I hoped they'd believe it was a clumsy attempt to make them think we'd gone downhill. The tracker would then start looking for signs of a camouflage blind or other illusion nearby. He would give subtle signals to the others to fan out and start beating the brush, revealing us. Then the chase would be over.

At least, that was what I'd hoped. Best case scenario, he'd waste a good twenty minutes searching the area before realizing that the entire trail was staged. At that point, they'd gallop back toward the origin of the trail and begin looking for the real one. Even traveling along the tree roots as I was doing wasn't foolproof.

My boots had left subtle impressions in the bark despite my careful maneuvers. To me, they were glaring and obvious, but that was because I'd made them. Aura might tread lightly, but Hannah didn't have the same skillset. The palomino centaur would almost certainly check the tree roots at some point and discover the deception.

Using the scope on my staff, I scanned for heat signatures and spotted faint movement toward the slope where I'd tossed the rocks. I considered waiting here until the palomino centaur came into view and sniping him. If he was their most skilled tracker, it might throw them off our scent. Waiting for the centaurs to pass by here, however, might take quite some time. It made more sense using the time to put distance between us and them instead.

I banished the staff and continued up the slope toward the next ridge. It didn't take long for me to spot a row of depressed ferns and a set of faint footprints at the top. Spattered and smeared blood made the trail visible to even the worst of trackers. Hannah and Aura had apparently stopped using the tree roots once they reached the top.

I knelt and examined the ground, noting only one set of foot-prints. Hannah was carrying Aura. It was no wonder they'd stopped being careful. Since there was no sense in me being careful either, I ran after them and caught up moments later. Aura was slung over Hannah's shoulder like a sack of rice.

Hannah was stronger than the average person, thanks to her fledgling god strength, but hefting dead weight while walking uphill wasn't easy regardless. By the time I caught up, I also realized Aura wasn't just unconscious—she was dead.

11

Aura's death was only a minor setback, considering she'd reincarnate. But it was a big deal in the sense that now we had to lug a corpse around until midnight.

Hannah stopped and turned toward me. Glowing white energy in her eyes faded, replaced by relief. "Oh, thank god, Cain." She dumped Aura unceremoniously on the ground. "I don't think I can carry her much farther."

"I threw the centaurs off the trail, but not for long." I touched the tracking sigil and felt a northwesterly pull. The signal wavered and fluctuated in strength. Either the blood was too old to maintain the spell, or something else was interfering. It could also mean Baura was utilizing a mushroom portal. Either way, we didn't have much time to catch up to her. "I'll carry Aura for now." I bent down and slung the limp elf onto my shoulder. The cooling flesh of her arm touched me on the cheek as I adjusted her position. "How long has she been dead?"

"Ten minutes at least." Hannah shuddered. "She was too weak to walk, so I carried her. I think she passed away not long after that."

I finally got comfortable with the load. Aura wasn't terribly heavy, but walking around with an extra hundred and twenty pounds on my shoulder would eventually feel like a ton of bricks, even with my body tattoos giving me extra strength. I touched the tracking sigil again and sensed the same strange fluctuations in the signal.

If worse came to worst, I could just leave Aura behind. She was an elf, so the centaurs might just leave her body alone. However, if centaurs buried their dead, it was possible they'd bury her too. That would be a nightmare scenario because she'd suffocate seconds after resurrecting and repeat the process every day unless and until someone dug her up.

Despite the shit Aura had put us through in the past, she didn't deserve a fate worse than death.

Hannah slung Aura's backpack over a shoulder, and we started off at a brisk pace up the slope. Once we reached the crest, the hill flattened out. The trees in this section of forest seemed even bigger than the ones below.

Speed was more important than not leaving a trail at this point, so I walked in a straight line, occasionally touching the tracking sigil to make sure the target hadn't changed direction. The fluctuations in the signal stopped for several minutes, then started again by the time we cleared the edge of the forest.

If the spell was losing power or cohesion, the fluctuations wouldn't have stopped until the spell went dead. Traveling via mushroom portal wouldn't cause fluctuations. If the target traveled to another plane or out of physical distance of the spell, then the pull of the tracker would just stop.

It meant that the target was still in Feary and still somewhere ahead. It meant that whatever was causing these fluctuations was an enigmatic anomaly I hadn't experienced before. It might be something caused by Baura's proximity to apocalypse weapons or other artifacts from the armory. That meant the spell might be working just fine and that I didn't have to worry about losing the signal.

Only time would tell.

The land ahead grew hilly and mountainous. The forest thinned into a grassy savannah with scattered copses of trees here and there. A strange gray-green mound, perhaps a quarter of a mile away, caught my eye. It didn't look like stone or dirt. I summoned my staff and peered through the scope.

I flicked through several modes. Whatever it was put off no heat and had no auras. But it definitely wasn't a part of the natural landscape.

Hannah frowned. "Why are you looking at that hill?"

"Because it's not a hill." The cries of a pair of vultures drew my attention upward. They flew in from the east and began circling above the mound. It was at that moment that I knew exactly what the mound was, even if it seemed impossible for it to be there.

The grass started knee-high but was all the way up to our chests the further we walked. I remained wary of hidden predators, but there didn't seem to be animals of any kind, which further confirmed my suspicions about the mound.

We finally reached the enigmatic lump on the landscape and pushed through the tall grass to reveal exactly what I'd thought it was. A giant stared at us with huge, lifeless eyes, its swollen tongue lolling grotesquely to the side. The ground squelched under our feet, soaked with the blood of the deceased.

There were many kinds of giants on Feary—some humanlike, others animalistic, and, of course, giant trolls. This was one of the former—a human giant with gray-green skin. The side of its neck was puckered where it had been stabbed, puncturing the carotid artery. There were other puncture wounds along its skin, leading me to believe it had been shot by arrows first.

I found a dry spot of grass and laid Aura's body in it, then approached the massive corpse. The giant was nearly forty feet tall— about average for giants—and had feet large enough to squash a bull elephant like a bug. Giants would eat just about anything, elephants included. This area was typically full of wildlife, but the presence of a giant usually drove away anything that wanted to live.

Some giants were intelligent and peaceful, but most of those lived in the north. The ones in this area were brutish and dumb, mostly humanoid, and deadly to just about anything they ran into. The only saving grace was that once they latched onto a territory, they were very unlikely to leave it unless they ran out of prey. In such cases, they'd wander into another giant's territory and challenge them to a death match.

These kinds of giants were typically long-lived, provided they weren't killed by another giant. They were only driven to mate once every few decades, which was a spectacle in and of itself. During our training for the Oblivion Guard, we'd been dropped into the middle of giant territory during mating season and tasked with survival.

Mating season was the one time when this type of giant didn't care about territory. Drawn by instinct, they'd gather in the middle of the mountains for a giant orgy in all senses of the word. I'd watched giants fuck from a safe distance, because during the times in between sex, they ate anything they could find. Unfortunately, many fellow trainees became munchies for the giants because they underestimated their sense of smell.

Giant skin was incredibly tough, as I'd learned during that exercise. Not even the sharpest swords could penetrate their hide. We hadn't yet been given oblivion staffs since we weren't full recruits, so a normal sword and a bow were all we'd had to defend ourselves against the giants.

During the mating season, the giant children from the previous cycle were brought along by the females. The children didn't interact much with the adults if they were lucky. Some of them were torn apart and eaten if the giants ran out of food, so most of them ran off and hid during the entire ordeal.

I'd encountered one of the kids—a twenty-foot-tall brute with a slack jaw and crossed eyes—while hunting for something to eat. Giants loved eating tiny humanoids more than anything and could sniff them out like nobody's business.

During the fight, I'd discovered that my sword would barely prick the humongous bastard's skin. Most of my arrows had likewise simply bounced off. I'd finally lured him to the edge of a cliff and tricked him into rushing me, dodging aside at the last instant and watching him plummet a thousand feet to his death.

Staring at this giant corpse, it made me wonder who or what had been able to kill him.

Hannah stepped next to me. "Aside from the dead giant, what are you thinking about, Cain?"

I produced a dagger from Aura's backpack, went to the giant, and stabbed down as hard as I could on its arm. The dagger scratched the skin. I powered my body sigils and bore down on the blade. It finally pierced the skin and slid in.

"Wow, armored hide?" Hannah took the dagger and drove it down as hard as she could. It struggled and finally broke through. She pulled it out and wiped the blade on the grass. "How in the world did someone else kill this thing?"

"Good question." I walked along the body looking for other signs. "They must have had magically tempered arrowheads and blades to do it." I took a closer look at the skin around the arrow wound. "Or maybe they knew exactly where to aim."

Hannah tilted her head and looked at the wound. "It looks like the skin was scarred there previously."

I nodded. "Good eye."

She beamed. "Scarred skin is weaker?"

"Yep." I walked over to the neck wound. There were several wide scars along the skin there. "Looks like this giant was bitten by another giant at some point. The wounds scarred over, but the skin is weaker." I took the dagger and jabbed it into a white patch of skin. It resisted the blade, then gave way with marginally more effort.

Hannah studied it. "Wouldn't scar tissue be thicker and harder, though?"

I shook my head. "Their skin is like a bullet-proof vest. Once it's been damaged, it's weaker even if it heals."

"The molecular structure changes." Her eyes brightened. "Once a shield is cracked, it's never as strong, even when mended. I learned that in school."

"Weaponry and Defense class?"

She nodded. "It's not as exciting as it sounds."

"I never went to a human school, but my training included similar subjects."

Hannah perked up at the unexpected offering of information about my past. "Did you go to school with fae kids?"

I snorted. "Hardly. The high fae don't really do school. My magical training was in the equivalent of a school. The elves, drow, and low fae who studied there tried to bully me at every opportunity. It certainly made me a better fighter and encouraged me to learn magic even faster than them. I earned top marks in most of my classes, and that only made them hate me more."

"God, you're just like Mr. Spock." Hannah shook her head. "The Vulcans bullied him because he was half human."

"Um, sure." It probably explained why he was one of my favorite Star Trek characters, but now wasn't the time to delve into the trials and tribulations of my childhood. "Let's get back to the matter at hand." I cleaned the dagger off on the giant's skin. "The person who killed this giant is probably the same person who scaled Prometheus's Rock."

She snapped her fingers. "They found the weak spots in the rock and in the giant."

"Yep. Whoever it is, they're extremely dangerous." I looked at the ground. "Judging from the still damp blood, I'd say this fight happened less than a day ago."

Hannah's gaze went distant. "You think this person has a score to settle with Baura?"

I nodded. "I'm certain of it."

"Maybe one of Athena's agents?"

"Maybe." I mulled it over for a moment. "Baura made a lot of powerful enemies when she killed Athena. Considering how she slaughtered the merfolk for no reason, I'd say it's highly likely she did the same to others in our dimension. Someone found out she was a prisoner on the rock and went to extract vengeance."

"Someone really skilled and smart," Hannah said. "Scar tissue or not, they killed a fucking giant."

"Yeah." I knew plenty of people who could kill a giant, but most of them were in the Oblivion Guard. There was no reason a guardian would be stalking Baura unless the fae had somehow been wronged by her. I was almost certain it had to be someone sent by the gods.

More vultures gathered overhead, eager to plunder the corpse. They had their work cut out for them. The belly of the giant was swelling dangerously large as gasses built up inside the decaying corpse. Within the next few hours, this body was going to explode like a whale carcass on the beach.

I retrieved Aura's body and slung it over the other shoulder. It wouldn't be long before the centaurs found our trail since there were enough of them to fan out and search a wide vicinity. Soon enough, they'd stumble upon the trail left when Hannah had to start carrying Aura.

Our feet would also leave crimson footprints, thanks to the bloody mud around the giant. Not that it mattered since it was nearly impossible to not leave a trail in the tall grass covering the savannah.

We covered a decent amount of ground for bipeds, reaching the mountains within an hour. My shoulders ached from carrying Aura, but I pushed aside the pain and climbed on a boulder for a look at the terrain behind us. The centaurs were only just emerging from the forest, galloping toward the dead giant with the palomino centaur in the lead. It had thankfully taken him longer than expected to discover our deceit.

The tracking sigil still led in the same direction—seemingly straight up the mountain. The slope started off gently but grew much steeper a quarter of the way up. It seemed likely that Baura had chosen to go deeper into giant country because it was the perfect place to hide. What didn't make sense was why she was hiding.

If she had Earthmaker and the other apocalypse weapons, she could have carved a path through the mountains at a whim. Trying to divine the reasoning of a madman was just about impossible. The mere fact that Baura had traveled all the way to the weapon stash and then returned here to kill merfolk was evidence enough that logic didn't dictate her plans.

I just needed to catch up to her and deal with her before her insanity caused her to unleash a fatal blow against Gaia and Feary. During the walk, I'd spotted traces of blood left in the grass by the person who'd killed the giant. They had also left a few footprints and other signs of passing here and there. The giant killer clearly didn't care about leaving a trail. Then again, they probably didn't think anyone would follow them.

Baura had also left multiple signs of passing. Grooves in the dirt looked as if she'd dragged something along the ground behind her. She had also defecated and wiped her ass on the grass. For some reason, I doubted the giant killer would have left their droppings in plain view, but it could have just as likely been their shit.

Here at the base of the mountain, the trail of clues diverged from the pull of the tracking sigil. The signal indicated they were on the other side of the mountain, but the trail continued around the base of the mountain. That made sense. Scaling the mountain without gear would be extremely difficult. I had the gear, but even so, the mountain was so steep that climbing it would take more time than walking around its base.

After a brief hesitation, I decided to follow the trail rather than the sigil. It was possible Baura had taken a pass or other shortcut through the mountain. That suspicion bore fruit moments later when the trail led to a rocky outcropping. Hidden behind thick brush, I found a cave entrance.

Hannah looked inside. "Are we about to walk through the mountain?"

"Probably." I cast a light spell and headed in.

"Are there goblins in these mountains?"

"Yep."

"Great." She scuffed her foot on the floor. "And we've got a dead elf to carry around."

I sent the ball of light ahead, illuminating a chamber about fifty feet in diameter. There was no tunnel leading through the mountain. In fact, there was nothing but a dead end. Footprints led to the center of the chamber and nowhere else. I directed the light ball to the middle. It reflected off a faint, pulsating bubble in the fabric of reality right where the footprints ended.

The fluctuations in the signal and the divergence of the path from the tracking sigil immediately made sense. And I didn't like what it portended at all.

Baura had somehow made a portal and left it open, and there was no telling where it led.

12

B aura and her stalker had gone through the portal if their footprints were to be believed. And I believed them. I didn't know how Baura had managed to open a portal, much less leave one open. The only way I knew of to open portals was with an oblivion staff, but those only remained open for a few seconds.

Entering the portal was extremely dangerous. I had no idea what waited on the other side. For all I knew, it could be a trap leading to a pit of quicksand or a thousand-foot drop into a volcano. There was, unfortunately, no way to know without going through. I couldn't simply stick my head through for a look because the portal would suck me through the instant I got close enough.

An open portal certainly explained how Baura had managed to steal the weapons from the warehouse and return to this place so quickly. The question that lingered in my mind was why hadn't she opened a portal closer to the ocean if her sole concern was returning for vengeance? And why leave the portal open?

I dumped Aura's body on the ground.

"We're going in, right, Cain?" Hannah stepped closer to the rippling air.

The tracking sigil indicated Baura was somewhere on the other side of the portal. That was the only clue indicating there wasn't certain death waiting on the other side.

I put a hand on her shoulder. "Wait here." I approached the ripples. The air bubbled out as I stepped within a foot of it. There was an instant of nothingness, a rush of frigid air, and then I stood in a small valley surrounded by beige cliffs and scrubby trees. The air was warm and humid. There was a strange scent in the air, like a fire burning in a swamp, but I saw no smoke.

Summoning my staff, I scanned the vicinity. The area appeared empty and silent. Devoid of life. I sensed nothing malignant, but that didn't mean anything. Judging from the trees and vegetation, I was on Gaia, not Feary. It was likely Baura had chosen a remote area on Gaia to hide in while she devised another plan to kill the gods.

I examined the portal with the true sight scope. A web of glowing lines anchored the shimmering gateway to the ground and the air around it. I didn't know how something could be anchored to thin air, but Baura had obviously figured out a way to do it. Perhaps there was another device from the armory that was capable of such a feat.

Or maybe I had such a device with me. The orb on the end of my oblivion staff had come from the lost armory and made my staff more powerful than it had originally been. It allowed my brightblade to absorb incoming attacks and use the extra energy for a devastating attack. It allowed the scope on the staff to see through god-level glamour. Maybe the orb also upgraded its portal-making power.

Maybe Baura possessed an oblivion staff and had upgraded it the same way I'd upgraded mine. If that was true, she was dangerous even without the apocalypse weapons.

The pull of the tracking sigil felt much stronger here. The only reason I'd been getting a signal at all was because the open portal bridged Feary and Gaia. It was why I'd felt so many fluctuations. Now that I was on the same plane as Baura, I sensed that I was only a few miles from her. That meant she'd probably reached her destination and was no longer on the move.

I took out my cell phone to confirm this was Gaia. The signal strength was only one bar, but it was there. This was excellent news.

If things went well, I could deal with Baura and be back home in time for dinner.

First, I had to retrieve my companions. As I stepped up to the portal, it bubbled out and engulfed me, delivering me back to the cave where Hannah waited with an anxious expression.

"Oh, thank god, Cain!" Hannah blew out a sigh of relief. "What if that thing dropped you in a volcano?"

"I can safely say that it didn't." I retrieved Aura's corpse. "Let's go."

We traversed back to Gaia. Hannah looked around in puzzlement.

"Where are we?" Hannah said.

"Somewhere on Gaia." I checked the map apps on my cell phone. It took a moment to locate us with the weak signal, but eventually a dot formed on an island south of the Greek mainland. We were just south of Heraklion and in the same relative geographical location we'd been in on Feary.

Baura must have chosen the cave for the portal because it lined up with the valley. That didn't explain how she knew it was a safe place to cross in the first place. I could open portals between the planes using my Oblivion staff, but since they opened in the same relative geographical area on the other planes, there was no telling what lay on the other side unless you took painstaking care to scout each area.

Stepping through a portal without knowing what was on the other side was a good way to die instantly. If the portal opened in the middle of a solid object like a tree or solid rock, that was where you'd end up.

When we'd practiced planeswalking in the Oblivion Guard, one of my fellow trainees had decided it was safe to open a portal a few feet away from the marked safe area. His body traveled into a pine tree. The sudden presence of new matter occupying the same spot as the tree had caused a powerful burst of energy, splintering the tree and causing it to topple.

The trainee, of course, was already crushed and dead before he even knew what happened. Long story short—never ever open a portal unless you know beyond a shadow of a doubt what's on the other side.

Baura was insane but clever. There was a fifty-fifty chance that she'd either performed due diligence or had just opened a portal and hoped for the best. She might not even know the dangers of planeswalking.

The cave with the portal was small. A dozen feet to either side would have taken the traveler into solid rock. I refused to believe she'd simply gotten lucky with that location. Either an artifact gave her a way to find safe crossing spots or she'd been able to test another way.

That kind of ability would come in extremely handy. If I could open portals to anywhere between the planes, my enemies would never catch me. Unfortunately, that power was now in the wrong hands. I'd hoped I could keep the apocalypse weapons and other artifacts from Beta safely for my own use. Baura had now shown me the error of my ways.

If I'd destroyed everything from the Beta armory like I should have, Baura wouldn't be nearly so dangerous. But no, I'd kept them, and now she could devastate Gaia within a day. I had to catch up to her before my mistake cost us our world.

We weren't far from something called the Spilia Venetian Aqueduct. The images on the map app displayed ancient ruins. It seemed strange even for someone of Baura's mental state to leave an open portal right out in the open, especially on Gaia where a human could accidentally walk into it at any moment. This looked like the typical place to find tourists hiking. On the other hand, this might have been the only safe spot to open a portal for miles around. Maybe that was why she'd gone so deep into giant country, because this was the only place the geography lined up perfectly for a portal.

Since I had no way to close the portal, I started walking in the direction the tracking sigil pulled me. My true sight scope hadn't spotted any magical traps, and judging by the straight line left by Baura's stalker, there probably wasn't anything to fear in the vicinity.

Hannah caught up to me. "Cain, I don't know a lot about portals, but I didn't think they could be left open like that."

"Me either." I shifted Aura's body to the other shoulder. "Baura must have an armory artifact that lets her do it."

"You look tired."

"I am tired." I set Aura on the ground and stretched my back, trying to get the kinks out. Carrying her all that distance was starting to wear on me. I wondered if I could take her body to the warehouse. Taking inanimate objects seemed to work. Maybe a dead body could go through as well. It would be a convenient place to store her, provided I remembered to retrieve her before midnight when she resurrected.

"Maybe we can just leave her here." Hannah shrugged. "Looks safe enough. Plus, if we run into anyone, you'll look awfully suspicious carrying a dead body."

"I'm going to try something." I put Aura on my shoulder, slid on Panoptes, and willed myself into the warehouse. Aura was still on my shoulder when I arrived. I leaned her against a nearby shelf and would have breathed a sigh of relief if not for the maddening dizziness caused by the ring. At least that was one problem off my shoulders.

I crossed back to the valley and yanked off the ring.

"So, it works for dead people." Hannah pursed her lips. "Not very practical."

Rolling my neck to loosen the tired muscles, I gave the riddle of the ring some thought. Inanimate objects could travel to the places the eyes watched. I'd taken food through as well, so organic things could travel. Even though Aura was dead, the cells in her body still lived on for a time. But cells were also very simple living things. Maybe more complex organisms couldn't travel together.

"Let me try something." I put my arm around Hannah's shoulder. She grinned. "Aw, did you need a hug?"

I slipped on the ring. Holding Hannah as close as possible, I willed myself through...and arrived alone. "Well, shit." I went back to Hannah.

"Maybe the ring doesn't like hugs," she said.

"There's something I'm missing, but I can figure it out later." I took off the ring and stowed it in my utility belt, then knelt and examined the slight traces of footprints in the dusty soil. "Let's go find Baura." I was more than ready to get this over with.

We continued through the valley, reaching the ruins of the ancient aqueduct moments later.

Hannah frowned. "Is it just me or are you weirded out that we haven't seen another living soul yet?"

"It isn't just you." A deep thrumming emanated from somewhere to the north, but it didn't sound like traffic or the ambient hum of a busy city. Heraklion was a city of about two hundred thousand, according to the maps app. We should hear traffic at the very least.

Hannah's eyes widened. "Do you think Baura destroyed the city?"

I blew out a breath. "I wouldn't put it past her." There wasn't anything we could do about it except catch up to the mad elf and deal with her before she initiated the wholesale destruction of our world. I picked up the pace, climbing up the slope of the small valley so I could get a better view of the surroundings. The cliffs afforded a decent view of the barren terrain. Sparse vegetation and scrubby trees dotted the landscape.

"It's beautiful!" Hannah beamed a smile. "I love the little stone houses!"

I started climbing another slope with a higher peak that promised an even better view. The view was much better, but it was also worse. Where the map showed roads and the outskirts of Heraklion, there was now a massive crater filled with blue-green water. It looked as if an asteroid had struck part of the city, casting buildings aside like toys and creating a new extension to the Gulf of Heraklion.

"Oh, my god." Hannah hissed a breath between her teeth. "She annihilated the city!"

I peered through the scope on my staff and zoomed in on the distant area. Parts of Heraklion were still whole and untouched, but a major section of it was now underwater. There were no signs of life that I could see. Only the incessant thrumming, the source of which I couldn't pinpoint.

Hannah took the staff from me and looked around. "That fucking bitch! She's wrecking our world, Cain!"

I nodded grimly. "Let's find her." Judging from the pull on the tracking sigil, she was close. Probably somewhere in Heraklion for reasons unknown. Or maybe the reasons were so obvious that I hadn't even considered them.

Baura had destroyed Gaia Beta. As a spinoff dimension, that didn't seem to have drawn the ire of the gods. But destroying Greece on Gaia Prime, the pride and joy of Zeus and the Olympians, seemed like the perfect way to draw the attention and anger of the gods. Baura was intentionally smashing up Crete just to piss them off.

It was brazen and foolish. Apocalypse weapons or not, Baura didn't stand a chance facing down a god. She'd acted directly against Athena, and that opened her up to direct divine retribution from the Olympians. As Mars had proven with Layla, it only took an accidental stumble into one of them to allow them to murder you.

Alternatively, it was possible I was, yet again, underestimating Baura. Insane or not, she'd shown incredible cunning, calculation, and patience. She'd killed a goddess. No doubt her training with Eclipse had given her the tools she needed to take down her mark. Reminding myself of her accomplishments early and often was the best way to ensure I didn't underestimate her again.

I spotted a nearby parking lot with dozens of cars to choose from and made my way toward them. Driving wasn't the stealthiest option, but it was the fastest way to catch up to Baura. That, and my legs needed a break. We had about four hours until sunset, and I wanted this to be over before dark.

It was probably wishful thinking, but it gave me something to aim for.

Most of the vehicles parallel parked along the cracked and broken streets were compact diesels. Due to the destroyed roads and rough terrain, we'd need something that could handle off-road action. I finally found a Jeep with oversized tires and rugged suspension parked in a driveway.

"These roads look really bad even without Baura jacking them up." Hannah leaped over a pothole that was deep enough to bottom out a regular car. "I'm surprised more people don't drive SUVs."

The Jeep's top was down, and the doors were off. Judging from the buildup of dried mud in the wheel wells and the undercarriage, this thing saw a lot of use. The seats were covered in dust, just like everything else around here. I wiped off the seat with my hand and climbed in.

The Jeep's old-school ignition required a key, which was good if I needed to hotwire it. The newer push-starts were more of a pain, thanks to the anti-theft safeguards built in. I lowered both sun visors, but naturally, the keys weren't there.

"It's never like the movies, Cain." Hannah snorted. "What idiot hides their key in the visor?"

I shrugged. "I mean, they had to get the idea from somewhere."

"It's called lazy writing." She pulled herself up into the passenger seat and looked in the glove box. "Hey, I found the keys!"

I gave her a look. "No need to rub it in."

She grinned. "You're so worldly and wise until it comes to looking for keys in visors, Cain."

"Well, as long as it's limited to that, I'm doing pretty well." There were several ways I could start the Jeep. I could use magic. I could hotwire it. I could probably even pick the ignition. This Jeep looked as if it were no older than fifteen years, meaning the key probably had a chip on it that was required for it to start.

Finding the key was the easiest way to handle this. Failing that, I'd try to hotwire it.

I jumped down, went to the front door of the house, and noticed it was hanging open. I went inside and grimaced at the sight. The walls were spattered with blackened blood. Human bones were scattered across the tile floor, some of them cracked open as if whatever did this had sucked out the marrow.

Hannah gasped. "Oh, fuck!" She knelt next to smaller bones. "Were these kids?"

"Explains why the cars were still outside." The Jeep keys lay on the floor alongside personal effects scattered from a torn purse. Four suitcases sat near the door. It seemed these people had been preparing to evacuate when something or several somethings had slaughtered and devoured them.

"Do you think animals did this?" Hannah wrinkled her nose. "Maybe escaped tigers from a zoo?"

The bones were picked so clean, there wasn't even a hint of gristle on them. I knelt and examined them closer. Had creatures really picked these corpses so clean that there was nothing left, or had this happened longer ago than I thought? Maybe Baura had done this before her encounter with Athena.

That scenario seemed unlikely. Though I didn't pay attention to the nub news, I surely would've heard about such cataclysmic destruction. The magical community would've been abuzz with rumors.

"What are you thinking, Cain?" Hannah looked concerned. "Does it have something to do with how clean the bones are and how it looks like this town has been abandoned for months?"

It wasn't normal for Hannah to see something I'd overlooked. I'd been so preoccupied with catching up to Baura that I'd not been paying attention to obvious indications that things were not as I'd assumed. "Good observations, Hannah. You noticed something I didn't."

She flinched. "Wait, what?"

I stood and mussed her hair. "Seems impossible, I know." I retrieved the car key and went outside. This time, I took a good look at the gray concrete houses, the weeds growing through cracks in the streets, and the amount of dust and debris building up on the cars. If I'd seen the same thing in a neighborhood of expensive homes, it would have struck me immediately. Instead, I'd thought that was just the general state of a poor area.

I frowned. "Something doesn't add up."

"It looks like Baura destroyed this place months ago, not recently, and she's only been free for a couple of weeks at most, right?"

A sneaking suspicion crept up on me. The hairs on my neck prickled, and I realized it wasn't the only thing creeping up on me. A scratching noise drew my attention to the neighboring house. The door creaked and swung inward, revealing a shadowy shape inside.

13

A low yipping emanated from the doorway and then a creature the size of a large dog stepped outside. Its moist, pale skin was covered in what someone might mistake for spots but were actually eyes. Its mouth hung open, sharp teeth dripping with gelatinous saliva.

"Holy shit, Cain. It's a shoggoth!" Hannah drew her clockwork rifle, pressed the butt to her shoulder, and took aim. Despite the imminent danger, she practiced trigger discipline, keeping her booger picker off the bang switch.

It was indeed a shoggoth, but it was smaller than the ones we'd encountered in the Dead Forest. According to Lovecraft's journals, they came in many shapes and sizes, but all of them were deadly.

The creature shook its head, flinging saliva as it stepped out into daylight. Its skin was wrinkled and baggy, hanging loose on visible ribs. Whatever else this thing might be, it was starving.

It yipped again, steadily walking closer to us, nostrils flaring, every eye on the front of its body swiveling to look at us. Other yips echoed from nearby streets. The shoggoth paused, swiveling its head left and right as it sniffed, then focused back on us.

It was hungry, and competition was coming. I drew my brightblade an instant before it did what any hungry predator would do. It charged straight at us, mouth wide, tentacle tongues flailing.

Hannah fired a single round from her rifle and jumped to the side. The bullet missile zipped straight into the open maw of the shoggoth. I stepped in the opposite direction and slashed sideways, lopping off the front leg of the monster. It screeched in pain and plowed face-first into the asphalt. The incendiary round Hannah had fired exploded. Blood spurted from the shoggoth's mouth. It spasmed madly for several seconds, then went still.

I considered taking cover in the house and decided against it. While the concrete structure might provide a sound place to fight off a possible horde of shoggoths, taking off in the Jeep looked like the better option. I climbed inside, twisted the key in the ignition, and the diesel engine miraculously rumbled to life on the first try.

Hannah flung her rifle into the backseat and climbed into the passenger side. "Go!"

I shifted into gear and hit the accelerator just as six more shoggoths stampeded around the corner two houses down. Some of them saw the fallen creature and made a beeline for it. Nostrils flaring, others targeted us as the more delectable prey and pursued the Jeep.

The pothole-ridden street led to a highway, but if I'd hoped to go full speed, this road only led to disappointment. Cracks ran across the asphalt—the results of Baura playing god with Earthmaker. Even though the section of land she'd pummeled was miles away, the aftershocks had traveled far and wide.

The first cracks resembled nothing more than typical wear and tear, but they grew progressively wider until there were gaps even the oversized tires could barely handle. Driven by hunger, the shoggoths were closing the distance fast as I veered around upraised sections of asphalt.

Hannah slid into the back seat and stretched the seatbelts so they crossed over each other. She buckled each one into the opposite latch, creating a harness. Then she picked up the clockwork rifle, took aim, and fired on our pursuers. A shoggoth howled and flipped head over heels in the rearview mirror as an incendiary round exploded.

I skidded around a bend and sucked in a breath as the road suddenly dropped out from beneath us. We flew a good twenty feet and slammed to earth, bouncing wildly on the huge tires and raised suspension.

"Holy shit!" Hannah barely held onto her rifle.

"Sorry," I muttered.

A look in the mirror showed that this section of road had dropped a good ten feet lower than the previous. The shoggoths leaped from the higher section without pause, tentacle tongues lolling and dripping slimy saliva. Hannah gripped the rifle and fired several shots, but the Jeep was bouncing over too many ruts for her to aim properly.

A cliff rose to the right, and to the left was a sheer drop into the bay. Just ahead, the asphalt tilted up at forty-five degrees, and I couldn't see the rest of the road beyond. For all I knew, it dropped off into nothing. I slowed down so I could look before leaping.

Hannah gripped my shoulder. "Cain, there's more of them!"

I glanced in the mirror and confirmed that the number of shoggoths had doubled. Not only that, but there were others racing along the clifftop. We couldn't go left or right. We couldn't scale the cliff. There was no choice but to hope that there was more land beyond the broken road ahead.

Images flashed in my head. The Jeep hitting the asphalt with a jolt. The front end rising up, then dropping. A twenty-foot gap between us and the next section of road. Us plummeting toward the rocks and water below.

I blinked and focused back on the road, no doubt in my mind that this cliff led to a long, deadly fall. I had no idea what in the hell had just happened, but something told me not to question it. There was just one major problem—we had nowhere else to go. The cliff to the right was at least thirty feet tall, but I didn't know if that was enough to dissuade the shoggoths up there from jumping down. If they were as desperately hungry as the ones from town, I didn't think they'd let anything get in the way of a square meal.

Options, Cain, options!

But there were none, and we had less than a minute before reaching the jump that would fly us straight into the afterlife. If that fleeting vision I'd had was accurate, the road on the other side was much lower than this section, but the Jeep was still too slow and heavy to make a jump like that. And even if we did make the jump, the landing would be disastrous.

There was only one option—stop and fight. The two of us couldn't defeat this many shoggoths head-on, so I had to use every trick in the book to give us a fighting chance.

"Cain, why are we slowing?" Hannah leaned between the front seats and looked at the road ahead. "Is that a dead end?"

"I think so." I stopped right where the road slanted up and put the vehicle sideways as a barrier. Then I jumped out and looked over the edge. Sure enough, it was exactly as I'd seen it in my premonition. There was no time to wonder how I'd seen a glimpse of the future, so I unzipped a backpack and pulled out another rifle.

The shoggoths at the top of the cliff reached us first, crowding so close to the edge that two of them fell over the side. One landed on its feet. Bones cracked, and the monster howled in pain. The other bounced off the end of the road and plummeted into the abyss on the other side. Another fell, landing heavily on top of the first one. Blood spurted, and more bones cracked, and the first shoggoth went still.

The one that landed on top of it rolled onto its feet and prepared to pounce.

Shoggoths, from what I'd read in Lovecraft's journals, were sentient. But in the crazed world of eldritch horrors, they didn't even remotely think the same way as sentient beings from our world, which was why they didn't hesitate to start jumping down one at a time on the corpse of their fallen comrade.

Hannah and I took cover behind the Jeep and started unloading on them with the clockwork rifles. Incendiary rounds found their targets, burrowing into flesh and exploding. Shoggoths shrieked in pain, but there were too many to deal with, and we didn't have enough exploding rounds left.

I dropped my gun and summoned my staff, switching it to long-shot mode. I powered the staff, focused my will into a coherent ball of energy, and fired. The burst of energy blasted a hole through the head of a shoggoth, and the creature went down. I focused and fired again, dropping the next.

Hannah and I dropped ten of them, but there were still more jumping off the cliff and onto the corpses below. Shoggoths slipped in the bodily fluids of the fallen. Some of them lapped up the blood and tore into the bodies, cannibalizing the dead. But most of them saw us as the ultimate prize and kept coming.

The ones that had been chasing us down the road caught up, plowing through the others. One leaped over the Jeep, flew overhead, and fell off the cliff behind us. A fight broke out among them. The weakest ones went down first, throats torn out. The roiling mob of monsters slammed against the Jeep, threatening to shove it over the side.

Hannah ran out of bullets and jammed another magazine into place. I kept firing shots, trying to thin the mob before they devoured us or pushed us over the edge. But I was tiring quickly because focusing this much power into the staff was no easy feat.

Gunfire exploded. Shoggoths howled and fell from the top of the cliff, blood and guts spraying like rain. The ones on the cliff focused on whoever was attacking them and charged out of sight.

Another shoggoth separated from the horde and lunged through the air. I cast a shield just above us. The creature slid across the slick surface and plummeted over the cliff. Another beast jumped toward us. The shield cracked and shattered and the shoggoth fell right behind me and Hannah. We braced our backs to the Jeep and delivered a synchronized kick to the monster before it could regain its feet, sending it to join the others who'd fallen onto the rocks below.

An object sailed off the cliff and landed on the road in the midst of the shoggoth horde with a metallic clink. The creatures stopped their infighting for an instant and the object exploded. Body parts and fluids sprayed the road. A heavy caliber machine gun erupted, and the rest of the monsters fell.

A figure in a black, hooded cloak appeared at the top of the cliff and silently regarded us for a moment. Then they leaned down and produced rope. Metal clanged as a hammer drove a spike into the top of the cliff. The figure rappelled down gracefully despite having a belt-fed machine gun strapped to their back.

Standing in the puddles of blood among the shoggoth corpses, the figure stared at us for a long time before approaching, the light machine gun still slung across their back.

They didn't seem to be a threat, so I spoke first. "Thank you for your help."

They said nothing as they picked their way through the bodies.

"Who are you?" Hannah said.

The figure stopped a short distance away and lowered the hood.

Hannah gasped.

The dead giant and climbing gear on Prometheus's Rock suddenly made sense. One of the deadliest assassins I knew had been tracking Baura, and I had a pretty good idea as to why. "Well, now I know why you vanished. You wanted vengeance."

Layla Blade nodded but offered no quip or sarcastic response as usual. "That bitch is going to pay for what she did to me."

Hannah grimaced. "You don't sound like yourself. Are you okay?"

Layla's head remained facing me, but her eyes turned to Hannah. "No. I'm not sure I'll ever be okay after my time in Soultaker."

I understood her anger. "Mars is the one who killed you, not Baura."

Her nose wrinkled. "Baura?"

"Aura Beta," Hannah said. "That's what we call her."

"Baura." She practically spat the name. "Her clever plan got me killed. I'm going to find her and see how she likes an eternity of torment."

"Sounds like our interests are aligned." I wasn't sure how to talk to Layla anymore. She'd returned from Soultaker a different person. I'd hoped giving her space and time would help, but she'd vanished soon after her resurrection. She'd come back to life, learned that Baura had escaped the rock, and apparently decided to do something about it.

"They are." Layla's reply was calm and cold. "That's why I rescued you."

Hannah frowned. "How did you even know we were here?"

"I heard the shoggoth howls from a mile away." Layla booted one of the corpses with a combat boot. "They've already eaten just about every living thing in the vicinity, so I came to investigate."

"How long have you been here?" I asked.

"Two days." Layla shrugged. "Long enough to realize that Baura is going to be nearly impossible to catch by myself, at least on this world."

My suspicions about our location returned to the forefront of my mind. "Have you been off this island yet?"

She shook her head. "There are monsters in the water. Traveling by boat is a death sentence. If they don't kill you outright, they'll drive you mad."

A deep, haunting wail echoed in the distance, sending chills down my spine. There was nothing to see in the blue waters below, but cold existential dread crawled up my back.

Hannah shivered violently. "I don't like whatever is making that sound."

"Bitch hasn't even been free for two weeks, and she's already fucked Gaia Prime in the ass." A hint of snark returned to Layla's voice, but she didn't so much as crack a smile.

"I don't think she's done anything to Prime." I took out my staff and scanned the bay. "Apocalypse weapons or not, Baura hasn't had enough time to do what happened here."

Layla stared at me with dead eyes. "What are you saying, Cain?"

Hannah's pursed her lips. "I think it's pretty obvious."

Layla looked around. "If this isn't Prime then that means..." she trailed off as another distant howl reached us.

I nodded. "This is Gaia Beta. The world Baura destroyed."

14

Baura had bragged about destroying her Gaia. With the apocalypse weapons, she was a one-person wrecking crew. But even if I'd known this was Gaia Beta, the presence of shoggoths was a surprise. I'd imagined a world hammered by Earthmaker, drowned by Tidebringer, and thrashed with Airbender. But if the world was overrun by eldritch monsters, that hinted at an even worse fate.

Hannah shook her head. "I still don't understand how we went from Feary Prime to Gaia Beta. I thought portals like the one we used only took us to other planes in the same dimension."

"Baura probably has the Tetron from Beta." I banished my staff and turned to the others. "Or she has an upgraded staff like mine, and it's capable of making interdimensional portals that can remain open."

Hannah nodded. "Or maybe she's using both at the same time."

The Tetron had been a device used by Noctua, the clockwork owl, to spectate the events of our worlds and planes across the dimensions. We'd found out the hard way that it could also transport you to another parallel world and had ended up on Gaia Alpha, a world where one small change had led to mechanist domination.

Trapped as we were, we had no choice but to find a way home by stealing the Tetron from the mechanists. Instead, we'd ended up liberating the Gaia Alpha. My alt on Alpha currently led its reconstruction, and magic was no longer a secret kept from the nubs.

Gaia Beta, on the other hand, had seen an even grimmer fate. Baura had infiltrated the mechanists, stolen the apocalypse weapons, and apparently, slaughtered most of humanity. Using Panoptes, she'd spied on us in Prime so she could kill Athena. Powerful gods like the Olympians existed across all dimensions simultaneously, but they only paid attention to Prime, allowing the splinter dimensions to survive or fall on their own. According to Fate, most alternate time-lines quickly hit dead ends and were extinguished. Others like Alpha and Beta were just as alive as the Prime that birthed them.

It seemed the gods hadn't realized what kind of threats such parallel dimensions could spawn. The mechanists had planned on invading other dimensions, asserting their rule in all the worlds, but they'd been nowhere close to becoming a threat as dire as Baura.

Baura had also done something that seemed senseless at the time, but a reason clicked into place given the context of this monster-infested world. Baura had destroyed the Rlhala I'd taken from Alpha. It was a stone totem that allowed me to control Cthulhu through his dreams. At first, I thought Baura simply wanted to ensure I couldn't control Cthulhu. But now I wondered if she was trying to consolidate her control over the Great Old One.

What if the Rlhala was what kept Cthulhu sleeping in R'lyeh? What if it was the only thing standing between us and a world driven mad by the Great Ancient One rising?

The Rlhala I'd had in Sanctuary was from Gaia Alpha, meaning the one on Prime presumably still existed somewhere in the depths of the Pacific Ocean. But Cthulhu hadn't risen on Alpha after I'd taken the Rlhala to Prime, nor had he awakened after Baura destroyed the Alpha Rlhala. I'd used the Rlhala to bend Cthulhu to my will and told him to only obey my orders and those of Cain Alpha. Perhaps the rules I'd given using the totem remained in place despite its destruction.

It seemed likely that Baura had found the Rlhala on Beta and used it to control Cthulhu, and through him, his minions. I just hoped she couldn't override the commands I'd given Cthulhu on Alpha and Prime.

It was a frightening thought, and one that made me realize that even the destruction brought on by apocalypse weapons paled in comparison to what Baura could do if she commanded Cthulhu.

Hannah eyed me worriedly. "What are you thinking about, Cain?"

"The mechanists used the Rlhala to control Cthulhu on Gaia Alpha. I think Baura might be doing the same thing here." I shook my head. "But in this case, she's just letting the monsters run amok."

"Seems that way." Layla offered none of her usual mockery and walked around the Jeep, examining it. "This is noisy. It's no wonder you attracted every shoggoth in the vicinity."

"To be fair, we only used it after shoggoths attacked." I shrugged. "I think the howls of the first ones are what attracted the rest of the mob."

"Probably." Layla walked back to the rope dangling off the cliff. "Just leave it. We need to be stealthy from here on out."

Hannah looked at the piles of corpses. "Do we? I think we killed every shoggoth for miles."

"Shoggoths are the least of our worries." Layla gripped the rope, planted her feet on the cliff, and quickly scaled it.

Hannah put on her backpack, clipped the clockwork rifle to it, and followed.

I grabbed the rest of the gear and climbed the rope to the top. Layla waited near a pickup truck. I raised an eyebrow. "What makes this any better than the Jeep?"

"It's electric. Virtually silent." She patted the hood. "Gets good range too."

"Yeah, but how do you charge it?" Hannah waved a hand around. "Does electricity work during the apocalypse?"

"Solar does." Layla climbed into the driver's seat of the crew cab.

I took shotgun, and Hannah got in the back.

The pickup began moving with nary a sound except a barely

audible whine. Layla took us cross-country a short distance until we reached a highway that was in considerably better shape than the one we'd left. If I'd taken a right turn back in town, we would've ended up on this one instead of the highway to hell.

We traveled through a canyon and took a turn down a gravel road that led a short distance into the countryside. On arrival, we found a sprawling Spanish-style villa. The roof was covered liberally in solar panels and the outside grounds were sprinkled with the corpses of shoggoths and humanoid figures with the fishy features of deep ones.

I blew out a breath. "I take it you found this place and made a stand here?"

Layla nodded. "Unlike you, I didn't raise holy hell the moment I arrived."

I rolled down the truck window and peered at the bodies. "Then where'd all these monsters come from?"

"I saw shoggoths eating one of their own when I arrived in town, so I skirted them and worked my way around, figuring I'd pick up Baura's trail on the other side." Layla shrugged. "Something caught my scent and started stalking me." She stopped the truck next to the body of a creature with at least a dozen tentacle legs and tentacle arms with scorpion stingers on the tips. Countless eyes covered the bulbous head. An orifice of sharp teeth gaped open, tentacle tongues lolling.

"What is it with tentacles and eyes?" Hannah gagged. "That thing smells like rotten tuna."

I examined it. "It looks like a migyo with a few modifications."

"Whatever it was, it followed me all the way here." Layla continued driving up the brick-paved driveway. "It must've attracted some other monsters along the way, because the rest of them came out of the darkness not long after I killed it."

I nodded toward the pickup bed which was loaded down with duffel bags and guns. "Where'd you get all the weapons?"

"From here." She parked in the garage, got out, and plugged a thick electrical cord into the truck. "I think this place was owned by the mafia. There's an arsenal in the basement and a room full of cocaine and heroin."

Hannah's eyebrows rose. "Sounds like a fun time."

"Have you seen any humans?" I asked

She shook her head. "Closest thing I've seen are deep ones."

Deep ones were humanoid fishlike creatures that were used as foot soldiers by the eldritch gods. What I knew of them consisted of information from the journals and notes Lovecraft used to write the book *The Shadow Over Innsmouth*.

Deep ones and their human hybrid offspring worshiped Father Dagon and Mother Hydra, both of whom were, at the very least, immortal deep ones, or at most, Great Old Ones. The deep ones I'd encountered during my time as Death worshipped Nyarlathotep, the Crawling Chaos.

The most important thing I'd learned about deep ones was that they were much easier to kill than shoggoths. Their humanoid form came with all the weaknesses one would find in a human—namely that a headshot would put them down in a hurry, whereas with a shoggoth, a headshot might just piss them off unless the blast came from my staff.

The duffel bags in the bed of the pickup were full to bursting with weaponry—mostly light machine guns and semiautomatic rifles. AK-47s and M-16s were in the majority, but there were others I didn't recognize. Nub weaponry had never been an interest of mine except in cases where one of my targets might employ such defenses.

There were also grenades and other explosives, but sadly no rocket launchers. If I wanted to blow up a horde, I'd have to do it with grenades.

Layla patted her machine gun. "It's primitive, but it works."

"As if daggers and arrows aren't even more primitive," Hannah said.

Nub weapons were loud and messy. I preferred hurling bullets of magical energy instead of brass and lead but had to admit that guns would work much better when facing mobs of shoggoths.

Layla opened the door to the house and went inside. We followed her into a room with a handcrafted wooden bench and racks for hanging coats. She continued on to a kitchen. The appliances were stainless steel and industrial-looking, but the countertops were dark granite, the cabinets mahogany, and the tile an expensive-looking stone slate.

This was definitely the house of a mobster or maybe even a corporate CEO—basically the same thing.

Hannah stroked the countertop, leaving a trail in the accumulated dust. "This is beautiful, Cain. Maybe it's time to upgrade your kitchen."

"Meh." I didn't care for the glitter and glam as long as I had what I needed to make breakfast and sandwiches. This mansion, while spectacular, was dirty and unkempt. There were no bodies or dried blood on the first floor, but that wasn't a surprise. I doubted a search of the top floor would yield any corpses either. The owner was rich and had probably chartered a flight out at the first signs of trouble.

I wiped dust off a stool and sat at the kitchen bar. "What's the sitrep?"

Layla laid her machinegun on a counter and leaned against a wall. "Crete is overrun with shoggoths, deep ones, and gods know what else. I lost Baura's trail when I had to skirt around the city and haven't been able to pick it up since."

"Any idea how or why she left open a portal between here and Feary?"

She shook her head. "No, but if I had to guess, I think she wants to take an army of these monsters back to Feary with her. Her trail goes straight toward Heraklion as if she doesn't have a worry in the world about them eating her."

"Well, that mostly confirms my worst fears." I pressed my lips together. "Baura knows about the Rlhala, otherwise she wouldn't have gone through the trouble of destroying the one that was in my possession. She must have done that to prevent me from fighting for control over Cthulhu's minions if she decided to invade with them."

"Great, an interdimensional monster war is the last thing we need." Hannah narrowed her gaze. "Why doesn't Baura just use the apocalypse weapons on Gaia and Feary Prime? It doesn't make any sense."

"Makes perfect sense," I said. "The second she uses an apocalypse weapon, the gods will home in on her and snatch her. If she hides on Gaia Beta and unleashes an army of minions, then the gods can't do much."

Hannah laughed scornfully. "The gods could easily destroy shoggoths and deep ones."

"I'm not so sure about that. If the creatures don't act directly against them, then the gods may not be able to directly react." I tapped my fingers on the countertop. "Anyway, the shoggoths and deep ones are just foot soldiers. There are mind-wrenching creatures like the ones we encountered in the battle at Lake Lanier on Gaia Alpha. Creatures that could drive humans and other beings completely mad without even having to fight. Those are the ones I'm really worried about."

"Oh, yeah." Hannah grimaced. "I forgot about malgorths."

I snorted. "How do you forget about malgorths, ganthagons, migyos, and salkos? Those things left a lasting impression even on me."

"We've just fought so many monsters that I lost track." Hannah shrugged. "I don't even remember what those things look like except that some were big, and they all had tentacles."

Layla remained quiet, watching us closely.

I turned back to her. "It's in our dimension's best interests if we stop Baura and take control of the Rlhala. Clearly, this wasn't even remotely a consideration in my plans to capture her. I thought we'd run her down in Feary and be done with it."

"Likewise." Layla folded her arms across her chest. "But here we are. I want revenge, and you just want to save the world."

I held up a finger. "Correction. I want to preserve the place where I live. It won't do any of us any good if Gaia or Feary are destroyed."

Layla grunted.

Hannah shook her head. "Jesus, Layla, you're worse than Cain now. Did Soultaker really fuck you up that bad?"

Layla's gaze flicked to Hannah. "I was dead, transformed into a mindless soul that was forced to fight and die countless times, then resurrected with a memory of almost everything that I went through. So yeah, it fucked me up. I'm not the same happy-go-lucky assassin you once knew."

"Oh." Hannah's shoulders slumped. "That's really sad. I loved to hate the old Layla. Now you're just kind of there. You don't even call me girl anymore."

Layla focused on me. "Are we going to reminisce about the good old days until the monsters eat us, or do you have a plan for tracking down that murderous bitch?"

"I have a tracking sigil." I touched the stone. "It's pulling me toward Heraklion."

She grunted. "The good news is that the shoggoths have devoured just about everything on the island and are so hungry, they'll eat each other or any other monsters they find. There are probably less monsters around now than there were back when Baura unleashed them on the world. The bad news is that we're walking delicacies. Once one monster gets our scent, the others won't be far behind. Traveling into Heraklion will be extremely dangerous."

"Duh." Hannah rolled her eyes. "Maybe we need to bring back reinforcements before storming the castle."

I briefly considered it. The only reinforcements I trusted would be Oblivion Guard. Erolith would certainly help since this involved a direct threat to the high fae. But there was no way to reach him except by returning through the portal to Feary Prime and then traveling to the nearest mushroom portal to Faevalorn. That would take days, during which time Baura might unleash unholy hell.

There was also the matter of the centaurs who were still out for our blood. They might be waiting on us back in Feary. It was also possible they'd followed us through the portal and were tracking us here.

There was no way we could return to Feary for help. The hard reality of our situation was that we were on our own against a world infested with monsters.

15

We might be surrounded by enemies, but that didn't mean we had no options.

I'd survived by creating allies out of nothing. Leaving the Oblivion Guard required me to start an insurrection resulting in the Beast War. I'd escaped from Hel by raising an army of dead warriors who wanted to earn a ticket to Valhalla.

The problem with this world was that there weren't many potential allies left. But what if we could turn an enemy into the perfect shield? Nothing would be better than using a small army of centaurs to keep the monsters off our asses. The only question was whether I could convince them to help us or if we'd have to trick them into it.

Layla raised an eyebrow. "You've got an idea."

I nodded. "Reaching Faevalorn so I can talk Erolith into bringing over the Oblivion Guard is nearly impossible even if there wasn't a centaur army between us and them. But maybe the centaurs could be put to good use as either friend or foe."

"Good plan." Layla's gaze went distant. "But we need them ahead of us. Maybe you can use one of your magic tricks to make that happen."

"Possibly, provided they followed us through." I nodded in the direction of the town. "I'll need to go back where we came from and confirm their location."

Layla checked the time on her phone. "It's going to be dark soon. We need to wait until morning."

Hannah's forehead pinched. "Since when are you afraid of the dark?"

Layla motioned us to follow. She led us through the house and to a back deck with a huge swimming pool stretching from one end to the other. A humanoid creature black as pitch lay on its back at the far end. She opened the french doors and walked over to it. "Since this."

It was hard to tell if the thing was alive or not because its head was perfectly smooth—no eyes, ears, nose, or mouth. The only features on the head were two horns curving upward and inward from the sides, the tips reaching toward each other but not quite touching.

It had a long whip-like tail with feathery barbs at the end—the kind that looked fine as thistle needles and would easily lodge in the skin. Prehensile claws served as feet and hands, and a pair of bat wings spread nearly twelve feet from tip to tip.

I'd seen the creature in Lovecraft's writings but couldn't remember the name, so I took out my phone and searched images I'd downloaded from the internet.

Hannah circled around it. "What is that thing?"

"I don't know, but they're absolutely silent." Layla's eye twitched as if remembering something vile. "It tried to grab me." She displayed a red welt on her rib. "And its tail rubbed against me like it was trying to tickle me. But it was like being tickled with steel wool."

"It's a nightgaunt." I showed them a matching image on my phone. "They capture their prey and torture them by tickling them with their barbed tails."

"Tickling?" Hannah looked aghast.

Layla grimaced. "I put all the allergy medications I could find on this, and it still itches."

"That's the stupidest thing I've ever heard!" Hannah knelt and ran a finger along the creature's smooth, rubbery skin. "How does it eat without a mouth?"

"Lovecraft theorized that it feeds on emotions and electrical currents gathered by the tail." I scrolled for more information, but there was nothing else on the subject. I turned to Layla. "This is why you don't want to go out at night?"

She nodded. "I never saw this thing coming when it grabbed me. If I didn't have incredible reflexes, it would've carried me away. Not even my finely honed senses triggered until the last second when a breeze from its wings hit me."

"The scope on my staff can see their heat signatures." I examined the skin of the nightgaunt but didn't see any puncture wounds. "How did you kill it?"

"I broke its neck." Layla booted the head, and it lolled to the side, revealing a jagged bone pressing against the inside of the skin. "It wasn't easy, but my legs did the trick."

She was half fae, which gave her enhanced strength and reflexes. Even so, the fact that she somehow got the upper hand on something that tried to fly away with her was impressive.

"I think it's best if we scout for the centaurs right now." I shrugged. "We'll be safe in the truck."

Layla scowled. "Just don't blame me if you get caught and tickle-tortured to death."

"I thought I saw some night vision goggles in the duffel bags," Hannah said. "Can't we use those?"

"Depends on their rating." I went back through the house to the garage and found the goggles Hannah mentioned. There were enough pairs for a small army, probably because the former owner of the house had dozens of security personnel. I examined the manufacturing label on the bottom. "These have a range of three hundred yards. That should be plenty to keep an eye on the sky."

We each took a pair. I checked out an AK-47 with a night scope and brought it to my shoulder. I'd trained with nub weapons frequently in the Oblivion Guard but only to familiarize myself with the primary weapons of Gaian humans in case of a war. It was almost as if the fae queens had known the Fae-Human War was a certainty before it happened.

I examined several magazines to make sure they were full, then checked the chamber of the rifle to ensure it was clean. I didn't know much about the care of the weapons and couldn't break them down like I'd seen in nub movies, but I could aim and fire, and that was good enough.

Once we were geared up, Layla climbed into the driver seat, and we headed back toward town. I rolled down my window and listened to the mournful basso trumpeting calls coming from somewhere to the north and west. I couldn't tell if it was one creature or many.

"Same sounds every night." Layla kept her eyes on the road. "I tried to get closer to the source and heard chanting. The voices sounded almost human, but I didn't want to find out."

"Probably going to find out whether we want to or not since Baura is in Heraklion." I pursed my lips. "Might be deep ones. They're known to hold rituals for Father Dagon and Mother Hydra."

"Maybe that's what they were doing." Layla shrugged. "I didn't try to get any closer to town because of roaming packs of monsters." She parked on a cliff overlooking the part of town where we'd encountered the shoggoths. I summoned my staff and scanned the area. There were no centaurs and no signs that they'd passed through the area. Dozens of hooved beings would have left a trail even a blind man could follow, but the area looked untrampled.

Hannah scouted with a pair of binoculars taken from one of the bags. "Doesn't look like they followed us."

I pressed my lips together. "Strange. Why follow us so far if they weren't going to go the extra mile to kill us?"

Layla cocked an eyebrow. "How in the hell did you end up with a centaur army on your ass anyway?"

"Our trip through the labyrinth didn't go smoothly." Hannah grinned. "And Cain got donkey-kicked by a minotaur."

A small smile broke through Layla's grim façade. She blinked as if surprised by it. "How did that happen?"

I sighed. "What I want to know is how you made it through the labyrinth and Crete without attracting any attention."

"I'm half fae." She shrugged. "I told them I was passing through on official business, and they escorted me right on through."

"Easy peasy lemon squeezy." Hannah shook her head.

"Let's go to the portal." I banished my staff. "We're going to need those centaurs one way or the other."

Layla shifted into drive and drove on. Aside from the crackling of gravel and vegetation under the tires, our progress was nearly silent. That thought caused me to shift my gaze skyward. A slight shock of unease ran through me when I noticed a pair of distant nightgaunts spiraling in the sky even though it was still daytime.

I'd assumed nightgaunts were nocturnal, but that obviously wasn't the case. I'd have to rely heavily on my sigil tattoos to warn me of their approach. They might be silent, but at least they were visible, unlike the Nyx assassins I'd encountered in Feary. I just had to be extra vigilant.

After navigating rough terrain, we reached the cliff overlooking the canyon where the portal was. The area around the bubbling pocket of air was covered in hoof tracks. It looked as if a few centaurs had come through, looked around, and then returned to Feary.

I got out of the truck and summoned my staff.

Hannah hopped out after me. "Cain, what are you doing?"

"I'm going in."

Layla followed me. "That's dumb. You don't know what's on the other side."

"At the worst, a cave full of centaurs." I shrugged. "But if they didn't follow us, I'd be willing to bet they're not in the cave." I navigated down the cliff using the slope to my advantage.

"Cain, wait!" Hannah stopped at the edge of the cliff, hands outstretched.

I strode to the portal without pause. The air bubbled and sucked me in. I emerged back in the cave to the sounds of bedlam. The cave was empty, but the ground was shaking. Shouts and cries of pain echoed from outside. Holding onto the cave walls for support, I poked my head out of the entrance.

A humanoid giant stomped the ground, roaring furiously as centaurs fought to snare his legs with thick ropes. The giant's belly was huge and sagging, its legs stubby and twisted. A massive head perched on a tiny neck, the face little more than a wide mouth with two tiny eyes and a stub nose.

It was deformed like many humanoid giants and not terribly bright as it tried chomping on the centaurs who were trying to take it down. Its mouth looked big enough to hold an entire horse in it, but the giant's stubby legs were an impediment.

This situation was no good. I needed the centaurs free to pursue us so I could use them as shoggoth bait. I switched my staff to long-shot mode, aimed, and blasted the side of the giant's kneecap. It was little more than a pinprick, but the blast of energy penetrated the skin and found the sensitive tendons. The pain was just enough to make the leg buckle.

The centaurs shouted in victory and toppled the giant with a concerted pull on their ropes. The giant fell with a basso cry of surprise and slammed to earth. Spears jammed into the giant's eyes. Battleaxes hacked at the tough skin around the neck. The giant struggled, but the centaurs swarmed it, stabbing and beating it until it went still.

The palomino centaur pulled out one of the giant's large flat teeth and held it overhead like a trophy. A single tooth would earn a small fortune if sold in Faevalorn. The giant skin would also fetch a good price since the leather was extremely durable. The centaurs likely didn't care about money and would probably just use it for themselves.

Now that the sounds of battle had died down, I decided to announce myself. I whooped and cast a flashbang spell to get their attention. Their celebration went silent as all eyes turned to me.

I considered taunting them but decided to try diplomacy first. "I must stop a great evil from attacking our worlds and require the help of the mighty centaur nation."

The palomino reared up on hind legs, the giant tooth raised in one hand. "Capture the intruder so I might skin his hide!"

I sighed. "Can't we just cooperate for once?"

The herd galloped toward me, battle cries resounding through the hills. I turned tail and ran back through the portal. Banishing my staff, I clambered up the cliff side. "They're coming!"

Hannah's eyes flared. "What took you so long?"

"A giant." I was nearly to the top when Layla reached down, grasped my shirt, and yanked me up.

"Why the hell don't you just ghostwalk up the cliff, Cain?" Layla shook her head. "You really don't use that ability enough."

"If it was that easy, don't you think I'd ghostwalk everywhere?" I brushed off my pants. "Plus, the top of the cliff was out of range." Ghostwalking had its limits, and it wasn't cheap to use either. It required a surge of power that could be put to better use elsewhere, especially when I might have to fight centaurs.

The palomino burst through the interdimensional bubble first, the giant's tooth tucked casually under an arm even though it probably weighed a hundred pounds. I drew my staff and aimed it at him. "Hey, up here!"

He looked up, eyes blazing with anger. "I will tear you apart, little man."

He was speaking Faeicht, and Gaia didn't have the ambient magic to translate for us, so I switched to speaking the same language. "I'll blow your head off if you don't shut up and listen to me."

He gripped the giant's tooth. "Try your luck."

"Feary is in grave danger." I waved my hand toward Heraklion. "There's an elf who was imprisoned on Prometheus's Rock by the gods because she murdered Athena. Now she's free and is planning to unleash the end days on Feary and Gaia if we don't stop her here. How about we join forces and stop her together?"

More centaurs piled through the portal. The palomino trotted forward to make room while bearing the tooth as a shield. "You trespassed in our city, killed our warriors, and now you lie to avoid the consequences?"

I gritted my teeth. "I didn't kill anyone. You killed yourselves by firing a fucking rocket launcher and causing a landslide!"

"We will visit our wrath upon you and your companions." His gaze narrowed as Layla stepped close enough to the cliff to enter his view. "You? We granted you safe passage through our city, and now you are with this human?"

Layla held up her hands in surrender. "Cain isn't lying. There's an insane elf who unleashed eldritch horrors on this Gaia, and she's planning the same for Feary. If you join us, we can get to her before she destroys your entire city."

Palomino wasn't having any of it. He shook his head vehemently, giant's blood spraying from his shaggy beard. "We will hunt you to the ends of the world and have our vengeance."

I shrugged. "Then why didn't you follow me through the portal earlier?"

"The giant attacked our flanks, so we fought it off." As he spoke, his fingers flicked in an almost unnoticeable pattern.

Having used sign language to convey wordless messages in the Oblivion guard, I knew exactly what was about to come next even as it happened.

Centaurs raised their bows and fired.

16

Arrows whistled through the air.

I threw up a shield, and wooden shafts splintered against it. We backed away from the edge of the cliff, the shield guarding against arrows.

I turned to Layla. "Looks like we're doing this the hard way."

She nodded. "Dumbass centaurs."

Hannah scowled. "They're so bullheaded."

I grunted. "Stubborn as mules."

"Bunch of horses' asses." Hannah flipped them off.

Hooves thundered in the canyon below as the centaurs raced back and forth, looking for a way up.

We climbed in the truck, and Layla gunned it, taking us back the way we'd come. I kept an eye on our rear and saw no signs of centaurs. That was good and bad. I needed them for monster bait. It was clear I'd have to come up with a better way to get them to go where I needed them when the time was right.

We made it back to the house at dusk. I set up a wide perimeter of sigils that would warn us if anything crossed them while Hannah watched the sky for nightgaunts and other terrors. I considered laying explosives as traps, but the detonators required wiring, and I didn't have time for that.

Back inside the house, we set up defenses. The windows were already barred and bulletproof, adding further evidence the former owner was a mafioso. The house was a prepper's wet dream with solar energy, underground food stores, and tons of weaponry. Unfortunately, not even all of that would have been enough to help the former owner survive the eldritch apocalypse that struck Gaia Beta. I just hoped it was enough to help us bring this quest to completion.

Most of the bedrooms upstairs had french doors leading to covered balconies. They were perfect places to setup defenses with the light machine guns because they offered a good vantage point and provided protection from aerial attackers like nightgaunts.

We turned off all the lights in the house and used only camping lanterns, which I shielded with sigils, so the light was only visible from one side. That allowed us to keep some rooms dimly illuminated while also making the house look dark from the outside.

Using my scope, I checked for auras and infrared signatures in the night while Layla and Hannah used the night vision goggles to do the same. The centaurs were nowhere to be seen, which meant they were likely setting up camp for the night and would resume hunting us tomorrow.

My plan was to kite them along and hope the shoggoths and deep ones took the bait, opening a path for us into Heraklion. Considering the Centaurs' unbridled aggression, it seemed the easiest way to manipulate them into becoming our unwitting allies.

Hannah sat down next to me on the southern balcony, a bag of chips in her hand. "Are you going to get Aura's body before midnight?"

I took a sip of one of the beers I'd found in the cellar and gave the question some serious thought. Aura and Layla didn't mix well under the best of circumstances. With Layla on a revenge quest against Aura's doppelganger, the tension was bound to be particularly bad. But we also needed an extra body to fend off monsters, and Aura was capable.

Hannah chuckled. "Tough decision?"

"Yeah." I held the beer bottle toward her. "Want a sip?"

She frowned. "Is sharing your beer one of those father-daughter bonding things?"

I had no idea what she was talking about. "Nub parents bond with their kids by giving them alcohol? That sounds like a strange ritual."

"Yeah, I heard other kids talking about it in high school." She shrugged. "I don't really understand it either. Then again, I was little when Mom died, and you're the only other family I've ever known."

"Then let's bond." I gave her the beer.

Hannah took a sip and grimaced. "Ew. This is nasty."

"You can have it." I got up and turned to head inside.

She laughed. "You didn't like it either, did you?"

I shook my head. "Nope. But I feel like we've really bonded."

Hannah rolled her eyes and followed me. "Are you going to tell Layla about Aura?"

I pressed my lips together grimly. "Yep."

Layla was watching the eastern approach since the north and west sides were protected by a steep cliff. She took off the NV goggles and turned around. "See anything?"

I shook my head. "No. I came here to tell you that Aura is with us."

Her right eye twitched. "Aura? Where?"

"She died earlier, so I put her in a safe place. I'm about to go get her, and I thought it would be wise to tell you beforehand."

"Smart." She set down the goggles and rose. "Is it our Aura or the one from Alpha?"

"Aura Prime."

Layla scowled. "Why in the hell didn't you bring this up earlier when we were out? We could have gotten her body then instead of having to go back out in the dead of night!"

I produced Panoptes from my utility belt. "We don't have to go anywhere." I slipped on the ring and winced as my vision split and dizziness washed over me. I willed myself into the warehouse, then quickly retrieved Aura's pale, lifeless body and went back through to the room.

Layla stared at me in slack-jawed confusion. "What in the fuck just happened?"

I dropped Aura on the bed, then took off the ring and held it up. "This ring allows me to travel to places that it's watching. I can't take anything living with me, but I can take bodies."

"Where did you get that ring?"

"Baura."

Layla stiffened. "That's how she pulled off her caper, isn't it?"

"Yeah." I put the ring away. "It allowed her to spy on us and take Aura Alpha's place at the last moment so she could kill Athena."

"Smart fucking bitch." Layla's fists clenched.

I leaned against the wall. "I feel like I need to reiterate that Baura isn't the one who killed you. It was Mars."

"She's the one who caused it to happen." Layla remained tense as she stared at the body on the bed. "And I can't very well get revenge on the god of war."

"Not unless you're willing to take the path of Baura."

Hannah watched her closely. "You're not that crazy, are you?"

Layla glared at the corpse, then abruptly looked away, her body suddenly relaxed, seemingly at ease. "Unless I suddenly come into some god powers, I'll be satisfied taking down Baura."

"I'm worried about you, Layla." Hannah's forehead pinched. "Did Soultaker strip away everything that made you who you are?"

Layla shook her head. "I'm not in the mood for counseling, but, yes, this mission is about healing. Getting Baura will go a long way toward that."

"Wow." Hannah's eyebrows rose. "That's a really direct and honest answer coming from someone who usually hides behind sarcasm."

"My soul was laid bare and brutalized." Layla bared her teeth while a lone tear trickled down her cheek. "I have no shields left."

Hannah blinked, and a tear of her own pooled in her eye. She walked over to Layla and hugged her.

Layla flinched as more tears spilled. Then she wrapped her arms around Hannah and hugged her back.

I watched the raw emotions flash across Layla's face with unease. I utilized emotional shields all the time. They weren't simply to keep others from knowing what I was feeling, but to protect myself against the horrible things I'd done. They were part of my training. They were tools of survival that protected me from myself.

When and if Layla recovered, I had a feeling she'd regret this moment of candor. Or maybe, this was just what she needed to help herself recover.

Hannah took a breath and backed away. "I don't have many friends, but you are one of my best frenemies, Layla, and I'd like you back the way you were. I'll help you get your revenge on Baura, not just to save the world, but for you."

Layla wiped her cheeks dry and nodded grimly. "Thank you, girl."

Hannah grinned. "You're welcome." She turned to me. "Don't look so uncomfortable, Cain. Even you have your moments."

I left the room and went downstairs to see if there was any better alcohol to be found in the cellar. That was when I felt one of the perimeter sigils trigger on the western side. The alarm spell was simple, so it didn't tell me anything about what touched it—size, shape, or how many tentacles it might have.

Anything living would set it off by stepping across it. Since most of the wildlife had been devoured by shoggoths and deep ones, I doubted it was anything as innocent as a bird or a cat.

I ran up the western staircase and followed the hallway to a room at the end. Rather than summon my staff, I picked up a pair of NV goggles sitting next to the machine gun we'd stationed there and put them on. The world lit up in green. I zoomed in and saw a lone centaur galloping along the perimeter.

The warrior must have circled the fence to reach the western side where a cliff guarded the western approach. The fencing on that side had fallen over some time ago, granting him access to the mansion grounds. Even from this distance, I heard the clop of his hooves on the rocky grounds near the cliff.

Glowing orbs popped up over the cliff. Another pair and another appeared soon after. It took a moment for me to realize it was the night vision goggles casting reflections off nocturnal eyes. I zoomed in, and the grainy image revealed pale creatures creeping over the side of the cliff behind the centaur. The creatures resembled adult-sized kangaroos, but they had no fur and weren't remotely cute. Their skin was pale and wrinkled. Their faces looked human despite the lack of nose or ears. Their crooked arms bore three clawed hooks instead of paws.

The centaur spun in place, brandishing a battle-ax, and backed away from the creatures.

More of them popped up from a crevice near the cliff edge, emerging like angry ants from a disturbed mound. They hopped in disturbingly irregular patterns, sometimes running into each other and staggering drunkenly. The air filled with guttural coughing as if they all suffered from phlegm-clogged throats that needed constant clearing.

The centaur turned tail and ran toward the mansion.

These disgusting creatures were called ghasts, according to Lovecraft's journals. A quick look at my notes filled in the blanks. They were subterranean creatures that were supposed to reside in a place called the Vaults of Zin. And yet, here they were invading the backyard of our temporary home.

Ghasts had a very keen sense of smell. It seemed our unwanted centaur guest had not only made enough noise to wake the dead, but his odor had tickled the noses of our underground neighbors. In a world where most of the native food supply had been devoured, the centaur probably smelled like a veritable feast. And now he was leading a horde of ghasts right toward our hiding place.

The centaur ran across the backyard and began hacking at the fence with his battle-ax. The fence, however, was made of reinforced steel, and not even a centaur was going to simply bash his way through it. The centaur turned toward the house, apparently identifying it as the easiest way out.

While he was busy mulling it over, I summoned my staff, aimed, and fired a longshot. The back of his head exploded, and the centaur went down in a heap. I just hoped the body was far enough away from the house to keep the ghasts from smelling us. I could use a sigil to mask some odors, but it couldn't cover up the odors of the food we'd cooked earlier.

The creatures swarmed the centaur's body and tore it to pieces in a matter of seconds. When there was nothing left but bones, the ghasts turned toward the house, nostrils flaring, hooked arms flailing. They had our scent.

I banished my staff and raced to the eastern side of the house where Layla stood sentry.

"All clear?" I asked.

She raised an eyebrow. "Yeah, why?"

"We've got company from the west."

She blinked. "The west? But there's a cliff there."

"A centaur found the house, and it looks like he woke up some monsters along the way." I showed her and Hannah the illustration of a ghast. "These things are coming from somewhere underground."

"Fucking great." Layla gripped her machine gun. "Just one centaur?"

I nodded. "It's possible Palomino lost our tracks when we hit the road, so he sent scouts to fan out and search nearby areas. I shot the centaur, and the ghasts devoured it in seconds. Now they're coming toward the house."

She mulled it over a moment. "You realize that if we start a firefight here, every monster for miles around is going to hear us?"

I nodded grimly. "The bars and bulletproof windows might be enough to keep them out, but we need to be prepared if they try to enter."

Layla tapped a finger on her rifle. "Can we fight them with swords? I'd use arrows, but I ran out of those the first day I got here."

"Doubtful. We're looking at upwards of fifty bogies." I envisioned the lay of the land. "There's no good place to funnel them into, or I'd suggest a Spartan defense."

Hannah still had my phone and was reading my notes. "They're cannibalistic."

Layla grunted. "I don't think they'll spontaneously start eating each other when there are better meals to be had."

"What if we gave them a better meal?" Hannah tossed me back my phone and ran out of the room.

Layla and I exchanged a look, then followed her downstairs. Hannah continued all the way down to the cellar and started looking at the shelves. That was when I realized where she was going with this.

I also didn't think it would work. "If you lead them away with food, they'll just eat it and come back here."

She ignored me and pulled a large plastic bucket from the shelf, then turned it so we could see the label—*Lard*.

Layla grinned. "Cain, get the sealable plastic bags."

"What?" I looked from the lard to Layla. "I thought I understood the plan, but clearly, I don't."

Layla grabbed a box of plastic bags and went back into the kitchen. She filled a pot with water and began heating it.

Hannah opened the bucket and began scooping lard into the Ziplock sandwich bags, then sealed them and put them in the water. "I didn't think about melting it, but that's even better."

"Just enough to liquefy it," Layla said. "The splatter will be more effective."

"We're making lard water balloons to throw at the ghasts?" I watched in disbelief. "What kind of mad plan is this?"

"God, I love it when I feel smarter than Cain." Hannah cackled with laughter. "He's kind of cute when he's confused."

I paused to put the pieces of their plan together. Then I realized it was a damned good plan. "You're capitalizing on their cannibalism."

Hannah nodded. "Yep."

I helped her fill more bags while Layla warmed them in the pot until the fat was liquid enough to splatter. Hannah found an empty bucket and put the warm bags in there. Something squeaked against glass. I peered around the corner and saw ghasts pressing their ghastly faces against the french doors, nostrils flaring, mucous streaking along the pane as they tried to reach a meal that would satisfy their hunger.

"We've got to lure them away from the back doors." I gripped the bucket with the bags of liquid lard and ran toward the staircase.

The susurrus of guttural coughs increased in excitement as the ghasts saw me running past them. Their hooked claws clacked against the glass as they desperately tried to push through the windows. The french doors had thick metal rods holding them in place, but they wouldn't be able to withstand the mass of bodies for long.

I ran upstairs and to the first bedroom on the west side, slipping on night vision goggles as soon as I reached the balcony. Dozens of ghasts mobbed the back patio. Some had fallen into the pool and were coughing in panic as their brethren blindly walked over them, shoving their heads underwater.

Reflective eyes twinkled like stars as ghasts looked up at me on the balcony and began hacking and coughing loudly. I plucked a lard bag from the bucket and threw it toward the back of the mob. It hit a ghast in the face, splattering all over it. The creatures went silent, nostrils flaring as they spun.

The ghast I'd struck extended a long wart-covered tongue and began licking lard off its body, coughing in a way that sounded a lot like "Om-nom-nom!"

Then its companions lunged at it, clawed hooks tearing into its hide. The creature coughed piteously as it was torn open, its innards slurped up by those nearby. Another ghast that the lard had splattered on met the same fate.

"Oh, god, it sounds awful!" Hannah shivered as she put on night vision goggles. "Sounds like an orgy with chain smokers!"

Layla appeared with another bucket of lard bombs. "Well, looks like this is gonna be easy."

The ground to the west rumbled. The crevice where the ghasts had come from exploded into a gaping pit. A beast with biceps the size of my body leaped from the hole and thudded to earth. Covered in coarse black hair, it towered nearly twenty feet tall. Its face split vertically down the middle, revealing rows of horizontal fangs, like a Venus fly trap turned into animal form.

Its massive arms split into two more arms right around the place an elbow should have been. The secondary arms swiveled and moved independently on double joints. It slammed all four hands on the ground and roared.

17

The ghasts looked up from the remains of their former comrades and coughed in alarm as the newest monster made its presence known. They turned and slammed against the rear doors and windows as if the only escape wasn't by running around the mansion, but through it.

Hannah watched the creature in awe. "Cain, what in the ever-loving fuck is that thing?"

"It's a gug." I only knew that because it had been mentioned in the same notes as the ghasts. "It eats ghasts and anything else it can get its hands on."

The gug rushed toward the mansion, propelling itself much like a gorilla with its arms. The swarm of ghasts outnumbered it at least a hundred to one, but that didn't seem to lend any bravery to the smaller monsters. The gug bulldozed through a retaining wall around a small rose garden and sent bricks and debris flying into the pool.

It abruptly stopped, the nostrils on the sides of its face-mouth flaring. Reflective red eyes beneath the gaping maw turned toward us. The creature roared and ran at us. Layla reached for a machine gun just as the towering monster slammed into the side of the mansion. It was so tall that its head was nearly even with the balcony.

Bricks and mortar crumbled from the blow. I shoved Hannah off the balcony and back into the bedroom as a pair of hands grasped at us, the tender morsels that we were. The gug's giant hand gripped both buckets with our lard bombs and tossed them into its maw.

Layla and I dove into the bedroom as the balcony gave way and rumbled to the ground.

"Well, there goes our brilliant plan!" Layla shouted above the din and fury of the beast.

We clambered away from the gaping hole in the side of the mansion as another set of arms grasped for more delectable treats. The side of the house shuddered with the impact.

I thought fast. "Get to the cellar. We can shelter down there."

Layla balked. "But we'll be trapped."

"Better than being eaten by that thing." Hannah dashed downstairs.

Layla gritted her teeth. "I'm not going into the cellar. I'd rather make a last stand in the kitchen."

I frowned. "Whatever you want."

She narrowed her eyes. "Okay." Then she ran after Hannah.

I followed her and stopped at the bottom of the stairs. The french doors were leaning dangerously inward from the weight of the ghasts and the constant pounding of the gug. The creatures coughed in excitement when they saw us run past, hooks clacking madly against the bulletproof glass.

The doors creaked and groaned under the added pressure.

I ran into the kitchen where Hannah and Layla were throwing down sacks of food in a vain effort to make a barricade. The thick wooden cellar door hung open behind them. The stairwell led down a brick corridor to the wine cellar at the bottom. There was barely room for two ghasts to run abreast in the narrow space, making it a perfect bottleneck.

Stepping back, I almost tripped on the bucket of lard Hannah had been scooping from earlier. It was still half-full. I motioned toward the cellar door. "Set up at the bottom of the stairs. The ghasts will funnel in, and you can kill them one by one. I'm going to see if I can even the odds a little bit."

Layla gripped a rifle. "We'll back down into the cellar when we have to, but I'm not going to lock myself away down there." Her face paled. "I won't be trapped again."

I put a hand on her shoulder. "Do what you want, but try to stay alive, okay?"

"Cain, what are you planning?" Hannah pushed between me and Layla. "How are you going to even the odds against all those monsters?"

I picked up the bucket and poured some of the still steaming water from the pot into it, then stirred it into a thick soup. "I'm going to toss this on the ghasts and get them to eat each other."

She nodded. "Be careful."

"I'll be back in a minute." My plan was simple—toss the soupy lard through the cracks in the french doors. But as soon as I ran into the living room, I saw it was too late. A crushed ghast was pressed against the nearly fallen doors, its brown blood smeared across the glass and puddled on the deck out back.

I'd barely made it there when the doors finally gave way, and the ghasts poured inside. I gripped the bucket by the bottom so I could splash it across them, but then the entire wall shook as the gug slammed it again. I dodged falling pieces of ceiling, the bucket handle gripped in one hand.

My brightblade hummed to life, drawn by pure reflex. It slashed down, severing a ghast's head from its body, then reversed to remove the arms from another. I changed direction and ran upstairs, determined to lead the horde away from the kitchen and into the west wing where I could exit through a window and climb up to the roof.

I passed the first bedroom. The gug had annihilated the wall and was groping madly inside the bedroom. Its red eyes found me. It lunged harder, collapsing more of the bedroom. That was when I realized the inevitable outcome of this battle. Even if the ghasts ate each other, the gug would still be around. It would dig us out of the cellar and devour us like truffles.

As ghasts stampeded upstairs and into the hallway, I improvised another plan—the only plan that might give us another day of life in this nightmare world. I ran to the end of the hallway and entered the door on the right. Thanks to the fire code regulations, there was another stairwell here—a narrow one that led to an exit at the bottom.

I yanked on a lever to release the iron bolts holding the door shut, and it sprang open into the backyard. A lone ghast looked up from the carcass of a comrade and hacked with excitement like a pneumonia patient trying to laugh at a joke. I dodged left, slashing with the brightblade in my right hand, and took off its hooked claws. Another swipe removed its head.

Once outside, I grimaced at the enormity of the gug still trying to claw its way further into the mansion. It pulled out a gaggle of ghasts and tossed them, cough-screaming, into its maw like a handful of popcorn.

Taking a deep breath, I steadied my heartbeat and focused on the mission at hand. This was no worse than fighting giant sand scorpions or being eaten by sea serpents. Then again, maybe it was. Oblivion was an apocalyptic world of monsters, but Gaia Beta was a full-on nightmare.

I raised the brightblade and waved it humming overhead. "Hey gug, if that's your real name. Come get your Turkish delight!"

The gug backed away from the ruined wall and spun toward me. Its maw split open, and it roared, sending unchewed ghast entrails and limbs spewing. It lowered its maw and charged me. I banished my brightblade since it was interfering with the night vision goggles and readied myself.

A hum and a loud click drew my attention to the mansion. Powerful floodlamps snapped on. The brilliant lights blinded the night vision goggles. I threw them off, blinking away the spots in my eyes. The gug thundered right over me, its mouth narrowly missing me since the sudden lights apparently blinded it as well. I barely had the presence of mind to keep the bucket handle gripped tightly in my hand.

I ducked, spun, and using both hands, splashed the lard soup all over the gug's backside. But there was a problem. The ghasts were creatures of darkness and the light panicked them. They were funneling into the dark house to escape. I dropped the bucket, drew my staff, and switched to longshot mode. A quick blast took out a floodlamp. The others clicked off before I could take them out.

Then I had another problem. I didn't know where I'd thrown the night vision goggles.

Switching to night vision on the scope of my staff, I swung it around and saw a constellation of reflective eyes swarming my way as the ghasts raced toward the fresh odor of warm lard. The ground shook. The gug spun and roared. I spotted the goggles, but they were right next to the gug's giant feet.

Casting a quick scent camouflage sigil on myself, I ran into the gaping hole the gug had made in the side of the mansion and ducked behind the remains of a brick wall. Coughing rapaciously, the ghasts hopped toward the gug. The giant beast bellowed and charged, lowering its vertical maw like a scoop.

It swept a group of ghasts into its gullet and chomped down. Blood sprayed. Ghasts swarmed the gug's legs, hooks digging in, sharp piranha-like teeth tearing at flesh and coarse hair. The gug spun to dislodge them, but the hooks only dug in deeper. It stomped a ghast to paste and roared, spitting out the half-chewed ghasts it had chomped a moment ago.

But the ghasts were as numerous as ants, driven insane with desire for the delicious odor of the lard. A few ghasts paused near my hiding spot, nostrils flaring. The odor camouflage wasn't enough to hide me entirely from their sensitive noses.

A pair of night goggles had fallen to the ground from the upper floor, so I slid them on and powered them, then drew my brightblade. The ghasts recoiled at the bright light, then slumped dead a moment later as their heads rolled.

Shrieking howls sounded in the distance. Despite our attempts to keep the skirmish silent, shoggoths had heard the din of battle or smelled the blood in the air. We were about to have even more unwanted company.

Another ghast invaded my hiding spot. I cut it down and retreated further into the mansion, climbing over rubble and squeezing through a hole where the door had been. The living room was covered in ghast corpses. Layla and Hannah stood among them holding katanas dripping with blood.

I blinked. "Where did you get swords?"

"They were with the other weapons in the cellar." Layla wiped the sword off on the corpse of a ghast, but the pale flesh only smeared the blood.

"Unfortunately, the gug has drawn the attention of shoggoths." I went to the broken french doors and looked outside where the ghasts were swarming the giant beast. They were tearing into the gug, but it was smashing scores of them at the same time. "I recommend we prepare a retreat into the cellar."

Hannah watched the fight outside, pumping her fists whenever the gug crushed another ghast. "Yeah, kill those nasty things."

"Uh, we want the gug to die," Layla said. "I'd rather fight shoggoths and ghasts than that thing."

Hannah pursed her lips. "I think one big target would be easier than a swarm."

Layla seemed to reconsider. "In this case, you might be right."

I nodded. "You killed a giant, so that thing should be easy, right?"

Hannah's eyes flared. "Layla killed that giant by herself?"

"Giants are easy if you find their weak spots." Layla narrowed her eyes as she watched the gug. "That thing looks a lot tougher."

Several alarm sigils tripped at the same time as more monsters invaded from the east and north. I ran to the front door and watched shoggoths smash through the gate guarding the driveway. I counted fourteen, all of them coming from different directions. They skirted around the mansion and toward the fight in the backyard.

I joined Hannah and Layla in the kitchen. Shoggoths pounced on ghasts, tearing out their throats and slurping on their guts. One went for the gug and was pounded to paste by a giant foot. Blood spattered, bones cracked, and monsters died. A shoggoth ripped at the gug's ankles, shredding tendons.

With a bestial cry of pain, the gug fell to a knee, arms flailing as it fought off the ghasts and shoggoths. Bodies flew, slamming against the mansion, splatting on the back patio, and splashing into the pool where drowned ghasts floated.

Another shoggoth tore at the gug's throat. The gug gripped it with a set of hands, squeezing until the shoggoth exploded in a shower of guts and blood. Blood pouring from the throat wound, the gug moaned and toppled forward, silent at last. The only sound was the phlegmy coughing of the ghasts and the moist sounds of feeding.

I counted the living—two shoggoths and seven ghasts. The odds looked much better than before, especially since the monsters were too busy feasting to pay attention. A camouflage blind wouldn't work well since the shoggoths had eyes all over their body, and I'd learned the hard way that they noticed the slight blur in the air.

But I cast a blind anyway, hoping to give myself at least an extra second or two of advantage.

The nearest shoggoth raised its head from the ghast it had been feeding on, the eyes on its sides blinking as they watched me approach. Their night vision was apparently just as good as their day vision for them to notice a slight blur on the move.

It spun and crouched, teeth bared, tentacle tongues slithering in and out like a snake sensing its environs. I cast a sigil five feet to my left, and an illusionary version of me appeared. The shoggoth lunged. I ignited my brightblade and slashed off its legs midair. It howled in pain and skidded across the ground.

I drove the brightblade down through its head, and the creature flailed violently in its death throes.

The other shoggoth raced toward me. Layla sprang high into the air and drove her katana with all her downward momentum into the beast's head. It shrieked and ate dirt. The katana twanged as the blade stabbed into the ground and snapped.

A few ghasts looked up from their meals and began coughing

greedily, ready for dessert. Hannah impaled one through the chest, and it went down. She tried to cleave the head from another, but the katana just wasn't sharp enough. She ducked beneath the claw hooks and rammed the blade into the neck of her attacker.

"These katanas are junk." Layla tossed aside the remains of her broken sword. "I think we can use guns now, right?"

"Better if we don't." I cleaved down two more ghasts. "Who the hell turned on the floodlamps earlier?"

"The ghasts hit the switches when they broke in." Hannah stabbed another ghast.

My sigil tattoos tingled, and it wasn't because of the ghasts. I looked up at the last instant as a nightgaunt swooped toward Hannah.

18

I picked up Layla's broken blade and threw it like a dagger. It thunked into the nightgaunt's back just as its claws extended to scoop up Hannah. Noiselessly, it tumbled until it hit the ground with a wet smack. It flailed, prehensile paws gripping at the hilt protruding from its back.

Hannah shouted in alarm, narrowly ducking the claws of a ghast. She abruptly reversed her stance and tried to impale the nightgaunt with her sword, but the eldritch horror rose on all fours and strafed nimbly to the side. Its wings flapped, and it rocketed upward, silent as death.

I quickly dispatched the remaining ghasts, then looked skyward. Two more nightgaunts circled above with the one that had attacked. Something flashed toward me. I jumped back as the broken katana blade narrowly missed me and plunged into the ground.

"Get inside, fast!" I took my own advice and started running.

The nightgaunts dove in unison, claws outstretched. We dove through the broken back doors an instant before they reached us. They landed lightly on the back patio, watching us with smooth, featureless faces, heads tilted slightly. One was slightly taller than the other two. Another's head was slightly more elongated, the horns smaller than the others. Blood trickled down the leg of the one I'd injured.

I held my brightblade menacingly. "Come try me, you fucking tickle-bitches."

Hannah snorted. "Did you just call them tickle-bitches?"

I strode toward the door, hoping to taunt them to come inside where they'd be easy to deal with, as opposed to outdoors where they had air superiority.

They continued watching us, tails lashing like agitated cats.

I lifted my shirt to display my bare skin. "Want to tickle me, Elmo? Come and get it."

Layla sighed. "Cain, your trash talking needs some improvement."

"Seriously!" Hannah barked a laugh. "Tickle me, Elmo?"

The nightgaunts sprang into the air one at a time, apparently also unimpressed by my taunts. I banished my staff and groaned. Something hurt more than it should. I touched my leg and winced. My fingers were covered in blood. The protective clothing had held up, but something had jabbed me hard enough to break the skin beneath.

"Cain, are you okay?" Hannah inspected my leg. "Can we get some real lights on? I'm sick of these goggles."

"Into the cellar." I headed through the kitchen and waited next to the thick oak door as the others went downstairs. I closed the door and wasn't surprised to discover a heavy iron bar that could be used to secure it from the inside. There was probably a hidden saferoom somewhere down here as well.

The lights flickered on below as I limped downstairs toward the others. The wine cellar looked like something one would find inside an ancient castle. The brick corridors were lined with alcoves, each one holding dozens of wine bottles. There were giant casks at the far ends and stacks of wine barrels against the outer walls.

I removed the goggles and looked at the bloodstain on my leg. It seemed a ghast claw had struck me sometime during the fight, and I'd blocked out the pain automatically until the danger was past. I continued down a corridor and turned left where Layla and Hannah waited outside the armory.

The room was mostly empty since Layla had put almost everything into the pickup truck, but there were still plenty of weapons and ammunition if we needed to make a stand here.

"Cain, that looks bad." Hannah knelt next to my leg. "We need some bandages."

"No time right now. We need shelter, and there's probably a safe-room down here." I summoned my staff and examined the cellar with the scope. I switched to aura mode. While it was intended to see the auras of living beings, it also highlighted energy sources, revealing sigils and electricity. The electrical cables showed up as thin glowing lines even though they ran through conduits in the brick walls.

A bundle of glowing lines that was separate from the rest ran from the back corner and up to one of the giant wine casks. I banished the staff and inspected the wine rack next to the cask. I pulled out several bottles. One of them came out halfway and stopped with a click. A section of brick popped open to reveal a numerical keypad that went from zero to nine with an asterisk and pound button like an alarm panel or a phone.

"That's so cool." Hannah sighed. "I want a giant mansion with weapons and hidden rooms."

Layla grunted. "Too much upkeep."

I took a small spray bottle from my utility belt and misted liquid on the keypad. Oily residue glowed greenly on four numbers and the asterisk button.

Hannah peered at them. "So, there are sixteen possible combinations?"

"Unless one number is used twice." I pointed to the extra residue on the number three key. "Five numbers, but three is in it twice. Asterisk probably confirms the code."

Hannah puzzled over it. "Well, we know the numbers, so just twenty-five possible combinations?"

I nodded. "Let's just hope there's no failsafe that'll lock us out if we don't get it right the first few times."

Hannah reached for the keypad. "Can I do it?"

"Be my guest." I stepped back.

She tried a sequence of numbers, and a red light flashed over the keypad. The second sequence did the trick. The latch clicked and the front of the giant cask swung open a crack. Layla pulled it open to reveal a heavy metal plate on the backside of the wood and another door in the back. A red button on the inner wall presumably released the latch from the inside and a thick sliding bar offered a non-electrical method for securing the door in case the electricity was totally cut.

Another keypad guarded the next door. Hannah tried the same combination, but it didn't work, so I misted the keypad to reveal the numbers. All but two keys glowed.

"Crap." I looked at them from different angles to see if there was a difference in the amount of residue on the keys, but it looked as if they'd all been touched at some point. "This can't be an eight key combo."

"The owner probably used the room when the apocalypse first started and forgot the combination to this one." Layla peered at the keys. "Might have taken him a few tries to remember it."

"That's a lot of possible combinations." Hannah grimaced. "Why not use a spell to unlock it?"

I went to the latch on the cask door and inspected it. It wasn't magnetic like I'd first thought but used a mechanism to release the latch. That way, the door wouldn't open even if the power went out. But how would the owner get into the room if the keypad wasn't functioning?

"There's a mechanical latch holding the door shut." I shook my head. "I could short out the keypad with a spell, but that wouldn't open the latch."

The ceiling shuddered and dust rained down. Wine bottles rattled in their nooks.

"What in the fuck was that?" Layla stepped out of the cask.

The mansion shook again.

I pointed to the other keypad. "Hannah, start trying five number combinations on the keypad. I'm going to see what's going on upstairs."

Layla strode past me and jogged toward the stairs. I pushed aside the pain in my leg and jogged after her. The roars of battle echoed down from above, giving me all the information I needed before I even saw what was happening.

The rear floodlights had clicked back on somehow, probably due to a short circuit somewhere in the destroyed walls, and the scene they highlighted was as terrifying as I'd imagined.

A pair of gugs fought over the fresh meat littering the ground while dozens of shoggoths pitched smaller battles among themselves. The backyard was crawling with even more monsters than before.

The battling gugs slammed into the mansion, shaking the building to its foundations. The top floor was going to collapse at any moment. And that was when I remembered I'd left Aura upstairs. "Oh, shit."

Layla raised an eyebrow. "We left the elf upstairs, didn't we?"

I nodded.

She looked at my injured leg and sighed. "Get back downstairs. I'll get her."

"Thanks."

She booped my nose and blinked in confusion as if she couldn't understand why she'd just done that. Then she abruptly turned and ran up the crumbling stairs to the eastern wing. I hobbled back down into the cellar as the pain in my leg refused to let me ignore it any longer.

Hannah was glaring at the keypad when I reached her, obviously not having any success. "What's happening up there?"

"More gugs and shoggoths showed up. We might be safe in the cask if we can't get into the saferoom." I rapped my knuckles on the steel wall. "Or it might end up being our coffin if the house collapses on top of it."

Hannah pounded out another failed combination and banged a fist on the wall. "Won't the saferoom be a coffin too?"

"Maybe, but anywhere is safer than being upstairs."

Layla jogged down the cellar stairs, Aura's corpse slung over her shoulder. "They saw me."

I frowned. "The shoggoths?"

"All of them." She tossed Aura into the cask. The corpse flopped and rolled against Hannah.

"Ew!" Hannah grimaced and shoved the body away. "Can't you see I'm trying to concentrate in here?"

Layla unfolded the two legs at the end of the light machine gun for support and went prone, aiming the rifle at the cellar doorway. "They're coming."

I grabbed another machine gun and crouched next to her as growls and shrieks filled the room. A pair of shoggoths dove simultaneously toward the doorway at the bottom of the stairs and became wedged against each other and the brick frame. Howling, shrieking, tongues lashing, they tried to wriggle free.

Hannah punched in another combination, and the keypad rejected it with a beep. "Cain, use a damned spell on the keypad!"

"I told you it won't do any good." I fired the rifle in controlled bursts at the shoggoths. The shockwaves pounded against my eardrums in the enclosed space. Blood spurted from their heads, but they continued wriggling through the opening, unfazed. "The latch isn't magnetic, so disrupting the electricity won't work. The keypad controls a mechanism that opens the lock, and I don't have a spell to pick something like that."

Layla fired full auto into the shoggoths until her magazine emptied. The shoggoths went limp, still firmly wedged into the doorway. Shrieks and howls echoed in the stairwell, and the bodies began to move forward as the monsters behind them tried to push through.

"Keep trying, Hannah." I looked back at her. "We'll lock ourselves in the wine cask if we have to."

The house shuddered so violently, wine bottles flew from the nooks, smashing on the brick floor. Electricity crackled, and the lights blinked out.

"Double shit!" Hannah shouted in the pitch black. "Now what?"

I cast light balls and sent them drifting through the cellar until I could see all the way to the stairwell blocked by the shoggoth corpses. "I don't know. We'll have to lock ourselves inside here."

Layla grabbed bags of weapons and tossed them into the cask. Then she ran to a shelf, plucked an armful of wine bottles, and stuffed them into another duffel bag.

I shook my head. "Really?"

"I'm not doing to die sober if I can help it." Layla ran to another shelf and selected more wines as if idly browsing her local grocery store while a horde of eldritch beasts was vying to burst inside and devour us.

The shoggoth bodies blocking the stairs abruptly skidded across the floor. Their friends burst into the cellar. Tentacle tongues whipping, the new shoggoths homed in on us and shriek-howled.

"Fuck!" Layla ran inside the cask with an armful of wine bottles.

Grimacing, I rose to my feet and limped inside, then swung the heavy door shut and twisted the handle inside to secure the steel bar.

Hannah slumped against the back, defeat on her face. "I failed us."

The cask rocked as shoggoths rammed against the door.

I cast a brighter light ball overhead and sighed. "Look, it was just about impossible to guess the combination with that many keys."

"But I got the first one so fast." She bit her lower lip. "This setup is so stupid. Why would you bet your life that the electricity wouldn't be out, making the keypads useless?"

I frowned. She had a great point. Dual keypads doubled the risk of failure. It made sense to have a backup just in case the power went out. The keypad was installed flush into the wall, but there was a thin seam in the stainless steel around it. A flat-headed screwdriver or a thin-bladed dagger could probably pry it open.

Layla hovered behind me. "Want me to smash it open?"

"Smash open the keypad?" I shook my head and inspected the keys. I pressed each of the buttons. They felt springy and normal except for the asterisk key, which clicked when I pushed it. I pushed harder. It clicked, but nothing happened. I pressed the zero key, but it felt normal. The pound key, however, clicked when depressed.

The solution became obvious.

I pressed both keys simultaneously until they clicked. The panel popped out. I pushed the keys harder, and the panel protruded further until I was able to pry it loose with my fingers. A bundle of wires connected to the backside. Most were probably decoys to prevent hot-wiring the lock, but none of them mattered without electricity.

What I was looking for was just below the wires—a keyhole.

"Ooh, so there is a backup." Hannah looked over my shoulder. "But what if they forgot the key?"

"I can pick the lock." Layla dug into her utility pack and produced a set of lockpicks.

The cask shook. Metal squealed as the bolts holding it to the wall began to break. The cask was never meant to be a safe room. It was just decoration—a fancy way to hide the real door. The room rocked. Concrete rumbled, and countless wine bottles broke. I peered through the scope so I could see through the door with infrared. A pair of massive gug legs dominated the view. The beast was right on top of us.

That thing was going to tear the cask loose from the wall, then tip it back like a cup and toss us in its mouth.

"I can't pick the lock with all this movement!" Layla shouted over the din.

I took out my sprayer and misted the back wall, starting in the upper corner and working my way down. Fingerprints glowed green in the corner about halfway down on the side opposite the keypad. Peering closely at the area, I noticed an almost imperceptible seam in the stainless steel. I pushed down where the fingerprints were, and a sliver of metal slid from a slot.

Using thumb and forefinger, I pulled out a key. Its top had been perfectly flush with the slot, hiding it. Pushing down on the top released a latch inside so a spring could push it out. It was an ingenious design.

I handed it to Layla. "Try this."

She blinked. "Where in Hades did you get this?"

I ran a finger over the coin-sized slot. "They hid it in here in case of emergency."

"Thank the fucking gods." She put the key in and twisted it. The cask rocked violently. The bolts and weld seams cracked and broke.

The saferoom door clicked open. "Get inside!" I pushed Hannah through, then tossed Aura's body and weapons bags after her.

Hannah grabbed them and pulled them out of the way as the cask rocked so violently that Layla and I were thrown against the walls and into each other. Just as the last bag was through, the cask rolled to the side, tossing us around like clothes in a dryer. The edges of the cask rolled past the door, and suddenly, we were trapped with nowhere to go.

19

Something slammed the side of the cask hard enough to ring it like a bell. The room rolled. Layla and I ran like hamsters in a wheel to remain upright. A gug roared, and its massive claws gripped the back edge of the room. The cask rattled as the monster dragged it sideways so it could get to the open end and the juicy treats inside.

"We've got one chance." I held my staff at the ready but didn't ignite the brightblade since I didn't want to accidentally chop me or Layla to bits. I stumbled to the cask door and twisted the handle to release the bar just as the cask was yanked sideways again.

A gug's vertical maw glistened in the dim illumination of the light balls I'd summoned earlier. It roared in triumph. Another gug slammed into it, and the cask spun like a bottle.

"Fuck!" Layla grabbed the back door handle to steady herself.

My injured leg gave out, and I fell against her. The door swung open, and we tumbled out, landing on our backs. The cellar ceiling was gone as was most of the house above. A nightgaunt flew above, its black form highlighted by the full moon.

Layla yanked me to my feet. "Stop napping, Cain!"

The gugs grappled with each other near the back wall as shoggoths mobbed the cask we'd been in. They spun toward us, suddenly realizing their prey was in the open. With a mighty roar, the battling gugs slammed into a pair of giant wine casks. A flood of red wine rushed out, upending shoggoths and carrying them right at us.

Layla jerked me to the side, running and dragging me out of the way of the unholy flood.

Hannah stood at the open door to the saferoom, a machine gun at the ready. She ran just outside and unloaded every bullet at the battling gugs while shouting, "Get to the chopper, Billy!"

I'd never felt prouder in my entire life.

I found my feet and pushed aside the agony in my leg long enough to reach the open door of the saferoom. Layla and I dove inside.

Hannah jumped in after us and slammed the door shut. She lowered a heavy metal bar into a slot to secure it, then dropped rifle and hugged me. "My god, I thought you were lunch meat!"

"Yet you still had the presence of mind to quote Schwarzenegger?" I mussed her hair. "The Force is strong with this one."

Layla looked up at a dimly glowing light bulb. "I thought the power was out."

"Must be battery powered," Hannah said.

I inspected our new environs. The saferoom was large and rectangular with four bunkbeds against the left wall, a shelf with food on the other, and various kitchen conveniences. A small metal box with a camera icon printed on the side connected to a large television on the wall, presumably so the occupant could see what was going on outside.

A vicious impact shook the door. It rattled again and again. It might be four feet thick, but after seeing what the gugs did to the wine cask room, I had little doubt they could break into here with enough effort.

"Gods be damned." Layla slapped another magazine into her machine gun. "Guess this is our last stand."

The room was built into bedrock beneath the house, so it seemed unlikely even the gugs could pull it out of its recess. The door was too small for them to fit through, but they could reach their arms inside. It wasn't the worst place in the world to make a last stand, and we certainly had plenty of ammo to work with.

But I didn't think this saferoom was the last trick the previous owner had up his sleeve. This room looked like a place where his bodyguards would hang out and monitor a situation, not a place where someone accustomed to the best in life would be content to live for even an hour.

I continued my inspection of the room and found the next trick inside the small pantry at the back. There were shelves on every wall but the back one. I located an inset handle and pushed on it. The back wall swung open to reveal a ramp descending into darkness.

"This dude just didn't know when to quit." Layla stepped into the tunnel and an emergency light flickered on as the sensor detected us. A lithium battery pack on the bottom seemed to be the source of power. The tunnel had been smoothly bored through solid rock. There was a charging station with an image of a golf cart nearby, but the cart was gone.

There was yet another thick steel door that could be slid into place along metal rails to block anyone from the first saferoom from entering this tunnel.

Hannah ran her fingers along the stainless steel. "Why didn't he close this door if he came down here during the start of the apocalypse?"

I had another theory.

Layla beat me to it. "This is an escape route. He either came down here to die, or this tunnel keeps on going."

I nodded. "That's what I was thinking." The saferoom door rattled again and again as the monsters tried to break it down. "Let's get our stuff and close this door."

We formed a human chain, me in the saferoom and the others in the pantry and tunnel. I handed the bags to Layla, and she passed them to Hannah who slid them into the tunnel. I grabbed Aura's body last and limped to the tunnel.

I closed the pantry wall and slid the next door into place. A heavy-duty latch on the right side locked it down, and a pair of thick bars on the other side prevented it from sliding even if the latch failed.

"Let's scout ahead." I placed Aura on the floor next to the bags of weapons and Layla's wine, and we walked into the darkness.

Emergency lights flickered on as we passed and went dark once we were out of sight of the sensors. The tunnel sloped down at fifteen degrees and ended a few hundred yards later. There we found an electric golf cart parked in front of an ornate wooden door.

We opened it and entered a chamber that resembled the foyer of the mansion above. The floor was polished marble, and there were couches, a television, and all the creature comforts in the den beyond.

Several bedrooms, including a master suite, were located off the foyer. There were showers and sinks all with running water. It was a virtual replica of parts of the mansion above but with one story instead of two.

Hannah whistled. "This guy went all out."

"Can't blame him." Layla rinsed blood from her face and arms with water from the sink faucet. "Might as well hide in style." She looked at my leg. "Take off your pants, Cain."

"Not yet." Fighting off the stiffness in my leg, I opened the door that was analogous to the garage door upstairs. There was no garage on the other side, but there were three spots for golf carts. One of them were gone. The others were plugged into a charging station.

Layla grunted. "And that's how he got out."

"Yeah." I closed the door. "That's how we'll be leaving too."

Hannah walked around the room, a frown on her face. She put her ear to an air vent. "Layla, do you hear that?"

Layla leaned against the same vent and grimaced. "Sounds like ghasts coughing."

I groaned. "Well, they did come from underground. This might have been built in a natural cave."

"I'll search this place from top to bottom to see if there's a way in." Layla blew out a breath. "Last thing I want to worry about are those fuckers swarming us here."

"Hannah and I can get the supplies." I went back through the front door and climbed into the golf cart.

Hannah slid onto the bench seat next to me. "Think we'll be safe for a while?"

I turned the cart around and headed back up the tunnel. "I think we can handle ghasts in close quarters unless an entire section of the wall collapses."

She shook her head. "Anything is better than gugs."

"Agreed." I pulled up to the supplies and began loading them into the flat cargo bed on the back of the cart.

Hannah slid Aura's body onto the backseat and buckled it in. "Don't want it flopping around."

We went back to the underground house and unloaded the supplies, carrying most of the bags to the golf carts in the escape tunnel since we'd likely be using it sooner than we wanted to. I placed Aura's body on the couch and then took the time to examine my own wounds. I pulled down my pants. The athletic underwear underneath rode low on the injured thigh so I pulled up the material for a look.

The skin beneath was deep purple and crusted in blood. The bruise was consistent with the shape of a ghast claw. They might not look like much, but those monsters hit hard. The protective enchantment on the clothing might have prevented penetration, but even it couldn't absorb the entire force of the blow.

Aura gasped and jerked upright. Her pale skin flushed with renewed health, and the grievous wound that bled her dry vanished without a trace. She looked over at me with horror. "Cain, why are your pants down? Did you—" She shivered. "Never mind. I don't want to know what you did with my corpse."

I watched her with a deadpan gaze. "I hope you're not serious."

Hannah slapped Aura on the back of the head. "I ought to beat your ass for even suggesting that Cain is a necrophiliac!"

I pulled up my pants then retrieved my backpack and went into a bathroom, closing and locking the door behind me. I took off my clothes and showered all the grime and blood away. Despite the pain in my leg, it felt great to be clean, and hopefully safe for the moment.

I located a thick gel potion in my utility belt and coated the wound with it. The pain receded as it sealed the skin and began working on the damaged tissue beneath. It wouldn't heal the wound immediately, but it would accelerate progress. I put on a fresh pair of enchanted clothing.

The others were eating in the kitchen when I returned.

Hannah paused chewing on some dried beef. "The fridge is empty. All we found were dried and canned foods."

Aura slurped canned beans like a ravenous animal. "Did I miss anything exciting while I was dead?"

Layla gave her a dirty look. "How about you stay alive next time so we don't have to do all the work?"

Aura walked toward the propane tank attached to the stove. "I'm going to heat up these beans and boil the ramen noodles."

I shook my head. "The last thing we want to do is spread the scent of food. If the ghasts aren't aware of us now, they will be the moment they smell food."

"Ghasts?" Aura's forehead wrinkled. "What are you talking about?"

Hannah grabbed another hunk of dried beef and gnawed on it. "We got to meet some awful new monsters while you were dozing. Nasty hook-handed ghasts and giant gugs."

"Those words sound made up." Aura went into the pantry and pulled out a can of Vienna sausages. "What do they look like?"

While Hannah brought Aura up to speed on the past few hours, I turned to Layla. "Find any weaknesses in the structure?"

She shook her head. "The walls are solid. No secret doors that I could find. I took the covers off several of the vents. They seem to go diagonally up in all directions, probably as some sort of redundancy so they can't be easily found and blocked. The coughing ghasts we heard seem to be that way." She pointed west which was in the same direction as the crevice the ghasts and gugs had come out of.

"Probably a network of caves nearby. The vents must run through them." I opened a bag of dried banana chips and tested one. It tasted fine. "Hopefully we're in a section the ghasts can't get into, but it's best if we sleep away from that side of the saferoom."

"Agreed." Layla stood and stretched. "Wouldn't hurt to place a few wards."

"Already planning on it." I ate the banana chips, then opened a package of ramen noodles and put them in cold water to soak. Hannah was still regaling Aura with our monster adventure, so I left them and began tracing alarm sigils on the walls in the western bedrooms. Using my scope, I looked for thermal signatures, but if there were any ghasts in neighboring caves, the walls were too thick for them to show up on infrared.

I placed more wards around the front door and then a couple on the eastern side just in case. My noodles were soft enough to eat when I returned to the kitchen, so I mixed in the flavoring and ate the cold concoction. It was filling, but I needed protein to help the potion heal my wound. Thankfully, there was plenty of dried beef in vacuum-packed bags in the pantry.

Once I'd had some meat, I decided it was time to sleep. Layla had already claimed the couch, so I dragged a mattress from one of the smaller beds and put it near the escape door in the kitchen. I could've slept on the rock floor, but there was no sense in roughing it when I had creature comforts available.

I took off my pants, opting to sleep in underwear since my wounded leg needed fresh air to heal faster. Then I placed a loaded machine gun and a pair of NV goggles next to the mattress. A handgun and knife went on the other side. If the ghasts broke in, I wanted to be ready to fight. Despite the looming possibility of another ghast invasion, sleep found me the moment I lay down and closed my eyes.

MY EYES FLICKED open to pitch black. My body sigils tingled in dire warning. The room was dead silent, all except for a moist sucking noise from somewhere to my left. A strange odor stung my nose and the air felt heavy to breathe. I was normally fully alert when my sigils woke me, but drowsiness pressed heavily on my consciousness, trying to drag me back into slumber.

I traced a silencing sigil and cast it, then reached over and picked up the night vision goggles. I held them up to my eyes and powered them on. There was barely enough ambient light to see anything. A haze hung heavy in the air nearly blocking out all the light from the overhead lamp and the adjacent rooms.

A dark silhouette near the couch caught my eye. It looked as if someone were hunched over the occupant. A slender, needle-like appendage extended from the form and toward Layla's silhouette. Blackness flickered in my vision as I faded in and out of consciousness. The haze in the air was probably a gas, robbing us of oxygen or drugging us into sleep.

I tugged off the goggles and reached back to summon my staff. I passed out again and woke, my arm still moving. Gritting my teeth, I forced myself to remain awake and summoned my staff, pressing the indentation on the handle and igniting the brightblade.

The air burst into flame, and a creature of pure nightmare became visible for an instant before everything went black.

20

My lungs burned, and the odor of singed hair filled my nostrils from the burning gas. I blinked away the spots in my eyes and thrust the brightblade forward. Lumps of black mold spotted the floor, each one emitting a black, smoky gas.

A slug-like creature with blubbery, gray skin hunched near the couch, a slender needle-like protuberance extending from the top of its body and into Layla's neck. Veins pulsated blue along the length of the needle as it sucked fluids from her. Its countless legs undulated in waves with each slurp.

I was still drowsy, and my skin felt raw from the flash fire. The creature stared at me with three huge black eyes on rotating stalks atop its head. It quivered and shat out a lump of black mold as if trying to put me back to sleep again. The gas crackled as it came into contact with my brightblade.

Shaking my head as if that might clear it, I stepped toward this new nightmare, ready to cleave the needle off its face. The skittering of feet drew my attention just as my tattoos warned of impending danger. Another of the monsters crawled across the floor toward me at an astonishing speed. Or it might have just been normal speed, but my senses were too addled from the noxious fumes from the black mold.

It bounded forward with surprising agility, a needle extending from a slit in its top. My reflexes took hold. My brightblade hummed, and the needle fell to the ground smoking. The creature sucked wetly through the truncated tube. I staggered and drove my blade down through its head. It quivered violently and went still.

Adrenaline now fueling consciousness, I slashed the needle off the one feeding on Layla, then slashed it down the middle, bisecting it. Black innards spilled out, spewing more gas into the air. Blood trickled from the needle still protruding from Layla's neck. I yanked it out but inhaled a lungful of gas in the process. Consciousness faded just as I saw two more of the monsters squeezing out of the air vents and wetly plopping on the floor.

Somehow, I stumbled toward the duffel bags in the kitchen. Dropped to my knees and dug my hands inside for something I'd noticed earlier—a gasmask. I pulled it out and slipped it on. The plastic visor fogged. Dizziness swept over me again. I steadied myself on trembling arms.

One of the creatures skittered toward me, black eyes rising on stalks. Its front half rose, skin flaring to the sides like a cobra readying to strike. The needle jutted from the slit and jabbed toward my neck. Either it was moving incredibly fast, or the gas had so slowed my senses that I couldn't quite process what was happening.

I couldn't stop it in my current condition, so I did the only thing I could do. I bent my elbow and fell forward. The needle grazed the back of my neck. My skin burned for an instant and then went numb. Thankfully, there didn't seem to be a paralyzing agent. The gas mask finally delivered a breath of clean air. My mind began to clear.

My tattoos tingled, so I rolled away from the creature. The needle jabbed against the stone floor with a clink. Another breath further cleared my muddled senses. I saw my brightblade humming a few feet away, the tip sizzling through a mound of the black mold.

The creature struck again. I tried to roll away, but the needle stabbed into my bare thigh—the one that hadn't been injured earlier.

Pain lanced through my leg and then it just as quickly went numb. I could still move it, but only felt pressure. I tried to crawl toward the brightblade, but it was just out of my reach. Using its numerous legs to anchor itself, the monster began to drag me toward it, a fish caught on a hook.

The haze lifted from my thoughts as I drew in another breath of filtered air. Using a trick I'd discovered recently, I cast a pair of shields to clamp the handle of the brightblade between them. At least that's what I tried to do. Instead of shields, I felt a strange connection between me and the brightblade as if it were clenched in an extension of my hand. I yanked it toward me with a burst of will. The brightblade slid across the floor, spinning wildly, humming with energy.

I jerked my hand back just in time to keep it from being sliced off, then caught the handle with my other. The needle in my leg pinned me and prevented me from turning around, so I swung the blade back without looking and felt it cleave through the appendage. The creature slurped wetly through the severed proboscis.

I rolled and drove the blade into its belly, then slashed upward in a ragged pattern. Oily guts spilled out. Black gas roiled up from them, igniting into flame when they struck the brightblade.

The remaining slug skittered toward me, eyes undulating atop their stalks. I flicked off the brightblade, switched to longshot mode, and rolled onto my stomach. With an effort of will, I unleashed a blast of energy. The shot ripped through the head and the bug collapsed, innards steaming.

I swept the staff from side to side searching for another target, but that seemed to be the last of them. Exhausted and still dizzy from the gas, I rolled onto my side and looked at the proboscis jutting from my leg. It was stiff but slightly flexible. The edges were smooth and thankfully not barbed. Gritting my teeth, I gripped the thicker side and pulled it out of my leg. The entire area was numb, thanks to the glistening anesthesia on the skin.

The bugs might be dead, but my job wasn't finished yet. I limped to the duffel bags and pulled out three more gas masks, then slipped them onto Hannah, Layla, and Aura. They were all breathing gently, so it seemed the gas only put them to sleep. Hopefully there were no long-term side effects like brain damage. Once they were protected, I considered our next steps. I could clean up the gas-emitting turds, but there was no way in hell we could remain here when more of those bugs might come.

I inspected the freshly bleeding wound. I hadn't been wearing enchanted pants, which might have protected me. I rubbed a healing potion over the wound and hoped the proboscis hadn't injected other toxins into my bloodstream. Some of the insects on Oblivion injected digestive acids into their prey. It'd be really inconvenient if I began to dissolve from the inside out.

All things considered, I still felt mostly okay.

I put on my pants and protective shirt, then slipped on my shoes. I didn't want to be caught with my pants down if more slugs paid us a visit.

Hannah moaned and sat up. She gasped and pulled at the gas mask.

"Keep it on." I limped over. "How's your head?"

"Ugh, I feel nauseated." She gagged and heaved. "I feel hungover." She saw one of the dead bugs and shrieked. "Jesus Christ, Cain! Is that a giant slug?"

I put a hand on her shoulder. "It's something much worse. We need to get out of here now. Help me wake the others."

Lips peeled back in a grimace, Hannah nodded uneasily and pushed to her feet. She walked over to Aura and shook her until the elf began to stir. I went to Layla and checked her pulse. It was strong despite having had a pint or more of her blood drained. I rubbed healing potion on the wound in her neck to stop the bleeding, then shook her.

Layla moaned, and her head lolled to the side. The gas mask prevented me from slapping her cheeks, so I slapped her shoulder instead. Her eyes flicked open, and her hand gripped mine. If she still hadn't been drugged out her mind, she probably could've broken my fingers.

"W-what happened?" Aura staggered upright. "Oh, gods, what are those things?"

Layla drew in a ragged breath and sat upright. Her face was pale with tinges of green around the edges. "Why do I feel like I just partied with Bacchus for a week straight?"

"Just get up and move." I stood and held out a hand. "We've got to go."

"Cain, maybe we should just go back to our world." Hannah shivered violently. "This place is a fucking nightmare."

"Get the weapons and go to the escape tunnel." I pointed toward the exit. "We need to get out of this room, because I don't think these gas masks are filtering out all the turd gas."

Layla stood unsteadily. "I'm going to puke."

"Me too." Hannah gagged again. "I've never felt so nauseated before."

"Puke in the escape tunnel!" I managed to put some force behind my words. "Go, now!"

Miraculously, the others shambled zombie-like toward the exit without retorting, each of them grabbing their backpacks and duffel bags and dragging them through the door. I gathered my things and dragged equipment into the tunnel after them. When I returned for the last bag, black eyes on stalks regarded me from across the room.

Another slug crawled down the wall, followed by several more from the other air vents. I could have probably blasted them with longshots, but my mind was still unfocused and woozy. I needed to spare some strength in case we ran into something even worse on the road ahead.

I closed the door behind me. The others had already piled into the two golf carts and loaded them with supplies. We'd stuffed as much food into the bags as possible since food was obviously in short supply in this world. I just hoped we lived long enough to need it.

"More bugs coming." I slid onto the passenger side of the golf cart since Hannah was already behind the wheel. "Go."

Hannah hit the accelerator, and the electric cart whined to life. Aura drove the other cart after us. There were no more emergency lights in the tunnel ahead, so Hannah turned on the cart's head-lamps. They were dim but did the job. I took off my gas mask and enjoyed a gulp of unfiltered air.

I turned to Hannah. "Feeling better?"

She took off her gas mask and nodded. "Yeah, but I still want to hurl. What the hell were those things, Cain?"

"No idea." I leaned back and opened my searchable collection of Lovecraft journals. There were a number of bug-like races in his writings, many of which had never made it into his stories. I'd never seen mention of giant slugs.

I finally found a drawing and description buried deep in one of Lovecraft's many sketch books. It described a proboscis appendage and blubbery bodies. There were no pictures, unfortunately, since cameras of the day weren't exactly portable. One of his travel assistants had created marvelous drawings of Cthulhu and other creatures, but he'd unfortunately been devoured during one of their excursions.

Lovecraft labeled the creatures *thropids* and described them as crawling horrors which could squeeze through the narrowest of cracks like cockroaches. The black goop was indeed fecal matter that emitted what he called mind-suffocating fumes.

Hannah glanced over at my phone. "Why are you grimacing, Cain?"

"Because those things used their shit fumes to keep us asleep." I put away the phone. "This quest is turning into a real Lovecraftian field trip, and I'm not enjoying it one bit."

"Is this what'll happen to our world?"

I nodded grimly. "Baura would've done the denizens of Gaia Beta a favor if she'd actually killed them all. The people here probably met fates worse than death."

"I really want to know how she did it." Hannah shuddered. "Does she control them with the Rlhala, or did she just set everything free?"

"Hopefully we live to find out." I touched the thigh injured by the ghasts. "This makes the Dead Forest look like a picnic."

"Maybe we can find some face-hugger semen to rub on us." She offered a wan smile. "But I doubt it."

"If only it were that simple." It was evident that this quest would be all about slogging through an army of monsters just to capture one person. The smartest play would be to find a way to bait Baura back to our dimension, but setting that up would take time we didn't have. She might duck over to Prime at any moment and unleash another apocalypse. But the odds against us were stacked so high I didn't know if we could overcome them.

Hannah abruptly hit the brakes, and the cart skidded to a stop just a few feet away from a dead end. I cast a light ball ahead. It illuminated a metal door that spanned the width and height of the tunnel.

I got out of the cart and pressed a red button on the wall. Predictably, it did nothing since there was no power. There was, however, a pulley and chain on the side offering a manual option.

"You sure we want to open the door right away?" Layla slid out of Aura's golf cart and approached on unsteady feet. "It's still dark out and none of us are in fighting condition. We need to rest."

I looked back down the long, dark tunnel. "And what happens if more of those things show up?"

"All I know is that we're better off fighting a few of them in here instead of fighting off nightgaunts and shoggoths outdoors at night." Layla leaned heavily on Hannah's golf cart. "Strategically, this is the right move."

"I agree, Cain." Hannah sighed. "I can keep watch while you and Layla sleep." She conjured a light ball and tossed it back into the darkness.

"Fine." I nodded. "We need some warning sigils."

"No, we don't." Hannah threw another light ball further down the tunnel for a clear view of about a hundred yards. "You'll only tire yourself more if you use more magic. Go to sleep."

She was right. I'd pushed myself to the limit during the fight with the ghasts and gugs and surpassed it against the thropids. If I didn't sleep, my body and mind wouldn't recover. I'd pushed myself harder and further during my time with the Oblivion Guard, but I had a feeling this infested world still had trials ahead that would test me beyond even that.

I put my backpack on the ground to use as a pillow and lay down on my back. "Let me know when you want me to keep watch."

Hannah rolled her eyes. "Aura can take over when I'm tired."

Aura nodded. "I've been dead most of the day, so I'm rested."

That sounded just fine to me. I closed my eyes and began meditating to put me to sleep faster.

"Thank the gods." Layla settled down next to me, sharing my backpack to rest her head on. Her arm touched mine.

It was comforting having her there and hearing some of the old Layla back in her voice. I shut out the world, the pain, and my worries and let sleep carry me away.

Hopefully, we would live to see the daylight.

21

My muscles ached, and my wits were duller than a rusty butter knife when I woke up. I felt like shit, but at least I'd survived the night.

Layla still snoozed on her back next to me. I took a moment to savor the touch of her arm and leg against mine, then forced myself to get up. Hannah was curled up on the bench seat in the golf cart, sleeping like a baby. Aura sat behind the cart, keeping a lookout for eldritch threats.

She looked up at me, then down at the time on her phone. "Was six hours enough?"

"Six hours?" I stretched. "Felt more like an hour, but it'll have to do." It was already eleven in the morning local time, meaning we needed to get a move on. I touched the stone with the tracking sigil and felt it tug toward Heraklion. The signal strength felt about the same, meaning Baura was still on the island.

I pulled some dried beef from a bag and gnawed on it while considering the challenges ahead. Untold hordes of monsters and the gods only knew what else lay between us and our goal. We knew very little about the terrain and the shape of the roads. And if we were being chased, where would we find shelter?

There was simply no way to plan for the contingencies. Hell, we didn't even know if there was a car or other transportation waiting on the other side of the tunnel door. Though we'd salvaged several duffel bags, most of our weaponry had been left in the pickup truck.

Aura walked over to me. "What are you thinking, Cain?"

"I don't know how we're gonna pull this off." I'd been dropped into plenty of rough scenarios, both training and live missions, but this eldritch-infested version of Gaia was even deadlier than Oblivion. Monsters ruled Oblivion, but most were few and far between. You could walk for miles without encountering anything, and just when you let your guard down, that was when something would surprise you for the last time. Gaia Beta suffered the opposite problem. We couldn't go fifty feet without bumping into something that wanted to eat us.

Stealth was our best option. A camouflage blind wasn't perfect, but it was better than nothing. It might be enough to help us avoid shoggoths, nightgaunts, and deep ones, but there were still plenty of other monstrosities that I couldn't account for. This was a mission into the unknown, much like the Dead Forest, but far worse.

I went to the tunnel door and pulled on the chain. The door was probably impossibly heavy to lift, but the chains and pulleys made it almost effortless, albeit slow. It took a few minutes to raise it high enough to crawl under. I lay on my stomach and looked through the crack. There was a gravel road but no car.

"Fuck." I climbed to my feet and pulled the door high enough for the golf carts to fit under, then went outside and scouted around. The door was set in the face of a cliff in a narrow canyon. The gravel road ran east and west. I took out my phone and consulted the map app using satellite view.

The canyon formed a small horseshoe with exits just south of us. From there, the road wended toward a highway leading to Heraklion. There didn't seem to be a direct route back to the mansion, which was little more than a quarter of a mile from us. Since there was no other transportation available, going back for the pickup seemed like the best option. At least most of the monsters in that area were dead.

Even if the pickup had been destroyed in the fighting, we needed to recover as many weapons as we could.

There was also the possibility that the carnage would draw monsters from all over the place to feast on carrion. But after the battle last night, I couldn't imagine there were too many more left in the general vicinity.

I followed the road east for a look around the bend. I listened for shrieks, howls, or any other indication that there were enemies nearby. All seemed quiet, so I returned to the tunnel. Hannah and Layla were up and munching on canned goods and dried beef.

Layla wiped her mouth with the back of her hand. "Find anything useful?"

"We'll have to take the golf carts back to the mansion to retrieve the truck." I pulled a bag of dried fruit from a duffel and took a bite of something that looked like a withered banana slice. "If the truck is still operational, then we're golden. If not, we'll have to find alternative transportation."

Layla nodded. "If we use stealth, there's no reason we can't reach that elf bitch by this afternoon."

"You know it's not going to be that easy." Hannah brushed cracker crumbs off her shirt. "A city like Heraklion will be jam-packed with monsters. I just know it."

"Maybe, but it's possible starvation has whittled down the numbers." Layla zipped up the duffel bag and climbed into the driver seat of a golf cart. "Let's go. We've already slept through most of the morning."

I climbed into the other golf cart with Hannah. Aura got in with Layla, and our little convoy moved out. The carts were quiet, but the weapons in the duffel bags rattled constantly on the bumpy road. I watched the clifftops and sky for threats while Hannah drove. We reached the highway and turned toward Heraklion for a short distance before finding the road that led to the mansion.

"The battery is getting low." Hannah tapped the charge indicator. The needle was already in the red. "We'll be lucky if we make it."

The cart's top speed was only twenty-five miles per hour, but it was still faster than walking. I had a couple vials of liquid mana in my utility belt, but converting it into usable energy for a golf cart wasn't something I'd come prepared to do. Dolores had a special kit that allowed her to use liquid mana for fuel, but the engine was of dwarven design—far outside of my expertise.

I swept my gaze around the open terrain, constantly on the lookout for threats. "Just keep going until we can't."

The mansion wall came into view. Using my scope, I zoomed in for a better look. The gate was bent all to hell, but what little of the house I could see through the opening seemed intact. The golf cart rolled to a stop about fifty yards out. Layla's ran out of juice a moment later.

I cast a camouflage blind to suppress sound and scent, then readied a rifle. The others picked up weapons of their own, and we quietly made our way to the gate. A quick peek around the corner revealed the mansion was little more than a few walls barely stand-ing. The structure leaned back into itself due to the collapsed cellar beneath.

Corpses littered the front yard, and the driveway was smeared with blackened blood and other dried fluids. Sounds of guttural feasting echoed from either inside the house or the backyard.

I motioned forward, and we quickly crossed the distance to the garage. There were four separate doors. Three of them were bent where something had rammed into them, but the heavy-duty panels had held up to the beating. A door to the side of the last garage door hung open. I peered inside and saw the electric pickup sitting at the other end near the kitchen entrance.

We entered and inspected the pickup truck. It was still in perfect condition. Unfortunately, the garage door behind it was bent out of the tracks. Had it been an ordinary light-weight door, we probably could've forced it up, but the security-conscious owner of the mansion had used heavy reinforced metal.

Hannah looked like she wanted to speak, but I put a finger to my lips. The silencing spell wasn't perfect, and we'd learned the hard way that shoggoths had very sensitive hearing. I wanted to avoid another fight if at all possible.

The garage was spacious, so it was possible to turn the truck and drive it out of the undamaged door at the other end. I twirled a finger in a circle and pointed toward the other door. Layla unplugged the charge cable, then climbed into the truck. It powered on with a slight hum.

I patted my rifle, then motioned toward the backyard to indicate that I was going to see what was back there. The garage door would make considerable noise when we opened it, so whatever was back there would likely come running. I wanted to be ready.

Hannah started following me, so I held up a hand and shook my head. Pointed at the truck and then at the ground. She scowled but nodded.

I eased open the kitchen door and looked inside. Parts of the floor had collapsed into the cellar, so I made my way around the edges until I could see through the gaping hole that had once been the back wall. Blackened and withered ghast bodies littered the back deck and floated in the pool. The sun had burned their sensitive skin to a crisp.

At least a dozen humanoids were gathered around shoggoth corpses, digging into the bodies with their hands and scooping mounds of guts into their mouths. I zoomed in with the rifle scope on one who was facing me. He had scraggly hair, two ears, two eyes, and no visible tentacles. Having encountered seemingly normal humans in Fyeth Elunore, I knew that outward appearances didn't mean anything. But if these were surviving humans, it was possible we could use them to our advantage.

It seemed worth the chance to approach them, but first I checked on the progress with the truck. Layla had turned it ninety degrees and was now trying to position it toward the door. I went to her and drew the others into a close circle.

"We might have human survivors in the backyard," I whispered. "Or they might be monsters in disguise. I'm not sure which."

Layla raised an eyebrow. "Cannon fodder?"

I nodded. "If they're human, maybe we can recruit them."

She nodded. "You try. I'll get the truck ready to roll."

Hannah patted her gun. "I'll back you up."

I gave her a thumbs up, then went back into the kitchen area. Navigating the broken floor was tricky, but I managed to get through a hole in the wall that gave me access to the back deck. Hannah and Aura set up positions and aimed their rifles.

Before saying anything, I scoped out the rest of the area and saw other humans feasting on corpses. The biggest red flag was that they were eating everything raw and seemed to make no distinction between meat or guts. Even if they were human, it was possible they'd been driven insane. Alternatively, they were probably just starving.

I dispelled the scent and sound camouflage and approached the nearest group.

One of them blinked in surprise when he saw me and croaked like a frog.

That's not a promising sign, I thought. I posed a direct question. "Who are you?"

The others turned slowly, blood and guts trailing from their mouths. Some had inhumanly large eyes or patches of gray skin around their throats. Many had webbed hands and a decidedly amphibian look to them. They looked at each other, and then at me.

"English?" a woman said in a scratchy voice. "English man?"

They were mostly human, but bore the traits of deep ones, much like the hybrid citizens of Innsmouth, a town from one of Lovecraft's journals. This didn't bode well, but I was determined make the most of it. At the very least, I could gather information.

I nodded. "English man. Are you related to the deep ones?"

The woman twitched, her bulging eyes blinking in a very froglike manner. "Father Dagon has made it so. You wish to worship at New Innsmouth?"

"New Innsmouth is Heraklion?"

"Father Dagon's city now." Her neck bulged like a balloon. "New Innsmouth."

I pointed toward Heraklion. "You are far from the water and Father Dagon."

"No, water is close." She pointed in the same direction. "The goddess made it so."

A male watching me with the intensity a lizard might watch a fly tilted his head and spoke in Greek. The woman responded in kind.

I had spells for language translation, but none for Greek. Since these were worshippers of Father Dagon, it seemed highly unlikely that they'd be willing to join us. On the other hand, they might be the perfect camouflage for helping us navigate the treacherous streets of Heraklion—or New Innsmouth as they called it. The goddess they mentioned was almost certainly Baura and they might know where to find her.

So, I took a gamble. "I must reach the goddess. Can you help me?"

The woman blinked. "Father Dagon can help. Feast with us and we will take you to him."

"I am a worshipper of the goddess and must see her directly."

"Not possible." The woman glanced at a male.

His tongue shot out at hyper speed, latching onto my rifle as if it were a bug and yanking it out of my hands before I could even react.

"Come with us to worship," the woman said. "Father Dagon welcomes all to New Innsmouth."

I backed up a step. "No, thank you. The goddess will be furious if I worship Father Dagon." I continued backing up. "I must go."

The male who'd taken my rifle struggled to free it from his long, sticky tongue. The woman simply stared at me and said nothing. I expected them to come after me, but most of them turned back to the shoggoth carcass and started eating again.

The woman simply nodded. "Father Dagon will see you. He is the gateway to the goddess." She looked at Hannah and Aura. "They will worship as well."

Then she turned away and dumped another handful of guts into her mouth. Another of the hybrid humans finally helped the guy who'd taken my rifle, tugging until he freed it from his tongue, then it tossed it to the ground and resumed eating.

I wasn't sure if I should be grateful or creeped out that they weren't coming for me. The woman made it sound as if finding Dagon was inevitable. Perhaps by going to Heraklion, it was unavoidable. I turned toward Hannah and Aura. Both looked just as perplexed as I was. Once I made my way back through the wrecked kitchen, we went into the garage.

Layla looked at us expectantly. "Well?"

"They're hybrid deep ones." I spoke in a normal voice since it seemed we didn't have to worry about a fight. "They want us to go worship Father Dagon with them."

She frowned. "Who?"

"Oh, a giant amphibian deity." I tugged on the manual chain to raise the garage door. The rattling was enough to wake the dead, but the hybrids already knew we were here, so there was no point in worrying about it.

Layla frowned. "We should kill them to be safe."

It seemed like a good precaution, but there were other considerations. "There might be more of them, and we're still exhausted and wounded from last night. It's best if we avoid another battle for now."

Layla touched her neck where the thropid had pierced it. She nodded. "Yeah, you're probably right."

"Since when does Layla listen to logic?" Hannah groaned and wrinkled her nose. "We could mow them down in seconds, and it'd be that many less deep ones to worry about."

"I doubt killing them would put a dent in their numbers." I shook my head. "Let's play it safe for now."

She shrugged, rolled her eyes, and climbed into the back of the crew cab next to Aura. "What do you think?"

"I think Cain is right and Layla is being oddly reasonable." Aura fastened her seatbelt. "And I'm ready for a power nap anyway."

I took shotgun and eyed Layla as she climbed behind the steering wheel. She didn't so much as glance at me as she navigated the truck out of the garage. Soultaker had really done a number on her. She usually bristled with bravado and snark, but now she was quiet and determined to get her revenge.

Layla drove us to the golf carts where we transferred the food and other gear into the pickup bed. The best route into Heraklion seemed to be by the highway we'd used to reach the mansion, so Layla started driving that way.

"Tell me more about this Father Dagon monster," Layla said.

I decided to do it in song. "Rising from the oceans, thirty stories high, breathing fire, his head is in the sky."

"Godzilla!" Hannah sang out.

Layla stared at me blankly for a second, then turned back to the road. "Father Dagon is Godzilla?"

"No, but he's a giant green lizard-like monster." I showed her an illustration of Dagon rising from the ocean. He was humanoid, but the similarities ended there. His huge fish eyes, gaping maw of razor teeth, and the reptilian design of his head were all very amphibian, much like the other deep ones. "Lovecraft says he's fifty feet tall, but some entries in his journals claim that he's even taller."

"He's a Great Old One," Hannah said. "So, he's kind of like an Elder Thing demi-god."

"He's really just a very old deep one." I glanced back at her. "They can grow to be godlike if they live long enough."

Aura leaned over for a look. "He's downright beautiful by eldritch standards."

"Don't the deep ones come from somewhere in Massachusetts?" Hannah peered at the image. "Why are they all the way over here in Greece?"

"Baura probably called them all here," I said. "They even renamed Heraklion to New Innsmouth."

"Gross." Hannah grimaced. "Heraklion is a way cooler name."

I nodded. "Yeah, it is."

"Why didn't they try to capture us or chase us?" She looked behind us as if the deep ones might be there. "I mean, we would've killed them, but I'm surprised they didn't try."

"They seem to think joining them is inevitable." I stared at the road ahead. Heraklion was already coming into view. "We'll just need to avoid them like everything else."

My tattoos tingled just as something moved at the edge of my perception. Layla had already sensed the same thing and hit the brakes. A group of heavily armed people burst from the foliage and surrounded the vehicle.

When I saw who they were, I knew we weren't getting out of there alive.

22

These weren't ordinary people. They were mechanists.

None of us had a particularly good relationship with them in Prime or Alpha. We'd stopped the mechanists from achieving world domination on Alpha and foiled their plans to steal the artifacts from Hephaestus's lost armory in Prime. I imagined our alts on Beta probably weren't besties with them either.

Layla hit the accelerator, apparently intending to plow through the mechanists blocking the road.

The rear end lifted, and the front tires squelched, unable to grip the road enough to tear free. I looked back and saw why. A man in a brass metal exoskeleton had gripped the rear bumper.

I tried to summon my staff, but the pickup tilted wildly as another man in an exo-suit lifted the truck from the side.

The truck was armored with bulletproof windows, but it wouldn't stand up long to exo-suits.

"You will turn off the vehicle and exit!" the man lifting the side of the truck shouted. "Or we will remove you by force!"

Duffel bags spilled from the back of the truck as it tilted even further. If not for our seatbelts, we would've all been piled against the right-side windows.

Layla bared her teeth and turned to me. "Fake surrender. Then we kill them all."

I nodded. "Do it." I considered slipping on Panoptes and pulling a vanishing act but decided against it since the mechanists had already seen me.

Layla took her foot off the accelerator and raised her hands. "We surrender."

The truck tilted back down to level as the man released it, but the exo in the back kept the rear tires off the ground.

I unbuckled the seatbelt and exited the passenger door. A pair of mechanists gripped my arms and guided me away while others escorted my companions over to join me. Other mechanists collected the weapons and loaded them back into the pickup.

It was interesting to note that the mechanists wore military camouflage of varying designs with very little uniformity. It seemed likely that they'd scavenged the uniforms from wherever they could. Some still bore arm patches bearing the flags of their originating countries. Only a scant few wore the royal blue mechanist uniforms that I'd seen on Gaia Alpha. There was one commonality among the outfits. Everyone wore a pair of brass goggles with lavender-tinted lenses.

A mechanist in a standard royal blue uniform approached us. "Well, it seems our scouts were correct. There are sane survivors still out there."

Layla raised an eyebrow. "What do you want with us?"

He looked confused. "We mean you no harm, but we are looking for every able-bodied human still alive to help us fight back."

She laughed. "Fight back? My gods, you've already lost!"

He stiffened. "As long as humans continue to exist on this world, we haven't lost."

I crossed my arms. "Explain to me how you intend to win."

"We will provide more information later." He offered a curt bow. "I am Lieutenant Millar, and I will guide you to our base." Millar looked at the bags of weapons in the truck. "I would also like to know where all these weapons came from. As you might imagine, ammunition of nub or mechanist design is in short supply."

Layla's finger twitched just enough to signal to me that she was getting ready to pounce. I replied with another hand signal and shook my head. Since it didn't look like the centaurs were going to blaze a path to Heraklion like I'd hoped, the mechanists might be a better option. I just had to figure out how to use them without getting ourselves killed.

"How are you even still alive?" Hannah shook her head. "This world is infested with nasties."

"As I said, explanations will come once we are at our base." Millar motioned to a soldier. "Take the vehicle."

The soldier climbed into the truck and drove away.

Millar motioned ahead. "Move out."

"So, we're prisoners?" Aura said as the soldiers pushed us along.

"You're in our custody for now." Millar shrugged. "I do not see why anyone would resist being taken to a safe place in this mad, mad world."

I didn't expect any answers, but I asked anyway as we marched. "How many battles have your people fought?"

"Countless." Millar stared ahead, gaze distant. "Earth is a worm-infested apple, rotten to the core. There are very few places that are safe from the horrors of the eldritch monsters. That is why it is so surprising to find survivors. We have many questions for you, but they are not for me to ask."

I glanced at one of the exos lumbering alongside of us and realized that it was making little to no sound despite walking on asphalt. The clockwork gears were typically quiet, but the metal feet should have been making a racket. The exo resembled a terminator skeleton, was brass colored, and stood ten feet tall. The pilots strapped their arms and legs onto those of the exoskeleton with their bodies protected by the armored ribcage. The helmets resembled skulls but with lavender-tinted lenses over the eyeholes.

Unlike other exos I'd seen and fought against, the skeletal feet on this one were covered in black foam that apparently deadened the sound. The mechanists had proven adept at adapting their machines to various terrain as I'd witnessed during a battle on Oblivion where they'd outfitted them with flat metal feet to make walking easier on the beach.

This model featured a minigun mounted on one shoulder and what looked like a rocket or grenade launcher on the opposite shoulder. But what interested me the most were the sigils inscribed in the metal. I couldn't see enough details to know their purpose, but if I had to guess, I'd say they were for protection.

Using magic on machines was completely out of character for mechanists. They despised magic, even though their machines were often fueled by liquid mana. It seemed they'd made unlikely allies out of magic users. If they were that desperate, maybe they wouldn't kill us after all.

I turned to Layla. "These exos are protected by magic."

She blinked and looked at the same one I'd studied. "Are those sigils?"

Millar stared straight ahead, apparently lost in thought or unwilling to answer.

"Yeah. Defensive ones, I think." I didn't want to get closer to the hulking machine because the soldiers might interpret that as an act of aggression. "Let's go along and see what this is all about."

Layla narrowed her eyes but nodded. "Could be our new cannon fodder."

Millar flinched and looked at us. "What was that?"

"You heard me." She smiled. "We'll give you more information when we reach your base."

He cleared his throat uneasily. "I sense there is more to you people than meets the eye. Magic users, no doubt." A shudder ran through him.

Hannah sighed loudly. "Are we there yet?"

He didn't answer.

The formation turned off-road and into a narrow canyon crowded with parked vehicles. Many resembled nineteen-thirties paddy wagons used by mechanist enforcers, but these were retrofitted for troop transportation.

They ushered us into the back of one of the trucks where we were split up to sit on bench seats facing each other. The soldiers piled in behind us and closed the door. Most of them pushed their goggles up to their foreheads and massaged the bridges of their noses as if trying to ease headaches.

Escape wouldn't have been hard, but it would've been bloody. Millar was just lucky he'd roused my curiosity, and as Layla had said, the mechanists might be the perfect cannon fodder to help us reach Baura.

The clockwork engine ticked to life, and we began a bumpy cross-country journey that lasted for nearly half an hour before the wheels found smooth pavement. Narrow slits in the side and back of the compartment offered an unsatisfactory view of the outside, but it was enough to tell that we'd entered a tunnel, and the downward tilt told me we were going deeper underground.

"I don't want to go underground again." Hannah leaned against me. "What if there are more bugs or ghasts?" She looked at the soldiers as if they might give an answer, but they remained silent, only sparing cursory glances our way that seemed to indicate they weren't sure if they should fear us or not.

"If they've survived this long, I doubt there are any monsters down here." Layla pushed a soldier out of the way so she could look through the window. She put her nose to the open slit and sniffed. "I think this is a mine of some sort."

The soldier tried to squeeze back onto the seat but couldn't budge Layla. Another soldier scowled but didn't move to help.

The soldier finally spoke in a foreign language and Layla relented.

She looked at me. "I think he said please, didn't he?"

I shook my head. "I don't even know what language that was."

"Pashto," a young solider said with a heavy accent. "I am from Germany. We are from all over."

Another soldier put a hand over the young man's chest. "Silence."

"What is the harm?" The young one shrugged. "We were normal people before. Now we are living a dystopian nightmare."

I leaned forward so I could look at him. "Some of you weren't mechanists before?"

Many of them shook their heads, but one woman in a navy-blue uniform banged her fist on the seat. "You will remain disciplined and silent! There is no room for your old nub ways if we are to survive."

"We are giving away no secrets," the German said. "And it is human nature to seek comfort in conversation. These are the first sane humans we have seen in months, and I would like to know how they survived."

I glanced at the goggles on the soldier next to me. "Why the goggles? It's not that dusty out there, is it?"

"Remain quiet!" the woman shouted. "I will report anyone who says another word."

There was a collective sigh, and the German and others leaned back in their seats and stared blankly.

Layla snatched the goggles from the soldier next to her and put them up to her eyes. The Pashtun tried to take them back, but she slapped his hand away. "There's something magic about these." She tossed them to me.

I examined them from the outside and then put them up to my eyes. There wasn't anything visible scribed into the glass, but as I peered through the goggles, I sensed something strange that had nothing to do with the slight lavender tint they gave my view.

"Let me see." Hannah took them and put them on. "Everything is purple now. Seems kind of dumb."

Aura frowned and slipped them off Hannah's head. She tapped a lens with her fingernail. "This is mithrium, a byproduct of forging mithril. Mount Hjrn was covered in it."

I remembered seeing crystalline chips mixed in with the red scrush, the toxic waste produced by dwarven forges. "It's just waste, right?"

She nodded. "Usually. It's only moderately stronger than glass, but the purple tint makes it undesirable, so the dwarves don't bother to reclaim it. Some people use it for art, but nothing practical."

Hannah frowned. "Then why make lenses out of it?"

The grumpy mechanist who'd silenced everyone folded her arms and pouted, refusing to answer. The others seemed too cowed to offer answers of their own.

The truck stopped.

The Pashtun held his hand out imploringly. Aura gave him back his goggles. He tucked them into a pocket on his uniform and looked at the backdoor as if eagerly awaiting his escape from us.

The mechanist woman opened the door and hopped out. He rushed out after her. Layla shoved her way past the other soldiers before they could rise, leading to a wave of surprised grunts and alarmed faces as their charge seemed to be making an escape. They hurried out after her, shouting in various languages.

I was content to wait until the soldiers disembarked before exiting behind Aura and Hannah. Layla stood just outside the truck, taking in all the details of our new environs so she could plot an escape if need be.

We were underground in a large bunker that was designed like every other military bunker I'd ever seen. It extended for a couple of hundred yards in both directions with about a hundred feet of head-room overhead. The walls and ceiling were neatly hewn stone, but the floor was a concrete slab sectioned off by various colors of paint.

An area outlined by red was home to stacks of military crates—probably ammunition. Another area cordoned by yellow lines served as the motor pool, crowded with nub military vehicles, clockwork trucks and cars, and civilian transportation. Next to the vehicles were two rows of heavy exo-suits.

I'd encountered various models of exos, but these were heavily modified with armor and weaponry just like the ones piloted by our escorts. The most common ones were only a little taller than a normal human, so they could be used indoors. They were powerful machines, capable of giving mechanists super strength and speed, but they'd never match up to the prowess of vampires or werewolves if it came down to a fight.

These militarized models, however, looked capable of destroying an attacker before they even got close. The mechanists on Gaia Alpha had even more advanced designs, but that was because they'd had unhindered access to the lost armory of Hephaestus. Baura had told me that she'd used the mechanists on Beta to help her reach the armory and then she'd turned the apocalypse weapons on them. It was surprising that any of them had survived.

"Come with me," the female mechanist commanded, motioning toward cinderblock buildings at the opposite end of the bunker.

I flourished a hand. "Lead the way, mein commandant."

She scowled, then motioned for the other soldiers to form up around us.

Layla rolled her eyes and started walking in the direction of the buildings ahead of our escorts.

"You will wait!" the woman shouted.

Layla shook her head. "You will hurry or be left behind."

"Yeah, you people are so slow." Hannah hurried after Layla.

"Stop them!" the woman shouted.

None of the soldiers seemed enthused about the command but gave a halfhearted chase. Aura and I followed behind, apparently forgotten in the rush.

"They're not very organized," Aura said.

"Looks like they recruited as many warm bodies as they could." I continued making note of everything I saw. "The question is, why are the mechanists here in Greece?"

"A better question is, why are we here? Why did Baura leave a portal open so anyone could follow her here from Feary Prime? Why wouldn't she close it so someone couldn't come after her?" Aura frowned. "Do you think—" She grimaced. "Gods be damned, Cain."

I raised an eyebrow. "What?"

"Baura and I were the same person until the event that split prime into two variants. We've had the same strategic training and same experiences working for Eclipse. We improvise, adapt, and overcome in the short term, but we also are excellent at long-term planning."

I rubbed the back of my neck. "Yeah. You conned me for years so you could get your hands on a demi."

"It wasn't a con, it was a plan, Cain." Aura blew out a breath. "The difference between me and her is that she leveled up. She started looking at things from a godlike level because she finally had the means to kill a god."

"Well, shit." I stopped walking because I figured out where she was going with this. "Baura knew we'd come for her once we realized she'd escaped. She left a trail to lure us to Gaia Beta."

Aura nodded. "Maybe she thought the gods would come after her and planned to fight them here, or maybe she counted on you tracking her once you found out she escaped."

"I think she knew the gods wouldn't bother chasing her to Beta. They're content to just let the splinter dimensions wither and die on the vine. Besides, the gods can probably open their own portals whenever they want."

"Baura probably counted on you coming after her for killing Layla." Aura nodded as if agreeing with herself. "She sees you as the threat she needs to eliminate first."

"It's the perfect trap." I sighed. "She knows that I can't just leave her alone, because she can literally destroy worlds." I continued walking since Layla and the soldiers following her were nearly to one of the buildings. "Baura is expecting us, and she plans to kill us."

"Definitely." Aura sighed. "She probably thought the monsters would kill us first."

The group ahead of us had stopped at a square two-story building. A man in a white uniform stepped out, looking at Layla and Hannah. He and I locked gazes, and recognition flared in his eyes.

It was none other than Horatio—the leader of the mechanists and the man I'd defeated in two different dimensions.

23

Horatio shoved his way through the soldiers and made a beeline for me. He stopped a few feet away, face flushed, hands shaking. "Cain Sthyldor!"

I readied myself for a fight I couldn't win once he commanded all the soldiers to murder us. "Hello, Horatio."

Tears dripped down his cheeks. "We are saved!" He turned and raised a fist into the air. "We are saved!"

My mouth dropped open. "That's not the reaction I was expecting."

Horatio turned back to me. "We thought you and the goddess had died in the battle of Thermopylae! How did you survive?"

The female mechanist from the truck did a double take. "He doesn't look like Cain."

Other soldiers looked curiously from Hannah to me as if trying to reconcile the differences between me and the Cain of this world.

Horatio looked closer at me. "True, your scars are gone, and you no longer have a beard and long hair." He looked at Hannah. "You are not as gaunt, and your eyes are no longer white."

I blew out a breath and hoped my next words didn't get us killed. "I'm not the Cain from this world."

Gasps rose around us.

"Then the invasion of Prime has already begun?" a young man said.

Horatio looked past me and froze. "By the inventors! Is that the doppelganger of the nemesis?"

I glanced back at Aura, then turned to him and nodded. "Yes." I was still trying to wrap my head around how my alt could have possibly been an ally of the mechanists. It was time for a game of twenty questions.

Horatio sensed what was coming. "Cain, I am certain you have many questions which I will be pleased to answer. If you are anything like your doppelganger, then perhaps we can save our world after all." He motioned toward the building he'd come out of. "Please accompany me inside, and I will tell you what I can."

"Thank you." I followed him through the door, Layla, Aura, and Hannah close behind.

Some of the soldiers knelt and bowed as Hannah passed, murmuring in what sounded a lot like prayers.

Hannah blushed and walked closer to me. "Cain, this is weird. Are they worshipping us?"

"They're worshipping you, kiddo." I repressed a grin. "Something tells me we're about to hear some interesting stories about our alts."

"Yeah." She skirted the hands of a woman reaching for her, but others tried to come closer until the female commander from the truck shouted orders.

"Leave the goddess be and return to your normal duties!" She slapped down the grasping hands of soldiers. "Move out! Move out now!"

Everyone dispersed, leaving only the Pashtun man. He looked hopefully at Hannah, pressed his hands together in prayer, and bowed. Then he hurried off as the commander glared at him.

Lieutenant Millar stood outside the door, a worried look on his face. "Sergeant Pat is rather intense. I hope she wasn't too harsh during the ride over here. Had I known you were Cain, I would not have put you in the transport truck with the troops."

I shrugged as I walked past him and inside. "It's no big whoop."

"Yeah, no big whoop." Hannah lunged as if she were going to hit him and giggled when he nearly fell over backward.

Layla shook her head. "I should've known the Cain on Beta wouldn't just sit on his ass while the world went to hell. I wonder how my doppelganger died."

"She probably ran away and is still alive," Hannah said.

Layla grunted. "Yeah, probably. I'm no hero."

Hannah rolled her eyes. "You are a hero, and you know it, even if you don't like the idea that you're not entirely selfish."

Layla glared at her, body tense. "This is a mission of vengeance. I'm not here to save the world."

"We get it. You're tough and don't care about anything." Hannah winked at her. "That's why we love you."

"I don't love her," Aura murmured.

The foyer of the building was crowded with stacks of papers and diagrams. A soldier sat at a desk in the front room—no doubt the gatekeeper for anyone who wanted to see Horatio. He stood and saluted, fist over chest, then sat down and continued sorting through a stack of papers on his desk.

We walked down a hallway past several rooms where mechanists in teal and ivory uniforms pored over blueprints or tinkered with clockwork contraptions. The room in the back was larger than the others with a plain wooden desk facing the door and several folding chairs arranged in front of it. A dilapidated couch sat in the corner as if moved to the side to get it out of the way.

"Apologies for the sparse accommodations, but there is not much comfort to offer in this world." Horatio took a bottle of clear liquid from a shelf. "Drinks, anyone?"

I nodded. "Sure. What is it?"

He turned the label to face us. "Aviation Gin. A nub drink, but quite good."

He handed half-filled glasses to each of us. Hannah took a sip, and her eyes flared with delight. I tasted it and agreed. This was some tasty gin, and I wasn't even a gin person.

Layla shook her head when he offered her a glass.

I raised an eyebrow, because Layla was never one to turn down a drink.

Aura took hers and Layla's and gulped them down in quick succession.

"Dude, this is the Ryan Reynolds stuff!" Hannah took another sip. "It's as delicious as he is."

I had no response to that, so I sat on a folding chair and leaned back. "I need to know the recent history of this world to understand how events deviated from our timeline."

Horatio sat behind the desk. He gulped his gin and sighed, then poured himself some more. "One day, a mysterious letter materialized on the desk of an apprentice. She immediately brought it to me after reading it."

The story sounded familiar to me. "It was from the Horatio in Alpha, right? Told you how to raid the lost armory?"

"Precisely. As a mechanist, there was no greater dream than finding the lost artifacts crafted by the god who inspired the creation of the mechanist order."

I nodded. "Though in your case, it was to exact revenge on the gods for killing your family."

"Indeed." He took another swig of gin and continued. "My doppelganger's letter detailed who I needed to speak with—Torvin Rayne, the Black Hand, and former assassin for the Oblivion Guard. He possessed an artifact that could disable the guardians of the armory. I sent a message to Eclipse—the assassination agency I was told he commanded—and received a message to meet him at Voltaire's."

This sounded very familiar. The mechanists of Gaia Alpha had formed an alliance called the Pandora Combine between mechanists, Dracula, and his vampire minions. They'd then allied with Torvin Rayne and changed the alliance's name to Umbra.

"Torvin did not show." Horatio looked at Aura. "The bartender— your doppelganger—approached me and told me why. Torvin had been killed by Cain Sthyldor and the goddess."

"Well, that's new." Hannah frowned. "I'd love to hear how that happened."

"I do not know the details, but the Aura of this world showed me images of Torvin's badly maimed body. She said she had worked closely with him at Eclipse and could aid our quest." He shrugged. "She also told me of her faction, the Enders, and that she would do anything to exact vengeance on the gods. She then showed me the artifact that would grant us safe passage past the guardians of the armory, and I had no choice but to accept her offer."

Aura frowned. "I didn't even realize there was such an artifact."

"I later learned that Torvin had possessed it for some time but didn't know what it was. We speculated it was a key Hephaestus had entrusted to someone long ago." Horatio twisted his glass. "We allied with Aura and the Ender faction. That turned out to be a terrible mistake."

I nodded. "So, I've heard straight from the lips of Baura herself."

His eyebrows rose. "Baura?"

"Our nickname for Aura Beta." I shrugged. "It's just easier to keep track of who we're talking about."

"And our world is what you call Beta?"

I nodded. "Our world is Prime. Loki interfered with a major event that caused two other timelines to spawn—Alpha and Beta."

"Fascinating. My doppelganger's letter went into some details about the split, but there was no mention of a Prime timeline."

I took another sip of gin. "Please continue your story."

Horatio leaned his elbows on the desk. "We used Cthulhu's deep-ways to reach Oblivion and the original Mount Olympus. The Enders mutinied and took over our submarines, slaughtering our people. We escaped the fate of our comrades because there were only two Enders on my submarine. We tried to follow the stolen vessels, but they had our weapons and nearly destroyed us. So, we returned to Gaia and warned Dracula and our other allies. But there was no place to hide, not even in the far reaches of Romania once Baura had the apocalypse weapons."

Aura sighed. "Because she instantly became a god."

"Which is why I was surprised that nothing happened for several weeks. I thought perhaps she decided to take a measured approach in her vengeance against the gods." Horatio shuddered. "And then everything happened at once. The skies rained fire, the earth swallowed entire cities, and the oceans flooded inland, drowning millions. And then something even more unspeakable happened—the Old Ones began to rise, and their minions consumed humanity with madness."

"Baura probably did have a more measured plan to kill the gods, but she was using an artifact from the armory—a ring named Panoptes." I blew out a breath. "It allows the wearer to see multiple places at once and to visit each location the eyes see. But it's too much for most minds to handle, and it drove her mad so gradually, she didn't even realize what was happening."

"I am familiar with the ring," Horatio said. "Baura had a list of items vital for our campaign to kill the gods. Panoptes was in the top ten."

Aura's brow pinched. "Where did she get a list? We had no idea what we'd find in the armory."

"Baura had a mysterious female advisor." Horatio shook his head. "Whenever confronted with a decision, her advisor seemed to appear out of thin air. I believe she's the one who provided Baura with all her information."

"Ooh, that's a classic mistake." Hannah winced. "Never listen to evil advisors."

Horatio's eyes narrowed. "What happened in your timeline? You seem to be on good terms with your Aura, so the outcome must have been quite different."

I changed the subject instead. "How did your people not recognize me, Hannah, or Aura when they detained us?"

"Our Cain had long hair and a thick beard, not to mention several scars on his face." Horatio nodded at Hannah. "And the goddess was gaunt, almost sickly looking, but the power she wielded was immense. She and Cain gave their lives to destroy the Great Old One,

Hastur, as he feasted upon the brains of thousands of humans at once."

I tried to recall the name Hastur and failed.

"Tell me more, please!" Hannah leaned forward. "We sacrificed ourselves for the greater good like Captain Kirk in Star Trek Two?"

Horatio looked a bit flummoxed at the mention of the movie but eventually nodded. "It was our greatest loss. Perhaps the final nail in the coffin of humanity on our world."

I hated to tell him, but this world had been a total loss the moment the Great Old Ones rose. "Did Cthulhu also rise?"

He shook his head. "No, he remains sleeping in R'lyeh. If he had risen, it would have been the end for all of us."

I decided to offer him a partial solution. "We need to kill Baura to stop the cancer from spreading. She intends to infect Prime."

Horatio nodded. "Our Cain surmised that she had attacked Greece in order to anger the Olympians, but since this world is not the original one, the gods did not care. Killing the nemesis was also our goal, but she has proven elusive and extremely canny. It is almost as if she anticipates our every move."

"Maybe Baura isn't the mastermind behind everything." I sipped some gin and let it sit on my tongue a moment. "Maybe it's this mysterious advisor of hers."

"Isn't it obvious?" Layla snapped her fingers. "The gods of chaos are actively helping her."

"See, I knew I wasn't that smart," Aura said. "I've been wracking my brain trying to understand how my counterpart could anticipate so far into the future, because even my best plans aren't that amazing."

"It would explain how she knew to leave open a portal and lure us here where it's easier to kill us." I finished off the gin and put the glass on the desk. "Tell me about the goddess's powers."

Horatio looked at Hannah. "The goddess glowed with power most of the time. Something happened to her during the early days of the apocalypse that unlocked her abilities, or so Cain told me. She grew beautiful glowing flowers that filled our former base with protective light and kept the monsters at bay. She created monstrous plants that devoured shoggoths and even killed gugs. And opposite her powers of creation, were formidable destructive abilities."

Hannah looked entranced. "What happened to her? How did she unlock her powers?"

"I don't know." Horatio's gaze grew haunted. "I discovered a terrible secret that she and Cain kept from me, though."

Layla suddenly looked interested. "Yeah? Were they making human sacrifices?"

"No, of course not." Horatio looked offended. "Using so much power is what took a toll on the goddess's body. We had just won a battle against hundreds of shoggoths and deep ones when I noticed Cain and the goddess had gone missing as usual. I detected a strange wavering blur in the air as I was helping remove our dead from the battlefield. I went to investigate and realized it was a camouflage illusion. Once I stepped through, I saw Cain standing over the bodies of deep ones. The tops of their skulls had been slashed off by his brightblade, and the goddess was devouring their brains."

24

"My alt was eating their brains?" Hannah gagged. "What the fuck, dude? I'm gonna be sick."

"Cain told me to keep quiet about it and that it had something to do with Hastur. He promised to explain the matter another time." Horatio sighed. "And then came the Battle of Thermopylae, and they died."

I looked up Hastur in my Lovecraft database. The description was somewhat enigmatic, almost as if Lovecraft didn't know exactly what the creature was. In one place, he was named the King in Yellow and described as vaguely humanoid with sharp tentacles used to pierce the craniums of sentient beings. There were several conflicting descriptions as well. A paragraph below his entry told me why.

Ambrose Bierce encountered the creature, Hastur, and described it in his telegrams but has not transferred the sum of his knowledge from his journals into the Chronicles. We must have a word about this in the next meeting of the Order.

-HPL

It was the first time I'd seen anything mentioned of the Chronicles or the Order. It made sense that Lovecraft hadn't been the only person chronicling eldritch creatures. One person simply wasn't capable of amassing so much information. And if all I had were Love-craft's notes, what more might there be in the Chronicles?

It was a question for another time. This world promised to offer far more encounters of the eldritch variety than any sane person would want. I cross-referenced *brains* and *deep ones* to see if there was mention of anything special, but the only reference was the mention of Hastur feasting upon the brains of deep ones as an offering from Father Dagon.

I looked up from my phone. "What did Hastur look like?"

"He was enormous, but also small." Horatio squeezed his eyes shut as if trying to remember something elusive. "He had a body like a man, perhaps thirty feet tall, and countless tentacles." His gaze went distant. "They whipped madly about, piercing heads, draining the minds of all they touched. The more he suckled their brains, the more brightly yellow he glowed. It was not the warm yellow of the sun but something sick and grim. The light defiled all it touched and threatened to overcome even our best protection with madness."

Horatio shivered and squeaked as if startled by his own thoughts. "The goddess fought with all her might, unleashing such destruction as I'd never seen, cleaving tentacles with pure rays of energy. But she weakened, and Hastur had fed too much. We were trying so hard to help, but our resources were stretched to the limit holding off an onslaught of malgorths, ganthagons, and salkos."

Hannah's eyes grew wide. "Keep going."

"Cain seemed to be arguing with the goddess. At first, I thought he was commanding her to retreat, but then a tentacle struck his head. The goddess slashed it, but Cain fell to his knees. He kept pointing at his head even as blood poured from the wound. Then he picked up the sharp tip of the severed tentacle and rammed it into his own head."

Hannah gasped. "Why?"

Tears filled Horatio's eyes. "The goddess screamed as Cain fell, then I lost sight of them in a swarm of tentacles. When I saw her again, she was rising from Cain's body, her face covered in brains and blood. Her entire body lit up like the dawn of creation. She gripped one of Hastur's tentacles, and energy ran along it and up into the monster's body. There was an explosion so brilliant it blinded me. When my vision returned, the goddess and Hastur were gone, and only a crater remained."

Hannah looked horrified. "She ate Cain's brains?"

"I believe so." Horatio poured a full glass of gin and drank it. "Madness seeps into our minds despite the mithrium lenses on our goggles. But I feel certain that what I saw was not a byproduct of madness. Cain sacrificed himself so that the goddess might take his power."

"I'm a fucking zombie!" Hannah turned to me, tears pooling in her big eyes. "I would never eat your brains."

Layla's lips peeled back in disgust and confusion. "This is some of the weirdest shit I've heard, and I've heard plenty."

Aura frowned. "Maybe whatever unlocked her powers gave her an insatiable appetite for brains." She looked up. "Did Cain and Hannah fight Hastur before?"

Horatio nodded. "I believe they encountered the creature some-time before joining us. The goddess bore a scar on her temple from the encounter."

Hannah gasped. "You think my alt got her powers from Hastur?"

"Makes sense," Aura said. "Hastur tried to eat her brains and got more than he bargained for. Maybe Hannah somehow absorbed that ability to give herself more power."

The logic was sound, but there were too many missing links for my comfort. "You're saying Hannah can leech abilities?"

"Something about the attack must have unlocked Hannah's true power." Aura nodded as if her own words made perfect sense. "We know Hannah has powers of creation and destruction, but maybe she can assimilate abilities as well. Hastur gained power by eating brains, so Hannah was able to do the same."

Layla nodded. "Okay, well, that's not so weird. I encountered a mind-eater cult once, but they ate brains to absorb memories, not power. And zombies eat brains to feel alive again."

I narrowed my eyes. "Your agreeing with Aura is weird."

"I know." Layla shrugged. "I just don't feel like disagreeing and being snarky because it's a waste of time. I'll be plenty happy once I squeeze the life out of her bitch alt."

Aura frowned. "Except she can't die permanently."

An evil grin spread across Layla's face. "Oh, I know. She's going to experience what it was like for me in Soultaker, but I plan to keep the pain going for eternity."

Horatio leaned forward, listening intently. "Cain, I sense that you're avoiding telling me about Prime for some reason. Is it because we've encountered each other before?"

Avoiding that unpleasant conversation wasn't realistic, so I decided to give him the highlights. "We've fought in two different dimensions, mostly over the lost armory and its contents. My companions and I destroyed all the items from the armory in Prime and Alpha to keep them from falling into your hands."

His brow pinched in worry. "Did you kill me in the other dimensions?"

I shook my head. "You survived. A lot of mechanists lost their lives, though."

Horatio looked at Hannah. "Because of her?"

"Because of all of us," Layla snapped. "And if you're upset that we stopped your alts, just take a look at what those weapons did to your Gaia!"

Horatio held up his hands imploringly. "I know, I know. The weapons always posed a grave threat to the world, but I was so consumed with vengeance that I never stopped to consider the consequences. I am glad you stopped me in the other dimensions, and now I hope you can help me and the remnants of humanity overcome the results of my foolish quest."

Layla groaned. "Gaia Beta is FUBAR, you idiot. We'll be lucky if we can get to Baura and stop her from destroying the rest of reality!"

"FUBAR?" Horatio frowned.

"Fucked up beyond all recognition," I said in a calm voice. "We'll see what we can do, but our priority is to apprehend Baura and prevent her from unleashing Armageddon in the other dimensions."

"I understand." Horatio rose. "And we will help you in any way we can."

"How?" Layla sneered. "All you have is a handful of ragtag recruits and a few exo-suits. Not even all of the weapons your people took from us will be enough to overcome the shit storm of monsters between us and Baura. All you'll be good for is the diversion we need to get to her. Are you willing to do that?"

Horatio's shoulders stiffened. "We will do whatever it takes, madam. But I think you will find that we're not as helpless as you think." He pointed vaguely east. "Heraklion is Baura's fortress. It is protected by Great Ancient Ones and hordes of lesser minions. We had hoped to penetrate the city and take her ourselves, but Hastur came for us in Thermopylae before we reached this island."

Layla shook her head. "What in the hell were you doing fighting there in the first place? Isn't that on the mainland?"

"We had been trying to form an alliance with other human remnants. One was a group of demigods led by a powerful girl named Daphne." His shoulders slumped. "She told us there was a gateway being built in Thermopylae that would allow more eldritch creatures to come to Gaia, and if we helped them destroy it, they would become our allies. But it was a trap. We faced Dagon, Hydra, and then Hastur, all of whom normally guard Heraklion. Despite their awesome powers, the demis all perished. Had it not been for the goddess, all would have been lost. At least with Hastur dead, we now only have Hydra and Dagon plus numerous lesser minions to worry about."

Layla huffed. "Only?"

"Daphne was a super powerful sun goddess." Hannah grimaced. "Was there a dark-haired girl named Shae with them?"

Horatio nodded. "There were three demis with lightning powers, several with incredible physical strength, and even one with super speed. The one called Shae was able to slow time and protect Daphne, but Hastur broke through their defenses and devoured their brains."

Hannah paled. "Poor Shae." A tear trickled down her cheek.

I almost told her that it wasn't our Shae, the one she'd dated, but I imagined it was still traumatic to hear. She seemed more upset hearing about Shae's alt dying than about the death of her own alt. So, I switched the subject. "Horatio, I need to know everything you know about Heraklion and a complete breakdown of your offensive capabilities."

He nodded. "All that is mine is yours, Cain."

The man looked ready to do anything, so I went straight for the brutal truth. "Getting to Baura will probably be a suicide mission for you and your people, because the only way to get to her is by drawing off her forces so a smaller group can infiltrate her stronghold and take her."

"I understand. But perhaps it won't be such a suicide mission if you can help me with something."

I spread my hands. "And that is?"

"I think you will be pleased with what I'm about to show you." Horatio gulped another glass of gin, then got up and motioned for us to follow him. He led us out of the building and to a clockwork car that looked like something from nineteen-thirties Germany. We piled into the car, and he spun the igniter crank on the dash to start the clockwork engine.

He drove past the buildings and into a tunnel in the back. The ground pitched steeply down, leading us even further underground. After a short time, we reached another bunker, this one nearly twice as long as the first and much taller.

"Welcome to the launch bay." Horatio gestured to the sides where semicircular enclosures had once housed missiles. The launch pads were blackened, probably because the missiles had been used to fight the monsters invading Gaia. All were empty except for three at the far end.

"Whoa!" Hannah leaned forward against the front seats. "Are those what I think they are?"

Horatio grinned proudly. "Yes, they're mega-exos, or megas as we call them."

Layla whistled. "Okay, now I'm impressed.

Aura nodded. "They're massive."

Hannah giggled and clapped her hands. "Cain, they're like the jaegers!"

"More like if you ordered your jaegers from Wish," I muttered. Jaegers were highly advanced giant robots used to fight alien invaders in Pacific Rim, one of Hannah's favorite movies. These clockwork creations were much smaller and looked far simpler.

The mega-exos were precisely what the name described—giant exoskeletons about fifty feet tall and nearly half as wide. Unlike the smaller skeletal suits, these were fully encased, hiding all the clockwork mechanisms behind armor. There were missile launchers on the shoulders and chain guns bolted to the arms. The hands were humanoid but with razor-sharp blades instead of fingers.

Unlike most mechanist inventions, the mega-exos were tinted silver rather than the standard brass brown their creators favored, probably due to infused mithril.

Horatio parked the car at the foot of the nearest mega-exo, and I took a moment to appreciate the sheer scale. The foot was at least double the size of the car.

I climbed out of the passenger seat and rapped my knuckles on the foot. "What kind of metal is this?"

"A titanium-mithril polymer." He shrugged. "We didn't have access to nearly enough mithril to construct them, so we had to compromise."

I ran a finger along the polished metal. "How do they perform in battle?"

His grin faded. "We have only used one. It fared well, at least until it ran out of liquid mana."

"I was just about to ask how in the world you power these things." Layla pressed her hand to the foot. "These things must weigh tons."

Horatio walked around the back and pointed to a pair of giant cylinders mounted on the back. "With both tanks filled, one mega can operate for hours. Unfortunately, we lost all our mana supplies except for what we could carry with us here. We drained the fuel from our submarines, and it was barely enough to fill one tank on the mega that saw battle. It defeated ganthagons and many lesser minions, but it was toppled when the fuel ran out. The pilot killed herself to prevent capture."

"See, that's a problem." I shook my head. "You can't tell us you have a secret weapon and then have no way for us to use it."

"What about rocket fuel?" Hannah pointed to rows of towering tanks with liquid oxygen labeled on the sides.

Horatio sighed. "Some of the weaponry on the megas was modified to use rocket fuel, but it cannot be used for the main power. Even if we modified the clockwork engines, they would need far more energy than liquid oxygen can provide."

"So, what are we supposed to do about it?" Layla looked around as if hunting for an answer. "Do you see any pixies around here? Or are we supposed to pull a thousand gallons of liquid mana out of our asses?"

Horatio winced. "We need two hundred and sixteen culeus of liquid mana to fuel our three remaining megas sufficiently."

I did the math in my head. The fae used furlongs, culeus, and other ancient methods of measure instead of imperial or metric. They were old school like that. "That's nearly thirty thousand gallons."

"Insane!" Aura looked at the mega in stunned disbelief. "These things are just giant paperweights."

"Did you leave supplies of liquid mana at another base?" Layla said. "Can we scavenge enough from somewhere else?"

"We have no way to return to those bases, I'm afraid." Horatio looked down. "Our submarines have no more fuel. We have just enough liquid mana to fuel our cars and the normal exos."

In other words, their great inventions were useless.

25

L ayla started berating Horatio again. I tuned out the verbal lashing and thought about our options. If—and it was a big if—we could get these things functioning, it would make our quest a hell of a lot easier. Dagon alone could probably wipe out the entire mechanist contingent if they tried to assault Heraklion on foot or in vehicles. We needed an ace up our sleeve.

But how in the hell could we get our hands on enough fuel?

Dwarfs produced liquid mana by refining pixie dust in a forge. It was sometimes referred to as fae oil since it was the most popular form of energy among the magic-using community. It was incredibly energy-dense. Just a tiny vial of liquid mana fueled my car, Dolores, for thousands of miles.

The fact that these metal monsters required thousands of gallons to operate was a testament to just how massive they were. Even the mechanist submarines could go great distances on only a few gallons.

Feary was the best place to get liquid mana, but since I'd baited the centaurs into following us to this world, they likely stood between us and the portal back to Feary Prime. And even if I could reach the portal to Feary, the nearest place to find that much liquid mana was in a specialized dwarven forge. The only forges I knew of were thousands of miles away.

Another option was to use my staff to transition over to the Feary of this dimension, but without knowing the geography on the other side, I risked crossing over inside of a tree or a mountain or perhaps plunging a thousand feet to my death. Blindly transitioning to another plane was suicidal.

Perhaps there was a third option.

I removed Panoptes from my utility belt and slipped it on. My vision split into a honeycomb, and dizziness washed over me. The warehouse, the winter and desert landscapes, and other unknown places appeared before me, answering one question I'd had—would the ring show me locations even if they were in another dimension?

The answer seemed to be yes. The eyes watched places across space and time and were still connected to the ring no matter where the user was. I could travel back to the warehouse, but the stores of liquid mana there weren't even remotely large enough to fuel the mega-exos. I was interested in two places I hadn't visited yet.

Rather than risk my physical body, I simply willed my gaze to focus on the winter world. Snow filled my view, and it was suddenly as if I stood in the middle of the frozen wasteland. There was nothing for miles, but then I rotated the view.

A trail of ice led into a dark forest. The trees were bare, their branches covered in frost and snow. They looked dead, but they were still alive and prospering, thanks to the ice dryads that lived among them. A mountain rose behind the forest, and on it sat an ice palace shining in the cold light of the moon.

This was the land of the winter fae—a place I'd visited many times before.

I willed myself back out of the winter frame, and the honeycomb of different places appeared. My head ached with the strain of seeing so many places at once, but I pushed aside the pain and focused on the desert frame. It filled my view, spreading out around me.

Ocean waves crashed somewhere beyond sand dunes to my left. Seagulls cried in the distance. I rotated the view to the left and realized that what I had mistaken for a desert was actually a beach. Beyond the dunes loomed a palace woven from trees and vines. A startling variety of flowers bloomed in glorious colors all along the parapets and domes. Pixies flitted about, spreading their dust to change the colors of the flowers or grow new ones.

This was no ordinary beach. This place was at the very heart of summer.

It was no coincidence that Baura had set her eyes to watch the winter and summer courts. Baura had probably considered asking for their help, or perhaps she'd considered killing the fae queens as well. Whatever her plans, I now had the opportunity to solve our problems and subvert her plans.

I switched my view back to the mechanist bunker and slid off the ring.

Hannah stood next to me, a concerned look on her face. "Cain, your face is white as a ghost. Why were you using the ring?"

I took a breath to clear my head and give the raging ache in my temples some time to relent. Then I went to the car, sat in the front seat, and closed my eyes. "I might have an answer to our problem. But it'll be tricky."

"Really?" Hannah put a hand on my shoulder. "Does the warehouse have liquid mana?"

"It does, but not nearly enough." I blew out a breath and opened my eyes to see the others approaching.

Layla raised an eyebrow. "What were you saying, Cain?"

"I can use Panoptes to reach the summer and winter courts. There are dwarven forges near each one where they distill pixie dust into liquid mana." I'd visited both facilities during my time in the Oblivion Guard since they'd been considered possible targets by humans during the war. They'd either severely overestimated the capability of the Gaian humans or thought that there might be sympathizers among the humans who lived on Feary, because no human ever got remotely close to the winter and summer courts.

The forges were nearly a hundred miles away from the palaces since the fae didn't want the stench of industry tainting their seats of power. Just one forge might have enough mana for our needs, but I wouldn't know for sure until I went there in person. The supply levels varied greatly depending on the season.

Panoptes allowed me to bring anything I could carry into the warehouse. But was there a size limit, or could I bring through anything I touched? I planned to answer that question in short order, because hiking a hundred miles through hostile territory would take days and probably get me killed. I was still considered an enemy of the state by both courts, and the moment I appeared in their respective kingdoms, it would only take one pixie to ruin the entire trip.

"I need to try something." I slid into the driver's seat of Horatio's car and put on the ring. I focused on the eye watching the warehouse and rotated the view to ensure I had enough clearance for what I planned to do. Then I gripped the steering wheel and envisioned bringing myself and the car into the warehouse.

A loud crash echoed, and metal clattered. Intense pain pierced my head, and my vision blurred. From all the ruckus, I half expected to be holding onto only the steering wheel and find the car in pieces around me.

I rubbed my aching eyes until I could see again and discovered that the entire car had come through with me. The bumper had struck a shelf and shoved it over, spilling its contents on the floor.

"Oops." I rotated the ignition crank, and the clockwork engine ticked to life. So far, so good. The good news—I could transport an object as big as a car through Panoptes. The bad news—it hurt like a royal bitch.

I took off the ring and massaged the bridge of my nose. The pain radiated from behind my eyes and along my forehead. Some say that the eyes are the window to the soul. Perhaps Panoptes was using its eyes as windows to anywhere they could see. It certainly felt as if I'd rammed an entire car through my eyeholes.

Once the pain subsided, I steeled myself and put the ring back on. I focused on the bunker and confirmed the others weren't standing where the car had been a moment ago. Thankfully, they'd had the sense to back well away from the area. I focused once again and willed myself and the car back into the bunker.

Intense pain stabbed my eyes again, and everything went black.

"Cain?" Someone shook my shoulder.

I jerked upright and blinked my eyes until I could see clearly again. The steering wheel was the first thing I saw. Then I looked to the side and saw Hannah. "Did I pass out?"

"Cain, your eyes are bleeding." She grimaced. "You look like you just woke up after an all-night bender."

"I feel like it." I wiped a hand beneath my eye and examined the crimson stain on my palm. "Hope I didn't permanently damage something."

Hannah winced. "I mean, tears of blood are never a good sign."

I examined my face using the camera on my phone. There were only a couple of drops of blood in the corners of my eyes. "It's not that bad." I wiped them clean.

"Not yet, anyway." She chuckled. "And, of course, you don't think bleeding eyes are a big deal."

My eyes ached, but the rest of my body felt fine. "Bleeding eyes or not, now I've got a plan."

Layla watched me, brow furrowed. "You're going to take a car to Feary, drive it to a forge, and put in an order for thirty thousand gallons of liquid mana? You've got tons of Gaian money, but not even you have the funds to buy that much mana."

"You're right. I don't." I closed my eyes and massaged them. "But I'm not planning on buying it."

Horatio looked flabbergasted. "Might I ask how you and the car vanished? What sort of magic is this?"

I had reservations about telling him, but it was necessary. "I have Panoptes, the ring Baura used; the ring that drove her insane."

His eyes flared. "Oh, my. Please don't drive yourself insane."

Layla smirked. "Too late."

I patted the hood of the car. "Is this the fastest vehicle you have?"

He shook his head. "It pains me to admit that there are several nub vehicles that are faster."

"I have the need—"

"The need for speed." Hannah smirked.

"Yeah, exactly," I said dryly. I summoned a mental image of the lands near the summer and winter courts. The roads were magically preserved, so heat or cold wouldn't affect them. The environs would be dangerous no matter which I chose. But since it was closer to summer now, the pixies of that court would be producing more pixie dust. That meant the probability of more liquid mana.

"Tell us more about your little plan before you go rushing off to die, Cain." Layla stepped in front of me. "You know I don't like being left behind."

"There's no way to take anyone with me through Panoptes unless they're dead, so I'll have to travel from the summer court to the forge by myself." I put a hand on her shoulder. "Once I'm there, bringing over barrels of liquid mana will be a team effort."

Layla raised an eyebrow. "How far from the summer court to the forge?"

"About a hundred miles." I patted the clockwork vehicle. "Depending on the nub vehicles available, I can drive like a bat out of hell and cover the distance in an hour. Once I reach the forge, I'll infiltrate their security and find the liquid mana storage facility."

She nodded. "And we'll take turns using Panoptes bringing over barrels of mana."

"Yep."

"Not the worst plan I've ever heard." Layla sighed. "Let's do it."

"Did you say barrels?" Hannah frowned. "Like wooden barrels?"

"Yeah, the dwarves are old-school." Aura pursed her lips. "And they're also big on security. Cain, how do you plan to sneak into their factory?"

"With the ring."

"Are you sure using that thing so much isn't already corrupting your mind?" Layla pressed her lips together. "I don't want to end up fighting you and Baura if you flip your lid."

"I'm fine." I turned to Horatio. "Show me your fastest vehicles."

Horatio looked at me uncertainly for a moment, then nodded.

"Yes, of course." We piled into his car, and he took us up to the main bunker. Gunshots popped in the distance like fireworks.

Layla looked ready to leap out of the car. "Are we under attack?"

"Constantly." Horatio sighed. "Vile creatures are always finding new ways in, whether slithering through the vents or crawling through cracks in the foundation. Without the goddess's protective flowers, there is no safe place to hide, so we remain ever vigilant."

"What a miserable existence." Hannah shrank into the back seat. "I wish I could make protective flowers like my alt did, because this world sucks."

"Perhaps our world won't be so terrible once Cain helps us." Horatio looked as if he wanted to believe that but couldn't quite convince himself to do so. He parked alongside the other clockwork vehicles and slid out of the front seat. "The nub vehicles are this way."

We made our way through rows of military trucks and reached an assortment of civilian vehicles. Most of them were nothing special, much like the other cars I'd seen back in town. Any of them would be a better choice than a mechanist vehicle, because most nub cars could outrun their clockwork counterparts. Mechanists went for style points, not speed or functionality. I just needed something that could go at least a hundred miles per hour.

"That's a sad-looking bunch of cars," Layla said. "Where'd you find them?"

"They were already parked here." Horatio inspected a compact car. "But any of them should suffice."

A glint of white near the back caught my attention. I made my way past a pickup and found an assortment of motorcycles. Some were dirt cycles used for off-road travel. The one that drew my attention was a police motorcycle. The fuel tank was splashed with dried blood, and there was a crack in the windscreen, but it looked otherwise intact. I turned the key and pressed the ignition button. It rumbled to life. I opened the gas tank. Miraculously, it was nearly full.

"This will do." I checked the saddlebags and found a flashlight, a taser, and spare ammunition. I dumped out everything except the flashlight and taser since I wanted the bike to be as light as possible. Hopefully taking through the mass of a motorcycle wouldn't hurt nearly as much as taking a car with me.

Layla put a hand on the handlebars. "What weapons are you taking?"

"Just my staff and my good looks." I patted the seat. "I don't plan on battling a horde of fae in Feary. My plan is to outrun anything dangerous."

"Well, if the fae finds out you're breaking the law, then they'll be free to detain you." She put her hands on her hips. "You're going into the heart of fae country, Cain. It's not going to be as easy as you make it out to be."

"I know, and I'm not pretending it'll be easy." I put my hand on hers. "Besides, Panoptes should keep our activities hidden even from the all-knowing fae. Does that make you feel better about our odds?"

She put her other hand over mine and looked mollified. "It does, a little."

I lifted her hand to my lips and kissed it. "Good."

"Good." She nodded stiffly.

Aura groaned. "Get a room, you two."

"You two are so weirdly adorable sometimes." Hannah rolled her eyes. "And dumb."

I smirked. "Yep."

Layla managed a small smile of her own, then reclaimed her hand. "What now?"

I revved the motorcycle. "Now we train." I couldn't exactly expect them to ferry over barrels of mana without going through some test runs and getting a feel for the ring.

Because there was no room for error in this little scheme of mine.

26

I started off by letting each of them wear Panoptes.

Layla and Aura took several moments to get past the dizziness but were able to focus on the various frames and shift their vision to them with a few tries. Layla, of course, traveled to the warehouse even though I told her not to and returned with a duffel bag of supplies.

"See? It's easy." She dropped the duffel bag as if dropping a microphone on stage. "This is gonna be a piece of cake."

Aura huffed. "I could have traveled there too, but I didn't want to risk getting stuck."

I gave the ring to Hannah. "Your turn."

She slipped it on and shuddered. "Ooh, it's like having bug eyes!"

Aura took a step back. "Are you going to throw up again?"

Hannah turned in a circle. "Nah, it doesn't feel as trippy this time." She turned to me. "So, I can travel to anything I see?"

"Yeah, but only go to the ware—" She vanished before I could finish talking. "That's annoying."

Hannah blipped back a moment later. "Wow, this is neat!"

"How's your head?" I asked. "Do you feel like throwing up again?"

She hiccupped. "My head is fine. My stomach feels a little iffy. Nothing hurts."

I raised an eyebrow. "Your god DNA must make this almost natural to you."

"I don't know. But it does feel a little uncomfortable now that I've worn it for a minute." She hiccupped and reached for the clockwork car. "Can I test with this?"

I nodded. "Yeah, but make sure there's enough room—"

She and the car vanished.

"Wish she'd listen just one damned time."

"Now you know how we feel when you do the same shit." Layla smirked.

Hannah and the car returned a moment later, the tires screeching as they settled back on the floor. "Okay, so that does hurt a little." She rubbed her eyes. "Feels like I shoved that car through my eye holes." She turned her head to the side and spewed puke across the floor, then wiped her mouth with the back of her hand and shrugged. "I don't know why it makes me do that. My stomach doesn't even hurt."

Aura wrinkled her nose. "Someone bring her a bucket so we're not slipping in vomit."

"My turn." Layla held out her hand, and Hannah gave her the ring. "Be back in a flash." She put a hand on the car and vanished. The car remained behind. Layla flicked back.

This time, I watched closely. It was as if the air around her blinked and made her appear, much like an eye blinking open and shut. I wondered if one of the eyes of Panoptes was there watching us invisibly.

Layla scowled and put a hand on the car. Closed her eyes and furrowed her brow. They both flicked away this time. Several minutes ticked past before they made a reappearance. Looking green in the face, Layla tore off the ring and fumbled it over to Aura. "I'm not going to lie. That hurts like a bitch." She squeezed her eyes shut and massaged them. "How many barrels do we need to bring back?"

"A lot." I watched Aura. "Ready?"

She shook her head. "No, but I guess that doesn't matter." She touched the car, wavering dizzily, and then they both vanished. She took longer to reappear than Layla had and looked just as discombobulated.

"No wonder Hannah pukes." Aura dropped the ring on the floor and leaned heavily against the car. "I need some aspirin ASAP."

Horatio looked fascinated and worried. "Did you want me to try as well, Cain?"

I shook my head. "I'll need you to coordinate moving the barrels and fueling the megas while we work."

He smiled. "I am so grateful you've chosen to help us, Cain, when I know you could just abandon us to our fate."

I had no response, so I walked over and picked up the ring. "Who wants to keep practicing?"

"Me!" Hannah raised her hand and bounced on her feet.

Aura and Layla looked green in the faces.

I turned to Horatio. "Do you have any barrels around here we could use for practice?"

He nodded. "Yes, of course."

Moments later, mechanists delivered large plastic barrels filled with water. They were marginally larger than the ones used for liquid mana, making them ideal for our run-through.

Layla and Aura were able to take through three barrels at a time without too much strain. Hannah was able to take through as many as she could touch, which was six if she lay on top of them. Thankfully, she didn't vomit again.

"What if they were strapped together?" Hannah said. "I mean, a car is a bunch of separate parts put together, so the same should work for barrels."

Aura pursed her lips. "Maybe it's not about touching them. Maybe it's more about willing them through with you."

"I'll test!" Hannah touched a single barrel, focused her gaze on all of them, and then flicked away. Only the barrel she touched went with her. She returned looking disappointed. "Man, I thought we had something."

We strapped the barrels together, and Hannah tried again. All eight barrels went with her.

She returned with them, delight on her face. "Maybe if we get a long rope, we can bring through dozens at once."

I nodded. "Depending on how they're stored at the forge."

We continued testing and practicing, then finally called it a night. Even Hannah was feeling the side effects of Panoptes by that time, and we needed to be as fresh as possible for the big heist. Horatio took us to a building that had been sleeping quarters for officers, giving us each our own rooms.

I fell asleep the moment my head hit the pillow.

DESPITE THE INTERMITTENT gunfire during the night as mechanist guards killed any intruding horrors, I slept well. After breakfast, I was ready to invade the heart of the summer court.

I drove the motorcycle to the lower level, parking in the open area between the three megas since it was the ideal place to deliver the barrels of mana. The others followed me in Horatio's car.

Hannah hugged me. "Cain, remember you can travel back to here with the ring if it gets too dangerous."

"Yeah, but I can't keep the ring on the entire time." I mussed her hair and kissed the top of her head. "I'll be fine."

"I'm beginning to think it'd be preferable to let the worlds end." Layla rubbed her eyes. "I've got a headache so bad, I can feel it all the way down in my feet."

"The old Layla would have said in her cooch." Hannah shook her head disapprovingly. "You're really slacking on the sex jokes."

Layla didn't respond.

Hannah searched the saddlebags on the motorcycle. "Don't you need a helmet? The windscreen is cracked, and the wind is going to be brutal at a hundred plus miles per hour."

"Take these." Horatio handed me a pair of mechanist goggles.

I peered through the colored lenses. "What's the deal with these anyway? Why not just use glass?"

"Mithrium is the only thing that prevents us from going mad when we see insanity-inducing eldritch horrors." Horatio shook his head sadly. "Most humans went insane within moments of encountering ganthagons and other horrors. Mithrium blocks the psychic emanations enough to allow us to resist their effects."

"Nice." I took the goggles and climbed onto the motorcycle. "See you later, alligators." I slipped on Panoptes. The overlapping honeycomb of windows appeared. Despite having done this multiple times, I still felt just as dizzy as the first time. I focused on the beach and willed myself and the motorcycle through. Warm air touched my face. Sweet odors of summer tickled my nose. Insects hummed, birds chirped, and wild animals called from the nearby forest.

I took off the ring and stowed it in my utility belt, then allowed myself a moment to recover my wits.

The Summer Road was somewhere near the palace. I vaguely remembered that it paralleled the beach for a short distance, then turned northward. I didn't bother casting a camouflage blind since pixies could see right through it. The beach sand was firm enough to give the motorcycle traction, so I twisted the accelerator just enough to get me moving without revving the engine too hard.

The waves crashing against the shore would cover the rumbling engine a little, but I wasn't counting on it too much. The palace was less than a quarter of a mile away, and they had ears everywhere. I was thankful that Baura had chosen this spot for Panoptes to watch since it gave me just enough cover to hopefully sneak away.

I did a quick scan of the environs as the motorcycle crept along the beach. A gentle breeze whispered through the trees, reminding me that pixies weren't the only eyes the fae had. Dryads were just as likely to spread rumors of a stranger on a strange contraption through the forest, reaching the ears of a pixie and eventually the fae.

Keeping low against the handlebars so the dunes would shield me from eyes in the forest, I slowly made my way down the beach until rocks and steep cliffs made further progress impossible. I turned toward the dunes, gunning the motorcycle out of necessity to give me enough speed to drive up them. The tires struggled in the loose sand but managed to scale them.

I finally reached the other side. The Summer Road was visible across a meadow—a highway of smooth stone built by the dwarves thousands of years ago. A woman with bark for skin watched me curiously from the edge of the forest. Other dryads appeared near their trees, murmuring to one another.

There was no choice but to smile, wave, and then race across the meadow toward the road. There was little else but forests and grasslands between here and the factory. I just had to hope the dryads took a while to report seeing me. If I were shorter, they might think I was a dwarf testing an invention, but my human features gave me away.

When the tires hit the road, I oriented westward, then pulled the goggles over my eyes. I glanced back at the palace rising in the distance, half expecting to see armed beings on horseback charging after me, but the road remained empty.

I twisted the throttle all the way, and the bike roared to life, tires screeching as it rocketed forward. I shifted gears quickly, reaching a hundred and twenty miles per hour in short order. The bike might go faster, but I didn't want to risk straining the engine too much.

The road took me past fields of amber grain, acres of magic mushrooms, and dark forests. The first forty miles passed quickly, but I had to slow as the road entered a hilly region with unexpected twists and turns.

Thunder rumbled in the distance, and the horizon grew dark with rainclouds even though the skies had been clear moments before.

I left the road, guiding the motorcycle down a steep hill and under a bridge. Not because I wanted to avoid the rain, but because it was imperative that I avoid the cause of the rain.

Lightning sprites were a normal part of weather patterns in Feary. By themselves, they were relatively harmless, but when enough of them gathered, they caused massive storms and weather events. It was no coincidence that a storm had just formed ahead of me. The fae knew I was here—or at least they knew an intruder was in their lands riding a machine from the human world.

Riding into the storm would be suicidal. A random bolt of lightning might deep-fry me, or extreme wind shear might throw me off the bike. I parked the motorcycle under the bridge and climbed the hill for a look. The storm was still a mile or two distant, but it was sweeping rapidly toward me.

Hiding under the bridge might suffice, but I didn't want to take any chances. I slipped on Panoptes, touched the bike, and traveled to the warehouse. Despite the piercing headache, I kept the ring on and switched my view back to Feary, willing the view to move up the hill and to the road.

From there, I watched the storm sweep over the road. Hundreds of glowing blue orbs crackled with lightning, sending a web of electricity through the air. If I'd tried to cross through the storm, that net would have electrocuted me in a heartbeat. The lightning sprites carried the storm at such a swift pace that it passed over my point of view within seconds, continuing back the way I'd come.

I gave it time to get a good distance away, then climbed on the motorcycle and traveled back to Feary. Then I tore off the ring and gave myself a moment to recuperate. A thunderclap snapped my attention to the storm. I summoned my staff and zoomed in to confirm what I already knew—it had reversed directions and was coming back at me, moving even faster than before now that it had a visible target.

"Well, shit." I revved the motorcycle and took off.

The wind howled, and the air vibrated with constant thunder. The side view mirror showed me a swirling black cloud that looked as if it were skittering along the landscape on legs of lightning. The motorcycle was tearing up the road at a solid pace of a hundred and twenty miles per hour, but the storm, fueled by insane winds, was gaining.

I wished the apocalypse weapons were still in the warehouse because Airbender would have come in awfully handy right about then. It looked like my only chance would be to put the ring on and slip back into the warehouse unless I could squeeze some extra speed out of my ride. The storm would, no doubt, remain in place and wait for me to reappear.

The motorcycle crept up to a hundred and twenty-five mph, probably due to the extreme tailwinds from the storm. Leaves and debris gusted past, caught by the powerful wind. In a matter of seconds, the storm would catch me.

The tornados would rip me off the ground while lightning charbroiled me to a crisp. It seemed I had no choice but to abandon this quest.

27

I was just about to put on the ring when a thought hit me. What if I could harness the power of the storm? Keeping one hand on the handlebars, I held the other one behind me and traced a large sigil, binding it to the back of the seat.

The spell was one I'd done so many times I could do it with my eyes closed. It was a simple shield spell, but I normally didn't make them this wide. It was easier to cast layers of smaller shields instead of one large one. But layered shields wouldn't do what I needed, which was to catch the full force of the wind.

This motorcycle was getting a sail.

The hardest part of tracing the shield while driving was giving it a concave shape so it would capture more wind. Shields weren't flexible. They couldn't billow out to hold more wind, so I had to alter the normal shape instead of going with the boilerplate design.

I glanced back to confirm the glowing lines of the sigil were able to handle the altered design, then tied off the final weave. Focusing my will, I powered it, and the shield materialized into translucent form. The wind slammed into it, and the back tire briefly left the road. Rubber screeched as it bounced back down to earth. The speedometer inched up another fifteen miles per hour, and the storm suddenly wasn't gaining on me so quickly anymore. It was still outpacing me, to be sure, but I'd bought myself some time.

Unfortunately, I still had another fifty miles to go to the forge. My odds of making it went back to a math problem I'd read in one of Hannah's old textbooks. That one involved two trains traveling toward each other. This one was a little more complex.

If a motorcycle is traveling at a hundred and forty miles per hour, and the storm chasing it is going a hundred and forty-two miles per hour, how long does the rider have before being brutally destroyed by lightning sprites?

The answer—not long enough to make it fifty miles. But I clung to a slender thread of hope. The energy output to maintain such a fast, powerful storm was phenomenal. It didn't matter if the creators were lightning sprites or gods. Using magic was like using a muscle. The body would eventually tire. My only hope was that the lightning sprites would run out of energy and falter.

I had no idea if that would happen in five minutes or thirty. If the storm continued at its current pace, it would catch up to me within the next fifteen minutes. The only escape left to me was to put on the ring and enter the warehouse.

But there was a problem even with that option. The storm was moving so fast that I didn't have time to screech to a halt before putting on the ring and traveling into the warehouse. That meant I had to perform the maneuver while still hauling ass.

If I willed myself and the motorcycle into the warehouse while traveling at such a high speed, I didn't have a chance of stopping before slamming into the heavy metal shelves only a few feet away. The only place with enough runway to stop was the main aisle. But in order to ensure I ended up there, I'd have to put on the ring and move the eye there to the precise spot. There was no way I could drive while doing that.

The frozen land of the winter fae offered plenty of space, but hitting icy terrain at such a high speed wouldn't be good for my health either. It would still be better than crashing into metal shelving at one hundred and forty miles per hour.

Having said that, there was still one fatal flaw with using the ring to escape. Simply putting it on caused intense dizziness and disorientation even while standing still. Sliding it on while driving at full throttle would likely send me careening off the road and crashing before I even had a chance to focus on a destination.

Somehow, I had to find another way to slow down the storm.

I reached the peak of a tall hill and got a good look at the surrounding countryside. The Summer Road continued straight ahead, intersecting with another highway that went east and west. The rolling grasslands ahead wouldn't do anything to slow the storm, but the highway to the east offered possible salvation.

The hills grew steeper in that direction, but they weren't what I was looking at. It was the towering trees of the Thystle Forest that caught my eye. If there was anything that would slow down a storm, it was a forest. But how in the hell was I going to take a ninety-degree turn east without slowing down and allowing the storm to catch me?

Once the lightning sprites realized I was turning, they'd simply travel diagonally off-road and overtake me. That left me little choice but to also cut diagonally through the tall grass and get back on the road. Unfortunately, traveling so fast through even waist-high grass would probably be enough to crash the bike or yank me off it.

I summoned my staff and prepared a longshot. Instead of a concentrated bullet of energy, I willed it to be flat and wide. As I neared the intersection, I aimed and fired. A blade of white energy skimmed above the ground, mowing down the grass and creating a narrow path. I stood on the foot pegs. The bike leaped off the side of the stone road and hit the grass.

There was a moment of panic as the wheels slipped in the newly shorn vegetation. Somehow, I managed to keep the bike steady, but my speed dropped noticeably as the makeshift shield sail turned away from the tailwind and instead began to drag. I fired another blast of energy, mowing down another swath of grass, then banished the staff and guided the bike to the eastern road.

The front wheel hit the side of the road and bounced. I wrestled back control and screeched onto the stone, risking a glance back at the storm. It followed my path, ripping up grass while lightning charred it to ash. It had gained a good fifty feet on me. I just hoped this gambit worked.

I gunned the bike up the hill as the wind caught in my shield sail once again, boosting my speed up above one hundred and forty. Giant trees with orange and red leaves formed a colorful canopy over the road ahead. Unlike many forests, this one was light and airy— certified safe to enter for most beings since it was a major trade route to the summer heartlands.

The moment I entered the forest, the wind at my back subsided. The storm rolled to a stop just outside the trees. The lightning and tornadoes dropped to a murmur. I stopped and wheeled around one hundred and eighty degrees to face the storm. It seemed that whoever was controlling the lightning sprites didn't want to destroy the forest just for little old me.

As the dark clouds cleared, an imposing figure on a horse of mist rode out. Long, silver hair whipped majestically in the wind, and eyes flashed with the power of lightning. Lord Aeolus, one of the ancient high fae, calmly regarded me with cold eyes.

He spoke in a voice that rumbled like distant thunder. "Cain Sthyldor, why do you despoil our lands with your traitorous presence and this human machine?"

I'd seen Aeolus several times before, but his visage still struck the chill of fear into my heart. He might be fae, but he was also considered a god in ancient Greek lore. The fact that he'd personally given chase to me was both an honor and a terrifying reminder of just how much the high fae despised me.

I gathered every shred of confidence I could muster and answered him somewhat honestly. "I come seeking aid for the Gaia of another dimension, which is overrun with eldritch horrors. The cause of this cataclysm is an elf who murdered the goddess Athena. Even now she seeks to extend her destruction to our dimension."

He pursed his lips. "If you seek aid, then why do you flee?"

The fact that he'd replied with a question was mildly comforting. I wondered if the fact that he hadn't raced across the distance between us was because doing so would cause another destructive storm. Glowing sprites hovered in the air outside the forest as if waiting for their master to give them the word.

I toyed with the idea of asking him for help, but there was absolutely no way he would stoop so low as to aid a mere human, no matter the cause. Branches creaked, and the hairs on the back of my neck stood on end. In that moment, I realized that his question had been a delaying tactic.

Gunning the motorcycle until the rear wheel smoked, I spun the bike back around. Dryads leaped from the trees on all sides, branch-like hands grasping. I accelerated past them before they reached me, casting shields toward those who got in my way and shoving them off the road.

Thunder rumbled. A quick look in the side view mirror told me that Aeolus had not reignited the storm, but his horse was galloping after me. Without the full power of the storm at his disposal, I was quickly outdistancing him.

Thankfully, the dryads ahead hadn't gotten the message to stop me yet. I assumed Aeolus had used a lightning sprite to tell the nearest dryads, and they'd spread the word. Despite the good news that I was out of immediate danger, I had other issues to contend with—namely that I was heading in the wrong direction and surrounded by trees.

Like most forests with huge trees, there wasn't much underbrush, and there was plenty of room between tree trunks. I swerved off-road, slowing so the blanket of leaves didn't cause the bike to slide out from under me. I swerved around a thick root, then hit the next one, launching the bike a few feet into the air before bouncing back on the ground. The wheels skidded in the thick leaves and collided with yet another root.

The impact flung me off the seat and toward the tree. I reflexively threw out a hand, intending to cast a shield to cushion the blow. But instead, I felt a strange tingle emanating from my fingertips. An invisible force stopped me almost instantly, and I landed back on the motorcycle seat. It was in the process of flipping over, but the force emanating from my hand shoved the wheels forcefully back to the ground, keeping it upright.

I was so surprised that the bike toppled the other way, and I fell to the ground, skidding through leaves and down a hill. I recovered quickly, pushing myself into a sitting position and sliding on my backside as the bike continued its journey down the slope. I reached out and felt the invisible force again, grasping at the bike.

It was the same force I'd felt when reaching for my brightblade while fighting the thropids.

I touched the handlebar through the kinetic emanations. The sensation was the same as if it were touching my actual hand. I yanked, pulling myself toward it. I reached the bike and held on, unable to stop it. The tires hit a thick root halfway down, bringing us to a halt.

I glanced up the slope and saw Aeolus staring down the ridge at me. Turning the handlebars sideways, I gunned the bike and brought it upright, then hopped on and steered it downhill. Dodging trees and jumping roots, I made it to the bottom in one piece, then turned west.

Rumbling thunder told me Aeolus was still giving chase. Once I reached the plains ahead, he'd be able to restart the storm, so my only hope was to gain as much ground as possible before that happened. Even thirty-five miles per hour felt too fast, but I revved up to fifty, jumping roots and ridges, swerving around trees, and hoping I didn't end up making a Cain pancake in the process.

Thankfully, I hadn't traveled that deep into the forest to begin with, so I reached the plains within minutes, then swerved diagonally up the steep hill toward the road. The street tires spun and slipped on the grass, so I angled up the rise to maintain as much traction as possible. The tires met the stone road, and I twisted the throttle as far as it would go, flicking through gears like a madman.

I looked back and saw no sign of Aeolus for several minutes. Then the sky near the forest darkened as if the sun suddenly vanished. Lightning combed the ground, and tornadoes twisted savagely. The reignited storm headed northwest, cutting across the plains to beat me before I could reach the intersection and turn north.

For a moment, I considered giving up and simply returning to the mechanist bunker with the ring. But Aeolus was really pissing me off, and I didn't want to give the old bastard the satisfaction. I swerved down the slope, cutting diagonally across the plains. Long grass whipped me, grasping at the bike and threatening to tear it from beneath me since I hadn't thought to draw my staff and mow it down like last time.

The bike ripped through the final patch of grass and bounced back on the highway. I looked to the right and gauged the storm's distance. The race was on again, and it looked like I was going to lose unless I came up with a brilliant idea.

"How is he so fucking fast?" I shouted above the roar of the tornadoes. There was nothing I could do. The storm would reach the road ahead of me. Unless I gave up and turned around, I'd be toast.

28

I had no clever plan to overcome the power of Lord Aeolus. There was no reasoning with him, no bargain to be made. The storm was going to swallow me whole unless I cut my losses and gave up.

Unless.

I slowed down and rewound the events in my head. He was high fae. My bargain with the high fae prevented them from acting directly against me. While Aeolus could ask the dryads of the forest to detain me, they were helping of their own free will and not being directly controlled. The lightning sprites, however, were directly under his control. If he struck me down with them, he would be breaking the bargain that bound him and the high fae.

The bargain had been bound in blood. If the high fae broke it, they would lose considerable power and magic. Since it had been bound by the queen's blood, that effect would ripple across Feary, weakening all fae.

They could indirectly harm me by using my enemies, but there were very few other loopholes in the contract—I'd made sure of that. Unless I acted directly against the fae, they were not allowed to kill me without breaking the bargain. I could, of course, be arrested for breaking laws, but the fae still weren't allowed to act directly against me under those circumstances.

I glared at the storm and gunned the motorcycle back to full speed. "Let's play a game of chicken and see who blinks first."

The storm crossed onto the road and remained in place—a maelstrom of tornados, lightning, and debris. If the sprites were doing this of their own free accord, then this was pure suicide. But lightning sprites weren't exactly sentient beings. They were elementals, meaning that a storm lord like Aeolus commanded them, and they responded. They had almost no concept of physical beings in the way that we did.

"Please be right," I muttered. "Please be right."

I had about sixty seconds before I found out. My mind naturally wandered back to the strange happenings in the forest and the bunker. How had I grasped my brightblade without using shields? How had I kept myself from flying off the bike? Was it a new ability I'd somehow unlocked? I'd been toying with shields, using them to manipulate things as a sort of fake telekinesis. Had I somehow created a new way to do the same thing but without sigils?

It didn't make sense. Sigils guided magical energies into shapes, forms, and purpose. Willpower and focus powered the sigils and allowed magic-users to cast them for their intended purpose. I hadn't even had a chance to cast a sigil, much less imagine one when I'd been hurled from the motorcycle. As Ekhsis, the descendants of the original humans from the previous universe, I supposedly had limitless ability to evolve. Was this a new phase of my evolution?

That was all the time I had to wonder because the storm rose before me, a wall of malevolent power wielded by a being far more evolved than me.

I shouted my puny voice at the storm. "Kill me, Aeolus! Kill me and break the bargain!"

I hit the storm front, and all went deathly silent. The clouds dissipated, and the lightning sprites scattered in all directions, suddenly freed from servitude. Aeolus and his steed of mist hulked in the middle of the road, eyes glowing like an angry thunder god.

Slowing the bike, I pulled up beside him since running into him while he stood there would certainly be a breach of the bargain on my side. I was tempted to stick out my tongue at him, but gloating was stupid and pointless. The high fae were assholes, but it was better to show a little respect, so they didn't go all out in their efforts to destroy me.

I nodded at him. "Well met, Lord Aeolus. May your winds blow eternal."

He straightened atop his steed as if caught off guard by my words. "Leave our lands, filthy animal, for there are other ways I can deal with you."

"I humbly accept your advice, gracious lord." I flourished a bow. "My business here will soon be complete, and I will sully the summer lands no more." I gunned the motorcycle and screeched away.

He turned his steed and began to follow me, but without the lightning sprites, he quickly fell into the distance.

I tried not to feel too smug, mainly because I'd been stupid enough to forget that he couldn't directly harm me. Though I hadn't known that he was at the heart of the storm originally, I should have realized the truth once he revealed himself. It was clear he'd herded me toward the forest so the dryads could apprehend me. He'd known that I'd try to use the forest to slow down the storm, or maybe I was just giving him too much credit.

Either way, I still had too much shit to do that could get me killed —namely dealing with dwarven security. They certainly had no bargain with me, and they were known to show little mercy toward unwanted intruders.

And if they didn't kill me, there were a thousand more ways to die on Gaia Beta.

The hilly landscape became steeper as I approached the Glurin Mountains. Smoke drifted from the peak of the volcano where the dwarves had their forge. The sides of the mountain were thick with virgin forests that had never seen an ax since the summer fae wouldn't allow deforestation so close to home. That was okay because the forge relied on geothermal activity for heat and not burning wood or coal. The dwarves considered metalworking with anything other than extreme volcanic heat as child's play.

The Summer Road continued through a tunnel in the mountains, but the route I wanted branched off ahead, entering another tunnel that would take me to the underground city of the dwarves. They were a strange species, not so different from humans or elves in that they liked sunlight and being aboveground, but their intense devotion to mining and crafting led them to spend most of their lives underground.

There was only one way into their city as far as most people knew, but as a former member of the Oblivion Guard, I knew of at least five passages leading inside, some of them more secret than others.

I reached the branch in the road, but instead of following it to the left, I went off-road to the right, entering the forest and driving a short distance before stopping at an outcropping of rock. I stowed the motorcycle behind some bushes. I could drive it through the passage, but the engine noise would echo far and wide through the tunnels, and I didn't want to raise an alarm.

Though the outcropping appeared to be solid rock, it was actually an optical illusion and not even the magical kind. Putting my shoulder to the rock, I looked sideways down the outcropping where I spotted a gap that was only visible from this angle due to the way a thin wall of rock overlapped it.

The gap was six feet wide and about twenty feet tall. But even from this angle, it was easy to miss. I stepped between the overlapping outer wall and stood inside the passage opening. This wasn't the most secret passage, but it was the one I remembered as leading most directly toward liquid mana storage.

The stone walls of the tunnel were meticulously carved into columns, statues, and mosaics by the artisan-class dwarves. It was all one piece though it looked as if it was comprised of multiple works of art. This was just some lowly hidden tunnel entrance, but the dwarves were all about doing everything just right.

Dwarves admired Hephaestus and worked all their lives perfecting their various crafts in the eternal pursuit of creating godlike masterpieces. The mechanists idolized both Hephaestus and dwarves but were far more focused on clockwork and other mechanical designs, ignoring the artistic roots of the dwarves.

A clockwork minecart with an open back waited in an alcove ahead. I stepped inside and pushed a bejeweled button. The liquid mana glowed and sparkled. I pushed forward on the lever, and the cart departed the alcove.

Unlike a minecart, this one didn't employ thick iron wheels rolling atop rails. Instead, the cart glided just above a thin vein of metal embedded in the tunnel floor. This wasn't magic—it was magnetism. At least, that was what one of the engineers told us during one of the Oblivion Guard's visits here. Small mana-fueled thrusters on the bottom provided acceleration.

I pushed the lever halfway to full, and the cart increased its speed, following the curve of the tunnel as it spiraled down. There was no other traffic, carts, or otherwise, but I cast a camouflage blind and ducked low behind the sides just in case. If someone spotted an uninvited human, all hell would break loose.

The cart reached the bottom of the tunnel and entered a round room with dozens of branching tunnels. Towering statues of dwarf kings, mythical creatures, and other artistic extravagances decorated what should have been a simple railway junction.

Other carts zipped past in adjacent junctions, but this part of the mine wasn't heavily traveled. This was an easy place to get lost in, and that was by design. Untold riches and death awaited intruders stupid enough to enter. There were dead-ends and traps aplenty in this place, most of them bearing the scattered bones of would-be thieves and adventurers.

Naturally, I'd memorized all the routes we'd taken during our visits here, not only as a matter of security but also because our training made it almost automatic. I pushed the lever to the right until the cart rotated toward a tunnel with the symbol of a flame carved over the entrance. There were three tunnels with nearly identical symbols over each of them, but there were minute differences that were easy to miss if you didn't know what to look for.

With the cart aligned, I pushed the lever forward and accelerated. The tunnel was wide enough for a dozen carts to fit side by side. Metal veins in the ceiling and walls allowed carts to shift tracks and avoid collisions. Dwarves were incredibly individualistic, and the mine cart system was designed around that trait. In fact, there was no mass transportation in any dwarven city that I knew of.

Dwarven carts were not only the best transportation system I'd ever seen—and I'd seen a lot of them—but they also played right into my strengths, allowing me to more easily infiltrate the maze-like fortress.

I pushed the lever to the right, shifting the cart to a wall track and then pulled up to move it to the ceiling as the tunnel branched. I guided the cart through a series of forks and then the tunnel opened into a cavern that spanned miles in all directions. The cart followed a track along the domed-shaped ceiling, taking me over the sprawling city below.

A fortress with towering walls and parapets dominated the center. Homes and other buildings also hewn from the bedrock encircled it in a precise grid of streets and alleys. Crowds of dwarves bustled along the streets, each one of them probably intent on their own tasks. From this height, they looked like ants. Up close, they were still small in stature, maxing out at about four feet in height.

Another cart approached across the great dome on a track next to mine. I ducked lower but shouldn't have even bothered because the dwarf inside was too busy staring at a blueprint to notice me even if I hadn't been using a camouflage blind.

The cart reached the other side, and I shifted it into another tunnel with the same flame symbol etched above it. The next chamber was nearly as cavernous as the one with the city. This one hosted massive vats for melting metals and ladles used to transport molten metal to casts.

Only the smaller vats were in use, probably because this mine had been stripped nearly clean of all precious minerals. Even so, there were hundreds of dwarves gathered around casts, each one working on their own projects. No one even looked twice at the seemingly empty cart as it glided past.

My journey continued for several more miles until I finally reached a cavern unlike any of the ones before it. The air went from cool to humid. Thick vines grew along the walls. Grass, flowers, and other vegetation covered the floors and walls. A small forest occupied the center of the cavern, the treetops reaching toward sunlight that beamed through portholes in the cave ceiling.

I slowed the cart and used my scope to scout the trees. Tiny houses were carved into the trees, and in those houses lived pixies. I saw dozens of them flitting about, tending to flowers and other plants. Among them, I spotted their even smaller kin, the fairies—definitely not to be confused with the fae.

Whereas pixies were about the size of a Barbie doll, the fairies were miniature even compared to them. Unlike pixies, fairies were mostly uncivilized, vicious little creatures. They spoke and behaved like their larger cousins but were wild to the core. That was why they were seldom seen around cities.

They were also known to attack any unwelcome visitors who wandered too far into a forest. Like pixies, they produced dust, but it was superior in every way. It was so pure and concentrated that it could produce triple the amount of liquid mana. That was why the dwarves went to such lengths to keep them healthy, happy, and under control.

During my first visit, I'd been mildly surprised to see fairies inside a dwarven city, but the dwarves had specifically created this oasis of paradise in the middle to increase the production of liquid mana by attracting fairies. The pixies were there to keep the fairies in line. Small tubes wound around the trees using suction to draw in dust and transport it to the production facility.

This room was also the most dangerous for me to traverse since my camouflage blind would do nothing to hide me from pixie eyes. I guided the cart to the track farthest from the forest and ducked until I was only peering over the top. After several tense minutes, the cart finally exited the dust chamber and entered the production facility.

Crystal vessels along the walls contained sparkling fairy and pixie dust that was gathered by the tubes in the previous room. Shaped like the top half of an hourglass, the vessels filtered impurities and funneled dust into the bottom where it fell into a mixing tank below. Secret ingredients were then mixed with the dust and churned until a golden honey-like substance oozed into shallow pools below where it settled and slowly turned into its glowing blue liquid form.

Dwarves walked around the pools, dipping rods into the mana to test its consistency or testing samples with reagents. One dwarf opened a sluice, and the liquid trickled through a canal and into a wooden barrel. Another dwarf added pale, yellow liquid, which diluted the concentration and then used a brass mixer on the solution. He pulled a chain, and a machine fitted the end of the barrel into place, sealing it.

A clockwork automaton clomped over on four legs. Its clamp-shaped head turned sideways to lift the barrel, then rotated it ninety degrees. It walked to the end of the bay and lowered the cargo onto a rack. The storage area was full to brimming with racks of barrels. There was more than enough liquid mana to fuel three megas, provided we could steal it without triggering dwarven security.

The clockwork cargo hauler was primitive and unadorned by dwarf standards, but the automatons guarding the storage area were not. They ringed the area, motionless as statues, but would spring to life the instant they detected an intruder. Each one stood ten feet tall, their bodies forged like dwarven armor, their faces molded into the shapes of former dwarf rulers, kings and queens alike.

It was a ring of certain death to anyone who tried to get past them.

29

The first time I'd seen dwarven sentinels, I'd quickly realized that they were symbols of wish fulfillment. Dwarves wanted to be tall, imposing, and impossible to defeat in combat. They'd challenged members of the Oblivion Guard to duel their metal warriors. The mithril-infused armor made them nearly impervious even to brightblades, and the dwarves had been delighted with our failure to so much as dent one.

What they hadn't realized was that we'd been ordered not to defeat them. The high fae who'd given the order didn't explain why, but it had seemed obvious to me. If the dwarves ever decided to create an army of these things, the fae didn't want them knowing we could defeat them. It was ludicrous, however, to think the dwarves would ever mount an insurrection against the fae. They were quite happy being left mostly alone.

One might wonder how to fight a sentinel with nearly indestructible armor. The answer was relatively simple. Even the carefully crafted joints on the automatons had seams and gaps in the armor. Otherwise, they wouldn't be nearly flexible enough to engage in hand-to-hand combat. The clockwork gears inside the joints were the weak points. Destroying the gears immobilized them. If they couldn't move, they couldn't fight.

I'd identified seven different areas to strike a sentinel the first time I'd seen one in action. The more intricately honed the machine, the easier it was to take it out of commission by disabling a few gears here and there—at least, that was the theory. I'd never tested it in practice.

The sentinels didn't operate on sight. They used infrared and vibration sensors to detect intruders. The dwarves had bragged that their creations could sense a heartbeat from a hundred feet away, even if they were in a noisy environment. I suspected fae glamour could fool the machines, but again, it was something I hadn't tested.

Despite all that dwarven technology, I had the one thing that would allow me to slip past them completely undetected—Panoptes. Once I was inside the ring of sentinels, it would just be a matter of transporting as many barrels as possible with me to the mechanist bunker.

I guided the minecart to a halt and crept out, keeping low to avoid being spotted by dwarves. There was nothing on this side of the chamber except for flatbed minecarts used to transport the mana barrels into a shipping area where merchants and others purchased and picked up barrels.

I slipped on the ring and let the wave of dizziness wash over me. In one frame, I saw Layla and the others pacing and talking in the mechanist hangar, probably wondering if I'd died yet. I could have traveled back to them and let them know I was okay, but I really didn't want the distraction right now. Instead, I traveled to the warehouse.

Once there, I shifted my view back to the mana chamber and guided the gaze of the eye toward the ring of sentinels. I passed by them and continued deep into the storage area, down rows of barrels until I was at least a couple of hundred feet from the machines. Then I traveled to the new location and took off the ring to allow my senses to recuperate from the disorientation.

I took a full minute to listen for the heavy stomp of metal feet, the whir of clockwork, or anything else indicating that I'd been detected. Aside from the distant churning of mixers and the clomp of the hauler automatons, it seemed I was in the clear. It was time to start the heist.

Starting small was probably best, so I touched three barrels, concentrated, and willed them to travel with me back to the mechanist bunker. I traveled through the frames, and the three barrels thudded to the ground on their sides now that the rack no longer supported them.

"Finally!" Layla threw up her hands. "Why didn't you check back in with us? We thought you were dead."

"I haven't been gone that long." I slipped off the ring and nudged a barrel with my foot toward a pair of mechanists on their way to retrieve it, then I knelt on the floor and traced a square in the dust with a finger. "The storage area is surrounded by dwarven sentinels. It's important that you stay as close to the center of the area until we start running out of barrels there, okay?"

Horatio's eyes lit with excitement. "I don't suppose you could bring one of those through, could you?"

I gave him a look of disbelief. "They're made of mithril armor and programmed to kill intruders. You sure that's a good idea?"

"No, you're right." His shoulders sagged. "Just being able to study one of those would advance our inventions by decades."

"I'll go get more barrels, then we'll start rotating, okay?" I slipped back on the ring.

"Be careful, Cain." Hannah touched my arm.

Layla rolled her eyes. "Cain is the last person you need to remind to be careful."

Hannah rolled her eyes. "You just yelled at him because he didn't check-in."

I traveled back through the frames and into the storage area. Each rack held about twenty barrels. I went to the center of the rack and touched the barrels there, then concentrated on bringing them all back through with me. My head reeled back as if I'd been punched in both eyes by a bridge troll. The entire rack and I flicked back into the bunker.

Staggering, I ripped off the ring and held it out. I was too disoriented to see who took it, and I really didn't care. I stumbled over to Horatio's car and lay down in the back seat to give the pain a moment to fade.

"Oh, fuck!" Layla shouted a moment later.

I sat up, wincing. Layla leaned heavily against a rack of barrels she'd brought back with her. Aura took the ring and went next. She reappeared seconds later and fell to her knees, another rack by her side.

"I'm not looking forward to this," Hannah said as she pulled the ring from Aura's finger. She slipped it on. "Whoa. I can't get over how trippy this is."

Mechanists in exos began hauling the racks toward the nearest mega to get them out of the way. I didn't even want to think about how many more times we'd have to make these trips just to fully fuel one of these giants, much less three of them.

Hannah blipped away and returned with two racks, one on either side of her. She rubbed her eyes, stepped forward, and flicked away again. She went four trips total, bringing back two racks each time before she keeled over onto the floor.

I knelt by her side and rolled her onto her back. "Hannah, are you okay?"

She nodded, her face screwed up in pain. "It was like being punched in the eyes by someone stronger every trip."

"Yeah, well, you're doing better than the rest of us." The pain in my eyes had faded to nothing, but I was already mentally preparing myself for round two. Bringing an entire rack through had been a mistake. I needed to pace myself with just a few barrels at a time.

Hannah gripped my hand. "How many barrels do we need, Cain?"

"Three hundred." Each rack held ten barrels, making the math easy. "We've got sixty so far."

Layla forced herself to stand. "Let's keep going. I've felt worse pain than this."

I put on the ring and went back to the storage facility. There was a big empty spot in the middle where the racks we'd taken had once been. I didn't want to risk getting too close to the perimeter and triggering the sentinels, so I went over one row to the left. I focused on taking back two barrels and traveled back to the compound, then came back for two more and took them. My eyes throbbed with discomfort, but it was nothing like the last time. But as I came back with barrels five and six, the discomfort ratcheted up another notch. By barrels nine and ten, the pain was almost right back where it had been the first time.

Every successive trip without a break amped the pain level until the trip with barrels thirteen and fourteen nearly knocked me out. I gritted my teeth and leaned against a barrel for support to combat my swimming vision.

Layla tugged the ring off, brow furrowed. "I'm guessing this method is no better than just bringing them all through at once?"

"I got four more barrels, but maybe that's because I didn't bring back the rack." I massaged the bridge of my nose. "But this method takes longer, so it's just a wash."

"Agreed." She pushed me gently out of the delivery area. "Go rest your noggin."

I returned to the back seat of the car and closed my eyes.

"Fuck, that hurts!" Layla shouted a moment later when she returned with a rack of barrels.

Aura and Hannah completed the cycle, and it was my turn again.

My head still ached, so I called a recess to give us extra time to recuperate. It took about thirty minutes for the pain to completely dissipate this time.

"Do you think we're giving ourselves brain damage?" Hannah asked.

Layla snorted. "Without a doubt."

Aura nodded slowly. "This kind of pain can't mean anything good. And why does it hurt my eyes so much?"

"The eyes of the ring are windows to other places." I shrugged. "The link with our eyes must cause some kind of magical feedback."

Horatio rubbed his hands briskly, a delighted grin on his face as he approached us. "The first mega is fueled, and we have enough for one tank on the second."

"So, we're halfway there." Hannah sighed. "We can do this."

A woman sporting a pilot's helmet that looked straight out of a museum strutted past us and began climbing the rungs up the side of the first mega. She opened a hatch on the side of the head and went inside. The solid facepiece became transparent just like the bow on the submarines did, revealing the inside. She strapped her arms and legs into a metal suit, then spun a large ignition crank.

A deep hum filled the chamber. Clockwork clunked to life, much louder than even that of a mechanist submarine. The pilot flexed her hands, and the giant hands of the mega responded. She moved her arms, and the contraption followed her lead, creaking and clanging.

"I'm impressed!" Aura looked at Horatio. "I was expecting her to have to use a complex array of levers and switches."

"Me too." Hannah shook her head. "You guys don't seem to believe in ergonomics."

"The engineers knew that optimal performance would be required in combat, so they mimicked the smaller exo-suit controls." Horatio's chest puffed out proudly. "These are our crowning achievements."

The pilot moved her legs, and the mega thudded out of its alcove and began walking toward the far end of the chamber. She rotated its torso, aimed its arms, and performed several maneuvers. The mega creaked and swayed, gears ratcheting loudly as they followed her commands. It looked as though the thing was going to topple over, but she swung out an arm or adjusted a leg in time to keep it upright.

Hannah's forehead furrowed. "Um, is that the best pilot you've got?"

"I'm afraid we don't have many pilots who are experts with the megas yet." Horatio watched as the pilot turned the giant exo in place and practiced punching. "We simply haven't had enough fuel to provide ample training."

Hannah wrinkled her nose. "How much fuel are they burning through right now?"

"I don't even want to think about it." I took the ring. "Let's finish the job."

A claxon rang out, echoing throughout the bunker.

Horatio's eyes widened. "That's the general alarm."

The radio on his belt crackled. "The outer perimeter has been breached, sir!"

He lifted the wireless radio to his mouth. "Assemble all forces. Get a scout out there immediately!"

"Already on it, sir." The radio went silent.

Hannah froze. "What now, Cain?"

I pressed my lips into a grim line. "Hannah, Layla, Aura—bring over as much mana as you can. We need those megas active now." I dropped the ring into Hannah's open hand.

Hannah saluted. "I'm on it!"

I turned to Horatio. "I'm taking your car to the motor pool. I need another motorcycle so I can see what we're up against."

Hannah tapped Horatio's shoulder. "How hard is it to pilot a mega?"

The massive machine whirled its arms to stay upright as the pilot nearly lost control again.

Horatio sighed. "Apparently quite hard."

"Let me try." Hannah tilted her head and watched the hapless pilot like a predator assessing its prey. "I can do better."

Horatio nodded. "Yes, of course." He clicked the receiver on his wireless. "Pilot, park the mega and disembark so another candidate can train."

The radio crackled. "Yes, Inventor."

Hannah turned to me. "I'll get more barrels, then come back and practice piloting the mega."

I watched as the other pilot wrestled the mega back to its pad. "Looks like they need all the help they can get."

Aura grimaced. "I hope their other pilots are better."

I climbed into Horatio's car and spun the ignition crank. He hopped in beside me, and I pushed forward on the acceleration lever while twisting the steering wheel. "Why in the hell can't you people use floor pedals, for gods' sakes?"

"It's far more convenient having everything controlled by hand," Horatio said as he gripped the *oh-shit* handle above his right shoulder.

I guided the car up the ramp and back into the main bunker. Red lights flashed. Mechanists scurried past, grabbing weapons and lining up in formation. Others climbed into exos and marched toward the bunker doors.

I parked the clockwork car near the off-road motorcycles and got out. "Any word from your scouts?"

Horatio spoke into his wireless. "Control center, I need a status update."

"Sir, we've heard nothing from the four scouts we dispatched."

"Bloody hell." Horatio wiped sweat from his forehead. "How did they find us?"

"We don't even know who found us yet." I hopped onto the dirt cycle and shoved down on the kick starter. The two-stroke engine rumbled and sputtered. Black smoke drifted from the exhaust. I adjusted the choke to keep it alive, and the motor finally revved to life. Horatio said something, but I couldn't hear him over the noise.

I slipped on the mithrium goggles and gunned the bike toward the exit. There was nothing waiting outside, but that didn't mean anything since the alarm perimeter was a quarter of a mile out. I guided the bike through the canyon, then up a narrow ledge to the top for a good vantage point.

Shadows flitted across the sky on silent wings. I'd nearly forgotten about the nightgaunts, but they weren't the ones who'd set off the alarms. The creatures responsible stood in the distance gazing at me with dead black eyes. They were elephantine with thick legs and green-gray bodies. But that was where the similarities ended.

These creatures were much taller than elephants, with massive, webbed wings that spanned nearly fifty feet. They were too small for flying, but that's because they were designed for underwater use.

Their imposing physical presence wasn't what scared me, though. It was the single black eye in the center of their heads that concerned me.

I'd encountered malgorths during our travels in the deepways, and their hypnotic eyes nearly sucked my mind dry. Even from this distance, it was possible to feel the draw, but the goggles seemed to protect me against even that faint siren call. I lifted the goggles, and dread washed over me as the full effect of their hypnotic stare hit me.

Fighting psychic traps was part of my training. I pushed back against the psychic emanations to stave off their hypnotic effect. It required a lot of effort, so I put the goggles back on and felt immediate relief.

I zoomed in with the scope to count the array of enemies before me.

Instead of an army, there were only three malgorths. The center one bore a single rider who stared back at me with a pair of binoculars. She lowered them, her lips curling into a smug smirk.

It was Baura.

30

I lowered the scope and stared at the distant figure. Baura hadn't come here with an army, but she'd brought enough creatures to protect her. There was only one reason to show up like this, and it wasn't to fight. Baura wanted to talk.

The question was, why?

She had apocalypse weapons and control over enough eldritch creatures to end civilization in Prime and Alpha. So, just what in the names of the gods was she doing? Playing with her food before killing it? She'd lured me to this nightmare, presumably to get me out of the way. This had to be a trap.

My tattoos tingled. I leaped off the bike and dodged to the side as a body dropped from the claws of a nightgaunt and thudded to the ground next to me. Another body landed beside the first. Judging from their steampunk attire, they were the missing mechanist scouts.

Each body bore a scrap of paper with a single word, forming the sentence, *Let's talk.*

Approaching Baura and the malgorths was stupid. I'd be out in the open, nightgaunts flying overhead, and the gods only knew what else was lurking in the shadows. But I was also extremely curious as to why she wanted to talk.

The wind whistled, and another body landed atop the others with another message. *Talk, or I attack.*

I raised the scope and looked at her looking at me through her binoculars. I pointed up and slashed my hand sideways. She nodded. The nightgaunts circling overhead flashed away into the distance until I couldn't see them even with my scope. There was hardly a cloud in the sky to hide them, so I at least knew they were truly gone.

It was one less thing to worry about, especially if I was about to talk with Baura. She had nothing to gain by talking with me as far as I knew, and it made far more sense for her to simply end us all with a single strike from Earthmaker.

So, why hadn't she?

I drove the bike down the ledge and jumped it to the canyon floor, then gunned it through the narrow passages until I reached open ground. Within a few minutes, I got as close as I dared to the malgorths. A hundred yards was near enough to talk and far enough away to run if I needed to. The mithrium goggles seemed to be working as promised since I didn't feel so much as a twinge of psychic-induced dread emanating from the malgorths' eyes.

A malgorth extended a trunk-like tentacle from its mouth and wrapped it around Baura's waist. It lowered her gently to the ground, and the tentacle slurped back inside its mouth like a giant strand of spaghetti. She stalked toward me, an insane smirk still on her face, and stopped twenty yards away.

I raised an eyebrow and waited for her to speak.

Baura crossed her arms, the smirk widening into a grin. "Finally, we can converse without the eyes of the gods on us, Cain."

I shrugged. "Here we are, just like you wanted. The perfect first date on a monster-infested world."

Her eyebrows rose. "You already knew that I wanted you to follow me."

"Right from the beginning." It was a lie, of course. "You knew that I couldn't simply let you run free." I waved a hand around. "I don't want our dimension going to hell like this one."

"Exactly!" Baura rubbed her hands together. "We can bargain our way through this, and everyone comes out happy."

"Bargain." I nodded grimly, giving her no doubt that I'd expected this all along even though I had no idea what she wanted. I wouldn't ask why she felt compelled to bargain when she had the might of the apocalypse weapons at her disposal. I still didn't even know how she'd gotten back into the warehouse and taken them in the first place.

The most likely reason for this bargain was because she'd completely lost her grip on reality. Maybe she forgot she had the weapons, or maybe she had an insane reason for not wanting to use them. Clearly, she didn't care about this world, so there was no reason for me to think she'd care about devastating Prime.

Baura narrowed her eyes. "I don't understand you, Cain. You have the power to wipe this place clean, but still, you hold back. Do you really think you can salvage this world?"

It took the space of a heartbeat for me to realize what she was saying. She thought I had the apocalypse weapons. I held onto my poker face. "You just want to kill the gods. Why drag humanity into this?"

She tilted her head slowly to the side. "You're good, Cain, but even you have your tells." Her eyes flared. "You don't have them, do you?"

"Do you really want to test that theory?"

Baura nodded. "Yes, Cain, I do." She grinned. "Fetch Earthmaker and turn this canyon into dunes. Raise Airbender and make it rain." She stepped closer. "Prove to me that you—"

I focused on the space behind her and ghostwalked. She stood just outside my range, but it was worth a shot. There was an instant of cold void and then I stood five feet in front of her instead of behind her. I lunged. Baura dodged back. I cast a shield behind her foot, and she tripped.

I ghostwalked again and this time ended up behind her. A swift chop to the side of her head and Baura went limp. I had her.

The malgorths raced forward, tentacles flailing. I drew my bright-blade and slashed through a pair that darted my way. Another made it through my defenses and wrapped around my ankle as I slashed at two more coming for my face. It snatched me off my feet and dragged me toward the creature, maw undulating and gurgling in anticipation of a meal.

I threw up a hand as if to cast a shield and squeezed my hand. An invisible force clamped down on the tentacle. The malgorth trumpeted in pain and released me. I rolled to the side, looked back toward the motorcycle, and ghostwalked. I blinked into existence ten feet closer to the bike.

The malgorths, however, no longer seemed concerned with me. They wrapped tentacles protectively around Baura, cradling her, and backed away, their great eyes glaring at me.

I blew out a breath and sat down on the rocky soil. The entire interaction had taken place in less than two minutes, but it answered so many questions. Baura didn't have the apocalypse weapons. She'd lured me here because she thought I had them. She'd probably planned to bargain for them, but with what leverage? If I'd had them, then I could have wiped out her entire army.

Baura wasn't stupid enough to have come here without a bargaining chip. She might be insane, but she'd just proven to me that it didn't hinder her ability to reason at all. What could she possibly have that I'd want badly enough to trade apocalypse weapons for?

The short answer: nothing.

Then I noticed the one malgorth that hadn't moved to help the others. The one that lurked behind them, its giant eye focused solely on me. Was it a special malgorth with the ability to pierce the protection of the goggles and psychically compel me to hand over the weapons? If that was the case, Baura probably would have led with that.

"Cain!" Baura rose from the mass of tentacles protecting her and glared down at me. "Did you really think you could just snatch me and run?" She shook with rage. "If you had, then you would've gladly brought me back to trade for my trump card." Baura pointed at the mystery malgorth.

The creature shuddered, and something wet and squirming fell from its underbelly. A tentacle retrieved it and raised it like a prize. A sheath of flesh fell away from the thing revealing a gaunt, naked human form. They were hairless, wriggling like a worm caught on a hook. Then I saw the face and hissed.

"Layla?" Not my Layla, of course, but the one from this world. One that looked as if she'd been starved half to death and tortured.

She raised her head wearily. "Cain? I thought you were dead."

Baura's glare morphed into a maniacal grin. "As you can see, I have someone you love, Cain. Someone you would do anything to protect. I'll offer you this one time and one time only—let's call a truce. You remain here with your dear mechanist friends and leave me be. It's not like you could stop me anyway."

I pursed my lips. "So, you thought I'd trade the apocalypse weapons for Layla? That was your brilliant plan?"

"I'm well aware of your fondness for Layla regardless of which dimension she's from, Cain." Baura sighed. "You used to be strong and callous. But Hannah and Layla have turned you into a loving, doting father figure."

Layla's head lolled, and she groaned. "Cain."

"Yes, Layla?"

"Do you love me?"

I nodded. "Yes."

With every fiber of strength left to her, she lifted her head and glared at me in the way only Layla could. "Do. You. Love. Me?"

"I do."

"Then you know what to do."

Baura's grin widened. "See, Cain? Even Layla agrees."

Layla gritted her teeth as if forcing her head to remain upright. Tears trickled down her cheeks. Not just tears of sadness but tears of desperation.

Baura watched her with glee. "You heard the lady, Cain. Agree to a truce, or the love of your life dies."

My lips quivered. She wasn't my Layla, but she was Layla. It didn't matter which dimension she came from; she was the woman I loved. I cleared my throat. "I love you."

Then I quickly raised my staff and fired a longshot. Layla's head kicked back with the impact. Blood sprayed, and she slumped, free at last. Tears filled my eyes, and the staff dropped from my hand, clattering on the rocky soil.

Baura stared in openmouthed surprise at the corpse, then turned to me, speechless for once.

"I didn't come here to bargain, Baura." I recovered my staff and banished it, then climbed on the motorcycle. "I came here to stop you from spreading this insanity any further. In case you forgot, I still have Soultaker. Don't think I won't unleash that army on you."

She motioned, and the malgorth dropped Layla's body on the ground. Baura regarded me silently. "I know you won't use Soultaker, Cain. The creatures killed by the undead army are absorbed by Soultaker and become part of the army. Outsider souls are able to resist the wielder of the sword and would fight against you."

"It's worth the risk." I tried to stare her down. Tried to convince her I wasn't bluffing, but I could tell she didn't buy it for a moment.

Baura laughed wryly. "I guess you do still have it, Cain." She glanced down at the body. "Your heart of gold still has a dark spot.

"You wouldn't understand why I did it."

Tears sparkled in her eyes. "I understand all too well why you did it. A part of me even admires it. You spared her further agony because you love her." Her teeth clenched. "And that's why the greatest evil must die, no matter the cost. Even if I must plunder a thousand worlds, I will see the end of the gods."

The malgorths flapped their great wings. A tentacle lifted Baura onto the back of the one that had been carrying Layla. Then they turned and left, a herd of eldritch elephants, bearing their mistress back to Heraklion.

I drove slowly across the distance to the gaunt corpse. From a distance, it looked like a sack of flesh with bones threatening to tear free. Layla looked even worse up close. One of her eyes had been burned. There were red sucker marks all over her skin as if roughly handled by tentacles, and there were bite wounds all up and down her body. She had been mistreated and tortured so extensively that it was a wonder she'd survived so long.

I suspected that the torture had begun due to the Cain and Hannah of this world. Baura had probably captured Layla and tried to gain information from her. Or maybe it hadn't been Baura at all. She'd been so preoccupied with killing the gods that perhaps eldritch minions had dealt this damage on their own accord.

It no longer mattered. She was finally at peace. I closed her eyes and rested my hand on her forehead. A part of me wished that the Garrick of this dimension would show up personally to claim her, but it was doubtful he would. As the Christian deity of Death, it was not in his job description to claim the souls of unbelievers.

Layla was half fae, half human, so there was no telling what kind of afterlife awaited her, if any. As an Ekhsis, I wasn't sure if there was anything except a void waiting for me. These were things I tried not to think about. I'd find out soon enough.

I lifted Layla's body and put it on the motorcycle. There was no graceful way to do it, so I slung the corpse over the back of the seat and strapped it down. Then I drove back to the bunker.

The klaxon was still wailing, so I made a slashing motion over my neck, and someone finally shut it off.

Hannah and the others watched me park with equal parts confusion and concern.

Layla was the first to ask. "That's not Baura, is it?"

I shook my head and unstrapped the body. When I laid it on the floor, Hannah gasped.

"It's Layla!"

Layla grimaced. "What the fuck happened out there, Cain?"

I told them.

"You killed Layla?" Hannah wiped tears from her eyes. "Just killed her in cold blood?"

Aura looked from the body to Hannah and nodded. "It was the right call."

"We could have saved her!" Hannah said. "Just shoot the tentacle and grab her or come get us and let us at least plan a rescue."

"He did save her." Layla reached over and put a hand on my shoulder. "Thank you, Cain."

"Yeah." My mouth went dry. I tried to resist the urge to touch her, but my hand slid over hers on its own accord. The touch of her skin against mine felt better than I wanted to admit. My Layla was still alive, but it did little to absolve me of the pain I felt from killing her alt.

She reclaimed her hand and cleared her throat. "I expect the same if I'm ever in the same position."

Aura nodded. "I'll do it in a heartbeat."

Layla turned to Hannah. "Why are you so broken up about my alt, anyway? It's not really me."

"It is you!" Hannah wiped tears from her eyes. "I don't always like you, Layla, but you are my friend. Knowing that Cain would just shoot you without even trying to rescue you makes me sick." She shot me a glare, then stormed away.

My insides knotted, but I didn't go after her. Baura was right. I'd become soft when it came to certain people. I wasn't sure I could have done the same thing if it had been my Layla in that position. I hoped I never had to find out.

Layla sighed. "I don't like having friends. I'm a killer, not some little girl's bestie."

"Hannah isn't a little girl," Aura said. "And having friends doesn't mean you're weak. It means you have something to live for."

"I'm not living for anyone else except little old me." Layla jabbed a thumb to her chest. "I died once, thanks to having friends, and I don't intend on doing it again."

I blinked. "So, that's why you've changed. It wasn't just being imprisoned in Soultaker. You blame us for ending up there in the first place."

Layla worked her jaw back and forth. "Yes, that's a big reason. Ever since I started going on these little adventures of yours, I've been taking more and more unnecessary risks. I haven't been looking out for myself like I should."

Aura frowned. "But you claimed on multiple occasions that these were the most exciting times of your life."

"They were." Layla's gaze went distant. "They gave me adrenaline highs that I couldn't stop chasing. Then Mars killed me, and I ended up in the purest form of hell imaginable. Fighting and dying over and over again. Feeling the agony as my guts were torn out day after day. Being nothing but a mindless berserker with absolutely no control over anything while the real me was locked up and screaming, a prisoner in my own soul."

Aura whistled. "You never put it like that."

"Yeah, because I don't want to think about it!" Layla shivered violently.

I reached out, but she held up a hand and backed away.

"No, Cain. I'm not living that high again either."

"Me touching you?"

She flinched. "You. Just you."

"Layla, you're okay now." Aura held out her hands pleadingly. "You can enjoy life again."

Layla looked toward the bunker door. "I'll enjoy life again when Baura is taken care of. I'll go back to my old life—killing, carousing, and copulation."

Aura blinked. "Have you been waiting to use that alliteration?"

"No, it just came to me." She sighed. "Let's figure out what to do next, okay? The sooner this is over, the better."

Aura opened her mouth to speak, but then her gaze locked onto Horatio, who was jogging toward us.

He stopped abruptly when he saw Layla's body. "Cain, what happened?"

"Baura doesn't have the apocalypse weapons, but she thought I did and planned to use the Layla of this dimension as a bargaining chip to get them." I shook my head. "Then she figured out I didn't have the weapons and tried to use Layla to strike a truce, so I killed her."

Horatio blinked. "She wanted a truce, but you killed her only bargaining chip, so now she will certainly attack?"

I opened my mouth and shut it again. "Well, when you put it like that, it sounds really shortsighted."

I could have bought us some time, but instead, I'd probably fast-forwarded Baura's attack on this base.

31

Maybe it had been impulsive of me to grant Layla a quick death. Baura had asked for a truce, and I'd shattered any chance of that by killing Layla.

"It was the right call." Layla booted the corpse as if it were common garbage. "Baura just wanted to delay us so she could launch Armageddon on our dimension."

Aura tapped a finger on her chin. "If she doesn't have the apocalypse weapons, doesn't that make her much less likely to be able to do that?"

"She has control over the eldritch beings here, so my guess is she controls the Rlhala or another artifact like it." I shook my head. "I already know that the Rlhala from another world works on the Cthulhu of our world. If she takes it over there, she could still unleash chaos with or without the weapons."

"I wouldn't be so sure," Horatio said. "Our order has extensively studied the Elder Things of Gaia. Though there are obviously some creatures that roam freely, most of them are trapped in pockets deep within the world. What you have witnessed here is what happens when all those creatures are freed from their prisons with the power of the apocalypse weapons."

"You're telling me that this world is only overrun because Baura freed them from subterranean prisons?" That was new information to me. "I assume your people found the Rlhala of this world?"

"Yes to both." Horatio pursed his lips. "We found the Rlhala during our search for R'lyeh. It was jutting from the ocean floor among other non-Euclidean structures." Horatio pressed his lips together. "It was to be the key to our plans for world domination, but Baura turned all our weapons against us."

Aura scowled. "Serves you right for trying to take over the world."

"I wanted to kill the gods myself." Horatio sighed. "Now I am doing my best to right my misdeeds."

I steered back to the topic at hand. "So, some monsters like Dagon and Hydra were free all this time, but the mass numbers of monsters were trapped?"

"Precisely." Horatio folded his arms and looked up as if recalling more facts. "Ghasts and gugs were constrained to the vaults of Zin. Hundreds of thousands of other horrors were frozen in ice or dwelling in subterranean pocket worlds. There have always been a goodly number of horrors loose in the world, but they were only remnants of what might have once been an invasion force from the Elder Things. Though they were trapped, they managed to hibernate or survive underground. The many horrors lurking beneath the oceans and the crust of our world were freed with the might of the apocalypse weapons."

"Great. So even our Gaia is infested with eldritch horrors." Aura bit her lower lip. "At least we know that without the apocalypse weapons, Baura can't free the monsters in Prime. I can't imagine she could create a gateway large enough to transport the army from here to Prime, or she would've already done it."

"Also true," Horatio said. "The Tetron might have the capability, but she has obviously not discovered how, or Prime would be overrun."

I'd used the Tetron to travel between dimensions but had never seen it used to hold open a portal as Baura had done. "If there's a way to do it, Noctua would know."

"We once had possession of the little owl, but Baura destroyed it to prevent us from utilizing her vast stores of information." Horatio shook his head. "All that Baura knows she learned from our research or discovered on her own."

I grunted. "Well, she was able to make a small permanent gateway somehow, so it might not be much longer before she figures out how to make larger ones."

"Fascinating." Horatio's gaze went distant. "I believe the Elder Gods are responsible for imprisoning the invading minions of the Elder Things. They are why Cthulhu slumbers and why we are not overrun with creatures. Only the apocalypse weapons were powerful enough to free them."

"Why not just kill them?" Layla said. "Seems idiotic to just bury them."

"An excellent question, but one I cannot answer with my limited knowledge." Horatio sighed. "I would love to know the answer."

I knelt next to Layla Beta's body. "I'm going to bury her and then we need to gather and discuss options."

"Why waste the time?" Layla said. "It's just a bag of flesh and bones."

I cradled the body and began walking up the ramp to the bunker exit. "Because I want to."

"I'm coming." Hannah appeared from behind a building, her face still flushed and angry. "Because it's the right thing to do."

Aura hesitated, then came after us. Layla remained behind an unreadable expression on her face.

The three of us walked outside the bunker and down the canyon until I found a small area just off the beaten trail. Using the bright-blade, I carved a rectangular hole in the rocky ground, then cast a wide shield and bound it to follow the motions of my hand. It slid under the soil and scooped it out like a shovel.

Hannah watched with a confused expression. "I've never seen you use shields like that."

"I haven't." I shrugged. "It just seemed like it would work."

"That's thinking outside the box."

I wondered if I could move the soil without shields in the same way I'd cut through that tentacle with my mind. I was either developing telekinesis, or I'd discovered a way to make shields without casting them. It would certainly be a useful skill to develop, provided I survived Baura's next move.

It didn't take long to dig the hole. I laid Layla's body inside, then picked up a handful of dirt in my bare hand and let it fall over the body like sand from an hourglass. "Rest well, Layla."

Hannah did the same. "Rest well, Layla from Beta."

Aura tossed a handful of dirt on the body. "You were probably a bitch like our Layla, but this still sucks."

Hannah rolled her eyes. "Eloquent."

Aura nodded. "Thanks."

I used another shield to scoop the dirt back over the hole, then brushed my hands together. There really wasn't anything else to say, so I gave Layla Beta a moment of silence before turning back toward the bunker.

Hannah strode alongside me. "What now, Cain?"

"Have you forgiven me for killing Layla Beta?"

She scowled. "I was just shocked. I thought for sure you'd try to save her first. I mean, you saved our alts on Alpha."

"I did save her, Hannah. Just not in the way you wanted me to." I put a hand on her shoulder. "Her eye was burned out. She was covered in sores and nearly starved to death. I had no chance of rescuing her from Baura. And..." I blew out a breath. "She asked me to kill her."

"Why do you leave important stuff like that out of your stories, Cain?" Hannah shook her head. "You just said you shot her. You didn't say Blayla asked you to kill her."

"Blayla?" Aura groaned. "We're just putting the first letter of the dimension in front of their names now?"

Hannah ignored her. "Use your words, Cain. Then maybe I won't get so pissed at you."

I changed the subject. "How did your mega pilot training go?"

She looked like she wasn't ready to let go of the argument, then blew out an exasperated breath. "It was fine. The controls are easy, but there's definitely some lag in the response. The trick is to keep the movements precise and not overcompensate, or you'll end up falling over. It's like fighting a bucking horse."

"That doesn't sound great." I headed down the ramp into the bunker. "Maybe it's better to let a mechanist deal with it."

She shook her head. "No way. I've always wanted to fight monsters with a giant robot."

I snorted. "Always?"

"Well, ever since you got me hooked on sci-fi movies."

Aura kicked a pebbled down the ramp. "Hannah controlled that mega far better than the mechanist before her, but it does seem risky putting her on the frontlines like that."

"It's riskier not putting me on the frontlines." Hannah narrowed her eyes at Aura. "We'll need every edge we can get, depending on what Baura throws at us."

"Our goal isn't to defeat her army," Aura said. "It's to capture her. We should let the mechanists be the diversion while we slip in behind enemy lines and take her. No reason you should die like Bhannah did."

Hannah wrinkled her nose. "Don't try to come up with nicknames for our alts, Aura. It's not your strong suit."

"As if putting a B in front of their names is any better!"

I veered the discussion back on topic. "It won't be that easy to capture Baura." I reached the bottom of the ramp and stopped to watch the mechanists scrambling vehicles, exos, and personnel into formation. Their response time left something to be desired, but it wasn't terrible considering what they'd cobbled together with rescued nubs. "I nearly had Baura, but the Malgorths protected her. I can guarantee she won't be vulnerable in her stronghold."

Aura folded her arms and stared blankly for a moment, lost in thought. "Maybe you can use Panoptes to surprise her."

"Maybe." It was the best stealth option we had, but the downside was that only one person could use it. "Navigating the eye to wherever she's located would be extremely taxing, and she's bound to have plenty of protection around her since she knows we might try something like that."

Layla joined us. "How was the funeral?"

"The pastor gave a heartbreaking sermon, and everyone cried." Hannah pretended to wipe tears from her eyes. "It's too bad her only family wasn't there."

"Well, that's wonderful." Layla turned to me. "So, any brilliant ideas about what we're doing next?"

"Nothing brilliant," I said. "Just a few half-assed thoughts."

"Great." She pursed her lips. "Maybe you should go back to the warehouse and search for the missing apocalypse weapons. One of those would be really handy right about now."

Hannah frowned. "Who could have stolen them if it wasn't Baura?"

"It sounds like something only a god could do." Aura let that sink in before continuing. "Maybe they finally took matters into their own hands."

"The gods aren't omniscient," I said. "They'd have to know where the weapons are to take them. Besides, I think once they were in mortal hands, they couldn't simply take them unless they were used directly against them."

"They let Cain keep Soultaker, so it's doubtful they'd steal the other weapons." Hannah nodded as if agreeing with herself. "Unless the gods of chaos did it."

"A god of chaos would've probably given them to Baura." I ran through a list of possibilities and pinned down one that seemed most likely. "The warehouse is supposedly abandoned, but maybe that's not true. Maybe someone else has access to it and made off with the weapons."

"Maybe they just hid the weapons somewhere else inside the warehouse." Layla produced a dagger from somewhere and began idly twirling it in her hand. "I say someone goes to the warehouse and scours the place for clues. Maybe the weapons are there but hidden."

"Do we have time for that?" Hannah said. "Baura might launch an attack at any minute."

"We can't afford not to at least try." Layla spun her dagger again. "Give me the ring, and I'll go look."

Hannah produced the ring from inside a pocket and held it out. "Knock yourself out."

The dagger vanished from Layla's hand as she took the ring and slid it on. "I'll be back."

I held up a hand to stop her, but she vanished. "Great. What if I need the ring to sneak up on Baura in the next hour?"

"I doubt she'll be gone long. Besides, she can keep an eye on things here." Hannah cracked her knuckles. "I'm going to train some more with the mega. Looks like we'll need to be ready sooner rather than later."

"Looks like it." I left them and went in search of Horatio. I located him inside his command center, huddled around a table with mechanists in royal blue uniforms. "Are we ready to defend against an attack?"

Horatio straightened and regarded me. "As ready as we can be. We're fully mobilized and waiting. If Baura attacks, there's only one way into the bunker."

I examined the map in the center of the table. The canyon leading to the entrance was marked with multiple dots. "What are those?"

"They were to be clockwork mine emplacements, but they were never removed from the submarine that carried them." Horatio ran a hand down his face. "It was a logistics oversight that may cost us dearly since there's no way to retrieve them now."

The map was marked with elevations and geology that might be challenging for human invaders but meant practically nothing to creatures that could squeeze through crevices as wide as the flat of my hand or crawl up and over cliffs as if they were nothing.

"How confident are you that the cracks in this place are filled in?"

A woman spoke. "We have identified hundreds of possible infiltration points for thropids and ghasts and sealed them all. That said, my confidence level is only eighty percent that they can't find another way in."

"Better than nothing." I jabbed a finger at the bunker entrance.

"That's the only bottleneck you need to worry about. Set up rear scouts to warn of danger to the flanks, but once the monsters start pouring in, unload everything into them. That will at least put a dent in their numbers. While you're keeping them busy, I'll try to snatch Baura."

Horatio nodded. "It seems to be our only option."

Murmurs of agreement rose from the others at the table.

I looked over a blueprint of the facility to reveal any holes in that defense. "Are the missile silo doors sealed?"

"Yes," the woman said. "We ensured not even a roach could get through the cracks."

"How are your food supplies?" I turned to Horatio. "Baura might siege us and try to starve us out."

"We have enough food stores to last a year," Horatio said. "The military rations aren't ideal, but they will keep us alive. However, judging from previous experiences, it's doubtful the creatures will try to starve us out. They have the sheer force of numbers and were willing to throw everything they had at us in similar encounters."

A radio crackled, and a woman spoke. "Drones and scouts report no activity."

"Keep me informed." I left the room and let them get back to it. There wasn't much more I could do, so I decided to catch a quick nap in the bunkhouse Horatio had provided for us.

I WOKE UP AN HOUR LATER, somewhat surprised that I hadn't been awakened by perimeter alarms or gunfire. I went to the main bunker and found the mechanist troops milling around and looking anything but battle-ready. I went back into Horatio's war room for an update.

"Still no signs of an impending attack," Horatio told me when I asked. "Even our long-distance drones have seen nothing."

I raised an eyebrow. "Well, that's concerning."

"Is it?" Horatio looked uncertain. "I thought it was a good omen."

"Maybe, but probably not." I blew out a breath. "Can your long-distance drones see into Heraklion? We need to know what Baura is up to."

"If we send them too far out, the nightgaunts will destroy them." Horatio sighed. "Our cameras can only zoom in to see the outskirts of the city, I'm afraid."

I grabbed a wireless radio. "I'll be back." I went to the motor pool and hopped on a dirt cycle, gunning it up the ramp and outside. I crisscrossed ledges and rode them to the top of a cliff for a better view. One of the mechanist drones buzzed above me, its old-timey brass camera clicking as it scanned the horizon.

There was nothing on the horizon. No malgorths, hordes of shoggoths, or shambling mobs of deep ones. I zoomed in with my scope, taking in the outskirts of Heraklion in the distance. All looked quiet on the northern front, and that disturbed me even more than if I'd seen an army marching on us.

Baura wasn't simply biding her time or gathering troops. She was up to something completely different—something unanticipated. That was the danger of trying to calculate the actions of someone whose mind rode the razor's edge between sanity and madness.

I'd killed her supposed trump card, but Layla Beta had been intended as a trade for apocalypse weapons I didn't have. If I didn't have them, then I was worthless in Baura's eyes. I had no means to stop her, and she had no reason to come after me. She'd offered me a truce to keep me out of the way of her plans—but what could those plans possibly be?

She'd lured me here in order to seize the apocalypse weapons because she needed them to free the eldritch on Prime. Now that she knew I didn't have them, there was no need to attack the mechanist compound. What did that mean for her next steps? Unless she could make a larger portal, it seemed doubtful that she'd try marching her army through the existing one. Besides, the existing one led to Feary Prime, not Gaia. It seemed highly doubtful that she'd lead an assault on the fae to start her conquest.

Baura, of course, wasn't completely rational, so maybe she would. Or maybe she'd create a new portal that went to Gaia Prime and begin trickling monsters through. Her options would be limited since anything larger than a shoggoth wouldn't fit. Without malgorths, her invasion force could be mowed down by nub military forces.

Anticipating Baura's next actions just wasn't possible. I had to go and find out what she was up to in person. Maybe she was pacing around her makeshift throne room also trying to decide what to do next, or maybe she'd made an impulsive decision and was acting on it. Or maybe she had a backup plan in case she couldn't get the apocalypse weapons from me—a worst-case scenario. I couldn't discount any possibilities with her because the wreckage of this world aptly demonstrated that she had no moral limits, no qualms about destroying anything and everything in her way.

Driving a motorcycle into downtown Heraklion would be reckless and stupid. But it also seemed like the only viable option if I wanted to know for sure what was happening since the drones couldn't get close. The dirt cycle's two-stroke engine was powerful and made for cross-country driving. The main danger would come from nightgaunts unless there were also giant dhole worms to worry about.

I mulled over the idiocy of the idea and decided it was worth it. A sound muffling sigil reduced the loud motorcycle exhaust to little more than a mosquito buzz. A camouflage blind reduced vision of me to a moving blur across the landscape. Those precautions might increase my odds ever so slightly.

The nightgaunts probably wouldn't be fooled, so I cast a shield overhead. It wasn't strong enough to withstand a full-on assault, but it'd slow down the silent menaces long enough to give me a fighting chance.

I took out the portable wireless and depressed the button on the side. "This is Cain. I'm going on a scouting run."

The radio crackled. "I don't recognize that call sign. Please repeat."

"It's not a call sign."

Horatio replied. "Cain, is that wise?"

"No, but I'm doing it anyway." We didn't have the luxury of sitting back and seeing what happened next because Baura's next move might be against Prime itself.

32

I slid the wireless clip over my belt and navigated the motorcycle back down the cliff. Then I headed northwest, angling toward the outer fringe of Heraklion rather than diving straight down the throat of the beast.

As it turned out, monsters were the least of my worries. The terrain was broken—shattered in places where the far-reaching effects of Earthmaker left their mark. Baura had reshaped the island, either on purpose or as collateral damage, when she'd gone on her original rampage. The dirt bike handled everything except gaping chasms and daunting drop-offs.

Navigating around the obstacles took me out of the way several times, forcing me to backtrack south or east. It was inconvenient, but I couldn't complain since I hadn't seen a single monster on land or in the air. The almost absolute silence was more than eerie—it was unsettling right down to my very core.

All wildlife had been wiped out by the invaders. There were bones and signs of former life, but the countryside had been eaten clean, leaving a void of sound once filled by insects and birds.

The lack of monsters was also cause for concern. If they weren't roaming the countryside looking for food, that meant Baura had commanded them elsewhere. It meant that maybe she was planning an attack and simply hadn't amassed enough creatures for her satisfaction. Or perhaps she had a secret way into the bunker.

It made me wonder how exactly she was controlling them. The malgorths had responded to her as if she'd communicated psychically. If she was using a Rlhala to command the creatures through Cthulhu, then it was possible she'd established a psychic link with him, and he was relaying commands even though she wasn't touching the Rlhala.

It was also possible she'd achieved a direct link to the monsters, but that seemed doubtful. The mental capacity to control so many beings at once seemed out of reach for those without godlike abilities. Unless the Rlhala conveyed such abilities to the wielder, it was unlikely that Baura controlled them directly.

She'd probably commanded Cthulhu to serve as her link whether she was touching the Rlhala or not. I'd never thought to do that with my Rlhala and probably wouldn't have risked it. Linking my mind with a powerful source of insanity was the last thing I would've willingly done.

I finally reached the western outskirts of Heraklion. Where there had once been a beach was now nothing but sand and a sheer drop of about a hundred feet to the blue waters. Crashing waves echoed far below, but another unsettling sound reached my ears from ahead.

I slowed and stopped. Cocked an ear toward town and cast an amplification sigil. What at first sounded like a low rumbling resolved into animalistic gurgling and growling. Goosebumps rose along my skin. There were words mixed in with the animal sounds, but I couldn't make them out.

"That can't be good." I dispelled the amplification sigil and let the warmth of not hearing it melt the goosebumps. Baura was up to something, and I really didn't want to find out what it was. The mithrium goggles might protect me against visual mind traps, but they did nothing against the slithering susurrus of insanity against my eardrums.

I cleared my thoughts and gathered my wits. My training allowed me to guard myself against psychic traps from most sources unless it was injected directly under my skin. I'd just have to be very careful, even going so far as to muffle my hearing if I had to.

I hated approaching danger without all my senses at full capacity, but sometimes there was no other way. I'd had to temporarily deafen myself to avoid the lure of a siren song once. It had been unpleasant but necessary. I wouldn't resort to such means unless it seemed unavoidable.

A twist of the throttle hurtled me toward whatever destiny lay in wait at the rotting heart of Heraklion. I didn't see any high-rise buildings with a superior view of the surroundings that might allow me to see the city center.

The land was flat, and the tallest buildings were no more than four stories high. The roads were cracked, the buildings slumped and leaning from the impact Earthmaker had delivered. Most of them didn't look safe for climbing. Then I spotted a cell tower to my southeast and aimed toward it.

The gurgling, growling, and chanting grew louder as I dodged wrecked cars and rubble. The sense of uneasiness grew into anxiety as the malevolent song of madness stabbed into the fear center of my amygdala. I resisted muting them and practiced self-control over my involuntary functions. The exercise reminded me of the most challenging situations thrown at me by the Oblivion Guard and how they paled in comparison.

This wasn't my first rodeo with maddening sounds. Shub-Nuggerath's dark young had one-upped just about everything I'd ever experienced. The cacophony echoing through the city streets wasn't as powerful, but it was bad enough.

I parked near the cell tower. It sat in a patch of green surrounded by what had once been painted concrete buildings but were now crooked slabs with rusting rebar jutting like bones from their remains. My brightblade sliced a section from the chain-link fence and cut the padlock from the door guarding the base of the ladder.

Climbing all the way to the top would take a while, so I only went as far as I needed for a superior view of the city. Finding the source of the chanting took little more than a glance at the northern shore. There were no more buildings in that section of town. Instead, there was a bowl-shaped crater that looked as if the earth had been neatly carved out by a gigantic melon scoop. The sides sloped gently down, ribbed with ledges of varying heights.

Geometry-defying shapes jutted from the center of the crater— twisting spires and crooked buildings that seemed carved from the bedrock. Foaming waves rushed through a wide canal leading from the sea and into the center of the crater where they crashed against the structures. The mind-bending creations were certainly the work of Earthmaker coupled with a mind that had been twisted by eldritch illogic. They reminded me of buildings I'd seen in R'lyeh and even in Fyeth Elunore.

That was when I realized they weren't just structures. They were temples carved with runes and glyphs that resembled those I'd seen on the Rlhala. I took out my phone and started recording, zooming in as far as I could without losing clarity.

Gathered around these unholy artifacts was a host of monsters— malgorths, shoggoths, deep ones, and more. The entire known bestiary of eldritch creatures seemed present at whatever was going on below. They glugged, ribbited, shrieked, and howled, verbalizing in a terrifying array of inhuman noises. They were the source of the sounds that set my sanity on edge.

The chin of a frog-like deep one ballooned out grotesquely before unleashing a thunderous croak. Another's entire torso swelled, raising spikes along its pink flesh like a pufferfish. An angler fish hybrid suckled greedily at the spikes as if they were nipples filled with mother's milk. I'd seen a lot of abominations, but the variety of deep ones never ceased to amaze and disgust me.

Down in the bottom of the crater where the ocean waters pooled around the structures stood dozens of humanoid figures in white robes. I zoomed in with my scope and focused on them. They were magical practitioners, maybe sorcerers, but it was hard to tell. Large symbols like nothing I'd ever seen had been carved into the stone around the semicircular platform around the spires.

New monsters with bodies resembling wrinkled old scrotums appeared from the left. They were pear-shaped and stumpy with huge feet and humanoid arms and hands. A single giant eye blinked in the center of their ballsack bodies. They didn't resemble deep ones or other typical eldritch creatures, and I didn't recall seeing them in Lovecraft's journals. I wished I could unsee them.

The walking scrotums escorted filthy, naked humans toward the circle of sorcerers, gave them each a prisoner, then waddled back to wherever they'd come from. Shouting the R'lyehian language in unison, the sorcerers raised jagged knives to the throats of their captives. In one synchronized move, they slashed from ear to ear and yanked back on the hair of the victims to open their arteries wide. Blood spilled onto the stone, filling the grooves of the giant symbol beneath them.

Two other symbols counterclockwise from the ritualists were already stained crimson. There were several more to go, but from this perspective, I couldn't make them all out.

The animalistic symphony rose in volume as the drained bodies were hauled away and disposed of somewhere I couldn't see. No doubt the shoggoths and others were upset to see good food wasted. Or perhaps they were excited for the feast to come once this ritual concluded. My concern was answered seconds later as nightgaunts swooped down and back up, corpses clutched in their claws, barbed tails tickling the dead to no avail.

They ripped the bodies to shreds, dropping the bits among the monsters. The gathering quickly devolved into a fray as creatures fought for body parts. The onslaught just as quickly died down once every morsel had been devoured. The ritualists around the symbol continued chanting, ignoring the feasting monsters until they completed their chant.

They knelt, touched their foreheads to the bloody ground, then rose and moved to the next symbol where they once again began to intone a ritual.

I looked up and around, ever aware of my surroundings in case a nightgaunt should spot me and come my way, but they were preoccupied with the proceedings below, and my camouflage blind still blurred me from sight.

Climbing higher, I reached a platform with a better view. I continued recording with my phone once I was situated. This time I turned my attention to the symbols around the R'lyehian structures. I noticed familiar patterns within the symbols and checked them against pictures I'd taken of a R'lyehian text from Fyeth Elunore.

These weren't giant symbols—they were entire phrases carved into the stone. The language was just so illogical to my human brain that I hadn't seen them for what they were.

Some of the symbols were in my R'lyehian dictionary, but not nearly enough to enable me to translate even a fraction of them. Noctua was the only non-eldritch being who could comprehend the chaotic language, but I knew what the first symbol grouping meant all too well.

Ph'nglui mglw'nafh Cthulhu R'lyeh wgah'nagl fhtagn.

That translated to, *In his house at R'lyeh, dead Cthulhu waits dreaming.*

The other symbol groupings referenced Cthulhu and R'lyeh, but my meager dictionary didn't have nearly enough information to properly translate.

Something massive stirred in the waters around the structures. A scaly green ridge jutted from the waters on one side. Blue-gray tentacles flailed on the opposite. A reptilian head emerged, huge fish eyes rotating. Its mottled green skin was covered in what looked like barnacles and squirming parasites. A guttural, gurgling purr spewed water and unidentifiable gray chunks into the air.

The head of the other creature appeared, blue-gray tentacles writhing atop it like living hair. A long spiky fin ran from its neck down to its tail. The second giant creature climbed out of the water and gripped the crooked spire on its side. The other monster clenched the opposite spire.

Gurgling and purring like sick cats, they rubbed against the spires, ejaculating thick green or blue slime from their crotches. The ritualists and monsters watched, entranced. Deep ones cried out, falling to their knees and worshipping as their gods performed grotesque acts for reasons I couldn't even guess. I kept recording, spellbound and sickened by kinky monster sex.

From my brief conversation with the deep ones at the mansion, I already knew who they were—Father Dagon, the green one on the left, and blue-gray Mother Hydra to the right. I lowered the mithrium goggles, and madness washed over me. Forcing myself to rely on my training, I let the sick feeling worm into my bowels and the crevices of my mind. The practice was necessary in case the goggles broke.

That, and I wanted to see if I could withstand the power of these Great Old Ones.

It took everything I had to resist the siren call of insanity—to fight the urge to throw myself from the tower, run to these gods, and debase my body and soul for their pleasure. I wanted to crawl into their maws and feel the comforting pressure of their warm gullets.

The fishy hybrid humanoids spawned by the deep ones had no such resistance. Many ran to the edges of the water, screaming and shouting at their gods. Hydra and Dagon ignored them at first but eventually ceased sliming the spires and turned toward their worshippers.

Hydra lowered herself back into the water and swam to the water's edge, her spiny back fin bristling. She raised her mouth and opened it. Eager worshipers leaped off the edge, falling inside the massive maw. She chomped down, masticating to cries of ecstasy from the deep ones who watched proudly as their offspring became one with their mother. Others did the same for Dagon, feeding the monster that looked like a mix between the Swamp Thing and baby Godzilla.

This was some of the sickest shit I'd ever seen, and I'd seen a lot of unholy rituals. What in the hell was Baura up to? Why was she allowing these monsters to perform a ritual instead of gathering her forces and wiping out the mechanists? Dagon and Hydra alone could probably destroy all resistance. The megas were huge, but these beasts were even larger.

I finally spotted Baura. She stood alone, tucked away from the monster madness, watching with a bored expression and seemingly unaffected by the psychotic waves emanating from Dagon and Hydra. Now that I'd been watching without the goggles for several minutes, those emanations were nothing more than spikes of anxiety in the back of my mind, pooling like curdled milk in the depths of my bowels. It wasn't pleasant, but I could live with it.

I contemplated blasting Baura's head with a longshot. It wouldn't permanently kill her, but it'd put her out of commission until midnight, which might buy us some time. It was a difficult shot from this distance, but not impossible for me. But it would instantly alert nightgaunts and other creatures that could reach me in seconds.

The camouflage blind might hide me, or it might not. Either way, I'd be trapped, and there was no guarantee that action would delay this mystery ritual. I watched the ritual for the next symbols from beginning to end. The sorcerers chanted, danced, and debased themselves, even disrobing and slapping each other's genitals relentlessly at one point. It took nearly an hour before they reached the blood ritual.

This time they didn't sacrifice humans. Instead, a group of hybrid deep ones stepped forward and lay face down on the engravings. The sorcerers carved bloody symbols on their skin, then drove daggers deep into their backs, piercing their hearts from behind. Once the grooves were filled with blood, Dagon and Hydra plucked the bodies and tossed them like withered grapes into their maws.

There were seven more symbol groupings, meaning at least that many more hours remained before the rituals were complete. Something told me that it was vitally important to stop the proceedings at any cost. With all of Baura's minions gathered in one place and preoccupied, now was the perfect time for an attack.

33

I climbed back down the tower, refreshed the muffling and camouflage sigils, and started back toward the mechanist compound. I took a more direct route since all the monsters were at the ritual. What I really needed was information from Noctua, but while the owl whistle she'd given me worked across the planes like Oblivion, Gaia, and Feary, it didn't work across dimensions.

The Noctua here was destroyed, and the one from Alpha was nonfunctional, leaving only the one from Prime available. I could go all the way back to the open portal, but first I needed to check in with Horatio and the others.

Layla, Aura, and Hannah weren't in the upper bunker, so I went to Horatio's command center and found him and others still huddled around the table watching drone video from a flickering projector.

I turned it off to a chorus of groans and surprised gasps from the others. "I found out what Baura is up to." With the video playing on my phone, I set it on the table and showed them.

"Disgusting!"

A woman gasped. "My gods, they're throwing themselves into their mouths!"

"This is horrific!" Another mechanist shivered and looked away. "What in the names of the Elder Things are they doing, Cain?"

Horatio stared in wide-eyed shock, then abruptly stood and began pulling yellowed scrolls from a shelf and unfurling them for a quick look before rolling them up and stowing them again. He found one with tattered edges and hissed a breath between his teeth. He laid it on the table and pinned the edges down with brass cogs.

A diagram in the center of the scroll matched the symbols and shapes of the structures from the crater. Dense Alder text encircled the diagram, each paragraph connected by a line to the symbol groups. I had to lean over so I could make out the words.

"Where did you get this?" I asked.

"It was taken from the library of Fyeth Elunore after our Cain and the goddess purged the Dead Forest of the minions of Shub-Nuggerath." Horatio shook his head. "We did it to win the fae to our cause, but war broke out among several kingdoms, and Feary devolved into chaos."

I leaned over the text and began reading it aloud.

"Dead Cthulhu, slumbering for his sins. Slumbering in death, an eternal punishment. Hear our pleas, oh, Cthulhu. Let our praise reach your dead ears." I moved to the next one. "You were a blessing on our world. A servant of Elder Gods no more, your slumber has soaked in the power of a million ages. Hear our pleas, oh, Cthulhu. Let our praise touch your mind."

Below each paragraph were instructions to go along with the chant. Dancing, singing to the precise tune required, sex rituals, and various bodily fluids of different creatures. The first required crushed sex organs of ganthagons and malgorths. The next, liquified brains from a dozen different creatures. Human blood was required to seal each ritual binding since Gaia was owned by humans, and only they could invite the desired madness.

And what they desired was to awaken Cthulhu.

"Our world is doomed unless we stop this." Horatio's face blanched until it was nearly green. He swallowed with difficulty and winced as his gorge refused to go down. "Why would Baura wish to raise Cthulhu?"

I didn't know the answer, but I guessed at one anyway. "He might be the only one powerful enough to allow her to open a giant gateway to our dimension. Or he might be the key to bringing other deities here who could do it."

"If she unleashes Cthulhu, I don't know if the mithrium goggles will be of any use." Horatio shivered violently. "We'll all be completely mad."

I'd seen Cthulhu in his dreams and experienced the creeping madness he inspired even in that state. The full living version of him supposedly caused instant madness. His countenance was probably akin to a hundred malgorths. Hydra and Dagon emanated harsher psychotic waves than malgorths, but even they likely paled in comparison to the behemoth specter of Cthulhu.

I quickly skimmed the rest of the text and discovered our only hope. The ritual had to be completed in a specific order and precisely. If it was interrupted for long enough or the wrong ingredients placed on the symbols, then it would have to be restarted.

At the end of the ritual, human blood would have to be spilled on the Rlhala. There was no mention that this needed to happen anywhere special, meaning it would be done wherever Baura had it stored.

We could target the Rlhala, or we could simply try to disrupt the ritual and hope it was enough to stop it cold.

We needed to invade and unleash everything we had into that crater. It was possible we could march there undetected since Baura's minions were so busy with the ritual. The tricky part would be navigating the terrain with the megas and vehicles, but the route I'd taken on my return would suffice with a few modifications.

I whirled a finger. "Round up your forces. We've got less than seven hours to stop this."

Horatio rosed on trembling legs and clapped his hands. "Make haste, people! Gather those under your command and assemble them outside of the canyons. Be ready to march within the hour."

The others scrambled out of the room, talking urgently into their radios.

I held Horatio back. "I need something that goes boom. The biggest boom possible."

"We salvaged several warheads from the remaining missiles in the silos," he said. "They're all conventional warheads but with powerful payloads. That should be more than enough to kill most of the monsters in the crater, provided a direct strike."

"Do you have any fully assembled missiles?"

He shook his head. "Even if we did, the systems to control their flight are no longer functional."

"Show me what you've got."

Horatio led me outside to his car. The bunker echoed with rumbling engines and bustling soldiers. Troops loaded into the backs of trucks. Military vehicles filed up the ramp and outside. There were a lot of frightened faces and wide eyes behind mithrium goggles, but the rag-tag army was in full motion.

A soldier held up a hand as Horatio drove us toward the ramps leading down to the missile silos. "Sir, please wait. The megas are coming."

Dull thuds echoed from below. Moments later, the first mega, this one piloted by Hannah, rumbled into the main bunker. Soldiers stopped and cheered, whistling and clapping as she navigated the giant robot. Grinning, Hannah waved, and the mega mimicked her actions precisely, albeit with a few milliseconds of lag.

Then she continued up and out of the bunker. The other two megas appeared moments apart. The pilots looked stressed to the max, wrestling the hulks with every ounce of grace and skill they could muster. Their megas stumbled more than they walked, but at least they remained upright. I had a terrible feeling that they'd be hard-pressed to function well in battle, especially if it came down to a fight with Dagon and Hydra.

Then again, we might not even make it that far. This might be a real quick trip to the afterlife if Baura had more monsters hidden and waiting in reserve.

Horatio drummed his fingers on the steering wheel while we waited, then gunned the clockwork car down the ramp after the last mega passed. He didn't look the least bit pleased about these marvels of mechanist engineering, probably because he felt as concerned as I did about the pilots controlling them.

The car zoomed down and around, then turned into the area opposite the mega docks. We entered a room piled high with munitions crates and benches loaded with clockwork cogs and gears of various sizes. Judging from the discarded crates and weapons parts, this was where the mechanists adapted the weapons for use with exos, megas, and other vehicles.

Three missile tips sat on another bench, the metal casing around them peeled open to reveal the computerized parts inside. They were about the size of my torso and head put together. I hefted one, but just barely. It had to weigh at least a couple hundred pounds.

"Well, this is no good." I powered all my body sigils and could barely carry it. "I'd hoped for something more portable."

"They're portable with an exo-suit." Horatio pointed to a non-weaponized cargo hauler.

I shook my head. "Let me explain. I need to be able to catapult these things into the crater somehow." An idea came to me. "Maybe a mega can do it."

He nodded enthusiastically. "Yes, I'm certain they could. I'll have the warheads hauled outside for you."

"Good. Can you get me to Hannah's mega? I'll need to do some test runs."

"Of course." He clicked on his radio and issued a few commands, then we went back to the car. Moments later, we left the bunker and reached the assembled army on the scrub brush plain beyond the canyons.

I hopped out and jogged over to Hannah's mega where she was trying to train the other pilots during the wait. Her instructions seemed to be having a positive effect since the other pilots no longer looked as if they were more likely to wreck their megas before they ever actually saw battle.

"Hannah!" I waved my arms to get her attention.

Her mega knelt smoothly, almost as if it were an extension of herself, and she grinned out from behind the transparent faceplate. "What's up?"

I motioned toward some boulders that looked about as heavy as the warheads. "I need you to pick those up and throw them as far as you can."

Hannah frowned. "Are we using boulders as weapons now?"

"No. I want your mega to throw missile warheads, but first I need to see how effective it is."

A delighted gasp escaped her mouth. "Oh, that sounds like fun!"

"Yeah, loads of fun." I nodded at the boulders. "Toss a few and let me see how you do."

She looked sideways, and the mega's head rotated with hers. "How big of a target am I aiming at?"

I pointed to a rocky hill in the distance. "Try to hit that."

Her mega rose to its feet and lumbered over to the boulders. Its giant hand clamped onto the largest boulder and ripped it effortlessly out of the earth. The extra weight caused it to stumble, but Hannah shifted the mega's feet to adjust. Carefully, she cocked back its arm, then threw the boulder.

It flew far and well wide of the hill, missing it by a hundred yards or more. Hannah lifted another and threw it. This one overshot the target. She continued, using up all the boulders in the vicinity. Only one came close to the target.

"This is going to take a lot of practice." She knelt so I could see her behind the faceplate. "How many warheads do we have?"

"Three."

She grimaced. "What if I miss?"

Judging from her practice throws, it seemed likely she would. "I may have to find another way."

A mechanist with a shaved head jogged over to us. "Sir, are you planning to use the megas like catapults so we can rain hell on the monsters?"

I shook my head. "No, I'm looking for a way to deliver weaponized payloads."

He grinned. "I'm a former airman from the United States. You tell me what you need, and I'll tell you if it's possible." He cupped a hand to his mouth, a conspiratorial look on his face. "These mechanists make shit way more complicated than it needs to be."

I held out my hand. "I'm Cain."

He gripped it and shook it. "Kyle Smithey, sir. Pleased to meet the famous Cain, or at least the alternate dimension version of ours."

Another man in olive camouflage hurried over. "Kyle, what's going on? I haven't seen you so excited since we blew up a malgorth with an IED."

I turned to him. "I need a precise way to deliver missile warheads without the missiles. Sounds like you two are experts in the field."

"Ground combat and recon for me," the second man said. "I jumped out of helicopters and raided compounds back in the day." He shrugged. "It was a living."

Kyle grinned. "I make the weapons, and Eric can get them anywhere you want them to go."

I took out my phone and showed them the video of the crater.

Kyle grimaced. "Holy Mary, mother of dog. I still can't get over how sick in the head these fuckers are."

Eric rubbed his hands together. "That is a perfect concentration of monsters, dude. One big payload in the right place, and we could frag hundreds of them."

I clicked on the radio. "Horatio, this is Cain. Where are the warheads?"

"They're being brought up with exos," he replied a moment later.

Eric and Kyle snorted in unison.

"Don't get me wrong, I love their robot suits, but trucks are better and faster." Kyle tapped a finger on his chin. "I don't think we have the equipment for a timed detonation, so we'll have to arm the warheads to blow on impact. They'll need to be armed just before reaching the target. If you hit a bump too hard with an armed warhead, you're just as likely to set it off by accident."

I hadn't even considered the possibility. "Can you two to work out a delivery system and get back to me before we move out?"

"Dude, we're so on it." Eric clapped his hands together. "This shit is as crazy as some of the D and D sessions I used to host back before the world turned into a live-action horror campaign."

"Man, I used to have a hummer with bloody handprints on it because I loved Halloween so much." Kyle sighed. "Twelve-foot-tall skeletons for Christmas decorations, coffins in the front yard, you name it. Much as I love horror, I kind of wish it was back to being make-believe again."

I clapped his shoulder. "Unfortunately, all those horrors were hiding right under your noses the entire time—vampires, werewolves, witches, and more. But at least they're human. These eldritch monsters don't care about humanity, and if they succeed in raising Cthulhu, then it's game over for Gaia."

"Gaia." Eric chuckled. "I still haven't gotten used to that term." He turned to Kyle. "Let's get cooking."

They walked off to meet with the exos, and I went back to examining the video footage of the crater, looking for any weaknesses I could exploit.

If this plan failed, we stood no chance against Baura's nightmare army.

34

It took the better part of an hour before all the vehicles, exos, and soldiers were assembled. Horatio and his commanders were inspecting their sections, readying them mentally for the trial to come.

I told Horatio to hold off on moving out until we had a solution for the warheads. Kyle and Eric found me not long after and led me to the back of the army, where I found the warheads strapped into the bed of an HMMWV.

"We've got some options for you," Eric said. "We could go for all the eggs in one basket approach. It's a bigger bang in one go but with more risk if something compromises the vehicle. The next option is dividing up the warheads between three vehicles. The downside is more moving parts, more that can go wrong. If the drivers don't time it properly, the bombs won't be delivered simultaneously, giving the monsters time to react and scatter."

"But a variation on that option is we approach the crater from three angles." Kyle led me to a patch of bare dirt where he'd drawn an outline of the crater. He placed three rocks at positions west, east, and south. "They synchronize and go full speed from these angles, jump the edges, and fall inside." He clenched his hands, then flicked his fingers outward. "Boom goes the dynamite."

I studied the diagram. "Will the hummers actually jump far enough into the crater? They'll need to clear a hundred feet or more."

"Yeah, that's why we A-Teamed this shit." Kyle led me to the back of the hummers and proudly waved at a pile of cylinders. "These are some spare rocket parts we found. If we bolt them into the beds of the hummers, we can give them a little extra boost to carry them the extra distance."

"Now I'm impressed." I nudged a rocket engine with my foot. "How long do you need?"

"Thirty minutes." He nodded at a group of mechanists nearby. "We just got the welders up here."

We still had a few hours before the ritual was complete, and it would take at least two of them for our army to traverse the terrain between us and Heraklion. "Do it."

They got to work, joining the mechanists to bolt and weld the rocket engines and warheads into place. It took longer than thirty minutes, but getting this right was probably our only chance to stop Cthulhu from rising.

Once the ritual was stopped, the megas and mechanist army would provide a diversion while Layla and I tried to snatch Baura. It was imperative that we finish before nightfall because then the ghasts and gugs would join the fray.

"We made some more modifications." Kyle nodded toward the hummers. "We shed as much weight as possible, and the mechanists attached glider wings to make the vehicles travel a little further."

I inspected the wings. "Is there a reason we couldn't have used the rockets to fly the warheads to the target?"

"We considered that and even discussed making mortar rounds, but our best chance is just ramming the warheads down the enemy's throat." Kyle patted a hummer. "And these babies will do just that."

Eric stood back to admire the work. "Yeah, that'll do just fine."

A mechanist ran his hand along the glider wings. "I must admit these nub military people know how to make do with very little."

"Improvisation is key to survival." Eric shrugged. "Keep it simple."

"Well, offer a prayer to whatever gods you believe in that this works." I glanced back at the army. "We're going to need all the luck we can get."

Kyle nodded grimly. "There's a downside to the plan."

I raised an eyebrow. "I'm sure there are plenty of them."

"Well, the terrain outside the crater looks pretty rough. There's no way to keep the hummers on a straight path without driving them right up to the ledge. The rocket boosters have to be ignited during the last few feet, and the warheads need to be armed in flight." He cleared his throat. "What I'm saying is, there's almost no chance the driver can eject safely at that speed since they'll need to keep the hummer on target and arm the warhead."

"It's a one-way ticket." Eric shrugged. "I'd rather die in a blaze of monster guts than get eaten by one."

"Same here." Kyle cracked his knuckles. "Those damned things took everyone I loved from me. At least this way I'll get to see everyone I lost in the afterlife."

Eric frowned. "Is there an afterlife? I've never been that religious."

"There are several," I said. "Just depends on what you believe."

Kyle looked hopeful. "Valhalla?"

"Yeah, it exists. I've been there before. It's not too bad if you're into constant war and drinking."

"Ooh, that sounds fun." He pursed his lips. "But my kids and wife probably aren't there."

"I hate to say it, but they're most likely in Hell." I winced. "That seems to be the default place people end up if they don't believe anything."

"Ugh, just what I need." Eric kicked a rock. "Maybe oblivion would be better."

"Well, the trick to Hell is that you punish yourself with your own insecurities and guilt." I shrugged. "If you can overcome that, then you can earn your way out, according to Lucifer."

"Man, you throw around names like Lucifer and Valhalla like they're nothing." Kyle frowned. "Is that normal?"

Layla appeared at my side. "Normal for Cain, maybe." She took my hand and put Panoptes in it. "I scoured the warehouse. The apocalypse weapons either aren't there, or they're so well hidden I can't find them."

"Worth a shot." I put the ring in my utility belt.

Layla raised an eyebrow. "Are we putting this show on the road, or what?"

I nodded. "I think we're ready."

Eric held out a fist. "I'm ready to take some monsters to hell with me."

Kyle bumped his fist. "Let's do it."

Layla went to the third hummer. "Let's do it, boys."

"Hold up." I gripped her elbow. "Didn't you hear them? This is a suicide mission."

Layla gave me a dead-eyed stare for a moment. "Cain, if you love me, let me go."

I blinked. "But, why?"

"Soultaker broke something inside me, Cain." She shook her head. "Or maybe it's just because I died and never should've come back to life. I feel hollowed out inside, and all I dream about is fighting and dying. It's like I never left Soultaker."

"That's no reason to throw yourself off a cliff."

"When you showed my alt mercy—when you killed her to end her suffering, it made so much sense to me." She took my hand. "I never thought I'd feel this way, but the agony of being trapped in Soultaker is just..." Her hand fell to her side. "I can't describe it. I just want it all to end."

I reached out and gently cupped her cheek but couldn't think of anything to say.

Layla put her hand over mine. "Just promise me that you'll get that bitch, Baura."

I swallowed hard. "I promise."

Layla smiled and kissed my lips. "That's my good boy." Then she climbed into the hummer and started the engine.

Kyle and Eric watched the entire interaction with concern, but they didn't say anything. They raised their thumbs to Layla and shouted, "For Valhalla!"

She returned the gesture. "Today is a good day to die."

I didn't want to think about it. The selfish part of me thought, *I became Death and went through all that work to resurrect Layla, and now she's going to kill herself?* But it was her choice. Being part of Soultaker's undead army had meant constant torture and death. It was clear that her resurrection hadn't cured any of that. Who was I to ask her to live with that pain?

She was still alive, but I already felt the pain of her absence. I unclipped the wireless from my belt and pressed down the receiver. "Horatio, we're all ready to go."

His voice replied. "All units, we are clear to move out."

Vehicles rumbled to life, and the convoy of troop transports, tanks, and more rolled into motion. The megas formed up to the left of the convoy, keeping a safe distance in case one of the pilots lost control and toppled over.

Aura rode over to me on a dirt bike. "Wow, they put wings on trucks?"

I climbed onto my dirt bike and kickstarted it. "Yep."

"And rocket boosters?" She watched as the hummers drove past. "Are we launching them into space?"

"Something like that." I accelerated to catch up with the convoy. Knots formed in my stomach when I realized that Layla's death loomed just over the horizon. I tried to ignore the pain, the grief, and the guilt. But there was no avoiding it. I could take small solace that Layla would die as she lived—in a brilliant blaze of glory.

Aura rode alongside me. "Cain, what's wrong?"

I shook my head. "Everything and nothing at all."

"That makes no sense."

"Yep." I gunned the bike to get ahead of the convoy and joined the other scouts on dirt bikes, who were finding the best route through the broken landscape. I checked the time and calculated we had another five hours before doomsday. As we neared the town, I circled back to rejoin the hummers. "Who's taking the western approach?"

"I will," Layla said.

I nodded. "I'll scout a path for you."

Another dirt bike pulled up alongside Eric. "I'm here to scout the eastern approach for you."

He gave another thumbs up to Kyle. "See you on the flip side, man."

Kyle returned the gesture. "See you in Valhalla, brother."

The convoy slowed to let the scout bikes and hummers take the lead at the outskirts of town. I'd considered masking their sounds, but the time and effort would've been considerable, and I had a feeling I'd need all my stamina to make it through the coming battle.

I turned northwest and guided Layla along the perimeter road. Rubble and wrecked cars blocked most of the side streets, but the route I'd taken into town the first time worked fine since both our vehicles were made for traversing rough terrain. I kept an eye out for nightgaunts and other threats, but it seemed the monsters were still entirely focused on the Cthulhu ritual.

That was a good thing, because the hummers and motorcycles weren't even remotely quiet. The raucous roars, growls, shrieks, and more echoing around the crater where the ritual was taking place were going to be the only reason the monsters didn't hear us coming until it was too late.

We reached the final stretch of road about three hundred yards away from the edge of the crater. I spotted a few nightgaunts perched around the edges, but none of them seemed aware of our presence.

"Eastern side in position," one of the scouts said over the radio.

"Southern approach ready," another said.

I clicked the radio receiver. "Western approach in position."

There was a momentary pause, then Horatio spoke. "You may proceed. May the gods have mercy on your souls."

Eric's voice crackled over the radio. "Leroy Jenkins!" His hummer engine roared in the background and then the radio clicked off.

Layla looked at me for a moment, then hit the accelerator, and the hummer rumbled forward. I gunned the motorcycle and paced her.

She gave me a sideways look. "What are you doing, Cain?"

"Keeping you company until the end."

She wiped at her eyes. "Love you."

"Love you too."

As we roared toward the edge of the crater, nightgaunts suddenly flew up and out, giant bats hovering just above the lip as they set their sights on us. I'd already prepared and summoned my staff, switching it to longshot mode.

The head of one nightgaunt exploded as the kinetic energy impacted it. I took down a second one, but three more were already zipping toward us. One swooped toward me. A dagger nailed it in the temple, and it slid lifelessly across the ground. Another dagger tore through the wings of the next one, and it spiraled out of control.

"Fuck yeah!" Layla produced two more daggers pinched between the fingers of one hand and threw them at the final nightgaunt. It tried to dodge, but the daggers slashed through its wings, and it fell like a brick into the road ahead. The meaty wheels of the hummer crunched its bones as they rolled over it.

I banished my staff as the lip of the crater approached at high speed. Layla hit the booster ignition. The hummer rocketed forward. I watched Eric's and Kyle's hummers doing the same thing from the other approaches.

Layla flicked the switch to arm the warhead. Her eyes flared, and she glanced over at me. "What the fuck am I doing?" The hummer hit the sloped ledge and shot up and into the void.

I slid the motorcycle sideways, stopping right at the ledge, and watched in what felt like slow motion as Layla hopped up from the driver's seat, ran to the back of the hummer, and leaped toward the ledge. She wasn't even close to making it. I reached for her, but the thirty feet between us might as well have been a mile.

There was a fifty-foot drop into a sea of monsters. The fall wouldn't kill her, but the horrors below certainly would.

I suddenly felt her hand grasp mine even though she was so far away. I yanked her toward me, and she floated up and over the edge as if tied to an invisible cord. Then the feeling vanished, and she tumbled to the ground a few feet away.

Layla stared at me in disbelief. "How did you do that?"

I looked over the lip of the crater and watched as her hummer detonated in a crowd of deep ones. Limbs and innards scattered into the air. Kyle's hummer slammed into the ledges and rolled half a dozen times, smashing through shoggoths and then coming to a rest at the feet of a malgorth. The monster gripped the hummer with a tentacle and reared back as if to throw it. The warhead exploded. The malgorth's massive dark eye burst. Tentacles flew everywhere. The shockwave leveled dozens of shoggoths. Crimson rained down on the crater.

The sorcerers performing the Cthulhu ritual must have made faster time than expected because they were chanting over the final group of runes. They kept going despite the carnage and explosions around them.

Dagon and Hydra waded from the waters and stepped onto dry land, crushing deep ones beneath their giant claws. Eric's hummer launched over the opposite side of the crater and slammed into Hydra's head. The explosion rocked her sideways. She stumbled, fell, and crushed a group of humans meant for sacrifice.

I summoned my staff and dropped prone on the ground, taking aim at the sorcerers. I fired, aimed, fired again, aimed again, and blew the heads off three of them before they finally quit the ritual and took cover behind rubble.

Layla went prone on the ground next to me. "Cain, how in the hell did you pull me through the air like that?"

"I don't know. It's a new thing."

"Aren't you going to make fun of me for changing my mind about dying?"

I shook my head. "I'm saving that for after we stop Cthulhu from rising."

"It won't be as fun then."

I leaned sideways and kissed her on the cheek. "I'm happy, Layla, okay? I don't want you to die just yet."

She kissed me back. "Fine. I guess the patriarchy wins this round."

I snorted. "As if the patriarchy ever won a round against you."

I spotted Baura shouting commands at the bottom of the crater. A herd of malgorths gripped humans in their tentacles and began running them around the water's edge toward the runes on the other side. We still hadn't stopped the ritual. The sorcerers might have completed their chant. Maybe all that was left now was to seal the runes in human blood.

The bulk of the mechanist forces arrived, scattering out of the backs of troop trucks and firing down into the crater. Rockets whistled through the air, crashing into monsters and sending body parts flying. They weren't nearly as powerful as the missile warheads, but they were enough to take out shoggoths and deep ones. The monsters scattered in all directions, panicked and fleeing, still reeling from the warhead explosions.

Dagon and Hydra roared and clambered up the sides of the crater. Mechanists panicked and fled as the giant creatures came for them. Hannah's mega reached over and gripped Hydra by her head tentacles and jerked violently. The monster shrieked in pain. Dagon leaped up and out of the crater as the other two megas joined Hannah's.

The battle of the goliaths had started.

35

Dagon punched the first mega, and it stumbled backward. Hannah kneed Hydra in the face and sent the monster toppling backward over the edge. Then she reared back and punched Dagon. The other megas fired rockets and incendiary rounds at the beast. Dagon roared in pain, but the weapons barely scratched his scaly skin.

Hydra crawled back out, a chunk of her head tentacles missing, and slammed into one of the megas. Hannah's mega twisted its fist, and a giant blade speared from the wrist. She thrust it forward and stabbed it into Dagon. His tough, leathery scales resisted, but the blow sent him tumbling.

The monsters in the crater that weren't dead or dying were racing up the ledges and attacking the mechanist foot soldiers. The mechanist lines broke, and chaos ensued as shoggoths and deep ones swarmed them.

Our forces were dying, but the diversion was working. "We've got to stop the sorcerers from completing the ritual." I slid over the lip of the crater and down to a ledge, then began hopping down each one. They were uneven in height and position, making the descent treacherous.

Layla dropped down behind me. "Guess I'll have a chance to die after all."

"Fun times." I slashed a shoggoth in half as it leaped from a chunk of rubble.

Layla spun and hurled daggers at deep ones shambling our way. They went down gurgling and clutching at their throats. "A small eternity of endless battles in Soultaker changed my idea of fun."

I parried an attack from a pair of shoggoths, ducked, and slashed the legs off one, then threw up a shield in front of the other. It collided with the translucent barrier and wobbled, stunned. A quick slash of the brightblade sent its head rolling. "Maybe you could retire to a nice beach somewhere."

Layla chuckled humorlessly as she plucked daggers from a freshly skewered shoggoth. "That sounds immensely worse, Cain." She booted the corpse of a hybrid deep one. It wore a Victorian-era suit like most of the male hybrids. When she was sure it was dead, she wiped the blood from the daggers on its torn suit.

I switched to longshot mode and took out a pair of deep ones, then ignited the brightblade to take out another shoggoth. Most of the monsters were headed toward the battle near the megas, but the handful in our way were slowing us down. The sorcerers had their human sacrifices halfway around the crater to the final rune, and we'd be hard-pressed to reach them in time.

"This isn't working." I climbed back up the ledges and out of the crater, making a beeline for the dirt bike. I hopped on and jammed down the kick starter. The engine rumbled to life.

Layla slid on behind me. "Is this thing going to support both of us?"

"It'll work." I spun the bike around and gunned it over the edge. The uneven positioning of the ledges made it a challenge to keep the front wheel from slamming into an obstacle. I angled downwards, riding the lips of the ledges and dodging rubble from the earlier explosions.

Every impact felt like balancing the razor's edge between life and death.

"Ow, my ass!" Layla's voice bounced in time with every bump.

We jumped off the last ledge and hit the bottom of the bowl where the runes were carved. A guttural roar drew my attention toward the battle between the megas and the monsters. Dagon, eyes glowing greenly, leaped from the lip of the crater toward us, webbed claws outstretched. The monster stopped abruptly, eyes bulging.

Hannah's mega had gripped the beast by the tail. Gears creaked and rattled with the strain. The other two megas were fighting Hydra some distance away. Sparks flew from the mega's arms. Metal shrieked. One of the arms tore loose at the elbow, and Dagon dropped heavily just inside the lip of the crater.

Gears burst from the other arm, metal shards flashing like daggers into monsters and mechanists alike. The mega toppled forward in slow motion.

"Hannah!" I reached out, hoping my new telekinetic power might stop the fall, but nothing happened.

The mega slammed down atop Dagon. The fuel tanks burst open, and liquid mana rushed out in a flood, cascading down the ledges. I glanced at the sorcerers and back up at Hannah's mega. There was no way I could ride the dirt bike up the ledges. No way I could reach her in time. But I tried anyway.

Layla pushed off, hit the ground, and rolled to her feet. "I'll stop the sacrifices. You go help Hannah."

I cast a shield like a ramp up the side of the first ledge and twisted the throttle all the way. The bike jumped up three levels. The front wheel slammed into the fourth ledge, and I tumbled over the handlebars, landing hard on my back.

Dagon shrieked. His claws dug into Hannah's mega and rolled it off him. Then he slammed his fist down on the head, over and over again, crushing the metal.

"Hannah!" I reached out again, vainly trying to activate my new abilities to no avail.

A nightgaunt swooped in front of me, Baura clutched in its claws. It gently deposited her a couple of ledges above me and landed, crouching at her side like a grotesque, faceless gargoyle.

Baura held up a fist, and Dagon paused, fists upraised, chest heaving, green drool dripping from his shark-like maw. Baura tutted. "And I thought I was the insane one, Cain." She trembled violently, head twisting so rapidly it almost looked like stop motion photography. "Obviously, I have my madness under better control than you do."

"I'm not insane." I drew my brightblade. "Just determined to stop the madness here before it spreads to Prime." My protective sigils tingled. I looked up and saw a pair of nightgaunts circling overhead.

Without looking back, Baura motioned with a finger. Dagon ripped the faceplate from the mega. His claws slashed.

Rage swelled inside me. "Hannah!"

Dagon gently plucked Hannah from inside. Her head lolled, but she seemed otherwise unharmed. Rising, the beast shambled toward Baura, Hannah dangling from his claws. Liquid mana splashed beneath his great feet as it continued pouring down the ledges toward us. Baura's nightgaunt flew up and hovered next to Hannah. Its barbed tail rubbed against her belly and ribs.

Hannah jolted awake with a tortured scream.

The nightgaunt landed next to Baura, its faceless head tilting as if it were watching my reaction.

Baura smiled. "Hannah, my dear, are you awake now?"

"Cain?" Hannah shook her head as if trying to clear her head. "What happened?"

I looked out of the corner of my eye and saw Layla battling the sorcerers. I didn't dare turn my head and draw Baura's attention to the fight. "Are you okay?"

Still dangling from Dagon's claws, Hannah nodded woozily and wiped blood from the corner of her mouth. "All things considered, yeah."

"We have a choice to make." Baura turned to Hannah. "It's a choice you once made willingly for Cain, so I'm sure you'll do it again."

"How about I rip off your head, you insane bitch?" Hannah bared her bloody teeth.

"Cain dies unless you willingly become Cthulhu's minion again."

Baura glanced over at me and smiled. "And then we become one big happy family."

"Don't do it, Hannah." I braced myself for a hopeless battle. "We're both better off dead."

Hannah's expression turned resolute. "Then let's die, Cain."

Baura's face went expressionless. "So be it."

Baura was out of range, but I did the only thing I could. I ghost-walked to the ledge just below hers and swung my brightblade. It slashed through her knees. Screaming, Baura fell sideways. Before I could lop off her head, Dagon's claw slashed across Hannah's neck.

"No!" I flung out my hand, but there was no stopping it.

Hannah slid straight down and out of the top of the pilot jump-suit. The claw grazed her forehead. She tumbled to the ground, rolled, and spun toward Dagon, eyes glowing white. The pools of liquid mana rose in droplets, suspended in the air as if gravity had stopped working.

Dagon roared, slamming his fists toward her.

Hannah screamed and flung her hands toward him. Globules of liquid mana flew into his gaping maw. Beams of white energy poured from her eyes and mouth. The blue liquid ignited with the force of a bomb. Dagon's head exploded. The circling nightgaunts were thrown to the ground by the detonation. Brains, bones, and gristle rained down on us.

One of Dagon's massive eyes landed on top of Baura, and her screaming went silent.

Hannah tumbled backward off the ledge and landed heavily on her back. Dagon's body toppled toward her. I thrust out my hand, reaching for her. I felt the telekinetic connection of my hand around her leg and pulled. She slid across the brain-spattered stone, stopping at my feet. I took a moment, trying to sense the part of me that enabled this new ability, but there was nothing tangible for me to seize on.

Dagon's corpse slammed to the ground and slid down a few ledges. Blood gushed from the ragged remains of his neck. Hydra shrieked in rage. Most of her tentacles were ragged or torn off, and her body was pockmarked from explosions. The last two megas lay in ruins just inside the crater.

I looked in the opposite direction and found Layla standing amid a pile of bodies. She'd stopped the final ritual, but we were about to have another boss battle on our hands, and without the megas, I didn't know how we'd beat Hydra.

The ocean water at the bottom of the crater bubbled and boiled, and a fresh wave of monstrosities crawled out. I suddenly realized why Baura had chosen this spot. There was a deepway entrance somewhere below the R'lyehian structures.

Explosions echoed from somewhere outside the crater as the mechanists continued battling the other monsters. We'd get no help from them. With Hydra turning her gaze on us and another army rising, we had nowhere to go.

I pulled out the ring and bent down to wake Hannah, but she was out cold from the blow to her head. I needed her conscious so she could escape with the ring, but that wasn't going to happen.

Baura dragged herself from beneath Dagon's eye. A nightgaunt swooped down to scoop her up. I leaped to the ledge and rammed my brightblade into her back. She screamed. I swept the blade up and lopped off the nightgaunt's head as it tried to retrieve her. Its body tumbled down the ledges.

Baura went still, dead at last. I put on the ring and grabbed her arm. We flicked into the warehouse. Even if I didn't survive, she'd be trapped here unless she knew the code to get out. I flicked back to the crater. Hydra was snaking toward us, but her injuries slowed her.

I considered my options, but there were none. I was about to be surrounded. My only escape was with the ring. Layla could get out by running. Hannah would be left behind to die. I wished I knew how to ignite the liquid mana as she had, but even dipping my brightblade into it only caused it to spark.

I was suddenly seized with one last option. If it failed, I'd be dead in short order. As monsters crawled out of the water, I knew there was no time to think about it—only to do it. Putting back on Panoptes, I traveled to a place I'd been all too recently—the dwarven forge. I ran straight ahead. Gears clanked, and lights glowed as a clockwork sentinel sensed me and came to life.

It spun just as I reached it. I ghostwalked behind it, gripped its metal shell, and took us back to the crater.

"Intruder alert!" it intoned in a robotic voice.

I traveled back to the dwarven forge and ran toward another sentinel. It clanked to life and spun seemingly even faster than the last one. I ghostwalked, gripped it, and traveled back to the crater. Dizziness nearly overwhelmed me as the many eyes of Panoptes threatened to overwhelm my mind. But I traveled again and again until I had two more sentinels in the crater.

Just as I arrived with the last one, I fell to my knees. This was it. The last sentinel would finish me off and then turn to fight the monsters.

A body collided with mine. I rolled, and something hard hit my head. The many views of Panoptes vanished, and Layla filled my vision.

"You're not dying before me, Cain." She bared her teeth in a fierce grin. "Now, get on your feet, you idiot."

Hanna lay next to me, still unconscious.

Weapons whined. Monsters roared in pain. I pushed to my knees and looked over the top of the piece of rubble Layla had thrown me behind. The sentinels stood in formation, jewels glowing on their metal arms. Beams of energy whined and tore into flesh, ripping the monster horde to shreds as they scrambled from the water and toward them.

I turned and looked up to see Hydra still slithering toward us, eyes burning with rage. With the sentinels taking on the horde behind us, we had a way out. I picked up Hannah and slung her over my shoulder, then started climbing ledges diagonally up and away from Hydra. She shrieked and began to follow. If not for the terrible wounds along her body, she would have been on top of us already.

A group of deep ones and shoggoths raced down from the top of the crater, captured mechanists squirming in their grasps. They crossed the path we'd need to get out of the crater but ignored us as they ran to the bottom.

"What the fuck?" Layla crouched and watched until they'd passed. "Why are they taking prisoners?"

"They're not." I pointed to a lone sorcerer in blood-soaked robes hobbling toward the final runes. "They're finishing the ritual."

"Can they, though?" Layla shook her head. "Don't they need all the sorcerers to do a final chant or something?"

"I don't know. The final ritual might be different." I hesitated, then blew out a breath. "Take Hannah. I'll meet you up top."

"Cain, it doesn't matter. We have Baura."

"Having Cthulhu roaming free even if it's in another dimension is a bad idea, Layla." I put Hannah on her shoulder. "Go!"

She scowled but took Hannah and hurried up the ledges.

I didn't have a clean shot on the remaining sorcerer, thanks to the deep ones and their prisoners, so I'd have to get up close and personal to end this.

This was going to be a suicide mission, but I had no choice.

Cthulhu could not be awakened.

36

The sentinels were still busy killing the endless swarm of tentacle monsters coming out of the water. One of the clockwork automatons had fallen, but the others were shredding enemies left and right.

I found the dirt bike. The front wheel was slightly warped, but it was better than running. I started it, then angled down three ledges and into the crater bowl. Hugging the edge of the bowl to steer wide of the sentinels, I zipped toward the deep ones. They didn't so much as glance back at me. Baura must have given them a command to finish the ritual at all costs, and that was all that mattered to them.

My sigils tingled. Something whistled through the air. I leaned hard left as a slab of rock slammed down where I'd been. The warped front wheel lost traction, and the bike flipped hard. I rolled to a stop, then immediately jumped up and dodged another stone slab. I spun around and found the source—Hydra.

She shrieked and picked up another slab.

I summoned my staff, switched to longshot mode, and fired a blast at her one good eye. She flinched as the shot hit her tough hide. But that flinch caused her to drop the slab. It slid down the ledges and out of reach. There weren't any other pieces of rubble close to her, so she'd have to come get me.

Thunder echoed, and the sky went dark. The ground rumbled, and a strange green hue lit the clouds.

I turned and saw the deep ones holding the mechanists in a circle around the final rune. Three human bodies sagged, their lifeblood pouring from slit throats. The sorcerer slashed the throat of another one and moved to the next. I aimed my staff and fired.

A deep one jumped in the way. Its head exploded. Shoggoths and other deep ones lined up, blocking my view of the sorcerer, staring at me with eyes devoid of concern for their own lives.

I scrambled for the dirt bike, but the front wheel was bent in half from the last wreck. A vortex of green energy began to form over the R'lyehian structures. The water swirled. It was too late to stop the Cthulhu train.

The only thing I could do now was run.

I'd done my best and failed. My only hope now was that the ritual was so corrupted that it would also fail. But judging from the light show at the bottom of the crater, things were going just dandy for the cultists.

Layla was three-quarters of the way to the top, her fae half giving her the strength and speed she needed despite carrying Hannah. I boosted power to my body sigils and ran as fast as I could, jumping up the crooked ledges one foot at a time as if they were giant stairs. My body was fatigued, my legs like jelly, but I pushed aside the pain and kept going.

I finally climbed over the lip of the crater and rolled onto my side, panting. Layla was there already, standing amid piles of monster and mechanist corpses.

The funnel of green light above the ritual structures swirled, synchronizing with the vortex of water below. The ground shook, and the sides of the crater cracked and broke apart. I pushed up and jumped back as a landslide claimed the ledge I'd been lying on.

The R'lyehian structures glowed bright green, humming with power. The ocean maelstrom rose like a giant water tornado until it reached into the sky. Clouds scattered as if fleeing what was to come. I should have taken it as a cue, but I remained rooted in place, unable to move.

Layla crouched next to me. "I'm gonna take a wild guess and say you failed to stop them."

Her words shook me from my trance. "We need to—"

Crooked spires rose from the crater, piercing the water funnel. An explosion shook the ground, and the tornado dissipated into a fine mist. Everything went quiet. The sorcerer and the deep ones stood to the side of the final blood-sealed symbols, still as statues.

The ocean calmed until it was nearly flat as glass. Sunlight sparkled off the blue water, and for the first time, the world seemed at peace.

"Maybe it didn't work." Layla sighed. "Holy shit, Cain, I think we stopped them!"

"Did we?" I dared to feel hope. Then just like that, the calm was shattered.

Out in the ocean, just beyond the crater, gouts of water shot hundreds of feet into the air. The water bubbled and boiled. Something shot through the canal leading from the ocean into the crater, something barely visible beneath surface. A massive green hand shot up and gripped the right side of the crater. Another hand rose and clenched the opposite side.

Giant wings broke the surface, and a head soon followed, shedding thousands of gallons of seawater as if they were nothing. Giant eyes glowed orange, burning coals set above a mass of writhing tentacles, each one large enough to clench an aircraft carrier and crush it like a tin can.

My body went cold as burning ice. I felt the blood vessels in my face pulsate like trapped worms. The veins in my hands turned black and squirmed madly. My brain slithered in circles in my skull, and the air tasted red.

Dull shouts rang in my ears. They smelled of fear. Perception turned inside. The void cried out for my bones.

Darkness.

Shouts.

Light.

Worms.

Blood.

Fear.

Joy.

Pounding, pulsating, palpitating pustules.

Beginning, ending, rising, falling. I am nothing but a writhing pile of maggots in rotting flesh.

I am—

"Cain!"

Pain flashed across my face. I rolled over and projectile vomited roiling green darkness onto bloodstained earth. The vomit squirmed like a pile of worms and burrowed into the earth. New life infesting the rotten core.

"Cain!" Layla gripped the side of my face. "Gods be damned, you idiot."

I felt myself being picked up and landed heavily on something metal. An engine roared to life. I bounced wildly, sliding across a corrugated surface.

My brain heaved. Dark liquid shot from my nose and mouth, splashing into the grooves, then turning into black moths and fluttering away.

A curtain peeled away. A translucent layer of darkness faded.

Sanity returned.

I felt weak, nauseated, and furious with myself. I'd looked full into the eyes of the risen Cthulhu and nearly destroyed my mind. How my sanity had survived was a mystery.

The ground shook, and the jeep we were in leaped off the ground and slammed back down, nearly tossing me from the back.

Hannah was strapped down in the backseat. I climbed over her and slid into the front, buckling myself in.

Layla glanced over at me. "Cain? Are you in there?"

"I'm here." I gripped the top of the door as the jeep bounced again. I glanced back and saw a hulking shadow rising from the crater. I turned back around before the eyes appeared. "I don't know how, but I'm here."

Layla stiffened. "Where's Aura?"

"Our Aura?" I looked at the carnage around us and spotted another contingent of mechanist vehicles racing away from the crater. "If she's anywhere, it's probably over there."

"We've got to get back to the portal. If Aura has any sense, she'll be going there too."

I checked my belt, but the radio was gone. The jeep had one in the dash, so I turned it on and clicked the receiver. "Aura, are you out there?"

The radio crackled, and Horatio spoke. "Cain, we failed! Cthulhu has risen!"

"Is Aura with you?"

There was a long silence and then Aura spoke. "Cain, I'm with the others. What happened?"

"Head to the portal. It's our only chance."

Horatio spoke. "Portal? The one you spoke of earlier?"

"Just follow us, okay?" I summoned my staff and fired a sparkly flare into the air. The other convoy veered toward us. Vehicles bounced in unison as the footfalls of Cthulhu shook the ground beneath them. "And whatever you do, don't look back, or you'll go mad!"

A cargo truck abruptly veered around and drove back toward the crater. Voices screamed incoherently over the radio.

"Don't look in the mirrors either!" Someone else shouted. "Don't look back at all!"

Fear was an emotion I'd dealt with all my life. I'd learned how to suppress it, push it away, and remain calm, cool, and collected. But there was nothing I could do to suppress it now. My skin was cold, clammy, covered in goosebumps. A knot of anxiety twisted my stomach with despair. Just the sheer presence of Cthulhu was enough to overwhelm even the most honed senses.

Vehicles in the convoy crashed or stopped, the people climbing out and turning to face Cthulhu, their minds already consumed in madness just from being so close to the source.

A high-pitched whine burst from a loudspeaker on one of the vehicles, giving me an instant headache. The anxiety and despair receded into the background, though it wasn't completely gone.

I clicked the radio. "Horatio, what is that?"

"A mithril chime we found on one of our expeditions." He cleared his throat. "We believe it was made by the elves of ancient times when they were trying to reclaim Fyeth Elunore from the creeping madness. It combats the psychic emanations."

It seemed to be working, as no other vehicles stopped or turned, but there weren't many of us left now. We found a road leading back to the town where we'd first arrived and veered onto it. The pounding footsteps of Cthulhu echoed behind us, the beats seconds apart as he ate up the landscape with his massive stride.

Cain Sthyldor. The voice echoed in my mind. *There is no escape. Madness is inevitable.*

"Well, that's not good." I dug around in the truck and found a pair of mithrium goggles.

Layla veered around a sinkhole in the road. "What's not good?"

"I hear Cthulhu in my head now." I clicked the radio. "Horatio, are the mithrium goggles working?"

"I don't know," he replied. "All of ours were broken in battle."

I blew out a breath and took a quick glance back.

Layla punched my shoulder. "What in Hades are you doing, idiot?"

The ethereal chime ringing in my ears and the strange tint of the mithrium goggles clouding my vision, I looked upon Cthulhu, bringer of madness, harbinger of insanity, and beheld his monstrous form. He looked just like I'd seen him in the dreams and the visions. A single stride ate a hundred yards or more of distance. He was easily Godzilla's height, maybe taller. His dimensions were so massive that my human brain could barely comprehend them.

The glowing embers of his gaze looked down upon me, but the mithrium and the chime seemed to hold my sanity in check.

You dared control my other self with the Rlhala in another dimension. I will consume your mind in repayment.

Why not just crush me like a bug and be done with it? If he heard my thoughts, he didn't reply. Gazing upon him was still twisting and pulling at my mind, so I turned around in the seat and braced as Layla took the jeep off a ledge where the road was broken.

The rest of the convoy had formed up behind us—twelve vehicles filled with an unknown number of people. We were probably all that remained of humanity in this world. Now Gaia Beta was firmly in the camp of the Elder Things. I was terrified about what having Cthulhu roaming this world meant. The only upside was that his presence didn't span the dimensions as the Elder Gods did.

There was only one Zeus, one Thor, one Hera, and they chose to keep their attention on Prime, though they could slip into any of the splinter dimensions if they wished. I wondered if they'd spare more attention for this world now or simply leave it be and hope Cthulhu didn't have the ability to traverse realities.

Dealing with a Great Old One of this magnitude was well above my paygrade. I had Baura, and that was all that mattered.

Shadows swept across the landscape. Shrieks and screams echoed from all directions. The blue sky turned crimson, and the sun became a blood-red orb drenching the horizon. The earth quaked and began to break apart.

"What's happening, Cain?" Layla dodged through an increasingly challenging landscape. "Is the planet about to explode?"

I gripped the door handle with one hand and braced Hannah in the backseat with the other. "This is the first time Cthulhu has risen as far as I know, so I have no idea!"

A loud explosion drew my attention back. One of the transport trucks had flipped and burst into flame. The terrain shifted, and another vehicle collided with broken road, spun out of control, and vanished. Cthulhu was less than a quarter-mile back. His strides were huge, but they were slow, and that was the only reason he hadn't caught up.

Layla tore through the small town we'd originally arrived in and turned down the road leading to the canyons where the cave and portal were. Then she slammed on the brakes. Barring our way was the centaur army. After failing to trick them into fighting for us, I'd nearly forgotten about them.

There weren't as many of them anymore. Most bore fresh wounds and scars. They'd evidently been fighting monsters, just not the ones I'd wanted them to. The centaurs looked just as surprised to see us as we were them. The palomino raised a battle-ax and trotted toward us.

I leaped from the jeep, staff in hand. "Get out of the way! We've got to get the fuck out of Dodge right now!"

"You!" The palomino reared on hind legs, weapon flashing. "You led us to this death world, and I will shed your blood for our lost warriors!"

The other centaurs formed up behind him even as the earth shook beneath our feet. Some of them abruptly looked up. Blackened veins writhed on their faces, and their eyes went black as pitch. The crimson sunlight made them look like sunburned centaur vampires.

The palomino screamed as the full insanity of Cthulhu's gaze caught him. Howls, screams, and gibbering sobs tore from the throats of his companions. Some began bucking madly; some ran straight toward Cthulhu. Most of them scattered, too consumed by madness to even see us anymore.

I climbed back into the jeep. "Go!"

Layla gunned it. "Well, that was super easy, barely an inconvenience."

"About fucking time something was!" I gripped the door as she made a sharp turn. Seconds later, we were at the narrow canyon leading to the cave.

Layla pulled off the road and screeched to a halt. I climbed out and unbuckled Hannah from the backseat, then tossed her over my shoulder. Horatio, Aura, and two other mechanists piled out of the car behind us. Another transport truck stopped, and a single woman slid out.

"Where are the other vehicles?" Horatio climbed onto the hood of his clockwork car and looked back. "They're gone!"

"And we will be too if we don't fucking run!" Layla scurried down the canyon, and I raced after her.

Panting, crying, shouting in panic, the other mechanists followed. We reached the cave and ran inside. The portal roiled like a pot of water on a stove. The air around it wavered and shimmered, sparking and arcing.

Layla skidded to a stop. "Something's wrong."

"No, you think?" Aura bent down, picked up a rock, and tossed it. It vanished into the portal with a loud pop.

Layla grimaced. "Was that a good or bad sound?"

The cave shook. Rubble and dirt rained down on us. "In a few seconds, it won't matter."

Cthulhu would kill us if we didn't move.

I steadied Hannah on my shoulder. "See you in hell." I ran toward the portal and hoped for the best.

37

M y flesh seemed to catch fire.

It abruptly cooled in the absolute void of in between. I flew through the air and landed heavily on my shoulder. Hannah tumbled from my grasp and flopped next to me. We were in the cave on Feary.

Layla burst from the portal, smoke trailing from her body and hair, and landed on top of me. The air burst from my lungs. Aura ejected from the portal an instant later at a different trajectory. She hit the wall with a dull smack and flopped to the ground.

Layla yanked me up and shoved me through the cave exit, then picked up Hannah and jumped outside as Horatio came through. Two more mechanists arrived, the last one her clothes on fire. The portal wobbled and spun on its axis, humming loudly.

A man flew out, flesh melting and burning. He screamed and rolled on the ground. Another mechanist followed behind. A gurgling shriek erupted from her throat. Blackened blood poured from her mouth. Her face was little more than a charred skull. One more flew out, flesh charbroiled to a crisp.

"Gods be damned." Layla shivered. "Good thing we went first."

The portal warped outward as if a human face were trying to

break free of a rubber barrier. Aura and the other mechanists ran from the cave as the portal continued to bulge and swell. A massive tentacle suddenly burst through a burnt body in its grasp. The body dropped, and the tentacle lashed out at the badly burned mechanist.

He screamed in agony. The portal bulged, and yet another tentacle shot through. Thunder clapped. The portal detonated, and the shockwave threw us backward. The giant tentacles flopped to the ground, writhing like dying snakes.

I picked up Hannah and moved away as the cave mouth rumbled and collapsed. When the dust cleared, it was me, Layla, Hannah, Aura, Horatio, and two mechanists. The portal was closed, and we'd somehow survived.

Unfortunately, we had a long trip ahead of us to reach civilization, and some of that walk involved going back through Minos. I wasn't about to do that while being this damned tired. I sighed wearily and started walking. There were no other signs of centaurs or dangerous wildlife nearby, so I chose a slightly elevated patch of land and set down Hannah.

"I'll be back." I slipped on Panoptes and went to the warehouse. Once there, I found the camping and emergency supplies and brought them back over.

Our bedraggled group set up camp and settled in, too tired to even complain about the canned food I provided. While they were setting up, I went back to the warehouse and grabbed Baura's body. I didn't want to have to deal with her when she resurrected, so I dumped the corpse into a heavy steel chest.

I stripped off her clothes and searched her for hidden tools and devices in places I didn't want to touch until I was certain she was clean. I closed the chest and locked the thick metal straps that held down the lid. Unless she could conjure a welding torch, she wasn't going anywhere.

After returning to the others, I pitched my special tent and put Hannah on the couch inside, then showered and stumbled into bed. Nothing mattered to me except for sleep. My mind and body were numb from exhaustion and the grasping tentacles of insanity.

Layla slid beneath the sheets and huddled next to me. She gently kissed me on the lips. "Good night, Cain."

I kissed her back. "Good night, Layla. I'm glad you didn't kill yourself today."

She smiled. "I'll save it for a special occasion."

And then it was lights out.

THE SMELL of bacon and eggs tickled my nose early the next morning. I left Layla in bed and went into the kitchen to find Hannah flipping pancakes. She grinned. "Hungry?"

My stomach rumbled. "Like you wouldn't believe."

Aura rose from the floor. "Fine, I'm up."

There was plenty of food, so I invited Horatio and the mechanists to join us. It seemed the least I could do for three people who'd lost their entire world to Cthulhu.

Horatio looked at the food, tears streaming down his face. "I never thought I'd see real bacon or eggs again, Cain. This is a gift."

"Truly, it is." The male mechanist bit into bacon and began to sob with joy.

"Eat up, because the next part of the trip isn't going to be easy." I sighed. "We've got to go through the labyrinth and survive the citizens of Minos."

Aura and Hannah groaned.

I shrugged. "Hey, it's better than shoggoths, ghasts, and gugs, right?"

Hannah pursed her lips. "Yeah, I guess you're right."

We packed up camp and moved out, making our way down the mountain and toward the plains and valleys. There were no centaur or minotaur corpses along the way, meaning someone had retrieved or buried them. It wasn't until we neared the beach that we saw signs of life. The merfolk, Maya and Rille, sat near the cliff overlooking the ocean. They jumped to their feet when they saw us.

"You're back!" Maya's eyes flared. "Who are all these people?"

Rille's lips peeled back, revealing sharp teeth. "Did you find the murderer?"

I nodded. "She can't die, but I can assure you that she'll pay for her crimes against your people."

"Where is she?" Tears poured down Maya's cheeks. "I want to look into the eyes of the beast who murdered my mate!"

I really didn't want to waste time here. We had a long road ahead of us. "She's locked in a steel chest in a place I can't take you. I know you want closure, but if I bring her back, I'll have to kill her first. Then we'll have to wait until midnight when she revives for you to look her in the eyes."

Maya clenched her teeth. "We have waited here every day since you left. I will wait one more for the satisfaction of looking her in the eyes while I slowly gouge out her eyes and torture her."

"Give her to us, child of man." Rille shivered, eyes filled with hate and rage. "We will torture her until the end of our days."

"I can't." I leveled my heaviest stare into them. "Her crimes against you are terrible, but she murdered a goddess, she destroyed an entire world and unleashed Cthulhu so she might spread madness to Feary, Gaia, and beyond. I am going to ensure she's incapable of harming anyone ever again."

Layla turned a grim gaze on them. "No disrespect, but that bitch got me killed and imprisoned in a hell world. I call first dibs on her punishment."

"Madame, I assure you that Cain will do what is necessary and just." Horatio stood a distance away with his mechanist companions. "It is a miracle he apprehended Baura at all."

Maya looked up at the sky, tears streaming down her cheeks, and then back to me. "What will you do to her?"

"I'm not sure yet, but I'll make sure she's never free again."

Rille clenched her fists and nodded. "The right of revenge is yours. I only ask that you tell us her final fate when it is done."

I nodded. "I will send word once it's decided and done."

"Thank you." Rille still didn't look happy, but fighting us on land wasn't a realistic option for them. Had we been in the water, this might have turned out much differently.

Hannah touched Maya's hand. "I'm sorry about your mate. Cain will make sure Baura pays."

Baura's actions had killed so many people that I didn't think there was a punishment worthy of her crimes. But I wasn't going to mention that now.

"We need to go." I turned toward Minos and started walking.

Rille and Maya watched us go, leaning on each other for support. Baura had wrecked their lives for no other reason than petty revenge for something the merfolk had no control over. Every last apocalypse weapon had to be destroyed so no mortal could wield such power.

We walked in silence for miles until the labyrinth walls appeared on the horizon, towering monoliths snug between the mountains. Road-weary and ready to stop despite it being early noon, we reached the walls over an hour later.

A pair of centaurs stood outside the wall, weapons on their backs as if guarding the entrance. They stiffened when they saw us approaching, then looked at each other and galloped toward us. It didn't take them long to cross the distance on four legs.

Long curving sabers appeared in their hands. They looked young, maybe in their early teens, judging by their human parts.

"It's them, Talvo," one said to the other.

"I can see that, Valen." The second one gripped the saber tighter as he glared at me. "Where are our people? What did you do to them?"

"Answer him or die!" Valen shivered, and tears pooled in his eyes. "Where is my father?"

"Oof." Layla grimaced. "That is not a pleasant story."

Judging from the palomino pattern on Valen's hide, it was obvious who his father had been. The question was, did I lie about what happened or give them the brutal truth that daddy dearest had gone insane?

I sighed. "It's better you don't know."

"I must know!" Valen slashed the weapon at me threateningly.

I held my ground and stared him in the eye. "Your father and his entire army decided to be bullies and chased us into the mountains. We entered a portal to a Gaia that is infested with eldritch horrors because we had a mission to bring a dangerous fugitive to justice. I tried to reason with your father and the others, but they would not help us. In the end, the monsters killed every last one of them."

Talvo recoiled. "T-they died? All of them?"

"All of them." I regarded them grimly. "Ask yourself, should they have followed me and my people, hounded and threatened to kill us simply because we passed through your city?"

"The gods punished them for denying travelers hospitality," Aura said. "Their sentences were death."

The saber dropped from Valen's limp fingers. "I was to join the army on my next birthday. I've trained all my life to become a warrior like my father. Now he is gone forever."

Talvo wobbled on unsteady legs. "My uncle, my father, my cousins. All dead?"

I nodded. "I am sorry."

"The gods cursed them." Valen wiped his eyes. "It is as the priestess said. Our lack of compassion for those who have wronged us will be our downfall. She warned our leaders so many times, and now the wrath of the gods has fallen on us!"

Horatio and the mechanists watched quietly, uncertainty in their eyes. Thankfully, they didn't speak.

"I am sorry for their deaths." I offered a slight bow of respect. "I request safe passage through your city, Valen and Talvo. Will you grant me and the others that which was denied before?"

Valen retrieved his saber and sheathed it. "Yes. Too many died for us to learn this harsh lesson. I will not repeat it."

"Nor will I." Talvo sheathed his sword and wiped tears from his face. "Safe passage is yours. But please go quickly, for it pierces my heart to see the cause of so much death."

"That ain't even the half of it," Layla murmured.

"What?" Valen said.

Layla's eyebrows rose. "What?"

"Did you say something?" he said.

"I'm sorry for your loss." She nodded toward the walls. "Please take us through."

We made it through the labyrinth and into the city quickly. The place was a ghost town, and it soon became apparent why. A crowd gathered outside a temple where a cervitauride stood atop a stone dais, arms upraised in prayer.

"Please bring our people back to us, for we know not where they are," the priestess said. "Answer our cries, almighty ones."

A familiar minotaur looked away from the service and saw us. Taurin trotted over to us, eyes wide. "Cain? Where did you go? What happened to our people?"

"The gods punished them," Valen said. "They are all dead down to the last taur."

"No." His bull nostrils flared. "All of them?"

"All of them." I sighed. "We didn't kill them." I gave him a brief summary of what had happened.

Taurin mooed gently. "Valen, Talvo, I will take them through the other side of the labyrinth. I am sorry for your losses." He motioned us to follow, and we veered away from the crowd outside the temple. "The priestess will be pleased to learn that nearly every warrior in the city is dead. She will soon make a power play and claim the city as her own. Of that, I am certain."

"I don't think we really considered the full ramifications of all those centaurs dying on Beta." Aura shook her head. "Have we upset the balance now that beings from Prime perished in another dimension?"

Layla snorted. "Ramifications."

I shook my head.

"Sorry." Layla cleared her throat. "Cthulhu has risen. The balance is fucked."

I had little doubt that she was right.

Taurin delivered us to the other side of the labyrinth and bade us farewell. "I cannot say it was good to meet you, Cain, for my people have paid a steep price."

"It wasn't my intention, Taurin." I shook my head. "In the end, they made their own decisions, and it cost them their lives."

His nostrils flared. "It is the truth, though I hate it to my very core. May you never have cause to come this way again, Cain Sthyldor."

"Amen to that." Layla raised her hands and waved them as if worshipping.

"I may send word this way about the fate of Baura," I said. "Can you ensure the message reaches Rille and Maya of the merfolk near Prometheus's Rock?"

He nodded. "Did she do them harm as well?"

"Great harm." I pressed my lips together. "She murdered most of their reef."

He closed his big brown eyes. "I will tell them, Cain." He opened his eyes. "I would also like to know the punishment of this evil being."

"As soon as it's determined, I will send word via griffin."

Taurin mooed softly. "Thank you."

Layla turned and looked at the scrubby plains and nothingness beyond. "Gods damn it, Cain. I'm not looking forward to this walk."

Taurin regarded me for a moment longer, then turned and walked back into the labyrinth.

"I feel so bad for his people even if they died being assholes." Hannah blew out a breath, then walked over to a stand of bushes about fifty yards outside of the wall. She pulled on the greenery. It wrinkled and flickered as she pulled off the magical camouflage cover, revealing a steam wagon beneath it.

It was a clunky vehicle designed by the humans of Feary. It resembled a wild west horse-drawn carriage, complete with a seat on the front for the driver. But there were no horses since it had a steam engine powered by liquid mana. The wheels had been modified with extra rubber for off-road travel, but it was still absolute garbage compared to most forms of transportation.

"That is quite a primitive contraption." Horatio examined the boiler. "Steam locomotion?"

I nodded. "Aren't you familiar with Feary transportation?"

"Not as well as I should be." His chin rose slightly. "Our designs are far superior."

"Yeah, not so sure about that." I opened the carriage door. "Let's get going."

Horatio and the mechanists climbed into the back with Aura. Hannah and Layla joined me on the driver's bench. A pull on a lever started the boiler. After a few minutes of waiting, steam began to vent, and enough pressure built to power the engine. Chugging like a train, the carriage lurched into motion. I turned the wheel and guided the vehicle east toward the nearest town with a fairy portal. The next few hours would be bumpy, miserable, and long, but anything was better than slogging through monster-infested Gaia Beta.

THE VILLAGE of Loofa spread out in the valley below us as we crested the final hill between us and a mushroom portal granting escape from the backwoods of Feary. Mushroom-shaped houses were scattered among giant oaks that had also been hollowed out into homes by the local tree elves, a smaller variety of the common elf.

I parked the carriage outside the rental hut, and a rotund human male came outside. "You didn't clean it." Grunting with effort, he leaned down and wiped mud off a fender.

Horatio and the others climbed out and stretched their legs while the man continued his inspection. The interior was just as filthy as the exterior since the others hadn't exactly knocked the mud off their boots before climbing in.

The man gasped. "By the gods! Do you have no respect for the property of others? What did you do to my wagon?"

"We took it off-roading." I dropped a pebble in his hand. "That ought to cover a good cleaning."

He rolled it around in his thick fingers. "Barely." He turned to the hut. "Get your lazy asses out here!"

A pair of brownies skipped energetically from the hut. They stood two feet tall and wore sackcloth shorts and rough wool shirts.

"What is it, master?" The young male pranced around the human, grinning madly. "Shall we clean the shit stains from your underwear this fine day?"

The female danced in a circle in the opposite direction. "Or did you piss yourself again from too much ale, Master?"

Layla laughed. "Did you strike a bargain with brownies, hoping for free labor?"

The human scowled. "Clean out the wagon, you useless shits!"

The male twirled and bowed. "Gladly, master." Then he and the female brownie yanked down the human's pants revealing a disgusting lack of underwear or grooming beneath. Laughing gaily, they skipped to the carriage and began wiping it down.

The human stumbled backward and fell on his ass. A resigned look crossed his face, and he just sat there for a moment, red-faced and wheezing. Then he turned onto his knees, drawing gags and condemnation from a group of passersby as they got an up-close and personal look at his butthole and sagging balls.

Hannah giggled uncontrollably. Layla snickered and elbowed me. Aura wrinkled her nose and looked away. Horatio and his companions didn't seem affected. Then again, they'd seen far worse on Gaia Beta.

I regarded Layla for a moment. She seemed almost herself again, but it was probably too early to tell. I'd de-pants a hundred men if that was what it took to see her laugh like that again.

"Well, let's go to the portal." I started walking further into town amidst the tree homes and mushroom houses, some of which stood no more than four feet tall due to the diminutive inhabitants.

A wooden shutter on a tree home opened, and a cherub-faced wood elf grinned at us. "Hello, neighbors. Would you like some cookies?"

Hannah's eyes widened. "I'd love a cookie." She glanced at me. "Is it safe?"

I nodded. "Tree elves are known for their cookies and their hospitality."

"Might I have one, kind sir?" Horatio looked hopefully at the elf.

"Of course, neighbor!" The elf produced a tray of colorful cookies and held them out of the window.

I took a red one for myself. "Thank you, neighbor. Might I return the kind deed with recompense?"

The elf grinned. "Only if you want to, neighbor."

I gave him a pebble. "It is my pleasure to do so."

"Very generous, neighbor!" The wood elf tucked it away. "This will certainly help my bakeries on Gaia to prosper!"

"The Keebler family has always been a good neighbor. It is my pleasure to help." I bit into the cookie and savored the sweetness. They tasted so much better right from the source.

Hannah tilted her head. "Wait, are you telling me that's the Keebler dude?"

I nodded. "He's a billionaire by Gaian standards, but I don't think he cares about the money. He just likes everyone to have cookies."

"That's so sweet!" She curtsied. "Thank you, Mr. Elf!"

"It's my pleasure, young lady."

I turned away and began walking toward the ring of mushrooms in a meadow not far from us. It was time for the risky part. Going to the mushroom portal and hoping there weren't any pixies who recognized me. If that happened, things could get unpleasant fast.

———

38

We continued to the mushroom ring in the middle of town where a line of carriages, people on horseback, and others waited their turn to travel. We took a spot in line and waited. I typically didn't like to travel by fairy portal since pixies were often quick to report my presence, but we were far from the royal courts of Faevalorn in this part of the world, and most of the pixies in these parts were wild and independent.

We also needed to be back near Faevalorn before transitioning back to Gaia, or we'd end up somewhere in Europe.

Horatio stared glumly ahead as we stepped closer and closer to the mushroom. He seemed to sag a little more with every step. His mechanist companions spoke in hushed whispers to him, but he simply shrugged and nodded, not offering verbal replies. Now that we were out of immediate danger, I had a feeling Horatio was experiencing an existential crisis.

We finally had our turn at the portal and took it to the southern side of Faevalorn near a safe place that would allow me to transition us to Gaia using my staff. When we reached the spot, I summoned my staff. "Everyone, stand close, so I only have to do this once."

Horatio slumped against a tree. "What am I even doing, Cain? My world is destroyed, and I don't know what to do with my life." Tears trickled down his cheeks. "I thank you for saving me, but what am I to do on your Gaia?"

I'd given some thought to his predicament, because I'd never planned to take him to Sanctuary. He might be a good version of Horatio, but I wasn't about to give up the location of my secret hideout to mechanists of any flavor.

"I have a place where you'll feel wanted, Horatio." I motioned him over. "I think you'll like it a lot."

His face grew hopeful. "Really?"

I nodded. "Let's go."

Layla frowned but said nothing. The other mechanists looked at each other, hope also blooming on their faces.

I slashed the air with my staff. It bubbled out, sucking our group inside. We passed through the cold void of the in-between and popped out in a forest on Gaia on the other side. I turned and took in the beautiful sight of Dolores, my 1970 Dodge Coronet Super Bee. I rushed over and ran a hand along her curves, then climbed inside and sighed with pleasure at her loving caress.

"Gods, Cain, get a room." Layla took shotgun. "The love affair you have with this car is perverted."

Hannah grinned as she slid into the back. "You'll never compare, Layla."

Layla grinned. "Unless his car grows tits, I'll more than compare, girl."

Horatio and Aura got into the backseat, but the other two mechanists had to get into the back of the station wagon.

I turned to Horatio. "I'm going to have to render you and your friends unconscious. If you don't want to do that, then you can wait here until I come back."

Horatio nodded. "Do what you must, Cain."

I took a vial from my utility belt, uncorked it, and held it under his nose. He slumped unconscious immediately, falling onto Hannah's shoulder. Using my thumb to cover the end of the vial, I climbed out of the car and went to the back of the station wagon.

The other mechanists dutifully took sniffs and promptly passed out.

Hannah shoved Horatio off her shoulder and over to Aura. Aura took the seatbelt and strapped the man in so he'd remain upright.

I drove us to Sanctuary and parked outside instead of the garage since I'd be leaving again shortly, then went inside.

"Cain!" Fred, aka Baby Cthulhu, jumped off the couch and ran over on stubby legs to give me a hug.

"Aw, Fred!" Hannah leaned down and hugged the little guy, giving his tentacles a tickle.

One of Fred's mouth tentacles touched my wrist. *Did you receive my help, Cain?*

I frowned. "Your help?"

I made a pearl and put it in your utility belt. But you left before I had a chance to tell you about it.

I blinked and remembered the pearl in my utility belt and the octopus in the aqueduct. "Hang on, that was your minion and not Cthulhu's?"

Yes. I am learning new things about myself. I have gone traveling and had adventures of my own so I can overcome these...limitations. He held out his stubby arms and turned his hands up as if illustrating what he meant.

I stared at him for a long moment. "You and I need to have a talk, then."

I would like that, Cain.

I turned to the others. "I'm going to take care of Horatio and friends."

Layla's eyes brightened. "By killing them?"

Hannah rolled her eyes. "Not even you are that heartless."

"I'll be back." I went into my bedroom, locked the door, and took a moment to enjoy being home. Then I lifted the table in my walk-in closet to reveal stairs leading into a tunnel. I followed the winding network of tunnels until I reached my hidden vault where I stored the Soultaker swords. It was also where I'd stashed the Tetron.

Thankfully, I'd not fully trusted the safety of the warehouse and kept some items from Hephaestus's armory here instead. The Tetron was presumably what Baura had used to open the interdimensional portal from Feary Prime to Gaia Beta. I didn't know how she did it, but I planned to have a long talk with Noctua about it when I had a moment.

The Tetron was comprised of three intricate clockwork devices, the Cubon, Spheron, and Pyron. When pieced together and activated properly, it allowed the wielder to travel not just between our local splinter dimensions but also among the many other dimensions that had broken from Prime eons ago. I stuffed the device into the largest pouch on my belt, then secured the vault and returned to my room.

I put on Panoptes. "Reveal yourself." The many eyes of the ring appeared. I found a closed one. "Watch this place."

The eye opened and stared, watching my room so I could fast travel here when needed.

I took a quick shower and changed into fresh clothes, then went into the den, where it seemed the others had already done the same thing.

"Did you crack the windows on Dolores for the mechanists?" Hannah said. "They've been in there a while."

"I left the climate on in the car." I headed for the front door. "Next stop, Voltaire's."

"Gods almighty, I could use some drinks." Layla hopped up and followed.

Hannah remained on the couch next to Fred, who was munching popcorn with the use of his mouth tentacles. "Cain, I'm just gonna watch some TV with Fred."

I nodded. "I'll be late."

She grinned. "I know."

Aura sighed and stood. "Guess you'll need a bartender."

"Yeah. I'm going to need a mangorita."

"Then I'll come too."

Layla snorted. "As if Cain was just going to let you stay here unsupervised."

The three of us climbed into the car. I drove to Little Five Points and parked just outside the fae safe zone around Voltaire's.

"You two go ahead. I'll be there in a minute." I looked at Horatio. "I'm going to deal with the mechanists first."

Layla raised an eyebrow. "What do you have planned for them, Cain?"

"Hopefully, something that will make them happy."

She shrugged, then followed Aura around the corner toward the hidden entrance of Voltaire's.

I popped the cork of another vial and held it under Horatio's nose. He jerked awake. I did the same for the other two and waited for them to get out of the car.

Horatio looked around, disoriented. "Where are we?"

"Gaia Prime. But this isn't your final stop." I led them into a vacant lot just outside the fae safe zone where no one would see us, then took out the Tetron. "We're going to Alpha."

"Alpha?" He looked confused. "Why?"

"You'll see." I twisted the pieces of the Tetron. "Join hands and touch me. Whatever you do, don't let go, okay?"

The two mechanists gripped hands, and the female took Horatio's free hand. I twisted the final piece of the Tetron and took Horatio's hand. Gaia fell away beneath us as if we'd rocketed into outer space. Horatio and the mechanists gasped and cried out.

The dimensional array spread out beneath us, three Gaias like blue-green marbles. Well, two of them, anyway. Beta was covered in greenish-red hues as if it were rotting. Thanks to Cthulhu, that probably wasn't far from the truth.

Horatio sighed with wonder. "Is this what it feels like to be a god?"

"This is just an inkling of what that must be like." I focused on Gaia Alpha and zoomed us down to the parking lot behind the Voltaire's. The old one had been destroyed when the mechanists originally took over. In its place stood a great Victorian mansion. Since magic was known on this Gaia, there was no need for magic users, vampires, werewolves, or other supers to hide.

A monorail glided above the street behind us. Clockwork vehicles resembling nub cars of the nineteenth century ticked by. Airships glided serenely through the skies, many filled with passengers partying as if it were the 1920s all over again.

The humans of this world had embraced mechanist engineering and magic. The mechanists had been delighted to discover they didn't need to dominate the world by force when they could bestow mankind with their gifts freely or for profit.

Horatio and his companions turned in circles, gaping at the sights.

"Is this paradise?" Horatio proclaimed. "Cain, you have brought me to a world of wonder!"

Tears filled the eyes of the other mechanists.

The female spoke. "It is a dream come true, Inventor. We are home."

Horatio nodded. "We are home." Tears of happiness trailing down his cheeks, he turned to me. "Thank you, Cain. You have brought us to a place that gives our lives purpose."

"Your other two selves are also here. It seemed the safest place to bring them to keep them out of trouble." I pointed to Voltaire's. "Go see the Aura of this world inside and tell her I sent you. She'll put you in touch."

Sobbing, Horatio hugged me. "Thank you, Cain. My world is lost, but there is still hope."

I didn't return the hug, but I nodded. "Yeah, there is. Now, get in there, you big lug. Make a difference in the world."

He released me and clapped his hands together. "I shall!" Then Horatio and the others hurried into Voltaire's.

I ran a hand down my face and stood in silence for a long moment. There was one more to-do item on my checklist, and I wasn't looking forward to it. Before leaving, I slipped on Panoptes and grimaced as dizziness hit me. Then I concentrated on the ring. *Reveal yourself.* The plain ring of metal shimmered and revealed its true self covered in countless eyes, some of them white with blindness.

Some of the eyes were closed, but many were open, the orbs rolling wildly or staring straight ahead. I'd worked out that the blind ones were useless and, when active, only showed darkness. I'd never tried traveling to their frames for fear I'd end up in a void, so I'd deactivated them.

The rolling and wild eyes could be used to watch places, but they sometimes roamed on their own and were unreliable. Those that stared straight ahead were doing their job of watching properly, and those that were closed were also functional but just unused.

I focused on one closed eye. *Watch this place.*

It opened, and a red iris gazed unblinkingly.

Keeping my focus on it, I sent it another command. *Reveal yourself.*

The air shimmered, and a massive eyeball appeared, floating a few feet above the ground and watching Voltaire's. I tried to touch it, but my hand went through it.

Hide yourself.

The eye vanished.

"Now, that is creepy." I hadn't been sure what to expect when asking an eye to reveal itself, but now that I knew, I envisioned giant eyes watching the places they'd been ordered to.

By leaving an eye here, I now had a shortcut to this world without using the Tetron. Panoptes was dangerous to use, but it was a good backup plan. As I reached down to slide the ring from my finger, I noticed fine, black veins writhing beneath the skin on my hand. I watched, entranced, and pulled up my sleeve to see the worms crawling up my arm just beneath the surface.

I flinched and yanked off the ring. The darkness receded, and my skin looked normal once more. Had that been a side effect of Panoptes, or was it a lingering after-effect of the gaze of Cthulhu? I didn't know, but I'd have to keep a close eye on things.

Using the Tetron, I went back to Voltaire's in Prime, walked downstairs to the door, and knocked.

The speakeasy panel slid open, and Durrug's eyes appeared on the other side. He grunted and opened the door without waiting on the password.

I stepped inside. "Greetings, Durrug."

He held up a book with a scantily clad cervitauride on the front. "I just get latest book from new favorite author."

I read the title. "Tales of a Trailer Park Centaur by Kimbra the Witch?"

He nodded. "She good. You tell Durrug in Alpha to read."

I nodded. "I'll tell him next time I'm over there." Durrug and his alt in Alpha liked one-upping each other with book recommendations, and it was handy being on the good sides of bridge trolls since they and their kin controlled access to a lot of places.

I joined Layla and Aura at the bar. A frosty mangorita already waited on me.

Layla smirked. "I promise I didn't drug your drink, Cain."

I raised an eyebrow. "You sound more like yourself after that failed heroic suicide."

"Nothing like a glimpse of true death to make you appreciate what you have." A haunted look flashed behind her eyes. "I'll never be the same after what I went through in Soultaker, but living is still more fun than dying."

Aura snorted. "Amen to that. I could go the rest of my life without dying again if it pleases the universe."

"Well, you're stuck living no matter what." Layla sipped her drink. "You'll never die even if you want to."

It was Aura's turn to look haunted. "Yeah, I've thought about that before. I'll never age, never die. If I have kids, will they be mortal? I wish I could ask Athena."

"Best not to think about it or have kids." Layla patted her on the back. "Last thing I want is more Auras running around." She turned to me. "What valuable lesson did you learn from all this, Cain?"

I stirred the drink with the plastic pirate sword. "Never start a land war in Asia, and never wake Cthulhu."

Layla winced and held up her glass. "I'll drink to that."

I clinked my glass against hers and Auras. "Here's to the end of at least one world."

"To the end of a world." Layla finished her drink and slapped the counter. "I need more. I want to get fae girl wasted."

"Shots?" Aura rose from her seat.

I nodded. "Shots."

A GOOD WHILE LATER, I woke up on the floor of Aura's private apartment in Voltaire's. Layla was passed out on the couch, and Aura snored peacefully on the bed. We were all clothed, so it seemed as though we'd managed one adventure without resorting to teen fantasy sex fulfillment that so offended some people's sensibilities.

I reached into my utility belt and took a potion to relieve my pounding headache and the lingering effects of so much alcohol. It was five in the morning, and I had one more responsibility before I could truly rest.

39

U sing Panoptes, I traveled to the warehouse.
I went to the chest with Baura and heard her whimpering inside. I unlocked the straps, and she gasped.

"Cain?"

"Don't do anything stupid."

"I won't. Just let me out of this fucking box!"

I opened the box.

Hands outstretched, Baura snarled and lunged for my throat. My brightblade sizzled into her chest, and she flopped back inside, dead once again. I banished the brightblade and looked at her corpse. Killing her was necessary because Panoptes didn't allow me to travel with a living person. The question remained, what did I do with her?

I couldn't just leave her locked up in a box. That kind of cruel and unusual punishment was too much, even for someone who'd destroyed an entire world for her revenge against the gods. I needed someplace secure, secret, and safe where she could live but do no harm. I needed a prison that routinely handled powerful entities.

There was another major issue. She somehow controlled eldritch minions without touching the Rlhala, meaning she'd given Cthulhu a command that allowed her remote control of his creatures. I didn't think the connection would work across dimensions, but there was no way to know for sure. I needed to mitigate that risk for all mankind.

I knew of only one person who could do that, so I made a phone call.

"Cain?" Fitzroy Simmons sounded wary, which was smart considering the situations I'd dragged him into.

I told him what I needed. "Is it possible?"

"It's horrific, Cain. I won't do it."

"Did I mention she wiped out humanity on Gaia Beta and raised Cthulhu? That she still retains control over him and could discover a way to bring him to Gaia?"

He paused. "Can she control the Cthulhu here?"

"I don't think so. She destroyed my Rlhala, so she'd have to bring the one from her world here in order to reach him in his dreams." I considered the possibilities. "Cthulhu exists separately in each dimension because he's not a full-fledged Elder Thing. We need to sever the connection Baura has just to be safe, though."

"I don't like it at all, Cain. It's abhorrent and goes against all my training." He sighed. "But for the good of mankind, I will do it."

"Thank you. I'll see you soon." I wished I'd placed an eye to watch Fitz's place so I could quick-travel there, but now I had to do it the old-fashioned way. I'd tried traveling across the globe using the Tetron. Sometimes it worked, but other times it didn't. I assumed that was because I didn't have the mental capacity required to master it.

I dumped Baura back in the chest and secured it, then traveled back to the parking lot and Dolores. I called a company at PDK Airport and chartered a flight. By the time I arrived, they were ready to depart.

I caught up on lost sleep during the flight and felt better when we set down at a small airport near Seattle a few hours later. A taxi delivered me to Fitz's house not long after. He answered the front door.

"I have been dreading your arrival all day."

I shrugged. "Sorry, but this has to be done."

He grunted and motioned me toward the gate in the fence on the side of his house. It unlatched at his touch and locked behind us. Using Panoptes, I traveled to the warehouse and returned with Baura's body.

Fitz examined her. "Cain, she's dead."

"She is, but she'll revive at midnight." I looked at her. "Not even burning her to ash will prevent that."

He frowned. "What kind of existence is that? What if someone buried her underground for eternity?"

"Or chained her to a boulder at the bottom of the ocean?" I grimaced. "Look, I don't want her suffering for an eternity. This will be a mercy to her and humanity even if it's horrible."

He nodded solemnly. "Memory alteration and mind-reading are black magic, Cain. It will harm her and stain my soul. Severe brain damage is unavoidable."

"We could just lobotomize her." I shifted the corpse in my arms. "Can you extract the location of the Rlhala from her? I also need to know where her Tetron and any other items from the lost armory are."

He nodded. "Her mind will be open to me during the process, so I will learn what I can."

"Once I know where the Rlhala and other items are, I'm going to try to recover them."

"That sounds extremely dangerous if Cthulhu is wandering the land."

"Can't be helped." I blew out a breath. "I need to see if I can reverse her commands."

Fitz tapped a finger on his chin. "Tell me this. If she dies, will her mind heal?"

I shook my head. "If I cut her and she doesn't die by the time the wound heals and scars over, the scar would remain." I lifted her shirt, but she didn't have the same scars on her abdomen that Aura from Alpha did. She did, however, have a long scar on the back of a leg.

Fitz nodded. "Let's secure her in the cellar, and I will perform the procedure once she resurrects." He pursed his lips. "What if we asked a vampire to compel her to forget everything?"

"I don't know a single vampire I'd trust, and compulsion isn't fool-proof." I shook my head. "I trust you, Fitz."

"Yes, well, that has gotten me into a great deal of trouble." He walked toward the cellar door. "I'll have to be very careful not to kill her during the process."

I hefted Baura's body and followed him downstairs into the root cellar. Rare, magical ingredients filled rows of shelves. He took me to the back, where I found a new addition to his workshop—a silver chair with restraints. Beyond that was a cage of similar metal.

"Where did these come from?"

"It seemed wise for me to purchase a mithril chair and cage in case you ever dropped off powerful deities for me to keep prisoner again."

"Smart." I put Baura's body in the chair and secured it. Then I stood back and regarded her for a long moment. She looked peaceful in death. It was a shame I couldn't make it permanent.

"I'm pleased that you look troubled, Cain." Fitz went to his work-table and began gathering ingredients. "Despite the horrible things you've done, you're still human after all."

"More or less." I sighed. "I have another side project I'd like to discuss sometime."

"Oh, dear." He looked up from his work. "What is it?"

"I want to kill a necromancer who murders young men and women and turns them into his playthings."

Fitz hissed. "Necromancers are a blight on the natural order. I will gladly help you with that." He sprinkled ingredients into his pestle. "Another time, of course."

"Another time." I walked toward the stairs. "Let me know if you need anything. I've got more errands to run."

"I'll let you know the moment it's done, Cain." Fitz waved good-bye, then returned to his work.

I went outside. This time I used the Tetron. When the dimensional array appeared, I focused on Oblivion Prime. I tried rotating the view to a familiar area like the beaches near Karnassas and the remains of Olympus but only managed to slightly shift my relative location.

The part of Oblivion I hovered over was barren and rocky, but it would do. I focused on it and shot toward the world, landing seconds later. I took in my surroundings and scanned them with my scope to ensure there were no lurking monsters like rock crabs or boulder giants. Once I was satisfied, I took out an owl whistle and blew it.

A feminine voice emanated from inside it. "Cain?"

"Hello, Noctua."

"We have not spoken in some time. I hope you are well."

I grunted. "I'm surprisingly well, all things considered. Can you answer some questions about the Tetron for me?"

"Gladly." She hooted gently. "What would you like to know?"

I summed up my adventure to Gaia Beta. "How did Baura create a portal and keep it open?"

"It is not possible as far as I know, Cain." Her beak clicked. "Only gods can do such a thing. The Tetron does not utilize portals, according to the records I possess."

"You're certain?"

"Quite certain." She hooted again. "Only powerful gods can create interdimensional portals and hold them open."

"Like Loki?"

"Perhaps. Most of the Olympians can."

"Yeah, but none of them would be helping Baura in her insane quest." I shook my head. "This sounds like the work of the gods of chaos."

"I agree."

Another thought occurred. "Can Nyarlathotep open portals?"

"I lack the information to answer that."

Either way, this was worrisome. It meant Baura almost certainly received help from a god. If said god had tried to lure me into a death-trap, why had they left open the portal? They could have closed it and trapped me on Gaia Beta. Then again, maybe they'd been too busy with other plans to return and close the portal.

On the upside, if Baura hadn't known I didn't possess the apocalypse weapons, then it likely meant her godlike benefactor didn't know either.

"Can you tell me how to select my arrival location when using the Tetron? For example, I'd like to land in another geographical location not relative to my location on the originating world."

"The process is simple, but it requires a great deal of energy," Noctua replied. "You must rotate the Spheron until you are aligned with your arrival destination. You can freely view the planet doing this, but once you commit to a destination, it will extract the energy needed to move you there."

"That sounds extremely simple." I frowned. "Where does the energy come from?"

"You, of course." She hooted gently. "I would be careful on your first try."

"I'll do that." I posed an unrelated question. "Now that I know my origins of Ekhsis, are you allowed to answer my questions regarding them?"

"Unfortunately, the knowledge is there but unreachable." She clicked her beak. "It is rather frustrating."

"There is a dragon named Tythus who roams the wastes near the Kameni desert. He has a collection of journals and other documents from my people. Can you meet with him and store that knowledge for me?"

"Gladly, Cain. Korborus and I are actually headed that way now." She hooted. "Did you know we found a lost tribe of crab people living among the coral reefs of Saginon? They look like crabs but talk like people. I would love to tell you about our adventures when you have time."

It only seemed polite since she listened to my adventures whenever we talked. "Yes. Let's plan to meet in person soon so you can regale me with yours and Korborus's adventures."

"This pleases me to no end, Cain." She hooted happily. "Gathering knowledge is great fun, but Korborus is not much of an intellectual. He is more about smashing and maiming monsters and other beings who threaten us."

"He's your best friend and doesn't want anything bad to happen to you."

"Yes, our bond is special, Cain." She went silent for a moment. "I think I have fallen in love with my companion."

I blinked a few times. "Um, that's amazing. I'm so happy for you."

A mechanical growling emanated from the whistle. "He says I am his darling owl, and any who dare oppose me will meet a violent end. He considers such threats romantic."

This had taken a turn I wasn't prepared for. "Let's talk about this when we meet. I'll buy you lovebirds a drink or something."

"As clockwork beings, we do not require sustenance, Cain. Our love is powered by magic and the gears ticking in our hearts." She hooted softly. "You brought us together, so we consider you our best friend in all the worlds."

I cleared my throat. "Thank you, Noctua. I'll talk to you again soon."

"Goodbye, my friend."

Korborus, the three-headed Mecha-Cerberus, growled in the background.

"Goodbye." I tucked the whistle away and stared out at the ocean, trying to process just what in the hell had happened. Noctua had always been factual and unemotional. Korborus had been created for the sole purpose of guarding the lost armory. It seemed their adventures together had bonded and changed them profoundly.

"If a clockwork owl and three-headed hound can fall in love, then I guess anything is possible." I let that sink in before using the Tetron. When the interdimensional array appeared, I zoomed in on Gaia Beta. I rotated the Spheron, and sure enough, the world below me rotated.

I circled the planet so I could get a good look at the damage.

Entire continents had been rearranged. Australia was cut in half by a jagged canal running from Sydney to the northwestern corner. Singapore and the other island nations to the north were just gone, replaced by masses of squirming tentacles. New Zealand looked oddly untouched. The story was the same in Asia and Europe, where vast swaths of land were now underwater or covered in swamps and blight.

A massive pit in northern Russia reminded me of something I'd seen in Fyeth Elunore. I observed it for a moment and confirmed my suspicion that it was a shudde m'ell—a cthonian worm. It regurgitated a host of dark young and shoggoths into the world, a new invasion force that was likely sent to challenge Cthulhu's current dominion. Over the next few hours, I spotted several more signs that Shub-Nuggerath was intent on wresting control of the world away from him.

We now had a world ruled by Elder Things in our own interdimensional backyard. The only upside was that it looked like they'd be busy fighting over Gaia Beta like a scrap of raw meat.

I'd seen enough, for now. I went back to the dimensional array and returned to Fitz's backyard so I didn't have to expend energy traveling to a new geographical location. Even so, I felt drained and mentally exhausted from having remained in orbit above Gaia Beta for so long. I set an eye to watch Fitz's place, then traveled to my bedroom in Sanctuary using the eye I'd set to watch the place earlier.

I was so tired that I could barely keep my eyes open. The Tetron and Panoptes extracted a heavy price for their use. I got out of my clothes and fell into bed.

THE GREAT EYES of Cthulhu glare at me, twin suns sizzling in a sea of red. I'm paralyzed, floating, bodiless above a vast army of minions. I can smell the blight, the rot, the blood.

I JERKED AWAKE, sweat beading my forehead and soaking my sheets. My skin crawled with sensations. I held out my hands. Dark worms writhed beneath the surface. I leaped out of bed and ran into the bathroom. My eyes were black as pitch. Blackness squirmed around my eyes. I splashed water over my face and blinked.

Just like that, my skin was back to normal. "That's not good." I sighed. The effects of Cthulhu's gaze lingered. Maybe they'd be with me forever. It was one more thing I needed to ask of Fitz. Maybe he could diagnose the issue.

My phone rang. I checked the caller ID and answered. "Speak of the devil."

Fitz spoke in a tired voice. "Cain, it's done."

I used Panoptes to travel to him. He was in the root cellar. Baura was secured in the mithril chair.

She looked up at me woozily. "Who is that?"

I raised an eyebrow. "I'm Cain."

A frown. "Am I supposed to know you? Fitz said I was in an accident."

"No, you don't know me." I cast a sigil to cover her ears so she couldn't hear us speak and took Fitz out of sight of her. "Were you able to find out anything?"

He nodded. "She has a cache of items stored beneath Mount Olympus in Greece. None of them are the apocalypse weapons you seek."

I sighed. "Clever woman."

"Too clever by far." Fitz yawned. "She honed her insanity into a doubled-edged, poisoned dagger, Cain. It is remarkable. I find it hard to believe she could even remain coherent, much less formulate world-dominating plans and the murder of Athena given her overuse of Panoptes and exposure to eldritch creatures."

"Probably because a god has been helping her." I felt an object in my hand and realized I was rubbing Panoptes between my fingers. I stuffed it back into my utility belt. I just hope I can get to her cache without too much trouble."

"Shouldn't the Tetron make it simple?"

"It should, but Gaia Beta is infested with the eldritch. Shub-Nuggerath and possibly other Elder Things are making a play for the world. I think all unholy hell is about to break loose there."

Fitz's eyes closed. He nodded off, then jerked awake with a start. "Cain, I'm sorry. I've been at this since midnight. I will keep her here for observation if you wish, but I think she's been neutralized." He sighed. "Now, I must sleep, for tonight, I must perform a cleansing ritual to wash the stain of black magic from my soul."

"You can do that?"

"For small stains, yes." He shook his head. "The larger ones do not come out so easily."

"I didn't even know there was such a thing as black magic." I folded my arms. "I've used magic to kill. Wouldn't that be black magic?"

"I am too tired to discuss this now, Cain." He patted my shoulder. "I'm going to bed."

"Before you go, I was wondering if you could diagnose a problem I'm having—not now, but next time." I grimaced. "I looked Cthulhu in the eyes, and I'm having, um, problems."

He sighed. "I hope you don't need a unicorn heart again."

"Me either." I put a hand on his shoulder. "Rest well, friend. I'll take Baura with me."

"Wonderful." He went around the shelf and to the mithril chair. Touching an amulet to the restraints released them.

"Why can't I hear anything?" Baura stared blankly. "My ears are fuzzy."

I dispelled the sigils. "Is that better?"

She smiled. "Oh, yes, thanks."

I peered into her eyes, trying to determine if this was real or an act.

Fitz touched Baura's temple. "Cain, her mind is truly stilled. She is not pretending, I assure you."

"You're 100 percent positive?"

"Yes. Unless her mind resets and heals at midnight, the damage is permanent."

"As long as she doesn't die before the end of the day, we should be good."

"Then keep her safe." He stumbled upstairs and left me alone with my new brain-damaged acquaintance.

I took Baura's hand, led her upstairs, and closed the cellar door behind me. It vanished behind a camouflage veil. I activated the

Tetron and took us into the dimensional array. She gasped in delight.

"It's the stars!" She reached out as if to touch Gaia. "Can I hold it?"

"You once held a world in your hand." I sighed. "Let's leave this one alone." I covered her eyes with a sigil and then rotated the Spheron until we hovered almost over Sanctuary, or at least where my home should be. All I could see were trees. No matter which way I turned the Spheron, I couldn't align us precisely over Sanctuary. It seemed the silver ring, wards, and other protections prevented me from traveling directly there. Caolan's druid magic was really damned strong.

I willed the Tetron to take me down. The air whooshed from my lungs as if an invisible fist connected with my chest. Baura gasped in unison with me, and we hurtled groundward. We landed on our feet but promptly dropped to our knees, gasping and wheezing. My legs felt like jelly, and my lungs felt incapable of drawing breath.

The cost of traveling with the Tetron was higher than I'd imagined. It seemed to have pulled energy from Aura as well. I wondered if we'd shared the cost, and if so, how bad off would I be right now if I'd done it alone. It was something I'd have to experiment with on an off day.

After a few minutes, I felt strong enough to stand up and pulled Baura to her feet. We were just outside the gates leading to my property. I disabled the wards and opened the gate.

"I can't see!" Baura stumbled after me. "What is wrong with me?"

She sounded so innocent and dumb that I began to feel more certain that Fitz's memory extraction had worked. He'd erased her memories as far back as possible and apparently caused a great deal of unintentional brain damage doing it. I led her down the road and to the old church that was my home, my birthplace, and the former location of a cult that worshipped Nyarlathotep.

You might say it had a little bit of history.

"What the hell happened to Aura?" Hannah did a double-take when we stepped inside. "Oh my god, that's Baura, isn't it?"

"Yeah."

Fred waddled over and touched her. "Broken Aura." He purred, and his eyelids grew heavy with contentment.

I raised an eyebrow. "You sense something?"

"Brain broken." Fred touched me. *Her thoughts are chaotic. I find them pleasurable.* His tentacles trembled.

"Wonderful. I guess you enjoy chaos like your father."

He nodded. *I am sorry, Cain.*

"Not your fault." I took Baura by the arm. "I've got to keep an eye on her overnight to make sure it sticks." I turned to Fred. "You can confirm her condition in the morning."

He nodded, mouth tentacles flailing. "Yes, gladly. Can I sleep with her?"

Hannah grimaced. "Fred, that's creepy."

He nodded, tentacles stretched in a grin. "I like creepy!"

"Uh, I'm not mentally prepared for something like that." I put a hand on his head. "Please, don't."

Fred looked downcast but nodded. *I would love to fill my mind with her broken thoughts for hours, but I will do as you ask.*

"Thank the gods." Keeping Baura blinded, I took her downstairs, through the library, and into one of the rooms that locked from the outside. The cultists of Nyar had apparently used the area as a dungeon. I'd remodeled and turned the cells into spare bedrooms but had kept the stout doors and exterior locks.

I pushed Baura gently down on a bed and removed the blind from her eyes. "You're my guest for tonight."

She blinked, looking up at me innocently. "Guest?"

I nodded. "My guest."

She looked at the bed for several seconds without speaking, then looked up at me. "Who are you?"

"Cain." I eased the door shut and locked it and then I looked at her through the barred window. "I'll bring you food later."

She flinched and looked up. "Oh?" Then she stared at the pattern on the bedsheets. "These are flowers!"

I went back upstairs and sat on the couch next to Hannah.

"We're gonna binge some Marvel movies, Cain." She grinned. "You in?"

I was still weak from using the Tetron. Vegging out on the couch sounded marvelous. "Sure."

Hannah glanced at the door leading downstairs. "What did you do to her?"

"Fitz erased her mind. It caused some major damage, but at least she's functioning."

"Oof." She winced. "Well, she deserved it. Too bad you can't just kill her."

"Yeah, it's too bad."

"Think she'll start shitting her pants? Do we need to get her adult diapers?"

"Gods, I hope not." I nodded at the television. "Let's do this."

Fred looked longingly at the basement door, then back to the movie. "I am sad."

Hannah patted his hand. "Maybe Cain will let you sense Baura's damaged mind tomorrow before he takes her."

He looked at me with huge eyes. "Please?"

I groaned. "Fine, Fred. Just give it a rest tonight, okay?"

I wanted to relax and enjoy this evening because tomorrow I'd be journeying back into hell.

40

Baura was still just as mentally defective the next morning. The brain damage was seemingly permanent. Fred gleefully confirmed her condition, purring softly, eyes closed with pleasure. I gave him a few minutes to enjoy his vice before taking her to what would likely be her eternal prison.

Baura had gone number two in the room's toilet but hadn't flushed. The fact that she was still potty trained was a win in my book. She'd also kept her clothes on and seemed able to function at the level of a five-year-old.

"Delicious, she is!" Fred said.

"Talking like Yoda now?" I patted his head. "It's time for me to take her."

A tentacle wrapped around my wrist. *More, please.*

"Fred, control yourself."

He sighed, releasing me and Baura. "Yummy brain, Cain. I want more."

"How about I take you to an insane asylum, Fred?" Hannah grinned madly.

"Don't you dare." I shook my head. "Behave while I'm gone, okay?"

Hannah and Fred looked downcast.

"Oh, all right." Hannah sighed and trudged out of the dungeon. Fred waddled after her on his short legs.

I was still exhausted from using the Tetron, so I took the long way to Feary, driving Dolores to my favorite transition spot in the forest not far from Sanctuary. Using my staff, Baura and I planeswalked to Feary, not far from a giant tree with claw marks. I put a hand on the marks and requested a ride into Faevalorn.

About thirty minutes later, a griffin landed. I paid her in gummy worms, and she took us to the city gates. I looked around and saw a pixie's eyes flare with recognition when she spotted me.

I waved my hand. "Can you please notify Erolith that I'm here?"

She dropped down and hovered just before my face. "Cain, I would not report you. You saved my cousin's life."

"You're related to Tempest?" I didn't remember seeing this pixie during my last visit here.

She nodded. "We're from the Fungus Forest tribe. Many of us are related, and we're grateful you saved the life of our dear Tempest."

Baura grinned stupidly. "What a pretty little girl. Would you like my candy?"

I sighed. "Ignore her. She has severe mental issues. I need to speak with Erolith so he can help me."

The pixie blinked. "Then I will gladly help you. Our tribe is eternally grateful to you."

"Eternally?" I didn't understand. "I saved Tempest's life, but that doesn't mean you're in my debt forever."

"We saved your life, so the debt was paid, but many of us are still grateful." She smiled. "That is different."

"It's certainly surprising. Pixies don't like humans."

"You've proven yourself to be special, Cain." She flitted upward. "I will announce your arrival to Erolith. May he have mercy on you."

"Horses!" Baura ran after a horse and slipped into a pile of manure. She sat in the mess, squishing it between her fingers, much to the disgust of a group of elves passing by.

"What a disgrace!" One of them said loud enough for all to hear.

I groaned and watched her, because I sure as Hades didn't want to touch her now.

A pair of Oblivion Guard, a drow and an elf, rode horses through the gates ten minutes later and regarded me cautiously.

The drow spoke. "Erolith sent us to retrieve you, Cain."

I pointed toward Baura. "She needs to come too."

It seemed to take all their training for their faces to remain emotionless. The drow dismounted her horse and gripped Aura by the arm, yanking her out of the manure.

Baura held up her disgusting fingers. "Want to play with me?"

The drow wrinkled her nose, then slung Baura over the back of her horse like a sack of oats and strapped her down. Baura struggled. The drow traced a sigil on Baura's forehead, and she slumped unconscious.

I looked at the elf still on horseback. "Can I get a ride?"

The elf reached down a hand and helped me up behind her.

"Thank you."

She didn't reply.

We rode in silence to Erolith's estate, drawing stares from passersby, either because they recognized the infamous Cain or were looking at the poop-stained Baura slung over a horse's ass.

Erolith was waiting outside his blocky modern home when we entered the gates. The drow unstrapped Baura and pulled her off the horse by the ankle. She caught her by the neck to keep her from flopping to the ground, then eased her onto the grass and removed the sigil that had knocked her out.

It was impressive that the drow didn't get so much as a speck of manure on her uniform. I dismounted the elf's horse and approached my adoptive father.

"Thank you for seeing me, sir."

Erolith glanced down at Baura. "This is the elf from Beta, I assume?"

I nodded.

"Then you have a story to tell me." His fingers twitched in the secret sign language of the Oblivion Guard. The elf and drow left without a word. Erolith turned and motioned at a pair of servants. "Please clean up our guest."

They wrinkled their noses, then stooped to pick Baura from the ground and took her away.

I followed Erolith inside and up to a simple room with two chairs and a table. He closed the doors and traced a silencing sigil to keep anyone from overhearing us. Then he went to a wooden chest on a shelf and opened it. "Would you share tobacco and drink with me, son?"

"Gladly." I sat on a chair. "What's this room?"

"I come here to think and be alone."

"Where is Mother?"

"She has gone to the Summer Court to investigate a disturbance at the mana forge there." He turned to me. "I suspect this is part of your story."

"Have you spoken with Lord Aeolus recently?"

Erolith paused, packing his pipe to regard me. "No. He does not deign to speak with city-dwelling fae."

"Well, that's a bonus." I accepted a glass of blue liquid from him. "Drow brandy? This is a treat."

He filled his own glass halfway and sat down opposite me before lighting his pipe. "A liquor so flavorful yet poisonous that only a select few may enjoy it."

I held up my glass. "Thank you, Father."

Erolith held up his glass and nodded. "You're welcome, son."

We sipped in silence for a moment, savoring the flavorful brandy. No one except a secretive group of drow and probably some high fae knew exactly how it was made or what gave it such strong flavor, but one key ingredient was a poisonous plant that grew only on a single mountain in Feary. It was a rare but potent herb used for potions, weapons, and also this brandy.

As a member of the Oblivion Guard, I'd imbibed many poisons to build a tolerance to them. After a raucous party night involving two bottles of drow brandy, I'd learned that my training also helped me survive drinking it, though I'd been so sick I'd nearly wished for death.

Erolith handed me his pipe, and I took a puff from it, holding the strong, bitter smoke in my mouth and letting it perfectly counterbalance the brandy. I gave it back to him and enjoyed this rare moment with the man who'd saved and adopted me, the last of the Ekhsis.

We leaned back in our chairs and embraced the silence.

After a time, Erolith set down the pipe and spoke. "Tell me what you need, Cain."

Over the next few glasses of brandy, I told him the story of Gaia Beta and my quest to capture Baura. And how we needed to ensure she remained a prisoner forever.

He said nothing until I was finished. "As usual, you have done what needed doing. I could speak with Queen Solara on your behalf about the liquid mana, but I am certain she will not be willing to overlook it, despite your just use of it."

"I know you must and will report this crime, as is your duty, but I only tell you this out of an abundance of caution." Erolith had already suspected I'd had something to do with it, and Lord Aeolus had probably already reported it to his queen. But I had another reason for telling him.

The briefest flash of pride crossed his face. "Duly noted, son. Tell me your concern."

"An entire army of centaurs from Feary Prime died on Gaia Beta, and I also stole a great deal of liquid mana and dwarven sentinels from Feary Prime. I'm certain this has upset the interdimensional balance in some way I don't yet know or understand."

Erolith pursed his lips. "The chaos effect is difficult to predict, but I suspect you are right. Liquid mana is a precious commodity, and moving so much matter from one dimension to another might affect the balance in ways we don't understand. Perhaps the splinter dimensions are so close to Prime that the effects will be negligible, or perhaps the ripples will form an unstoppable tsunami."

"It is why I propose recovering the missing materials by taking them from Feary Beta."

He raised an eyebrow. "That could balance the scales and wipe the crime clean from your ledger. But it is also an extreme risk that might not be necessary."

"It's something I'm considering. If I choose to do so, my task would be immeasurably easier if the dwarves shut down the sentinels here on Prime so they don't attack."

"That may be asking too much." Erolith pursed his lips. "There are rumors that the queens from Beta and Alpha have reached out to our queens for help. It seems there may be a fresh human revolt brewing on Gaia Alpha now that the non-magical humans are part of the community. Feary Beta, of course, came under severe attack from Baura. That is what little I know of the current state of affairs, but it is enough to know that the queens would be more likely to lure you into a trap than see you succeed at balancing the scales."

I took a sip of brandy and nodded. "Then I will leave it well enough alone. As long as you can ensure Baura is comfortably imprisoned, then at least that threat will be gone. All that's left now is to quantify the threat Cthulhu might pose from Beta."

"Indeed." Erolith rose. "The elf will be safe and comfortable in the Eternal Garden."

"Wow." I finished my brandy and rose. "That's practically fae heaven."

"Her mind has been ravaged. She is as innocent as a child now." Erolith emptied his pipe and cleaned it. "She can run free in a place she will never escape. Had you left her mind intact, I would have recommended the Eternal Frost."

"We needed to know all her secrets before erasing her memories. Her condition was an intended and necessary side effect since she can't be killed. It also means she's eternally trapped in a prison of her own body no matter where she is."

He nodded. "It is no less than what she deserves for her crimes."

I still had places to go and people to see, so I gave my father a curt nod. "Thank you for your hospitality. I have several more errands to run, so you'll have to excuse me."

"There are other matters we must still discuss, namely the missing apocalypse weapons." Erolith placed his pipe back into its wooden case. "Do you have any idea who might have taken them?"

I'd considered not telling him about the weapons, but since they were apparently loose in the universe somewhere, it seemed better that he be in the know so his extensive network of pixie spies could keep an eye out. "I have almost nothing to go on, but I'll investigate. I can't relax until I know those weapons are destroyed."

"And you don't intend to secretly keep them as you have been?"

"That was a mistake I don't intend to repeat." I shook my head. "There's no safe place to keep them. Destruction is the only solution."

Erolith watched me for a moment, then nodded. "I believe you're being sincere."

"May I ask that you send a message to Taurin of Minos and Rille and Maya of the merfolk near Prometheus's Rock?"

He raised an eyebrow. "These are the beings Baura wronged?"

I nodded. "Tell them how Baura has been dealt with."

"I will ensure the message reaches them."

"Thank you." I turned toward the door. "I need to go."

"I'll provide you with transportation."

The same elf who'd given me a ride earlier was waiting outside when we emerged from the house. She helped me up behind her, and we set off right away. We didn't say a word to each other, though I could tell from the way she kept looking over her shoulder at me that she really wanted to know why in the hell the infamous Cain had been in the home of the leader of the Oblivion Guard.

Erolith might be my adoptive father, but he'd never shown me favoritism. In fact, he'd tried to arrest me on several occasions and had sent the Oblivion Guard to reel me in when I revolted and tried to leave them.

The elf didn't stop her horse at the city gates but continued down the path in the forest toward the griffin tree. Her back muscles twitched, and that was when I realized there was something more going on than I'd realized. I shoved myself back off the horse and landed on my feet as a longshot whistled through the air where my head had been a moment ago.

I cast shields randomly in multiple directions. Three shattered from longshots instantly. I ghostwalked to a tree and dove behind it, then summoned my staff and ignited the brightblade. The air shimmered as the translucent energy of a longshot streaked from above. I whipped the blade up and deflected the magical energy. Some of it soaked into the staff, and the brightblade hummed a little brighter.

The sources of the attacks were hidden by fae glamour, but I knew they were Oblivion Guard. The question was, why in the hell had Erolith had them attack me here instead of in his compound where he could've easily taken me?

I rolled right and parried another longshot and another. My attackers were in the trees. I might not be able to see them, but there were other ways to sense their presence. The scope on my staff could see through fae glamour, but I couldn't exactly peer through it in the heat of battle. Instead, I resorted to other methods.

The guardians were invisible, but the way they affected the environment was not. I'd already pinpointed the branch the nearest attacker was on just from the angle of the longshots. I spotted two more branches jostled by the sudden movements of someone standing on them. They were at least twenty feet overhead.

I ran toward the nearest tree and used my momentum to run up the trunk. When I hit the apex, I ghostwalked higher and slashed the branch with my brightblade. The fae glamour also masked sound, so I couldn't hear if the move surprised them or not. The leaves below crunched and depressed as a body landed and rolled. The attacker was out of position but probably unharmed.

Still in the air, I cast a series of shields and ran along them like steppingstones to the next tree, jumped, and slashed the branch. The branch shook an instant before I hit it, and leaves fell from a lower branch as the invisible attacker presumably anticipated my move and jumped. I ghostwalked lower and rolled on the ground toward another tree.

If the attackers were visible, I might have a fighting chance, but there was little I could do with them still cloaked. Guardians usually uncloaked while attacking, since maintaining the glamour took a great deal of power even though the sigils were woven into their uniforms. It was also considered a matter of honor by some. This attack felt different as if the rules had changed.

There was only one way to escape, so I took it and put on Panoptes. I traveled to the warehouse an instant before another long-shot took off my head. Five more splintered the tree trunk where I'd been. Smoke rose from burning bark.

A drow shimmered into view. "Where did he go?"

"He does not have the uniform or the glamour." Another drow appeared, sweeping the area with the scope on her oblivion staff. "I do not see him."

The first drow narrowed his gaze. "He did not ghostwalk. This is something different."

Four more low fae guardians appeared.

One of them, a female with a hawkish nose and thin lips, sprinkled pixie dust where I'd been. The dust could uncover just about anything, no matter how strong the glamour, but it didn't seem to affect the hidden eye of Panoptes. Despite the dizziness from wearing the ring, I kept it on and maneuvered the eye back and away from the attackers.

I recognized the low fae female, and that was troubling. Because she'd died to the dark young of Shub-Nuggerath during the battle of the Dead Forest.

41

T he drow's name was Ena, and she'd been one of the hardline followers of Torvin Rayne, the sadistic former commander of the Oblivion Guard. I recognized others among them from Torvin's inner circle as well. Most of them had also died during the battle of the Dead Forest. The two drow, Anair and Gira, had been devoured by giant dhole worms.

That could only mean one thing. These guardians were not from my dimension.

I turned the eye toward the elf who'd given me the ride and wondered if she was the one from Prime or if that one had been replaced by her alt.

One thing was certain. Erolith knew nothing of this ambush because he hadn't ordered it.

"He possesses devices from the lost armory." Ena scowled. "He must have used one to escape." She turned to the elf who'd given me a ride. "You gave it away, Tisha. He sensed something was wrong and dismounted before I took off his head."

Tisha bowed her shoulders. "I gave nothing away. I don't understand."

Baring her teeth, Ena stepped closer. "Were Torvin alive, he would take your head. We did not go through the trouble of kidnapping your alt and replacing her with you for blunders like this." Her fists clenched. "I am certain that his next move will be contacting Erolith to find out why he would order such an attack.

Anair shook her head. "No. We have the numbers now to keep Cain from getting anywhere close to Erolith, and our pixies have infiltrated his spy network. We can intercept any messages before they reach him."

I had no doubt that was true. There was no way I could sneak within a mile of Erolith's compound, and unless I found another relative of Tempest's pixie family, there weren't any pixies I could trust with a message.

Ena banished her staff. "Spread out and search in case he is still nearby, but I suspect he is far away by now."

"So far and yet so close." I took off the ring as it threatened to overwhelm my senses and let my mind rest in the silence of the warehouse.

It seemed cross-dimensional overlap was already affecting Prime in ways I should have predicted but hadn't. The question was, how were those from other dimensions traveling to ours? Not even the queens were godlike enough to traverse dimensions, were they? They were powerful beings of nature, but certainly not gods.

The god that had opened the portal for Baura had almost certainly been helping these guardians. The only positive note was that Torvin from Beta was dead by Baura's hand, and I'd killed the ones from Prime and Alpha. At least I wouldn't have to deal with that ass hat anymore. But a rogue squad of guardians was still extremely dangerous, and they were hunting for me.

I had to figure out a way to warn Erolith. The Tetron couldn't drop me directly inside fae safe zones, and the entirety of Faevalorn was protected to prevent portals from opening within the city itself. If I used the Tetron, the closest I could get to Erolith's compound was going to be outside the city gates.

Before I did anything else, I had to recover Baura's Tetron and other artifacts from Beta. That meant getting out of here since the

Tetron didn't work inside the warehouse. I'd already tried using it to see where this place was, and all attempts had given me a severe nosebleed.

The other apocalypse weapons didn't work here either. There was a godlike dampening spell on this place that had probably been placed to keep the dangerous artifacts stored here from being used.

Despite that, Panoptes still worked, and I didn't know why. I suspected it was because Panoptes used ghostly eyeballs to watch a place. It seemed the eyes themselves were like point-to-point travel nodes. I also suspected that it linked to the wielder's eyes, which was why it hurt so much to bring through large objects like barrels.

Panoptes also ignored safe zones and other protections. I should have left an eye to watch Erolith's home, but it hadn't even crossed my mind. It was about high time I started using this ring to create my own information network.

Thankfully, I'd left an eye to watch Sanctuary, so I put on the ring, concentrated on that frame, and traveled there.

Darkness washed over my vision when I stepped into my bedroom. The skin on my face felt as if it were crawling with insects. I staggered into the bathroom as my eyesight waxed and waned with darkness and light. What I saw in the mirror sent a shock of fear into my guts. Blackened veins rippled across my face, spreading down my neck and eventually reaching my fingers.

Just as suddenly, it was over. My eyesight was restored, and my skin looked normal. But I obviously wasn't normal. Something was terribly wrong with me. Having Fitz diagnose me was already on my growing to-do list. There were more pressing needs to attend to first.

Hannah and the others were watching TV, so I sneaked out through the tunnels. I'd never replaced my motorcycle, so I had to hoof it for a quarter of a mile until I emerged aboveground through a trapdoor. From there, I walked to the protected gate and let myself out. I walked all the way to where I'd parked Dolores so I could touch her shiny metallic surface and feel a sense of rightness in the universe before taking the next step.

First, I set an eye to watch this place.

Then I stepped away from Dolores and withdrew the Tetron from its pouch. I manipulated the Cubon, Spheron, and Pyron. I flew into space, and the multiverse array appeared before me. I switched to Beta and zoomed in on Gaia. Even from this distance, things were looking markedly worse than yesterday. The ocean around Crete and Greece seemed to be boiling with new life forms. The gaping maws of chthonian worms were discharging dark young and other eldritch monsters at an incredible rate.

Shoggoths, malgorths, and countless other monsters fought bloody battles on Crete as the minions of Shubburath sought to overthrow Cthulhu's army.

Cthulhu himself was far out to sea, only the top of his monstrous head above the water. He didn't seem to care about the war. I averted my gaze since I wasn't wearing mithrium eye condoms and zoomed in on the spot where Baura had hidden her artifacts beneath Mount Olympus. The area looked clear.

I mentally prepared myself for the next step, then willed myself to travel there. The impact doubled me over. I landed on the ground and lay there for several minutes, trying to catch my breath. My entire body felt like jelly. Having a travel companion allowed them to split the energy usage.

It was a damned good thing there weren't any enemies around because I couldn't have so much as lifted a finger in my defense for nearly twenty minutes. Once I regained some strength, I climbed unsteadily to my feet.

Just to my left, a ladder led into the dark underground. Faint whispers emanated from below, leaving little doubt that there were ghasts and probably gugs in the tunnels below. I would have to make this quick. I cast a camouflage blind to cover my scent and sound. Gripping the sides of the ladder with hands and feet, I slid down mariner style and hurried to the left branch, a light ball guiding the way.

Judging from the bloodstains and rotten stench, this place had seen the deaths of untold numbers of people. They'd probably been sacrificed in the creation of the Cthulhu summoning runes. Baura had thoroughly desecrated Beta's Mount Olympus.

A right turn followed by two left turns led me to rooms carved in the bedrock, each one closed off by metal doors with food slots. I jogged to the one at the end and slashed it open with my brightblade. Inside were shelves with Baura's artifacts—the Tetron, dozens of spheres, including one that looked identical to the orb that Baura had used to destroy my Rlhala. Against the far wall was the Rlhala itself, this one stained with blackened blood.

Unfortunately, I couldn't travel from underground using the Tetron. I'd tried before, and it simply didn't work. If I wanted the Rlhala, I'd have to carry it aboveground. There was no way for me to do that without an exo-suit or superpowers. But not carrying it didn't mean I couldn't use it. Unless Baura had bound Cthulhu to never listen to anyone else, it was possible I could use it to turn the goliath against the eldritch invasion and possibly use him to cleanse the world.

Then I would put him back to sleep—or at least try to.

I placed my hand on the image of Cthulhu's head in the center of the stone cylinder. It should have instantly carried me into Cthulhu's mind, but instead, a powerful shock threw me across the room. My back hit the wall, and I fell to my knees. My hand felt numb as if I'd just grabbed a live power circuit but otherwise looked unhurt.

I rose to my feet and regarded the Rlhala. I knew very little about eldritch magic, but judging from all the blood in the runes on this thing, it seemed Baura had somehow enchanted it, probably locking it from being touched or used by anyone else. Or perhaps it could no longer be used in this dimension since Cthulhu was awake. Needless to say, that was bad. Very bad.

I couldn't even transport it using Panoptes if I couldn't touch it. Perhaps it was possible to indirectly touch it with a strap or something. That method had allowed us to transport barrels, so it would probably work with the Rlhala. Now wasn't the time to attempt it since I couldn't take the strain or pain right now.

"Just wonderful," I muttered. I added recovering the Rlhala to my list of things to do, then set an eye to watch this place.

Once done, I summoned my staff and scanned the room for protective sigils. It was clear, just as Baura had told Fitz, but I wanted to make sure myself. The runes on the Rlhala glowed greenly just as they had on my Rlhala, giving me no indication as to what protections the blood gave it.

I banished my staff, then filled my duffel bags with all the other items. There were no apocalypse weapons, though I was certain many of the spheres on the shelves could wreak serious havoc if used properly. I'd have to ask Noctua what they all did—yet another item on my list.

Hiccups echoed in the tunnels, meaning the ghasts were coming my way despite the protections of the camouflage blind. I imagined the slugs we'd encountered could also smell me through the veil, so I used Panoptes to travel back to Dolores.

Even though I only carried through a few duffel bags, my eyes felt as if someone had jabbed them with rusty daggers. They watered so profusely, I had to take a few minutes to allow the pain to subside.

Panoptes and the Tetron might be convenient ways to travel, but they were wearing me down physically and mentally. I had to find other means of travel, or I'd end up in the same insane boat as Baura.

I put the duffel bags in the rear of the car and drove home. It had been a long, eventful day, and I had so much more to do. But for now, our dimension was safe, and Baura was taken care of forever.

As with all my quests, it seemed rather than solving anything, I'd just created more problems for myself.

Thankfully, I knew just the way to ease my mind until I figured out the solutions. So, I got out of Dolores, hefted the duffel bag, and headed inside Sanctuary to store them in my underground vault. This place was now safer than the warehouse.

I'd been donkey-kicked by a minotaur, chased by centaurs, fought legions of eldritch horrors, and had my sanity torn to shreds by Cthulhu. It was time to take a break and drink an unholy quantity of mangoritas.

Because I deserved it.

BOOKS BY JOHN CORWIN

Join the Overworld Conclave for all the news, memes and tentacles you could ever desire!

https://www.facebook.com/groups/overworldconclave

Or get your tentacles via email: www.johncorwin.net

Fan page: https://www.facebook.com/johncorwinauthor

CHRONICLES OF CAIN

To Kill a Unicorn

Enter Oblivion

Throne of Lies

At The Forest of Madness

The Dead Never Die

Shadow of Cthulhu

THE OVERWORLD CHRONICLES

Sweet Blood of Mine

Dark Light of Mine

Fallen Angel of Mine

Dread Nemesis of Mine

Twisted Sister of Mine

Dearest Mother of Mine

Infernal Father of Mine

Sinister Seraphim of Mine

Wicked War of Mine

Dire Destiny of Ours

ABOUT THE AUTHOR

John Corwin is the bestselling author of the Overworld Chronicles and Chronicles of Cain. He enjoys long walks on the beach and is a firm believer in puppies and kittens.

After years of getting into trouble thanks to his overactive imagination, John abandoned his male modeling career to write books.

He resides in Atlanta.

Join the Overworld Conclave for all the news, memes and tentacles you could ever desire!
https://www.facebook.com/groups/overworldconclave
Or get your tentacles via email: www.johncorwin.net
Fan page: https://www.facebook.com/johncorwinauthor
Website: http://www.johncorwin.net
Twitter: http://twitter.com/#!/John_Corwin

Made in the USA
Las Vegas, NV
18 April 2023

70757927R00215